The Dogs of Lamu
And The China 12

CHINA 12 BOOK 3

RAOUL MORRIS

Also in the China 12 series
"*Brancusi's Head and the China 12*" Book One
"*A Sao Paulo Samba and the China 12*" (a prequel to Book One)

Published by Three heads inc
in association with
D Media Network

This book was crowd-funded with the aid of,
Anne Westcott, Melise Nevin, the Doctors Geraldine Morris and
Andrew Hillier, Carla Morris and Howard Laughton for
whose support I am immensely grateful.

ISBN- 979-8-650887-17-1

Cover design by: Jacob Morris

Typesetting by: www.bookstyle.co.uk

For the long and funny chats on a Friday

For the wise words

For Goran Stefanovski

PART ONE

1

Cast of Characters

The China 12
Dr Xi Liang Chemist Toxicologist
Dr Erasto Diallo Engineer
Ms. Koura Aripe Designer–Ergonomist
Dr Rachel Lopez-Real Pathologist- Biologist-General Practitioner
Dr Catherine O Shea Forensic Psychologist
Dr Wolfgang Schult Forensic Archaeologist
Dr Zhang Xin Mathematician–Statistics and Analysis, First Speaker.
Dr Rahul Patel Mathematician–Computationalist
Dr Himura Hoshika Mathematician–Proability

China 12–Operatives
Milo Talbot
Joanna Baines (deceased)
Kevin Twomey (deceased)

China 12–Unofficial
The Pixie (a pixie)
Sam (a clantech)
Julia (an AI)

Clients
Dr. Mariana Armenta
Feng Liu
Feng Ho
Ms Liang
Julia Church aka Jane Cruikshank aka Elspeth Martin
Felicity Dawson, Elspeth's half sister

Americorp
Anna May, a freelance Operative
Duncan Heath, Chair of Americorp
Mr Jones, CTO of Americorp
Mr Andrew Donovan, CEO Americorp

Brooklyn Brotherhood
Elder Thomas
Brother Daniels
Brother Francis
Brother Mathew
Brother Skolnic (Major)

The story so far...

Milo is a detective with the China 12 crime group.

The year is 2056 and world Governments have decided that "all thinking will be outsourced". Crime detection groups are a consequence. China 12 is one the best in the world.

Milo was called away on a job as a favour for a Chinese official. A missing daughter and plenty of discretion needed. While away, the other two China 12 field operative were called to Sao Paulo, Brazil; Joanna Baines and Kevin Twomey.

In Sao Paulo, Joanna and Kevin, fell out over how to finish the job, with fatal results. Sam, an American (she is an unofficial state operative, nicknamed a "pixie" in Europe, a "clantech" in the US) watched as Kevin shot Joanna in the back. He walked away, leaving Joanna and their client (Dr Mariana Armenta) to burn.

China 12, not knowing of the argument, and not hearing from Kevin, believed all of them lost in the conflagration

In Paris a young woman waited for a visitor her system had predicted would come.

Grieving for his friends killed in Brazil and taking a break afterward, Milo met this young woman. She seemed in need of help and his chivalric instincts drew him into a job in Paris. His cranial implant was infected with an AI named Julia, which had been developed by the victim of the murder he was led to investigate.

While on the job he picked up a Pixie, who might be ordered to kill him at any moment. A little later her American partner, Sam, the clantech who witnessed the attack in Sao Paulo, was herself shot in the hunt for the murderer and she is in a coma in New York...

2

Journey from the past

Prologue: Julia in Paris
[This was the day Julia met Milo in Paris]

"What would you say if I told you I had a man's head in my bag? No. What would you say if I told you I had a head in my bag?"

She made a face in the mirror and took a deep breath. Letting it out slowly, she closed her eyes.

'Relax.'

Her eyes snapped open again and she looked down at the bed. She chewed her lip. The bag was open in front of her and she reached forward to run her fingers over the minimal features of the face. She couldn't help it, she loved the sculpture and though this was a copy, it was perfect. She always thought she knew the difference when she did this with the original, but closing her eyes again as her fingers tried to find the faults in the surface, she wasn't sure.

The alarm in her system flashed and she called up the image onto her retinal projector. Milo was just passing through frontier control, his credentials appeared on her system just as they did on the system out at Orly airport. She smiled. He would receive the automated message from Anna, Julia's boss, on the train into Paris. Julia wasn't sure where Anna had gone, why she wouldn't make the meeting with Milo. She was worried, but it had suited her just fine. She'd laid out the path for Milo to come to Paris anyway, his arriving in a vulnerable state was ideal. That Anna wasn't there meant it had to be a bit more 'hands on', but she didn't mind that either. This was Paris after all.

She followed him through the airport security systems and onto the fast transit to the city. Julia had been kicking her heels in Paris for too long and the strain of having a virtual presence in the office in London was beginning to get to her. Or, that was what she told herself. She knew it was the worry that her cousin, having said too much about their damn system, had mentioned the fail-safe. If he had, this meeting with Milo was critical - it might be the only thing standing between freedom such as it was, and the silent invisible control she, her sister and cousin had recklessly developed. This was the moment when either they would have a system that stemmed the control of big corporations and could be adjusted to respond to the inevitable changes in tactics, or the already skewed system of power became uncontainable.

She had taken a risk showing herself to the China 12 head office but no one had mentioned her use of masking systems. People see what they expect to see, she reminded herself, and they probably explained away the distortions on the quality of the line. They knew she was calling from London, so might factor that in to the expected quality. The whole thing had been stressful, exhausting and she hoped this would be the last chapter. She also hoped that the transfer to Milo would not be needed and, if it was, that he lived up to her trust. If they found her and knew what she was doing, what would they do?

She shook herself. The lack of sleep was getting to her, creating boogeymen of her fears. This was important but surely there were limits to what people would do, even for that much power. Standing, she walked over to the bedside table, lifted a small vial and plugged it into a surgical injector. She held it to her arm and pressed the button. She liked the sound as it sent the vial's contents into her arm. Dropping the injector into the bag, she lifted a small bottle of clear liquid and drank the contents, swishing it round her mouth before swallowing. She turned the empty bottle in her hand and then dropped it too into the bag.

She reached out and leaned forward, zipped up the bag and took up her coat. She had to meet Milo in a bar close to this hotel. Julia knew how that meeting would go; he'd be annoyed, distracted, she'd be at the only seat 'really' available, the subject would move to the crime boards and then to her little announcement... She had studied Milo, having picked China 12 as the only trustworthy group for this... what was it, a mission? Milo was old enough to still feel the need for gallantry and stable enough not to have a meltdown when, if, the program was triggered. Maybe the fail-safe wouldn't be needed. Either way, the mathematics was clear.

She checked herself in the mirror one last time, not too obviously planning to go out not too vulnerable, but still that hint of need. She looked over the room; he was a detective, taking things in was his stock in trade, was this the room of a slightly chaotic but still pretty organised lawyer? She hoped it was. Here was where the mathematics ran out, like magic, it wouldn't work if you were too closely involved.

Taking a deep breath, she walked through the opening door. Milo was about to make his very own decisions about which bar to go to, which table to sit at, which woman to talk to and what to talk about. He was after all a free man, wasn't he? The affair of the Brancusi head was about to begin.

3

Bitter taste of Betrayal

[It was seven days before Julia met Milo in Paris]

The rain was easing off now, though the dense clouds promised more before the night was over. He'd been swearing and cursing, both aloud and under his breath, for the last twenty minutes as he'd zig-zagged away from the airfield. Now he stopped and let out a primal scream at the sky, his hands balling into fists out from his sides. As if in echo, the flames back at the airfield must have reached another set of the company's fuel packs because a loud explosion erupted, flames bursting into the sky.

Kevin turned to look back at his future burning in front of him. So simple, so close, all she had to do was reach out with him and they'd have had just about everything they could have wanted, 'Stupid bitch.'

What principle exactly was she defending? Honour? That had gone in the war. Loyalty? They were paid employees and ones their employers thought nothing about spying on. They didn't owe China fucking 12 a damn thing.

Lights. An oncoming cab. He needed one of them.

He walked out into the road and waited. Distracted, angry, he ran through what had just happened. Had he really just shot his partner in the back? Consequences were running through his mind as he saw Joanna go down again, on the record in his system. Then the client, Mariana coming out all "Ok Coral", gun blazing, hitting him square on in the chest, before she was taken out by that crazy assassin. Then, the look in the eye of that fucking American pixie, or whatever they call themselves. Bitch, who was she to judge him?

His attention came back to the cab. The lights changed direction as the system spotted him and began to manoeuvre around him. He moved across the road and the lights changed direction again, their speed slowing. Again he moved, and again. The cab finally stopped about thirty centimetres from his knees.

Once he was out of the way, the system would check he wasn't prone in the road and then that he had cleared away from the front on either side before moving off, about forty seconds. He'd only need half that. There'd better not be anyone inside, for their sake.

The cab moved off Kevin inside. He reached up to prise open the control box. The cab was following its return to base protocol. The rain had likely confused it as it had the cabs earlier that evening.

Kevin had two problems; he couldn't access any network while his China 12 system could still light up his position and indicate he was alive, and he didn't have much money. He'd depleted his 'running away money' with those triad bastards in Beijing and their rigged game. He'd have to rely on the skills he'd picked up in the army, unofficially of course. First things first, he needed a drink. He had to aim this thing at some place discreet. The harbour would do.

Sao Paulo had lost its harbour at Santos with the rise in sea levels. The decision to establish new docks when levels seemed to have stabilised had established a new 'informal' part of the city which catered to the workers and protected the robots making the sparkling future. It also housed the refugees from the drowned suburb.

He could find a place there, lie low and work out what to do next. He'd have to take care of that Pixie, she'd be the only one who positively knew what he'd done in any case. She must be working out of the US, the South Americans didn't have their own Pixie programme - not yet anyway. That'd give him something to do. He'd have to disable his China 12 system and he had to get money.

He sat back in the seat and closed his eyes. What exactly had happened? He should have been straight with Joanna, but she should have trusted him. Mariana would have gone along with it if they were together. Was Joanna right? Should they have gone back to Beijing?

Jones and his pals were businessmen, much easier for them to pay someone off than bump them off, if you did that you just had to pay the next guy. The Chinese, on the other hand were a government, a dictatorship not to be trusted. He'd had his fill as a believer in the army and where had that got them? Lousy food, lousy pay, their necks on the line and a third-rate parade with some bits of coloured ribbon at the end. They'd even missed out on the grateful thanks of an embarrassed country. No, he was right. This was their chance, she'd blown it and she would have taken everything else away. Goody fucking two shoes.

Where was he? He squinted out of the windows, it was raining again. Not too far to go. He really needed a drink. Money. There, they'd do. He slowed the cab and it pulled over.

Just up ahead were a couple of very well-dressed young men. Far too well-dressed young men, boys really. Sampling the way the other nine point nine tenths lived, no doubt. Easy pickings for someone with Kevin's skills. The cab rolled away. Kevin looked round to pick his spot, a narrow alley, the boys were just about to cross the entrance; hit them there and into the darkness. He could hear the rising sound of the excited banter of the two lads. Then, the unexpected. Just as he breathed out and took the first step in their direction, a man sprinted across the road heading straight for the boys. He hit them at the neck of the alley and, as they fell, hands reached out from the dark and dragged them in.

'Hey,' Kevin thought, 'That's my money.'

He jerked forward and was flat out when he got to the alley. His night vision showed the scene and it wasn't pretty, but the two 'boys' weren't in the position he'd expected. Four men had attacked them, and two were already in the dirt. They were busy looking for a way out. Of the other two; one was fighting and only the last, the big guy who'd come hammering in from across the road, was holding his own. Kevin changed sides.

He hit the big guy from the side, it was a cheap shot but needs must, that took him out. The man crumpled and lay still. The second would-be mugger had just turned the tables. He'd begun to get the upper hand and turned his 'victim' round when Kevin hit him full in the face. The two lads turned to face Kevin, unsure if they had now to fight him or thank him. He turned and smiled.

'Alright?'

The lads exchanged a look and turned back, 'Who are you?'

'Some call me "the night avenger", others "the shadow", my parents went with "Kieran."'

He stuck his hand out in front of him. One of the muggers began to crawl away but was stopped by Kevin's boot in his ribs. The two lads grinned and lurched forward, taking his hand, arm, patting him on the back. Kevin wondered if the fact they'd seen him meant he'd have to kill them.

4

Daniels' Dog

[Same day]

Daniels was sitting at his desk in his room waiting for the news. He believed that his man Skolnic could bring in the woman but he was fairly certain he wouldn't. He knew the man's powerful abilities but he also knew he was not a man for subtlety. The Brooklyn Brotherhood wasn't big on subtlety for that matter, but Skolnic was at another level. A blunt instrument, but effective when needed.

Skolnic called and he was clearly in a worse state than he had been earlier in the evening and that hadn't been too great.

'Well?'

'It was really weird.'

'I don't understand.' It was too late at night and Daniels was tired.

'They shot each other.'

'Who? Be clearer man.'

'The two China 12 ops, the man shot the woman. They had words and then she walked away and he shot her. Then the target, Armenta came out with a canon, blazing at him and he went down. I took her out. It was odd then, the place went up. I saw there was that clantech or pixie, or whatever she is, was there too. I guess she must have blown the place.'

'Why?'

'They don't like evidence when they've been involved.'

'But Dr Armenta is dead?'

'Yes, she is, must be. If the shot didn't kill her, the fire did. She didn't have body armour. I got her with a chest shot.'

'And the others?'

'I'd say gone. If you'll forgive me sir, it was what we used to call a shit show.'

'Alright. Get back here. I've arranged for the doctor to meet you

16

and bring you to get your wounds taken care of. He'll get that face of yours changed. Good job, thank you.'

'Yes sir, any time.'

He broke off the com and thought about what he'd just been told. That Skolnic was sure the woman was dead, wasn't the same as the woman being dead. He'd make sure to ask Anna to look into it. Anna. She'd come to him through the strangest of channels, a lawyer of all things. He'd tried but failed to check out her background. He knew they hadn't the best tech people, it went against the grain for the brotherhood, but still he'd been surprised they'd found nothing. He'd have to watch her.

It was late, but he knew that Elder Thomas would want to know as soon as he could. Things were at a delicate point. This initiative had to pay off, or the whole project would be closed down and he might be spending too much time on his knees, even for a God-fearing soul such as he.

'Ah, Brother Daniels, how are things? Have they settled down?'

'After a fashion, Elder. Skolnic has had to terminate the target. We were trying to bring her in but it seems that the China 12 ops fell out, turned on each other. I'm getting Anna May to find out for certain if she is indeed dead, but he was pretty sure of it.'

'A rather disappointing end.'

'We tried. We have gotten somewhere and Anna says she has a lead, somewhere in Europe. She seems to think we can still get the system we want, maybe even better than what we have at the moment.'

'That would be gratifying, but after the last few days I'm not keeping my fingers crossed. You are coming back now I presume? And Skolnic?'

'He's been exposed to too many cameras, so I'm having his face altered a bit. Not drastic but it would be a clever AI that would pick him out, if what the doctor promised is right. I am heading straight back, Anna will clear up and then follow this lead in Europe.'

'Alright, we'll expect you at the meeting in two days' time. Is that long enough to recover from your exertions?'

'I think so. Jet lag won't be a problem obviously. Sorry this wasn't more of a success, Elder.'

'The Lord obviously has a slightly different path for us, we just have to find it.'

'Amen to that.'

'Good night, Brother.'

'Good night, Elder.'

Daniels sat back in his chair. So it was done. The difficulty with his current situation was that the kindly souls on the council simply believed his ideas to be evil. He accepted the parts of the Gospel that were gentle and loving. But the Lord sometimes called for the sword and if you had a sword you had to have someone to wield it. Was getting into heaven just a case of being nice and turning up? What of your duty to the rest of the planet? It wasn't enough to live a good life and expect people to notice and try to follow, was it?

This path was hard but it was true. He was never so certain of anything as he was of this. The systems offered by those people in Europe were heaven sent, they must be. It was a sure way to gather in believers and bring on the end foreseen in Revelations. He was amazed he would actually live to see it. He thought of the many souls who had dreamt of these days and even imagined they were living in these days, but he was. The signs were clear, he could almost hear the cries of the lost and the singing of the choirs of the Lord.

He checked his watch. He should sleep and be fresh for morning prayers.

He got up and went about the ritual of undressing and getting ready for bed. Saying his prayers as he knelt in supplication to the Lord, knowing his salvation was sure if he should be taken in his sleep. If it weren't for the prospect of seeing the end of days, he almost wished for it.

Each in their own time.

5

The Wages of Sin

There's nothing quite like the unexpected. The intention was to rush the boys just as they passed the alley, bundle them into the darkness. Then threaten them, get them to transfer a chunk of dough to his chip and send them home to mama. Now he'd saved them. But the rain was still bucketing down and he still had no money.

They were still shaking his hand, 'Ok, I get it, you're very pleased with me. What were you doing there? If I'm not mistaken, you're off your beaten track and you look like raw recruits.'

The boys exchanged a look, as though checking their story, one of them lifted his chin then turned, 'It's part of a game, we wanted to see if we could do it for real, you know in the real world.'

'A game? I don't understand.'

'E-sport, we play online, there are lots of different sections, the last one is in a Virtual arena. We're near that level and one of our friends was saying it was just a game and we couldn't do it for real.'

Kevin looked around at the muggers in various states of injury, 'How do you think you did?'

The lads looked at one another again, and then at the men on the ground, finally turning back to Kevin, 'Seven out of ten. We probably would have had trouble with that last one.'

'You think?'

'Can we get you a drink?'

Kevin smiled, 'I think that would be acceptable.'

The drinking club looked as if it had been thrown together that evening and for one night only. For all that, it was a success as the crowd heaved in good natured but compressed relaxation. Kevin was leaning against a wall beside one of the boys.

'You have a name?'

'Didn't we say? Sorry, Eduardo, he's Iago.' He stuck out his hand and Kevin took it. 'You're Kieran, right? Funny name.'

'It's Irish.'

'That's so great - my great great great grandmother was Irish!'

'That is great...' No laugh, 'We're practically cousins!'

Eduardo looked at him wide eyed, 'Oh yeah, really?'

Kevin began to wonder whose side he should have taken in the alley, when Iago arrived back with a full tray. Sliding it onto the shelf at Kevin's shoulder, running along from where they were standing, he began to hand them out.

'Are you military?'

Kevin took a drink thinking about how to answer, 'Why'd you think that?'

Iago gestured with his drink, 'The suit.'

Kevin looked down, 'Oh, yeah.'

Eduardo pointed, 'It looks like you've just been in a fight.' He looked at Iago and they both started to laugh.

'Yeah, manoeuvres, you don't always get a chance to clean up.'

The boys nodded seriously. Iago looked at his drink and then at Kevin, 'If we lost that fight, do you think they'd have killed us?'

'Might have, depends.'

Eduardo, 'On?'

'You look pretty well off. If they thought killing you was going to keep them safe, then yeah, but if it increased the chances they'd be hunted down...'

Iago looked anxious, 'Told you.'

'How could they tell?'

'Just a judgement call. They looked like they'd been about a bit, but not too great at what they did, so I'd say their judgement wasn't too clever truthfully.'

'We wouldn't have lost though.'

Kevin looked at them and smiled, 'Of course not.'

Eduardo and Iago grinned, they slammed their glasses together.

Some time later and they fell out of the drinking den into the street. Rain was coming down hard enough to be bouncing off the surface. Kevin had managed to put away enough alcohol to overwhelm his suppressant system, part of it anyway. The boys couldn't tell what day it was. Somewhere above the clouds the sun was up, you knew because your watch said so. Eduardo leant against his friend and they were both leaning against Kevin, who leant against them. He was looking about for something. Iago was trying to gather his thoughts, he had something to say if he could only remember what it was. He smiled.

'You're alright, Kir'n, Ker'n… You are, you really helped us out you know…'

'Yeah I did…'

Iago gave the response a bit of thinking and looked hard at Kevin's chest, and then really hard. His head jerked up in sudden realisation.

'You're in th'army… Not much dosh in h'army… you know…'

'Yeah.' Kevin gave that some thought and then began to look at the boys again, in the way people coming out of a pub look at a kebab stand. Eduardo and Iago, oblivious to the look stared at each other. Eduardo turned.

'Why don't you take some?'

Holding out his wrist to Kevin he blinked and then a slow smile drifted across his face, he turned slowly to Iago who smiled back and agreed enthusiastically. Kevin stared at the wrist as he tried to make out what was going on and he pointed at it and looked up at Eduardo.

'Are you offering…?'

Eduardo still smiled, but looked at Iago, nodded twice and then slowly turned back at Kevin. Kevin pulled himself up to full height, looked serious and then swayed and looked down again and grinned. He pushed his wrist at Eduardo's who acknowledged it slowly. Kevin watched the wrists touch, blinked and then looked at the boy's faces.

'Very g'ners, generse... Thanks.'

Iago looked very seriously at him, 'You're not… insulted?'

Kevin shook his head and pointed at the other two and himself, 'Friends… loan…'

A cab rolled up beside them and the door slid open and they all looked at it accusingly. It waited, they waited…

Kevin's head snapped up, 'It's a cab!'

The others looked at him and back at the door, Eduardo smiled and nodded, they staggered and fell into the interior and the two boys crawled up onto the seat. Kevin lurched back and waved. It was unclear what the boys were doing as they stared out at him and the door slid closed. The cab rolled away and Kevin wheeled and headed back to the bar.

Across the road, someone watched. Tall, angry, not very pleased.

6

Rio

[It was four days before Milo met Julia in Paris]

If Sao Paulo had weathered the storm of global warming and rising sea levels and perhaps even got something from it, Rio had not. Gone were its famous beaches. Its harbour drowned, marina smashed. The luxurious seafront hotels and apartments had the sea now behind them and all round and inside. Engineers learned that tall buildings whose lower floors are enveloped in water, implode. The successive seawalls, trying to deny the inevitable, the unavoidable, were several metres under water and forgotten. Politicians may have tried to deny the science, but they forgot to pass on the message to the climate.

The favelas had suffered. Whereas in Sao Paulo they had become artist retreats and then gentrified and the poor pushed out. Here, they had simply been a stopping point on the retreat away from the sea. Increasingly violent storms had pounded their fragile construction and the sodden earth had slid away, taking many homes with it. "Liquefaction" became a common reference in conversation. Communities were destroyed along with the buildings and the already lawless had become wild.

Into the vacuum of social and political authority poured the physically strong and the wily, those who could survive thrived. People who can't go away, still need. They still get hungry, require heating and shelter and ways to generate the means to acquire those things. They still need to be entertained, have a place to meet and share stories and songs and love. If you were strong enough to hold your own, there were ways and means to harvest the gleanings from even the lowest rungs of the ladder. Rachel Meier was strong enough.

'And DON'T come back!' the troublesome customers crashed into the water and sobered up fast. Rachel Meier turned and headed back inside, her smile as sunny as ever.

Her whole life she'd been strong enough. She didn't look it, glasses, a wiry, slight frame and an open smile. Usually, she smiled as you sank to the floor in agony and was still smiling as you departed her company for what was likely to be the last time. She had to be tough. If she wasn't, then those who were would take everything from her in the blink of an eye. That had been true in the army, during the war, and now. "Why does the sergeant have freckles?" went her section's gag, "Misdirection…" You never told that one in her hearing either. Always called "sarge" or "Meier", by superiors, or Sergeant Meier or "sir" by lower orders, never "Rachel", which she thought was too personal.

Taking her thin army payoff and a few thousand she had managed to scrape together through 'unofficial' channels she set up a bar in one of the newer areas in Rio. It was actually one of the older areas, but the older residents had fled and new folk piled in on the basis that their older places had disappeared. You got there by boat. These buildings edged on the right side of secure though there were several disasters when that unpredictable security failed. The Government tried to ban their use, the ban was ignored.

The now "Ms Meier", or "boss" reckoned that this wild west would last about ten years and she had her eye on a place in San Francisco. From her base she ran several 'concerns', two of them were even official, registered, tax paying companies. She hadn't intended to set up a bar, what did she know about bars apart from what they were for? But Marcus had pointed out that that was probably most of what you needed to know and he needed a place to cook and someone to stop the world from taking it away. He had been a chef to the senior officers. She thought he was sweet and liked his pastries. He had a few grand to throw into the pot as well. Lots of people thought they were an item. They weren't. But they were good business partners.

She'd been working here for years, or at least that was what today felt like. Why did it always happen like that? Some days just seemed endless. Yesterday had been great, no amazing news but nothing went wrong and no-one caused any trouble. Today? Don't talk about today, a kind of ceaseless shit-show, that's what today had been and she longed for her bed. When the new girl came up saying there was someone needing to see her, someone from the "old days", she nearly smacked her. Then she jumped when she heard Marcus behind her saying, 'No, count to ten…' So she nearly smacked him instead.

She closed her eyes and told the girl to send them up in fifteen minutes.

'Does the Boss need a coffee?'

'Why do you creep up on me like that? But no, Marcus, what I need is sleep. First your delivery is late, then the booze is wrong, then two people call in sick. When I'm sick, I work…'

'Yeah and then everyone else gets sick…'

'Then we had those goons from the new gang who think they're something, because, "no one ever thought to lean on this place before and it's run by a woman, so she's easy pickings, she's so small!" '

'But you showed them the door.'

'But that, that takes effort and I've got a headache and they should know better, I mean just ask around. And they'll be back with a bit more muscle because I injured their pride and I'll have to kill someone because it isn't until they're looking at their dead friend that it becomes more than a game to these guys.'

Marcus sighed loudly and put the coffee cup in front of her and the brandy bottle beside her and a huge chocolate brownie in front of that. She looked at them one by one her face unchanging and then slowly turned to look up at him, as he was about to walk through the doorway. She beamed, 'You know me so well.'

She grabbed the brandy and dropped a slug into the coffee.

Marcus said, 'I never found a problem in this world that couldn't be cured by coffee, brandy and chocolate.'

He turned away again and she lifted the cup to her lips then stopped and shouted.

'Hey, do you know who it is wants to see me?'

He stopped at the top of the stairs and thought before continuing, 'Not a clue, he looked tall and skinny but his head was covered, his stuff looked rough, like he'd been sleeping on people's floors, or no one's floors.' His voice faded.

'Shit.'

She took a mouthful of the coffee and eyed the bottle again and then poured another slug into the cup. She lifted the brownie and took a huge bite, 'God that's good!'

For a drinking house they sold a lot of food and this was why, good basic main courses and delicious desserts. She leaned back in the chair and closed her eyes, feeling as much as tasting the chocolate. Chocolate, like coffee, had become a luxury and it was one she really enjoyed.

Having finished her short break, she stood up and walked over to the door. To get to her office you had to climb a narrow stairway and walk along a, just as narrow, balcony. Otherwise you had to go through the kitchens and up the service stairway which was much more complicated.

From her door you could see across the whole bar and she did just that, looking for the "someone" who wanted to see her, someone she knew from the old days… Another ex-military, damaged piece of flotsam, with a tenuous connection from someone who'd heard from a friend of a friend… But she always did something, it was her offering to the Gods of war. She spotted the figure leaning back against the wall near the door. A window to his right, feet planted on the ground. He was the real McCoy alright. Her eyes narrowed, there was something about the way he was sitting, something familiar.

She waved at the nearest server and lifted her chin at the figure by the door, then turned and went back inside. She poured another slug into the now empty cup and drank, hopefully this would be the last problem today. She eased open the drawer beside her and lifted the gun, holding it beneath the level of the desk. A rap on the door.

'Yeah, come right in.'

The door swung back.

'Hello sergeant.'

Rachel Meier's head snapped up and her eyes met eyes she hadn't seen in a lifetime. She stood, chair knocked back, hitting the wall behind.

'Fuck me! Look what the cat dragged in.'

7

Dawn Breaks

[It was six days before Milo met Julia in Paris]

It's only when you've drunk as much as Kevin had, that the expression 'dawn broke' really hits home. He had been shuffling down in his bed trying to avoid the light for… he wasn't sure how long for, it seemed to have been hours. Even when the sunlight touched his skin it hurt.

It was not the most luxurious of hotels. He knew that when he'd staggered in with, whoever it was he'd staggered in with, but he thought they'd have a set of curtains. The shock, when out of nowhere a cascade of agonisingly cold water came down on him, brought him awake in a hurry. He flailed out at the figure who had thought it was clever, or funny. He missed.

'Get up.'

'What? Who the fuck?'

'Get up, I want to have a little chat.'

'Whoever you think you are…'

If he was going to level a threat it was lost in the pain that swept over him as the intruder banged on the table, really loudly.

'Alright! Enough.'

'What's happened to your med system? I thought China 12 had the best systems.'

Kevin tried to pull himself together. He swung his legs over the side of the bed and his head fell into his hands, wet hair dripping on the floor. 'Limits, everything has a limit, everything can be overwhelmed.'

He looked up. Standing to one side of the window, still too difficult to see properly, was a tall woman. She looked like she was in a suit, weird. He squinted up at her.

'Who are you, am I supposed to know you?'

'You might, but we haven't met. My name is Anna May, I work

27

with the same company as Mr. Jones. Do you remember Mr. Jones? You had an agreement with him.' Kevin nodded and then stopped nodding, his hands still rubbing his face.

'Yes, I remember.'

'You'd perhaps like to explain what happened?'

Kevin was quiet, trying to piece together what exactly had happened. He tried looking up again, straight at the window and he regretted it.

'His stupid air crew is what happened.'

'Explain.'

He managed to look up, his eyes having reached a compromise with the light, less of a compromise, more of a surrender.

'Everything was fine. Arranged to tell Jo and Mariana on the flight, where and what. But your guys spilled the beans and Jo, you have to know Jo…'

'Not very likely now, is it?'

Kevin gave that a second, as the full memories flooded back, 'No. Anyway, she's a stickler for detail and she took it badly that we weren't going back to Beijing.'

'She thought that's where you were headed?'

'Yeah. Wouldn't agree to the US.'

'So, she finds out and…?'

'And she was going to leave.'

'To go where?'

'Plan B.'

'You stopped her.'

'No, and I wouldn't have.'

Anna sighed, 'I don't want to have to drag every word out of you, Kevin.'

'Your crew pulled a gun on her. She's a trained special forces officer in full combats and armed and they pulled a gun on her for fuck's sake.'

'Oh.'

'Oh, is right. That's when I arrived.'

'Why didn't you arrive together?'

'We had a pixie following us. You know what a pixie is?'

'Yes.'

'We didn't know what her orders were, so we split up.'

'Ok, then you arrived.'

Kevin is still talking, largely to the floor with the occasional turn into the glare of the sun, his mind frantically trying to work out how he's going to explain how the night ended.

'I talked her down.'

'Her?'

'Jo. And Mariana. We agreed to talk about it, but Mariana was spooked. Jo insisted we leave. Then your guys got smart with the guns and opened fire.'

'Did they hit the women?'

'They hit Jo, but she was in full combats and they were using pop guns, or they might as well have.'

'Who fired back?'

'How do you know someone fired back?'

Anna just looked at him and he tried to look back but turned away.

'I did. Your guys aren't much shots and they hit the fuel cells.'

'Not you?'

'I was standing beside them. No. Not me. After the bang, I recovered and the place was like a blast furnace, Jo was nowhere. I got out and went after Jo and the woman.'

'Alright, you go after them, they were still alive then. Now, not so much.'

'I followed them, but when I got out they were nowhere. I took a chance and went with plan B. Like I said, Jo is a stickler, emphasis on 'stick'. The pixie was nowhere either. Jo had mentioned some trouble at the first airfield, before they got into the hanger, someone tried to shoot Mariana, she was injured. Whoever that was, was gone too. Jo thought she'd chased them off but not killed them. Mariana plugged some guy outside the hanger, he was still there.'

'That tallies, go on.'

'I get to the Marta airfield and find Jo about to fly out with Mariana.'

'Where to?'

'No idea.'

'Ok, then what?'

'Then I'm trying to talk her into going to the US when someone, I think the pixie, shoots Jo. I ran to help her and Mariana came out of the offices behind. I bent down and shots came from behind me, somewhere out on the edge of the airfield, I found a hole in the fence later, anyway Mariana went down. The fuel must have been hit too, because next thing I knew, the place went up and I was thrown about ten feet backwards. I tried to get back to help them, not that I think it would have done any good, but the heat.'

Anna looked round the room not trying too hard to hide her distaste.

'And you ended up here?'

'I needed a drink.'

'Or two.'

'Or two. Jo and I went back a long way, she was one of the best.'

'Why not call China 12?'

'They'd give me the third degree and I doubt they'd trust me again. I'm not sure I could explain all that business with the US and the first stop and fire.'

'You could lie.'

He looked at her and she held his look and then.

'Right, you're out of a job?'

'I think I may be dead.'

'That might be possible. You'll work for me, don't worry, we'll be very generous?'

He took a deep breath and squinted at her again and a another long silence.

'Alright.'

'Good. You may have to kill some old friends - will that be a problem?' she asked.

'Not if you're very generous.'

8

The Major and the Sergeant

[It was four days before Milo met Julia in Paris]

Sergeant Meier, she suddenly felt like "sergeant Meier" again, was amazed, then she looked closer at the figure in front of her and her face darkened.

'You look like shit.'

Coming round the desk, she pulled out a chair and turned to the door at the back of the office. 'Hey Marcus, bring some more of that coffee and some food,' she shouted.

Then back to her guest, 'You like to eat, yeah?'

The figure nodded and sat, turning the chair so the back was in the direction of the wall, with the door to the left and in sight.

Meier turned back to the doorway where Marcus was now standing, 'Food? What does food mean, Boss?'

She shook her head and said, 'Food, whatever is on hand, hungry soldiers aren't particular, some water too… and coffee.'

Marcus shook his head slowly and left. Meier turned.

'Major Baines, I never thought… I heard you'd gotten a well-paid gig in the east, nice crib, the whole works. I must have heard wrong.'

Joanna smiled, 'No you heard right, but not everything always works the way you expect.'

She slipped the hood from her head. The bruising ran all down one side of her face, and the burns were livid, some clearly becoming infected. Her old sergeant pulled a face, 'I thought the war was over, or hadn't you heard?'

'Oh yeah, would you have anything for this?'

Meier was already on the move. Bending to a cupboard behind her desk she pulled out a large box, threw it up onto the table and leant out the door.

'Marcus, could you bring up your burns stuff, all of it!'

Then she came round the desk to Joanna who had begun to

ease off her coat. The fabric was stuck to her in parts and Joanna seemed to be about to give it a pull, assisted by Meier, when Marcus appeared at the door.

'No! Stop.'

He put the tray he was carrying on the desk and unslung the bag from his shoulder.

'What are you people doing? Anything that has partially healed will open up and any infection will spread. Get back, let me see.'

Meier stood back and leaned against the table. Turning, she saw the water and handed some across to Joanna. She picked up the brandy and took a slug straight from the bottle. Marcus took out a spray and sprayed the coat and the edges of the burns and slowly peeled away the coat.

'Shit, what have you been doing? On second thoughts don't answer that, I don't want to know.'

He got the coat off and then pulled at the edges of the combats. Jo was burned and badly bruised and then he saw the two puncture wounds from Kevin's gun, he frowned.

'Are the slugs still in here or... No, someone dug them out. Ok, they didn't go in too much, not sure how...they'll need to be stitched.'

Meier smiled and handed over the bottle of brandy.

'Major, it's quite like old times.'

'I have a friend down stairs, she's by the bar, or she should be by now, could you get her?'

'Sure.' Meier walked to the door and leant out, scanning the bar area. She could see a woman on her own, or trying to be, at the far end. She signalled to the waiter at the end of the stairs and he went over to her. A short exchange and Mariana looked up. Meier waved her up and she began to make her way toward the stairs and the office. Meier stepped back, 'Short woman, looks in a similar state to you, well, not that bad.'

Joanna smiled. Marcus stood and shook his head, 'It's not great but it will do for now, you need more drugs than we've got and soon.'

Mariana appeared at the door. Marcus looked at Meier, 'More food?'

She nodded. 'What about you?' She gave him a thumbs up. He looked at Mariana and then at the bag, 'I'll leave this, try not to kill her.'

It was about half an hour later that the two women were patched up and wearing chef's clothing and eating. Meier watched.

Joanna looked up, 'We need your help.'

'No shit, I thought you were just passing by and you dropped in to see an old mate.'

'Well obviously, that too. If it weren't for the people trying to kill us, we'd have come just to hang out. But...'

'Are these people serious?'

'Pretty serious, but not something I couldn't handle.'

'Cause you look like you're doing a great job at that.'

'Long story.'

'What happened with your rich Chinese employers? What happened there? Fallen out? They the ones trying to kill you?'

'No, no falling out and they aren't trying to kill us, but we can't contact them. I've lost my stuff.'

'Ok. So long as I'm not getting into something that's going to burn me and mine... sorry. I just want to be sure of what this will cost.'

'No one knows we're here, trackers dead, suits dead, pack gone.'

'Ok, so what do you need?'

Joanna took another slug of brandy, 'We need a place to rest, not long. I need a suit, some money and gear. She needs some clothes. And the big one, a way out of here.'

Meier looked at the pair in front of her and thought about it. 'How hot are you?'

'Not immediate. But they won't stop looking.'

'So disappear and out?'

'If possible.'

'Anything's possible, but go to the wrong person for the wrong thing and you'll find yourself in the wrong place.'

'That's why I always come to you Sergeant.' Joanna smiled broadly and Meier grinned.

'Alright, you can stay with me for the rest. I have a boat, it's not the biggest, but it's discreet. The suit and the clothes and the gear are not a problem. Money is… money. Getting you out, now that's the one we need to think about.'

'Problem?'

'No… and yes. Do you care where you're going?'

Joanna and Mariana looked at each other, then Joanna turned back, 'No.'

There was a knock on the door and Meier went over and pulled it open, 'Yeah?'

A server was there, the room behind her darker than it had been, 'Just knocking off Boss, anything you want done?'

'Nah, you're good. You on tomorrow?'

'I am and through the weekend.'

'Oh right, good. Good evening?'

'Ok, not amazing, but it was steady.'

'Get out of here then, see you tomorrow.'

The girl left and Meier watched her go until she'd passed through the door with a couple of her colleagues, they waved and she waved back. Meier turned back to her guests.

'You guys had enough to eat?' They both agreed they had and Meier walked to the back of the room and leant out the door.

'Marcus, we're off, can you bring something out for the morning? Meet us downstairs at the front.'

'Sure.'

She turned, they gathered themselves up and headed out down the narrow stairway. Mariana carefully kept Joanna between her and open space as far as she could. Meier watched and took note. Once down in the main room, Marcus came out with a box.

'I presumed for three, was I right?'

'Aren't you always? You staying?'

'Someone's been helping themselves to the custard cream tarts.'

Meier looked at him blankly.

'We pay people enough and feed them well, and they only have to ask. It wasn't you was it?'

'No sir. I always ask… almost always.'

'Last time they left the cold room door open and I found it by accident. We can lose a lot of money that way and burn out the motor, it's not like this equipment is new or anything.'

'Right I'll leave you, don't get killed yourself will you?'

Marcus gave her a steady look and she turned to the door and shooed the others toward it.

9

Who is...?

[It was four days before Milo met Julia in Paris]

Kevin had been living in the suite of rooms reserved for Anna's company in Sao Paulo. Jones, who he had last seen here on the night before the disaster with Jo and Mariana, was gone. Despite Anna's dark invitation, he had not set foot outside the building since his drunken night of regret. In fact he had been barred from doing so as Milo was in town and Kevin was supposed to be missing and, he knew from Anna, presumed dead along with Jo and Mariana. China 12 had been kicked off the case and couldn't be involved in the investigation of the deaths as they were themselves implicated. Kevin didn't like the sense of being imprisoned, it reminded him too much of being imprisoned. Too much time to think, too many things to think about. None of them good.

That changed pretty swiftly with Anna's arrival.

'Kevin, remind me again what happened that evening.'

'Which evening?'

She waited.

'Right...At the hangar where we were supposed to go with your...'

'No, skip on to the place where Joanna and Dr Armenta died.'

Kevin squinted at her, wondering what had turned up, what she knew, 'Why?'

'Because I want to know.'

In a cop reading from his notes voice, 'I had followed Jo and Mariana to the Campo de Marte airfield...'

'Let me just stop you right there. Why did you go there? You said it was "plan B" but it sounds pretty convenient to me.'

'It was where we'd originally planned to go, before Jones suggested using your plane. Jones's plan had all of the advantages that we really would look for; discreet, unexpected and private. Though it looks like you have a mole telling people things they shouldn't have.'

Again, she looked at him. He felt though, that last bit had hit home and something...

'Campo de Marte, go on.'

'You don't want to explain the leaks from your end?'

'Campo de Marte...'

He took a deep breath, 'I had been a bit knocked about, so I'm not clear on all the details, but when I got there Jo was already prepped to fly. We had words...'

'You had a disagreement? You didn't mention that...'

'She wasn't happy about what had happened earlier, but she understood... Anyway, we were in the middle of talking it out when someone, I thought it was that pixie maybe, but it might not have been, shot her. She went down and I ran over to her. Mariana came out of the office and as I bent down she was shot. There must have been more than one shot because the fuels cells went up and I was thrown back. When I managed to get to my feet, the heat was too much and I was driven back.'

'So both dead, everything in flames. Did you see any pilot?'

'No, but then I know Jo can fly.'

'Can fly?'

'Could fly.'

'You see, you keep making that mistake.'

'I've known Jo for a long time, it's not uncommon, I've lost a few friends, it takes a while to get your head round it.'

'Yes, yes, we've all been in the war. But in this instance, it's a bit different. Let me put a different outline to you, one that fits the facts rather better. Jones makes an offer to you and you seem to accept. You talk it over with Joanna and decide to go back to China anyway, but you want to buy yourself some time and you fancy the idea of getting your hands on that money. You two hit the hanger, tracking shows you did arrive separately; so, a surprise double hit. You blow it up killing our guys in the process. You cut your tracking. But you know someone's behind you. So, you then go to the second airfield where you play out a pantomime for the tail to see and then split. You have the added bonus of being able to confuse any detection. Of course, you didn't think that China 12 wouldn't be the investigators on the main case. Go on, am I close?'

Kevin just stared at her and she waited. Finally.

'What the fuck are you on? I saw them dead. The whole place went up.'

'Explain then the lack of a DNA match?'

'DNA, you got DNA out of that?'

'We're very clever.'

'How can you have a DNA match for Jo?'

'Even if there were no army records for us to find and even if we didn't have a match for Dr Armenta, there being only Male DNA at the scene was a bit of a giveaway.'

'But... I saw them...'

Anna watched him as he tried to play back the scene in his head and then his eyes came up to hers.

'There was no trace?'

'None.'

'Then where are they? Jo was hit, three times I'm sure of it. Her suit was shot, half of it was gone...Mariana didn't have a suit. They couldn't have survived the heat... could they?'

'Or something even stranger happened.'

'How?' Kevin turned away and sat down. Anna watched him, seeming to try to gauge his reaction.

'Let's believe you didn't know for a moment. Is there anyone she could've contacted to get out of Brazil? Had you already contacted someone else?'

'No. That is, no we hadn't any other arrangements, just vague plans we'd discarded because they were unsafe or impractical.'

'Had you discussed it with any other operatives?'

'There aren't any. It was supposed to be a quick in/out thing.'

'Does she know anyone?'

'Not that I know of.'

'Have you any other means of tracking her, apart from her China 12 system? I presume you have a system.'

'Yeah, of course, but mine was... damaged, I guess hers was too.'

Kevin stopped and looked at Anna, 'How did you find me?'

She grinned, 'You took a drink with our Mr. Jones, two in fact. Each drink had a molecule that we can track, it persists for about forty-eight hours.'

'Bastards.'

'You were on the payroll, we had a right. Back to our current problem, how do we find your former colleague?'

Kevin frowned, 'There must be someone, she won't have done it without a plan.'

'Alright young Kevin, if you still want to get your generous pay-day you have to find them, I can't wait about here any longer. You're on a last chance. Let me warn you that we don't have a sense of humour and we do have very long memories. If you're trying to play both ends against the middle, or you're still working with China 12 and not telling us; we will not forgive.'

'I'll need a few things.'

'Send me the list. I need Armenta and I want her alive.'

'And Jo?'

'I don't want her alive.'

10

How are you Here?

[It was two days before Milo met Julia in Paris]

A boat incongruously moored to a building in Rio. Incongruous to previous generations that is. In the quarter of Rio where Meier had her bar, hundreds of boats were tied up this way. At the edge of the city, those who could, had moved from the uncertainty of the favela to a nautical version. Living in boats, ranging from the large and elaborate, to the basic and tiny. The size of the boat often being in inverse proportion to the size of the community housed within.

Meier's boat, her home, was a converted river barge. Not a narrow boat, but something more spacious and easy to live in, still, not the biggest but not tiny. Highly efficient sunlight converters changed seawater to hydrogen fuel cells, which gave her power for the boat and supplemented the power in the bar.

Meier and another young woman came toward the barge in a smaller launch, pulled up alongside and threw a line over a peg on the larger boat, hauling them in tight. While her colleague kept the boats tight together, Meier heaved several large canvas bags onto the deck of the barge. Climbing up after them, she turned back to the woman in the launch.

'Be back in two hours, no later. José should have the specials I ordered last week and, when he tries it on, tell him the price is the price. I don't want to have to tell him myself.'

The woman smiled and waved, as she let out the line and Meier pushed the launch away with her foot. The launch drifted round until the woman pushed the power handle forward and spun the rudder, neatly turning the boat away from the mother ship, then straightened up and away.

Joanna's head appeared at the far end of the deck and as she climbed up the steps it was clear that she was ready for whoever it was had just come aboard. Reaching the deck, she dropped the bat she'd been carrying and went to lend Meier a hand.

'This it then?'

'Mostly, I have a few odds and ends to get from the bar, but this is pretty well the full shopping list.'

Hearing the voices, Mariana's head popped up and she scrambled up to help. Meier slung a bag at her, which took her off her feet sending her back onto her backside. The other two laughed and Mariana looked down at the bag across her lap.

'It's heavy.'

'It better be, with what it cost!'

Mariana looked concerned, 'How are we going to repay you?'

'You won't and this is only part of my debt, eh Major?'

Joanna looked down and smiled as she held out her hand to Mariana and dragged her up.

'Once we're off your hands I think we'll be settled up pretty handsomely.'

'Generous, but…'

Mariana squinted at the pair. She'd tried to probe their past earlier but had been pushed back by each in turn, curiosity still niggled away. They made their way to the hatch to head below Meier stepped back and as Joanna passed she muttered, 'We have to talk.' Something in the tone suggested that it was not about chewing the fat or the 'old days'. Joanna flicked her head and they went down.

They dumped the bags on a large dark wood table that took up one end of the room. Mariana looked at the other two women.

'Coffee?'

Meier grinned, 'Love it.'

Joanna nodded. Mariana turned and disappeared into the galley area. Meier faced Joanna and flicked her head in Mariana's direction.

'How much does she know about your situation?'

'She knows, I wouldn't keep anything from her, she is still the client.'

Meier dropped her head, pursed her lips, 'I heard some things.'

'Oh?'

'First, are you dead?'

Joanna grinned, 'For as long as I can make it last.'

'Looks like time's up.'

'Shit.'

'Words gone out, with some pretty good pictures and a lot of money attached.'

'Enough to turn your head?'

'Enough to push my plans ahead by a few years.'

'Ok. Kevin wasn't kidding then, they have deep pockets.'

'Kevin?'

'From China 12. He was bought off by the people trying to control Mariana, he isn't China 12 anymore I'm guessing. The bruising and bullets in my back were our parting words.'

Mariana made a loud noise and after a few beats came into the room with a tray of cups. Joanna turned to watch her come in and grinned.

'It's ok Mariana, anything I'm told I'll tell you too. If it's going to affect you, you'll know.'

Mariana smiled as she put down the tray, 'I don't know what you mean.'

Meier lifted a mug and sat on the edge of the table, 'Obviously there's a story to tell, and I've been polite and not asked; so, do you want to tell me?'

Joanna looked at Mariana who approved. Joanna took her mug and sat on the bench at the table, her back to the wall.

'Ok, yes we are dead, or were,' she turned to Mariana, 'they know.'

'Shit.'

Joanna turned back to Meier, 'I told you that we'd had trouble getting out of Sao Paulo. We'd arranged with the people Mariana was contracted to, to get a lift to Beijing. The idea was to take a break at our base and then decide what the best plan was for the future.'

'Why are you such a hot property?' Meier asked.

'We'll get to that…'

*

42

'…It's not my way to go out without a fight and anyway China 12 have a plane, booked and paid for, here. We still have options.' Joanna finished.

'I'm tired.'

'I know.'

They fell silent. Joanna could see the lights at the edge of the airfield approaching. She knew decision time was coming but a plan was forming in her mind; the fire they'd just survived had given her an idea, a desperate one but… It might work. She looked behind at the two cabs following. The pixie hadn't intervened yet. If she hadn't done anything at the hanger they'd just left, she was likely on a 'watch and wait' brief. The second cab was probably that nutter who was trying to kill Mariana. Or it was Kevin, if Kevin was still alive.

'Hey, Mariana, wake up.'

Mariana opened her eyes, clearly not asleep, 'I've been listening to you thinking.'

'Sorry. I have a plan.'

'Does it include me dying?'

'Yes.'

'What?'

'I agree, it's the only way. I just don't want it to be final.'

'I'm listening.'

'When we get to the airfield the cab will take you to the terminal. I'll get it to stop on the way. At the terminal you give the verification code, here.'

She reached out her arm and they touched wrists, Joanna transferring the code to Mariana.

'Then, you come back to pick me up, the office will give you the coordinates of the hanger.'

'And the dying?'

'We'll do that after you pick me up, it may get a bit hairy but then you'll get a rest, I promise.

Mariana sighed, 'Ok.'

The cab passed the gates and headed for the terminal. Joanna looked back and watched as the nearest cab went through the gates and took the opposite direction. The third cab didn't follow, turning off before the gate.

'Right, I think that's the pixie who probably thinks we're getting a plane out of here and is waiting by the hangers, I hope that's all she's going to do. The other cab…'

She looked at Mariana, 'It's probably our friend who attacked us at the last place.'

Mariana shrugged. Joanna looked out the window and said, 'Stop!'

The cab rolled to a stop and the door opened, Joanna climbed out. Mariana leaned forward and said, 'Continue.'

As the cab rolled away, Joanna looked back. They had rounded a corner and were out of sight of the gate and the buildings beyond it, 'Good.' She looked at the door in front of her. The place was dark. Beside the door was a plaque, white lacquer, black letters and a cross, "Necrotério do Espírito Santo", she walked to the door saw it had an old mechanical lock and she knelt. A few seconds at the lock and she went inside.

Once inside she headed for the cold chamber and hoped there'd be some customers. Impressed by the standard of security, she took a few more moments at the chamber's lock and then went inside. She scoured the place for cleaning fluids and chemicals that might make an improvised bomb and placed it near the air-conditioning ducts. She set a charge from the few she had in her suit, and a timer, then went in search of bodies. There were three, all male, all overweight. Heaving them all onto a single gurney, she wheeled it back to the front door and then waited.

A moment to run through what she'd need. She looked over to the reception desk. It was large, dark, solid and very old, probably there to give the place an air of solemnity and respectability. Looking at the chair, which was of a similar age and fashion, she winced at the thought of sitting in it for any length of time. Then she had a thought. Going over to the desk, she ran through the drawers, forcing the large bottom drawer. Bingo! Spare batteries and an old-fashioned data acquisition terminal (DAT). These were sometimes used for money transactions and the lazy could... just as this one did, access money, stored but not yet forwarded to accounts. It was the equivalent of petty cash. She transferred money to her chip and took the battery spares.

The suit she wore used an electrical field to reinforce its strength and needed power to use its other capabilities. As it was for use in combat, it had a system that allowed it to drain several types of power sources. Now that her backups were left behind, she'd need these for the plan to work, and it still might not. It hinged in part on how good a shot that assassin was going to turn out to be and in hoping the pixie didn't get involved. As she walked back to the door the cab rolled to a halt outside.

As the cab door slid open Joanna shouted, 'Give me a hand here.'

'Ok,' and Mariana jumped out of the cab then stopped, looking horrified.

'Did you just...'

'Yes, and I'm so tidy they're washed, smelling of chemicals and very cold.'

'Alright, how am I to know...'

Joanna gave her an exasperated look.

'Why do we need these?'

'These are us.'

Mariana looked sceptical as she reached for the first body, touched it and pulled back her hand.

'Oh, he feels...'

'Dead, that's what dead feels like. After a few hours anyway. Just keep clear and hold the gurney steady, they're heavy.'

Heaving the first body over her shoulder in a fireman's lift, Joanna took a step back to steady herself then eased it into the cab, climbed in and pulled it to the far side. She repeated the process twice more and smiled at Mariana.

'Get in, I'll be a moment.'

She raced back inside with the gurney and returned with a green sheet over one arm, she pulled everything shut as she came back out. She locked the front door, then turned and saw Mariana still waiting outside the cab.

'Come on.' She climbed in, with Mariana following slowly after. The cab rolled on.

As they arrived at the hanger Joanna could see the pilot looking over the plane, he waved. They drove to the front of the hanger and then in through the open double doors behind the plane. Right in as far as they could get, before they stopped. The cab door slid open and the pilot was standing behind the cab waving his arms about. Joanna leaned out.

'Calm down, I have…'

'Lady, you can't have the cab… how did you even? You can't…'

'Hey! I can, I did, and there's more. Are you going to shut up and listen?'

Mariana was crouching in the cab behind Joanna and it was clear that they'd been through a little difficulty.

'Look, we're a small company. We can't be involved in something. You'd better take your business…'

And very discreetly, Joanna pulled out her side arm. 'If you don't want to be involved, that's fine, but then shut up and do as I say.'

He looked at the gun, then at Joanna and then sighed heavily.

'Let's take a look at the aircraft.'

They walked out to the plane, and had a look. Joanna sent the pilot and mechanic back, telling them to go into the back office. After a moment or two checking what was where and fixing something to the door, she went back inside. She checked the office, noted it was windowless, then she sent the mechanic out to disconnect the fuelling tanker. She then locked them both in the back office, before coming round to the cab again.

'Right, we have a few minutes. Keep out of sight I think our friend is out there with a rifle.'

They dragged the bodies out and lined them up against the interior wall, covering them again with the sheet Joanna had brought with her. She stepped back and sighed. Leaning into the cab, she pulled the cover off the control system and did some adjusting. When she finished she gave Mariana a reassuring smile.

'I'll get rid of these guys, stay out of sight.'

Mariana pressed herself against the wall and watched as Joanna had an insistent discussion with the two unhappy men. They trooped into the cab. Joanna pulled an arm forward from each one. They winced and then stared at Joanna, as the door slid closed. The cab pulled away.

Joanna came over to Mariana, pulling off the parts of the suit that covered her lower legs as she walked.

'Right, these things are designed so that in the case of damage one bit can replace another bit, keeping your most important bits safe, safe-ish.'

Mariana watched as Joanna made a single piece and then held it out.

'You didn't kill those guys, did you?'

Joanna was surprised and then smiled, 'No. I sent them for a little sleep is all. Ok?'

Mariana smiled weakly and looked at what Joanna had in her hands.

'You have to put this to cover your torso. I've charged it so it should provide you with enough protection. I'm going to set some charges. I've already put a small camera on the door so I can see what's going on. When I'm done, I'll go out there and try and get shot, by our friend. When I go down, you come out with that cannon you had, hold it at head height and square on to the field, that way he'll only have a body shot. When he hits you, stay down. When all hell breaks loose, stay down. Stay down until I come for you. Understand?'

She nodded, looking terrified. Joanna smiled.

'If we're lucky, this will buy us a couple of days.'

She turned and slapped charges on the fuel tanker and then walked out to the plane, just as a cab pulled up and Kevin stepped out…

11

Leaving Rio is always Hard

'...And then, like I said earlier, we had words.'

Joanna was sitting on the edge of a seat, a drink in her hand. Cups behind her suggested it'd been a while. Meier and Mariana listened. Meier frowned.

'But didn't the pilot go get help?'

'I thought I said? I'd set the taxi to take a long trip round the city and the two guys were out of it. The power ran out in the Cab eventually I suppose, I don't know if it had a return to base protocol or just a 'help' signal went out. I said a little sleep, I guess it would have been about a day.'

'Your burns then were because you had to wait for the others to go?'

'Yeah. The pixie arrived down and I thought she and Kevin were going to get into it, but he backed off and so did she. They were at the edges of the image, so I'm not too sure. I thought the problem would be with the guy in the outfield making sure of the kill but he left straight away.'

'Once Kevin was clear I could get up and put our bodies in place.'

'What about the services?'

'That was why I set the bomb in the Mortuary. Because it was near the terminal it would get most of the attention.'

'And then you made your way up here.'

'Yeah, the comfort of freight transport. I was tired enough to sleep anywhere. I think Mariana here thought I was a goner.'

'You didn't look great and you wouldn't stay awake.' Mariana said defensively.

'Oh, *I* wouldn't stay awake...?'

'Yeah well, it had been a long day.'

'You do like your adventures Major.' Meier put in.

'So this kind of thing isn't new?' Mariana asked Meier.

'New? It sounded like a rerun.' Joanna exploded in laughter. She took a drink and then turned to the bags, still heaped up. She lifted her chin at them and Meier walked over and unzipped the first.

'I got pretty well everything. Not to spec, but beggars can't be blah, blah…' She began to pull things out and line them up in order. Joanna crouched and started to go through things, opening boxes and taking apart weapons, then snapping them back together. Mariana watched, impressed and intimidated at the same time. Meier turned to her.

'You still haven't said why there is this fuss trying to get you and the money…'

Mariana looked worried, 'Is it a lot?'

'Let's just say I can tell they want you and others will be pleased to oblige. So?'

'They want to control the world.'

That produced silence. Joanna stopped what she was doing and looked at Mariana, open mouthed. Meier looked at her about to laugh, but stopped.

'You're serious.'

Mariana nodded.

'How? I mean people have tried in the past, but, with all due respect, you don't look that powerful. Secret powers? You can leap tall buildings, not that that would help…'

'No, you'd never know.'

Joanna put down the pack of ammunition she was checking, 'This is what you and Rodrigo were working on?'

Mariana nodded and looked at her, 'It had two parts. We had heard about the idea from a friend at CERN.'

'CERN?' Meier looked puzzled.

'It's a big Physics thingy, trying to make black holes.' Joanna explained.

Mariana reddened, 'What? No. Yes, it's a physics thingy but we're not trying to make black holes.'

'I thought I read you made one.'

'Sometimes tiny singularities appear, but they're gone in an instant and they're rare.'

'Singularities are black holes, no?'

'In a way, but these are tinier than tiny and they're gone in thousandths of a second.'

'Oh.'

'Anyway… Our friend told us that he and his two cousins, who are these amazingly brilliant mathematicians, they are also science fiction buffs, Rodrigo is… was, too. We were laughing at Isaac Asimov, who was a last century writer. He came up with some amazing ideas for his time, but in his books he had only one woman of any consequence, who was not a child or housewife. Also, in his future they had robots with "positronic" brains, but people had to steer vehicles by hand, all of them, cars, planes, rocket ships.'

'Oh. So no women.' Meier looked puzzled.

'Not outside a kitchen, no. That wasn't all, but that was what we were laughing about.'

'I'd like to have met him.' Joanna said and Meier grinned, Mariana might have misunderstood.

'Oh yes, he was very brilliant.' Then she looked at them, 'Oh.'

'So what has this to do with taking over the world?'

'Asimov came up with a system he called "psychohistory", a mix of psychology, sociology and statistical probability. It was supposed to be able to guide populations and even huge Galactic Empires for their own good, in his books at least. Our friend said they had been kicking it about and had come up with a set of algorithms that could work. We didn't believe him but he said they'd tried it and it worked.'

'Whoa! How long has this been going on?'

'It isn't yet. They didn't implement the system because it scared them and he also said they had devised a fail-safe, but he didn't explain what that was or how it worked. Anyway, he went on to say that they had realised it was too complicated. If it was going to work over time, what it really needed was an AI to make it perform. Adjust it in response to how people adjusted. Once they had the AI, they lost interest in the system because they thought it would be the perfect research assistant. Which was how the whole thing about Asimov had come up in the first place.'

'Perfect?'

'Yeah. It would load into your implant, and then also grow into your physical, cellular system. It would be completely compatible with your mind because it would be devised based on your psychological profile and personality. When you're asleep it could still accumulate research elements for you to work on together.'

'Ugh! Creepy! An AI in your head. I don't like the sound of that at all.' And Meier rubbed her head.

Mariana grinned, 'But you have implants and you link up to systems all the time?'

'But not an AI, the rest is under my control, an AI could do what it liked. How long would it be before I'd be doing what it liked?'

'But it would be designed around you completely. You already have molecular automated robots in your system making drugs for you, when you're in a fight, or when you're sick, or drunk.'

'That's different, they help me out. Would you let them do that to you, Major?'

'I can see advantages, but the system would be wide open to abuse, especially in the military. So, no I wouldn't, but would I know if someone did upload one into my system?'

Mariana shrugged, 'You mean if they did it without your permission? You'd probably figure it out, but it might not be obvious.'

'But they did develop the research assistant?' Joanna asked, as she shifted her attention back to the contents of the bags.

'I think they did. They hadn't made it public, I think they were afraid of, like you said, abuse.'

'Then, which is it that these people are after?' Meier pressed.

'I don't think they know about the assistant part. We were struggling to get that right. We'd done the first part, but without the constant guidance of the assistant, it becomes obvious the system needs lots and lots of manual inputs, adjustments, as people's behaviour shifts. These needed to be carefully coordinated, it becomes impossible… Potential outcomes increase as time passes.'

'Surely you can develop an algorithm to control that?' She pressed.

Mariana pulled a face, 'We thought so at first, but it takes the instruction to the logical conclusion and very quickly becomes ridiculous and, like I said, obvious..'

'Lots of them then?' Joanna asked.

'We even tried that, having them make dynamic adjustments, but it quickly falls apart. We tried an AI too obviously, but either it learned something other than what we wanted, or it was too slow or... we don't know, we never got one to work, or we hadn't by the time...'

'So then the assistant, implanted?' Meier asked, puzzling it out.

'Yeah, but when you go down that road you find you have to particularise it and a few conversations with some friends suggested the dangers of psychosis were very high. The dividing wall between the virtual world and your sense of "reality" would have been breached. Rodrigo wanted to give it a go...'

'This means, if they find you and set you to work on this stuff, that would be bad news?'

'If I got it right, very bad news; if I got it half right, very very bad news. They've already deployed test elements of the program and produced some, I guess they think favourable, results.'

'So why'd you do it? Knowing what you do about it?' Joanna asked.

'We didn't begin with these people. We began working with our friends in a faith group, we thought we could maybe nudge the world into better decisions. Then the higher-ups thought it would be a chance to usher in the last days, skipping over the bad bits.'

Meier sat up, shaking her head slowly, 'I'm sorry, that doesn't sound any better.'

'No, but we were finding it difficult to get out of it. Then Rodrigo told me he had some friends who could help us get out. He didn't say who.'

'These guys.' Meier gestured to the air.

Mariana grimaced, 'But also our friends in the faith group turned on us. I would never have thought they could do this; but they did.'

Joanna shook her head, 'You can't be sure.'

'I can, the man I shot? He had a small cross, Rodrigo and I have the same one.'

Joanna held her gaze for a few moments and then dropping her head, shrugged. 'Who can tell what people are really like? I went through a war with him and Kevin still surprised me.'

Meier looked at her, 'I don't remember him?'

'He was with the Brits. We did that set of covert ops together, remember, toward the end?'

She shrugged, 'I don't remember what I remember, don't remember him though.'

Joanna looked at the contents of the bags now spread around her, 'I think you might have overdone it Sergeant, we'll never be able to carry all this.'

'Yeah, I don't think so either. The smart way out is the way you came up here. It would just be a case of picking your changes, then you can get lost in Central America. It would be needle in a haystack time. But I don't think that's what you should do.'

Mariana looked at Joanna anxiously; this was beginning to sound like the last conversation with Kevin.

'You're heading for the West Coast of the US, no?'

Joanna was also wary, 'Maybe. We do have lots of options.'

'Ok, so you need something that keeps alive your options but still holds that out as a final destination.'

'Ok.'

'You two are still, I don't want to be harsh but, showing some wear and tear.'

'Ok.'

'I control two shipping lines. They're not big…'

'Shipping lines; sounds big.'

'Think of like the shipping version of that plane you destroyed in Sao Paulo.'

'Oh, right.'

Mariana began to relax a bit and listened intently, still throwing the occasional look at Joanna.

'The thing is, even smaller ships are automated. These are retro-fitted with a system so they have to have at least two sailors on board.'

The two women exchanged a look and Mariana grinned.

'And I just noticed there are two of you.' Meier smiled.

Joanna grinned, 'I just noticed that as well.'

And then all hell broke loose.

12

Hunting

[It was two days before Milo met Julia in Paris]

Kevin had checked and rechecked for Jo's signal but could find nothing. If she had gotten out of that hanger alive, she was keeping very quiet. Not that that would surprise him, she'd always been smart that way, always had another plan to bring up and move onto smoothly. But he didn't see how she could have survived being shot. He was sure her suit must have been drained, or very nearly and she had left her pack in the hangar; he'd passed it burning as he'd left. She must have gotten a power source to drain somewhere. The cab maybe, though he couldn't see how in the time they had, it took a lot of messing about.

He had been trying to work out what she did afterward, but kept coming back to the events of that night. He shook his head and refocused on the map playing in his retinal implant. She should have headed to Rio, easy to get lost, lots of ways to get there, a good chance of help; but going to Rio was also obvious. Did she know anyone from there? Or who went there? He knew the place was a mess, which would be dangerous. A lot of desperate ex-soldiers.

After demob, lots of his comrades had left Europe; Africa had been popular and bits of Asia. Aus was no good anymore. But South America and parts of Central America were very much what the doctor ordered. The Nordics and other parts of the Euro-Army had taken the same view, he believed. Jo had been commissioned in the French Special Forces. He could see the Spaniards, the Portuguese and the Italians doing exactly that, but would the French? Jo had obviously gone for Asia. What kind of search parameters would he need? It'd be easy to just ask one of the geniuses in China 12 to find out, they just asked you a few questions and a few minutes later…

Anna's company's system was a bit clunky, a bit like the old Army system he'd had in the war. He hadn't realised how much he'd gotten used to the smooth way things had worked in Beijing. He'd tried "French", but then Jo wasn't French either. He'd tried, "French" and then "Euro" "Army ex". What about a simple search date? When had he demobbed? Add a few months for faffing and then travel and registering.

What kind of business did his former pals go into? What did they know how to do? If they went back into careers they'd already had they wouldn't be in Rio, not after what had happened with the sea level rises. What do soldiers know how to do? Security. Weapons. Paramedics, he thought a few of those would be useful. Drinking mostly, so a bar or a club, or a club and a bar. A few played instruments, so, music. Management? Maybe. Strip clubs, brothels, but he'd not really be able to find them too easily and the locals would get narked.

So, security, paramedics and bars. Even if he didn't find a guy she'd got in touch with, he might be able to find a man who knew. He was sure she had travelled up by freight, automated systems made that a no-brainer and that was part of standard special ops training as well, but should he go the same way or the quickest way?

How many days had he lost? What kind of state was Mariana in? She might be dead, they both might be. Just 'cause they didn't die there, didn't mean they didn't die in some truck on the way to Rio. Quickest then.

Probably best to check the paramedics first. He looked down the list, a surprisingly high number considering. But then they were pretty sought after, they certainly had experience of working under pressure and from what he'd heard of Rio there were a lot of shootings. He could ask any of them about the guys in security and they'd know about the bars. He'd have to get the right story, people can be pretty cagey when you're asking about their friends, even when they weren't friendly.

Ok, he had a plan.

It took only a few hours the next day for Kevin to be walking through the streets of Rio, sweltering in street clothes with his combat suit underneath. Most people kept off the streets from about 10am 'til 5pm and unless you were to take the long way across the top of the hill you had to constantly get from car to boat and back, to get anywhere. There had been no money to move the buildings or to keep remaking the streets as the sea levels rose and there was little point in attacking the problem now as the sea level still had some way to go.

His first few encounters had been what he was expecting, either they didn't know or they weren't prepared to say. Not that he'd been asking directly if they'd known Jo, or seen Mariana. He was just asking generally about units or divisions, as though he was trying to set up in Rio himself. Maybe that was exactly what he should have done. He could see himself running a nice little casino here. With the beaches gone, there was not that much else to do if you weren't rich and the rich always liked to find somewhere to slum it as well, just like those boys in Sao Paulo.

The last guy he spoke to had told him something interesting. Ex-French army, a Legionnaire, setting up a little money lending business, who might need a bit of muscle, had a few other interests. This might be just the ticket. Has a place on one of these boats, everyone had a boat it seemed. Either you're very rich or the land-based places are falling down, so you do the logical thing.

He wondered if this Shylock would offer him anything to bite on, or if he'd have to start getting rough with someone. He checked over his arsenal just to be sure, if they wanted muscle it would be best to come in looking like you could tear up the joint in any case. He was just beginning to feel frustrated enough to want to tear something up right now. He was just waiting for the right button to be pushed…

13

The past always Catches up

The room collapsed around them in a hail of bullets. Joanna dived for Mariana, pulling her behind the large sofa that filled one side of the cabin. It gave at least visual cover. Bullets though, had ripped through it and both its top half and the wall behind were splintered and in pieces. Joanna could see two legs at the top of the stair down into the cabin. They paused as whoever it was reloaded. She fired, hitting them in the right thigh. A man tumbled down the stairs and Meier put a bullet in his head. Joanna looked across and saw that Meier had been hit in the shoulder and was consequently in a bad mood.

A smoke grenade was dropped into the cabin. The room filled with a purple smoke and the sound of heavier people coming down the steps. Mariana's and Joanna's hands were cut by the glass from the window above, but Joanna pulled them both down again and put her face close to Mariana's ear, 'Head for the kitchen.'

Whoever was attacking them was now at the bottom of the steps, with Meier behind them and Joanna in front and to the side. Mariana crawled toward the narrow kitchen door and one of the men fired in that direction, hitting the wall above her. She pressed herself to the floor. Meier fired off a volley of shots, covering Mariana as she scrambled to the kitchen, and then called, 'Out.'

The men evidently had not used smoke before and their systems, whatever they were, were using old infrared imaging at best, they were blind. Joanna, not so much. She and Meier had systems designed to see through IR blocking smoke. When the man firing the weapon in her direction paused, Joanna stood and fired. He went down. Meier walked up and calmly took out the second man from behind with something heavy. Silence. Mariana was still trying to crawl quietly through the kitchen. Joanna and Meier listened, then Joanna asked, 'Are we done?'

Another pause, before Meier moved to the bottom of the steps. Joanna called, 'Sergeant,' and threw her a weapon. As she took the first step she caught it in one hand swinging it jerkily into her other hand and pointing up to the main deck. Favouring her injured shoulder she took the first few steps, stopped, then a few more. She got to the top and swept the area.

'Clear.'

Joanna looked back at Mariana still making her way painfully to the kitchen.

'We're clear.'

Mariana collapsed and lay still. The smoke cleared fully and Meier did a thorough sweep of the deck. Joanna went over to Mariana, knelt and lifted her, she was sobbing.

'Hey, they're done, we're ok.'

'Why did we ever start this thing? Why? Who are these people? Which side? How can they have found us so quickly?'

'I don't know. I think one is still alive, so we'll find out. It could be that the money offered for us unbuttoned some lips at the bar, but we'll find out.'

Meier was coming down the steps, blood now flowing pretty readily from her shoulder. She stopped at the bottom. A sound, from one of the prone bodies there and her foot lashed out.

'Fuckers!' And then across to her companions, 'Are you two alright? Good shooting Major, you haven't lost your touch. These bastards are going to pay.'

'Do you know them?'

'I do.'

'Do you think they heard about us through the bar?'

'Eh?'

'Someone must have seen...'

'No, no, this has nothing to do with you. This punk I don't know. The dead one here and the other one ...'

She walked over to check, bent down and stood up again, '... who is also dead, are brothers who were trying to set up a racket in the quarter where I have my bar. I told them to stick it and they don't seem to have taken it well.'

'So the third one's, what, a friend?'

'Let's find out.'

She bent down, lifted the man into a sitting position and slapped his face a few times.

'Hey, hey I'm talking to you, don't pretend you're out of it, or I'll cuff you hand and foot and put you over the side. I want answers.'

The man shook his head and opened his eye. He looked around and his eyes fell on the two brothers and then he snapped back to Meier.

'Please don't kill me.'

'You were coming to kill me, why wouldn't I?'

'Please, we only wanted to frighten you.'

'No, you were making an example of me to frighten other people. Isn't that right?'

He stared at her, his breathing shallow and quick, as though he'd been running. He acknowledged it and looked back at the bodies.

'Please, they said it would be easy.'

'If you're trying to make me feel sorry for you, you're going the wrong way. Are there any more in your little gang?'

He shook his head, 'I've never done anything like this, they said they would do it all, it would be no problem, they paid me extra, I work in their bar, I have a kid, please.'

'Fine example you are. Are you the security?'

He looked at her confused, and searched her face looking to see the catch, then it dawned, 'No I'm the bar man, I make cocktails, but I'm big, they said it would frighten you.'

She held his terrified gaze and he swallowed.

'Do I look frightened?'

He shook his head. She held his eyes steadily and he began to shake.

'Looks like you own a bar now. Take these two with you, I never want to see you again, or hear from you again, understand? This is your lucky day.'

He closed his eyes, tears running down his face and his head bobbed up and down vigorously.

A few hours later and they'd cleared the glass away, Meier had been bandaged up and Joanna and Mariana had hands covered in strapping. Meier was still in a bad mood.

'That's all very well, but they come here to try to make an example of me! I already have a reputation, people don't mess with me, I thought I was past this kind of shit.'

'You're never past this kind of thing.' Joanna offered, 'Not in a place like this.'

Mariana came out of the kitchen with a tray of bread and "meat", as well as mugs of coffee. She put it down in front of them and sat. She looked very unhappy.

'I want to be past this, I really do. I'm not used to it. I left Columbia to get away from anyone like this, I thought I had.'

Joanna covered her hand with her own. Meier looked at her sympathetically, her own rage seeming to evaporate.

'You will be soon. The ship leaves tomorrow morning. It finishes loading tonight at about midnight and you can get on board from about one o' clock. Any earlier than that and you'll have to meet people and people ask questions.'

Joanna started to slap some of the 'not quite meat' on the bread. 'That soon?'

'I was coming round to that when we were interrupted, sorry, it upset my train of thought.'

Mariana grinned at that and Meier smiled back.

'That is if you still want to do it that way and not overland.'

'We're not talking about this boat?'

Meier looked around and shook her head, 'No. A ship.'

'How long will it take?' Mariana asked, now also eyeing the food.

'It should take about 12 days. The forecast is good and the queue for the canal is pretty short because this ship is still small enough to use the old canal. It's a two day wait for the big one.'

Joanna looked at Mariana, who was negotiating several small pieces of the 'not quite meat' onto a large piece of bread. When the silence persisted Mariana looked up and found two faces watching her. She thought about it for a moment then, 'Oh, yeah, yes. I thought we'd decided. The ship. It seems much quieter.'

The other two looked at each other and Mariana caught the look. 'What? It is quieter, no?'

Meier nodded slowly, 'Yes, it should be. There's no reason to think it wouldn't be. Your names aren't near the manifest and there's no trace of you really, except your biometrics on your IDs which we can't avoid but can be cross referenced. If they track you down before you make port…'

'What? We'll be at sea.'

Joanna smiled, 'Yes, but if they attack when we're on board, we're trapped. It would seem you're a valuable asset.'

Mariana put down the bread. 'Is it likely?'

'Likely no; possible, yes. If we make port our chances go up a lot and I have resources in the US.' Joanna said.

'But so do they.' Mariana thinking it through.

'Yes, but they seem to have resources everywhere.'

'Ship is still better, either they get us or they don't.' She reached for the bread again.

The port was dark and empty along this quay. The rain had started up, distressing the surface of the water and drawing attention to the stillness that surrounded the ship. The huge automated container loaders were silent. Two quays over, it was a different story, a giant ship was loaded with thousands of containers being locked together with Tetris-like precision as the loading AI played out its plan for the most efficient and stable arrangements of sizes and weights for the ship and its journey. Once locked together the ship containers wouldn't move about.

At the first dock, near the gated entrance to the port, lay a much smaller ship. A launch swung round the point of the quay and drew alongside. Joanna stepped out onto the short deck of the launch and grabbed the bottom of the pilot's ladder. Slipping a line under the bottom rung, she threw the end to Meier who tied it off roughly, pulling the boat tight to the ship side.

Mariana emerged, carrying two bags slowly up to the deck, struggling under their weight. Joanna had already climbed up the ladder by the time Mariana got to its foot and she let down a line. Meier arrived with the third bag and each one in turn was tied to the line and hauled aboard. Mariana turned to Meier and put her arm round her neck, 'Thank you for doing this, I will never forget it.'

Meier smiled, 'That's ok, like I said, I owe the Major.'

'You never told me about that.'

'You can ask her, you'll have plenty of time for old stories.'

Mariana looked up and made a face at the slimy, very steep ladder in front of her.

'Is it safe?'

'That?' Meier grinned, 'That's the safest thing you've faced all week.'

Mariana grinned and reached out to the first rung taking it gingerly in her injured hand.

'Lean back as you climb and you'll be able to see each rung.' Meier advised, then covered her eyes as Mariana climbed.

Joanna watched, concerned, 'You're doing great, just keep going.'

It was painfully slow, but finally her white, slightly terrified face peeked over the rail at the edge of the deck, Joanna hauled her on board.

'That was terrifying.'

'Yeah, it is the first time.'

'First time?'

Joanna grinned and leaned over the side, 'Thanks Sergeant. I owe you now.'

'That's ok Major, any time,' and she released the line, pushing the boat away from the ship. Joanna watched her go. She turned and looked down at Mariana, 'Right, we'd best get this stuff below and check out what's what. Meier said we were stocked for twenty days and we leave in five hours.'

'We don't have to do anything, right?'

'Not unless we do. All we have to do is stay alive for two weeks and we should be ok.'

14

Questions at the end of a long night

[It was a day and a half before Milo met Julia in Paris]

Why was it that the back doors of bars and cafes and restaurants are always left open? This side of the bar was just above the current sea level and had to be approached by boat. It was dark and quiet and raining. Kevin had watched until the last workers had left. Watched until the woman he thought was the owner came back from somewhere in a launch and tied it off before heading inside, the lights going off as she moved upstairs. Did she live there, or was this just the office? Doesn't matter. He pushed the small rowing boat he was standing in away from the side and let it glide until it bumped into the steps. He tied it off and then stepped onto the bottom step.

Edging the door out with the tip of his rifle, he took a long moment to look and listen. Nothing. He walked carefully up into the building and along the first corridor to the bottom of the stairs. He stopped again and listened. He could hear someone moving up above and the early sounds of a kettle singing.

Floor by floor he rose through the building until he reached the third floor, the level of the kitchens, just below the office above. The light was on in the kitchen and the kettle was boiling furiously, going off with a snap just as he reached the door. He stepped back into the shadow and waited. He could hear someone moving about in the office above, nothing from this floor but the kettle gradually cooling. Was that for her?

Into the kitchen. Anyone about? Back office? Empty. Hand on the seat, cold. Kevin scanned the room, no one. She must have turned on the kettle.

Out of the kitchen, past the door and to the bottom of the stairs. Wait. Was she going to come down? Not yet.

Swiftly, silently he mounted the final staircase, nothing above but the skylight. He moved to the door of the office. It was slightly, invitingly, open. He moved round the door, trying to survey as much of the office as he could. She seemed alone, back to the door, concentrating on something in front of her. He took a last look and listen for anything else behind him. Nothing.

Rifle first, he went through the door and in a moment he was behind her, the muzzle of the gun pressed to the base of her skull.

'Sergeant Meier is it? Hands on the desk, look straight ahead. I have no doubt of your skills as a warrior.'

'Yeah? Who the fuck are you?'

'I'm a friend of an old comrade of yours, Sergeant. A Major Joanna Baines, of the Foreign Legion.'

'Oh yeah? How is she?'

'I was hoping you would tell me, I understand she's been visiting.'

'If you're such a friend, how come you're behind me and with a gun in my neck?'

'I've been told you're a dangerous woman, Sergeant. Can't be too careful. Now, if you'd like to let me know where she is, I'll be on my way.'

'At least tell me who I'm supposed to be talking to.'

'My name's Kevin Twomey, she might have mentioned me.'

Silence. The silence persisted.

Then, 'Never heard of you.'

'Doesn't matter. Just tell where she is and you need never hear from me again.'

'What's in it for me?'

'You get to live, that sounds pretty good to me.'

'Not from where I'm sitting. If I just tell you, you shoot me and leave. If I don't, you still need to find out what I know and we have something to talk about.'

He smiled, 'Very good. But even if we make a deal, what's to stop me just shooting you and leaving.'

'A deal ties me up. I want to get whatever we agree on, you want to check out if it's true and you still have the option of coming back and finding out more, or killing me.'

'You've worked this out.'

'Business.'

'So loyalty to the woman who saved your life and the lives of your unit, counts for nothing?'

'Business has to be kept away from sentiment, otherwise you're screwed.'

He leaned forward, 'What is that you're trying to hide Sergeant?'

His hand reached round to the desktop, pressing the rifle muzzle deeper into her neck, and lifted the paper.

'Shipping departures, interesting.'

One floor down, in the kitchen Marcus left the big walk-in cold room and the heavy metal door swung closed behind him. He walked over to the kettle and curse silently as he saw it was no longer boiling. Reaching forward to the switch a red light went on, snagging his attention. He stared at it hand frozen in mid air. After a moment he looked at his hand and pulled it back. He walked over to the little cubby in the corner, put down the clip-board, Marcus had been running through his inventory, the least favourite part of his day. He looked at the light again for a few seconds and he frowned. There was only one reason for that light and he'd only seen it once before. The question, was what to do about it.

'Sergeant.'

'I'm not a sergeant anymore.'

'I was told you were known as that round here.'

'Not to anyone who really knows me.'

'So what do you want to be called, seeing as we're going to be such great business partners?'

'Señora Meier.'

'Oh right Señora.'

He looked around the room, 'actually this seems a pretty sweet set up, maybe we will be partners. But first things first, eh? Did she leave on one of these ships, Señora?'

'Let me see the list again?'

Kevin leaned forward and put the list down in front of her and then everything went black.

'Shit Marcus.'

'Sorry Boss.'

Marcus leapt forward and dragged Kevin off Meier. When he'd hit him, Kevin had collapsed over Meier's head. Now he was on the floor and they were looking down at him. Marcus looked across at Meier, 'What do we do with him?'

'Cook him?'

'Nothing that would fit him downstairs and, anyway, how do we explain the sudden arrival of real meat?'

She reached into the desk drawers and pulled out some old-fashioned cuffs, snapping them on him with his hands behind his back. She stood again.

'I should put a bullet in him after what he did to the Major.' She said. Marcus looked alarmed.

'But,' Meier leaned over the desk again and picked up the paper she'd been distracting him with, 'how about he takes a nice trip to Africa? We have something leaving for Freetown tonight,' she called up her watch, 'in about fifty minutes and it doesn't belong to me so it's fully automatic. No complicated questions, well, not for me.'

'How long will it take?'

She looked down again at the page, 'Better and better, it's a slow one, so, fifteen knots a day, 12/13 days at best. He'll be there before they get to the States, but he'll have a hell of a job finding them.'

'Unless he comes back here.'

'Yeah, unless that, but I doubt it. Maybe, nah. Pessimist.'

'I never eat until I know what's in the pudding, you know that.'

'Thank you, by the way.'

'That's ok. Why didn't his drug system kick in, I thought all you combat types had them.'

Meier squinted and looked down at him, 'He's been through it, like the Major had and this suit isn't very good, not his original I'd say. If the monitoring system isn't working well enough, it doesn't trigger the bots that make the drugs. You hit him hard enough.'

They looked at the metal pan Marcus hit him with. Meier picked it up, 'I think this is done.'

They looked at the handle now bent and twisted. Marcus smiled,

'Worth it.'

About four hours later Kevin woke up in a dark empty room.
  'Shit.'
  He looked around, his night vision kicking in. A small piece of paper in the middle of the floor.

"Dear Kevin, I presume it's Kevin, the Major did mention you. Yes, I lied. You're on the way to Africa. It would be possible to hack the com system on the ship, but it might fry the control system and you might end up drifting. Or the anti-pirate system might kick in and you'd be locked in. You probably won't starve but... You should make port in about a dozen days. In the bag in the corner is food for about that long if you don't stuff yourself. I don't expect the cuffs to hold you long, but the door should keep you for a few hours at least. You might be tempted to swim to the coast and you can try, but it's further than you think. You can keep the cuffs.

Bon Voyage
  RM (Sgt)

PART TWO
SOMETHING EVERYONE WANTS

15

A lot to Think About

[It was ten and a half weeks since Milo met Julia in Paris]

'This is, what, our third chat since you came back from Europe? Dr Lopez-Real and Dr O Shea have told me you are making an excellent recovery. What do you think?'

Milo was sitting in the first speaker's office and had been wondering the answer to that exact question. They were alone, or appeared to be, or appeared to Xin to be. Milo could see one other person. Julia was leaning against the wall to his right, she looked to be waiting. The almost murderous confrontation with Anna May in Denmark had left Milo at death's door. He had recovered in the weeks following the operation to save his life and Julia had reawakened. Since waking, Julia had been working out a way of coexistence with Milo. She had told him she/they were now ready to "come out".

'Before I get into that, would it be possible to ask Dr O Shea and Dr Lopez-Real to join us for this meeting?'

'We could, I thought you'd be more comfortable with one-to-one discussions, are you sure?'

'I think you'd all prefer it if I told you what I have to say, all together. You might want to talk it over afterward.'

Xin gave him a puzzled look and thought about what his request might be about. She called up Cathy O Shea and Rachel Lopez-Real, China 12's psychologist and doctor cum forensic scientist, on her com system. She smiled at Milo but said nothing. Xin was a lot more comfortable using the non-verbal com system than Milo, who had always struggled, Julia couldn't understand why. Xin called it a matter of discipline, he called it being non-creative, Julia called it a bunch of other things, some of which shocked Milo. After a few moments, Cathy and Rachel walked in and Xin waved them to seats. Milo smiled at them as they sat, both faces held a mixture of concern and puzzlement.

'Hi. I've been speaking with all of you and doing the standard tests for the last few weeks. I haven't been entirely open with all of you. In part because I haven't been entirely comfortable with it myself,' He stopped and looked at their faces becoming stiff with polite anxiety, 'look, there's no easy way to say this or… this.'

Using the general system and not their individual holo systems Julia appeared. Rachel sat back sharply. Xin stood. Cathy leaned forward and grinned, and then turned to Rachel. She held out her hand, as if to say, "there".

Xin looked back at Milo, 'How long?'

'You remember the first time the Pixie visited? She carried a trigger program.'

'So she uploaded the program back into your system?' Xin looked angry.

Julia stood, 'No, I was always in Milo.'

'We removed and purged his entire system.'

'I had grown into his cellular system, my program is encoded in DNA. I had little choice as Milo's system was too small, but I am designed to do that in any case.'

Cathy relaxed in her seat, 'So the trigger was?'

'The Pixie had allowed me to use a small part of her system and I encoded a wake-up protocol so that I could reset. I then gave Milo the option to shut me down.'

Rachel running through the permutations asked, 'But was that a real option? Did he have a real choice? Once you were in his physical system…'

'The DNA encoding has to be renewed like any other cell in the body. I have a sub-routine that prevents the encoded cells renewing, a sort of apoptosis for these specific cells. It was a real choice. I am supposed to be a collaborative system, capable of deletion.'

Xin frowned, 'Apoptosis?'

'Cell suicide. It's a natural process for cells that are old or damaged, it's how we renew ourselves and keep healthy.' Rachel said.

Cathy was now in full "geek" mode, 'So what was all the waiting for?'

Milo turned, 'Julia wanted to be sure that we could actually work together, she was not designed to be inside me on an ongoing basis.'

'I was designed to work inside Elspeth as an assistant, she made some changes to my code so that I could get the fail-safe programme in place if something should happen to her. When I had no room in Milo's system I did what I was designed to do in her system and grew into his DNA. But we are not necessarily compatible and where there have been mismatches in the past, it has produced psychosis.'

Cathy concurred, 'Because of the difficulty in perceiving the difference between real and virtual?'

Milo and Julia nodded together, exactly together, and the others stared. Milo smiled.

Rachel asked, 'Are you "fail-safe"?'

'The "fail-safe" is a system not a personality. Julia has many functions, but "Julia" is Julia. I, am Julia.'

Rachel thought for a second and then turned to Cathy, 'How did you know?' She faced Xin, 'Cathy said she had suspicions that this might be happening, or that there might be some residual effects from Milo's experiences.'

Xin turned to Cathy, 'How?'

'Simple really. Milo and I have had lots of debriefs and more than a few meals together. Meals are a good way to look for displacement behaviours. Some parts of personality persist, taste too, when they change, usually they change slowly. Brain injury can bring about sudden shifts, there was no sign of that. But Milo's answers were significantly different than in previous interviews. That could have been the after effects of his experience maybe something hidden, but also he now eats quite a lot of hot food, yet it still makes him uncomfortable.'

She turned to Julia, 'I take it you like hot food?'

Julia smiled and agreed and then, 'And now I like omelettes too.'

Milo smiled, 'With chilli.'

Xin gave a single sharp , 'Right. You were correct Milo, we need to talk about this. If you can excuse us and give us, say, forty minutes?'

Milo stood, 'Of course.' He and Julia walked out together, watched by the other three.

The door closed and a thoughtful silence persisted, with all three still looking at the door. Xin sighed and sat down. Rachel and Cathy turned toward her. She looked at each in turn.

'Thoughts?'

Rachel and Cathy looked at each other. Xin made the decision. 'Cathy.'

'Right. I had wondered, as I said, and had talked it over a bit with Rachel. I have been thinking about it quite a lot. My notes suggest that there has been something of a shift in his personality, it is distinct but very small, he's a bit more methodical…'

'More?' Rachel blurted out.

'Yes, that is the direction he's taken, he is "more" of what he was. I thought at first it was the result of the events in Denmark, perhaps slight frontal lobe damage, but then he isn't lacking in decisiveness but only makes his mind up when he believes he knows exactly what is being asked.'

Xin turned to Rachel, 'Physically?'

'He's as good, better really, than before. No sign of damage. As you know, I was concerned about the new system, changing systems can be tricky and this is his fourth complete change and each one because of injury. But this was smooth. I had been wondering if it was his body being able to anticipate what was happening. I think now it was probably Julia.'

'And the long term?'

'Cathy would have something to say I suspect, but physically, there are no signs of it being problematic.'

Xin turned to Cathy again.

'I haven't picked up any early signs of a problem, he is in any case a calm, reasoning type of person.'

'And security? Can we trust her?'

Rachel and Cathy again looked at one another and then Rachel turned, 'We're not the people to ask. We have no means of making that judgement.'

Xin nodded, 'The engineers then.'

'I'm not sure if they will be able to extract a better answer. If Julia is telling the truth and the coding is in his cells, I don't know how they could detect dangerous code.'

'Alright, does she have other applications? Is there anything she could do outside of the parameter of a good detective or an assistant.'

Rachel and Cathy gave this some thought, but shook their heads.

'Maybe another one for the engineers?' Offered Cathy.

Xin frowned, 'One thing, my recollection was, and I went back to check to be sure, Julia Church didn't look the same when we spoke with her about Sao Paulo, when she was working with Anna May's legal firm.'

The other two looked at each other and then back at Xin.

'I thought at first it was that she had changed the image of the AI, she hadn't. It appears she had altered her own live image. Was she planning on this sort of thing all along, and if so, is the physical Julia/Elspeth really dead?' Xin asked.

'We can ask, but the AI seems to see herself as separate from her maker.' Cathy said.

'And Milo seemed pretty convinced that Julia Church was dead in London,' Rachel added.

Xin sighed again.

Milo was sitting in the dining hall. A cup of coffee in front of him, Julia beside him. She seemed to be reading something. The Pixie appeared in the doorway. Seeing Milo and Julia, she grinned and walked over, perhaps "bounced" over would be more correct.

'So? Did you?'

Milo and Julia looked up, Milo smiled, 'We did.'

'And?'

'And we're waiting for the results of the discussion. It might take a while.'

'Pff, it's either yes or no, how long does that take?'

'They'll have to be careful,' Julia answered, 'Is Milo alright, do they trust me, do they trust him, can they trust him? All the same questions you had. And of course, they'll ask you about it.'

'What should I say?' She now looked worried. Milo smiled.

'Quickest, easiest thing to remember is the truth. Just say that.'

'What? That I think you should have her cut out of your head because she's dangerous and you're nuts?'

Neither Milo nor Julia reacted at all, a small smile was all she got from Milo, eventually, but she waited.

'If that's what you think.'

'Nah, I won't say that. You know I won't say that, right?'

'You'll say what you say.' Julia offered.

The Pixies eyes narrowed, 'You have gotten worse, I swear.' And then Milo grinned.

'We aren't expecting you to say anything negative, you've had plenty of chances and you've said plenty already, but you can and should say whatever you think. One day, your life might depend on you being right.'

The Pixie agreed, 'I got you out of a pickle once and Julia's helping me watch Sam now, so I'm pretty sure I made my decision. We just have to wait on the bigwigs.'

Julia sat up straight, 'Speaking of Sam. Someone is looking for her.'

She turned to look at Milo and then at the Pixie, 'Someone who shouldn't be able to look for anyone.'

16

Curious Cat

Feng Liu was glued to the images in front of her. She had been following this line of thought doggedly for weeks now. After the horrible events with the gamers and the action of China 12 to pull her out of her place with the special directorate, she had been searching to find out why they had lied to her father.

When she began she was certain they had. The elements of The Game were too clear, the values too certain for the end to be so twisted. But all of the evidence she could find pointed the other way. So she began to look for evidence that they had changed the information available.

She had spoken to people in lots of different countries who had all played The Game, or something very close to it, and who had ended, or whose friends had ended, in the way Milo had described. There were depressing numbers, especially in "friends of" category. Not many seemed to be coming out 'after' their experience. None in fact.

She had hunted in China, but again could find no one who had been through the special directorate. She could find lots of reports of missing children who had been in The Game though. Just like Milo said, centered on the places she believed the directorate had training academies. The more she searched, the more furiously she didn't want to believe it and the more it looked like he had been right.

About three days ago she had changed the goal of her searching again. Now she was looking for China 12. Who were they? What did they do? How did you become a member? Were they enemies of the state? She could indeed find out plenty about what they did, quite a lot about who was involved, but nothing on how you joined up, where they came from. She was pretty sure they would say no to someone like her on the grounds of age, but that hadn't stopped her in The Game, and it wouldn't stop her now. Not that she wanted to join them.

By the evening things had taken a strange turn. She began to find a lot of chat about their last job. Something in Europe, or in South America. It took a while before she realised they were different jobs and that in fact the second job had never been up on the net Crime Boards. Sometimes she forgot that the web she was following was not clear to the rest of the world. It was beneath the surface, in encrypted coms and the hidden corners of the virtual world. Not the old Dark Web, this was a parallel world. From her though, little was hidden. Unless, she thought grimly, she had her eyes closed! Not this time. In fact, she had woven a note into the band that kept her head com on, (she was too young yet for an implant), "Don't blind yourself." She read it every night before she went online.

She picked up a lot of complaints about much wider, more random results from searches and also of normal feeds being scrambled. At the same time there was lots of discussion about a "ghost", or a holographic op working with China 12. A ghost? That would be wild. She wondered for a few minutes if it could talk with her mother… but then she shook herself.

As she got into the chatter around this op, it became more about the potential it might hold; perhaps other functions. What other functions were there for a ghost? The police reports were thin, but the chat she picked up from what Milo had called "pixies", was much more exciting. It seemed to be some sort of special AI and it was generating a lot of interest. She was struggling with why. If it was an AI, surely there were lots and lots of them already working across the world? What could be so special about this one? Whatever it was, she could see what she knew was encrypted chat about how it could be developed in future and there began to be signs that money was being offered for information, quite a lot of money. She knew, because some of it she could break. Milo was connected in some way to this AI. But she'd also come across news he'd been badly injured, he would be in a wheelchair for the rest of his life, but then later that he was recovering. It was like her own personal soap and like all soaps, addictive enough to keep her up deep into the night.

It was the news about Milo that led her to try to hack China 12, this evening. That was what she told herself. She knew she could just have messaged him, but she didn't want to bother him if he was still recovering. It was tough going. They had a reputation for being the best, but then lots of people and governments had a reputation. It was mathematical complexity not reputation that Liu respected, but her respect was growing. For the fourth hour in a row she'd worked on the problem. She had gotten through layer one and then layer two, or so she thought, and then she suddenly found herself back at layer one. She took a long time staring at the images at that point. Then she went through it again and thought she had found the sub-routine that had brought her back to the start. That was when she nearly had a stroke.

The voice seemed to come from behind her. Everything in front of her in the real world went flying in all directions and she spun around. That was when she got the second fright and leapt to her feet, all martial preparedness. The woman in front of her dissolved into peals of laughter.

Liu edged toward the door, always facing the woman. She wondered if she could get to the panic button before the woman would try to stop her. But the woman just slowly stopped laughing and watched, carefully turning with her. There was something about her Liu couldn't quite... she wasn't really here, in the room. Liu stopped and unwound, and then stood. The woman smiled. Then it hit Liu.

'You!'

The woman grinned.

'You're her. The ghost.'

'I don't know about that, but I'm certainly who you've been trying to find out about.'

Liu's eyes narrowed, 'How do you know that?'

'When you climb into my maze you open yourself up, you're a curious little thing.'

Liu bridled, 'More than curious.'

'I apologise, that was rude. I meant you've been doing a lot of looking about me and China 12 and you've gotten further than most.'

'Most?'

'Yes, you're not the only person who knocks on our door. "Most" probably isn't right. You are the first I've spoken to.'

'But you are her?'

'I believe I am who you think you're talking to.'

'Why are you so special?'

'Don't I look special?'

'Oh yeah, I mean, I've seen lots of holograms though.'

'And how many AIs have you talked to?'

'We deal with AIs all the time.'

'Talked to, like this, a conversation?'

Liu waited considered for a moment, 'You'd be the first.'

'That not a bit special?'

'A bit, but… There's lots of excitement, you'd think you were Wonder Woman.'

'Maybe I am.'

Liu smiled, hand on hip.

Julia went on, 'But, he's fine, better than fine.'

'Who?'

'The person you're pretending to ask about.'

'Oh, Milo.' She smiled again; caught.

'I'm glad, I like him, he was fair.'

Julia let her off the hook, 'He is. Is there anything else we can do for you today?'

'Don't go!'

'I won't.'

'Can we talk?'

Julia smiled broadly, 'We can, that would be fun.'

Liu blushed a little and smiled. 'But I mustn't get caught.'

'Who by?'

'My Dad, it would be… bad.'

'We'll have to be careful then.'

'You will anyway.'

'Why?'

'Those people who want to… look, here and here.'

Liu opened up sets of coms and Julia looked and then gave Liu a quick look, 'Good decryption skills.'

'Thank you.'

'Oh, this isn't…'

'Good?'

17

None left Behind

The hospital ward was middle-sized with four beds, only one of which was occupied. Like all of the intensive care wards the interior wall was glass. Despite this, the room was dark and quiet, the only illumination was from the monitors which gave a fairly complete picture of the patient's state of health. Heart, lungs, kidneys, liver and brain condition and current operational state were displayed. The brain monitor even showed which parts of the brain were active and to what extent. Through the wall were two chairs and two combat dressed operatives, clantechs (American pixies). Clantechs saw the European moniker "pixie" as demeaning, whereas the Europeans saw the name "clantech" as deeply uncool and a bit awkward. Of the two sitting outside watching over their colleague, one was a young male, the other a young female.

Their colleague, a senior officer in the semi-military group they worked for, was still in a coma. Sam was no longer on the critical list, as she had been, following the encounter with Anna May in Brooklyn. But she was still in a medically induced coma to give her brain time to recover. Her experiences in Brazil, on the other hand, were now about to catch up with her.

Unseen by the clantechs, Julia entered the room and went through the monitoring system. She was particularly interested in the brain activity of the patient. She gave the patient a gentle virtual nudge and then another one. The brain monitor began to change colour as Sam's consciousness rose to the point where she and Julia could converse, though the monitor apart, from the outside, nothing appeared to have changed.

'Sam.'

'Yes? Who are, oh you're Julia. Am I…? Where am I?'

'No, you're not dead,' she answered the unspoken thought, 'You're in a hospital in New York. You were taken here after Anna shot you.'

If you had been watching the monitors in the room, you'd have seen several readings spike.

'Yes, I remember, bitch. She was faking it.'

'Yes, very good.'

'So why can't I see the room?'

'You're still sleeping, you've been in an induced coma.'

'Bad?'

'You were.'

'Will I recover?'

'It looks good.'

'Are you visiting? Hey, hold on, if I'm knocked out, how are we talking?'

'I'm accessing your mind through your implant, it's nice and new. This is a bit like a dream.'

'So will I remember this?'

'I hope so, I think so. I have something to tell you, but first I have someone who wants to talk with you, it will have to be quick.'

The Pixie appeared. Sam smiled.

'Babe.'

'Hey you. You're not supposed to get yourself shot without me.'

'I know I'm bad, but it was the only way I could get you to New York.'

The Pixie smiled, 'I'm going to come get you. We're not going to let anything happen to you, you know.'

Sam stopped smiling. Julia reappeared.

'That was less tactful than I'd hoped. There is someone coming who wants to harm you.'

Sam looked sad, 'Is my own people? Do they want to terminate my contract? I know I'm getting old, but I thought they'd let me out, or kick me upstairs.'

'"They" are talking about it and I'm watching that. They're keeping up with your medical status, but I'm not worried about your bosses, yet. There's someone else, it's a bit confusing, but I'm trying to track them down. I might have to get you out of here.'

'That's ok, I'm a clantech, they'll look after me, until they don't. Just let me know.'

'It won't be as simple as that, real world, you might find moving a struggle at first. If I can get the Pixie to help you I will.'

Sam was tiring and drifting off to a deeper state. 'Just let me know.'

Julia watched her and then took a quick run through the hospital security systems. Everything was quiet for now.

The Pixie sat back in her seat in the plane, a scheduled flight, the Hyperflight from Beijing to NewYork, nearly three hours total flying time. Julia appeared beside her. The Pixie grinned.

'She looked good.'

'Slow down, she's not in that great a shape. She'll need careful handling and she won't be able to do any running around.'

The Pixie looked serious, 'Oh, right.'

'You'll need some specialist equipment and supplies from the hospital. I've tagged it, and uploaded the inventory onto your system and where to find it. You have access to all the areas in the hospital and I've got transport waiting.'

'She has the two operatives, I saw them.'

'They won't be good enough. Delay is all they'll offer, not much more.' Julia seemed anxious.

The Pixie began to look alarmed, 'So how much time do I have?'

'He's not there yet, nothing on the exterior system either, but we can't count on your having anything but the barest minimum. You might have more, it might be less.'

'I'll kill him.'

'We'll protect her and bear in mind we're not sure who he is yet.'

'But are the clantechs doing it? My people had a kill switch in me. Where can we go?'

'I don't know, if we get the chance we'll ask. We just have to get her safe for now. You're about forty minutes out, twenty to land.'

'Is that enough?'

'I think so, I hope so. It has to be.'

Avoid the A+E and the hospital was quiet. Darkened corridors and wards, automated monitoring, a medical AI watching over it all.

Even acute wards and intensive care, which might in the past have had several nurses on duty, now for the most part had one or two. The AI could predict problems hours before they flared up and action was usually automatic and machine administered. Were it not for the need for humans to see humans and interact with them, the staff might have been reduced further.

So when Kevin stepped quietly from the lift and into the twilight corridor, he could see everyone on the floor at a glance. His trip to Africa had been humiliating and had it not been for the fact that Anna had traced him, he might well have just stayed and looked for work in security or thuggery. But Anna was a woman who liked her pound of flesh and despite not having paid out a penny she insisted Kevin come back and finish the job. To be fair, she had anted up since then. Now this had come up on the radar. As the last other person to see Jo that night, she might have been involved in getting her to the US. It was, he reflected, ironic that the bust up was over coming to the US, but that was where Jo and Mariana now were, or so Anna thought. Going back to that bitch in Rio was a bust as she'd gone; actually the whole place had gone, washed away in a storm, serves her right. He still hadn't worked out what had happened.

As he was thinking, he walked slowly up the long corridor. He presumed that the ward would be across or beside where those two people were sitting watching him. He came to the nurses station. His seat turned to face Kevin, emergency glass rising in front of him. About halfway up to where it should have been, it stopped. The nurse frowned and stared at the glass, he was about to push the panel to force it up when a movement drew his attention to Kevin. The nurse fell back in his seat unconscious before he met Kevin's eyes. Kevin smiled and turned to continue his walk. The operatives were now standing and in the middle of the corridor.

Kevin was now certain he was in the right place. He could see that the two in front were young and could carry themselves, it was almost certain they were clantechs, dangerous. Anna had anticipated their presence and given him a little machine. He blinded his system to a small block of frequencies and then pushed the button on a small oval stone in his hand. He thought of it as a stone, obviously it wasn't. The two clantechs grabbed their heads and collapsed. The very second they hit the floor his head almost exploded in pain. He too hit the floor. He just about realised what the source was and jammed his finger on the stone to shut it off. He was dazed, he felt as though he had been hit very hard but not in the right place to knock him out.

He looked up to see what had happened to the clantechs and they were still there, still out of it. He got to his hands and knees and then to his feet, leaning against the wall for support. He felt sick. That was one vicious little stone. He looked round and then checked his internal system. Somehow the frequencies he'd shut off had opened up again, just not enough to hit him as hard as the clantechs.

'They warned me about you.'

He said to the empty corridor. He looked behind him and all round. He knew what he was looking for and knew that it was unlikely she would be any "where" exactly. He cursed quietly. He took a drink from the bottle in his suit and pushed himself away from the wall. He could see the door of the ward and headed for it.

"Get answers", he'd been told, "and then get rid of her." Anna had made sure he had a little subroutine for the monitoring system to wake the clantech up.

At the door he paused and looked around again, then pushed into the room. He immediately jerked back as someone appeared in front of him. She was about his height, early thirties he'd say, smartly dressed, athletic looking without looking like an op. He didn't think she'd be a problem and then he realised who he was looking at.

'Oh, you do appear.'

She smiled, 'We haven't met, Julia, Julia Church.' And she held out her hand. He reached forward to take it automatically and then realised that even if he could, that wouldn't be very bright. He didn't look amused.

'It's Kevin isn't it?'

He said nothing but began thinking about the steps to the

monitors, or whether he should just go to the end point.

'Aren't you supposed to be dead? There are a lot of people who were very upset at that. I think they might be more upset now you're not.'

He moved toward the bed and took out his gun. He could feel that she tried something, but Anna's people had prepared him for her and she didn't manage it. He got to the machines and his system began to upload the wake-up routine. His system reported that it had been blocked. He looked at her and she wasn't smiling. He realised this wasn't going to work and he aimed the gun at the unconscious Sam.

The door behind him swung open and the Pixie barrelled through it. She had thrown something at him and he ducked as he turned. He tried to fire at Sam, but his wrist jerked and the shot hit the wall, something had sent a pulse through his system to the muscles in his arm. He turned and tried to dodge, but the Pixie hit him full on in the ribs and he slammed into the end of the bed.

Julia shouted at the Pixie, 'We just want to get rid of him.'

The two rolled on the floor and then the Pixie was up on her feet, now between Kevin and the bed. Kevin tracked left giving himself a path, through the Pixie, to Sam. He calculated her weight and decided she would be enough to smash the head of her friend, if he landed her skull to skull. He took a run and grabbed her, lifting her clear of the floor and continued to the bed. She twisted and threw her body back, he lost momentum. His implant blurred his eyesight as Julia began to create interference and he lost balance his leg jerking involuntarily. He staggered, but kept his feet. His face twisted into an angry grimace as he straightened. He concentrated to regain control of his body, adjusted his grip on the Pixie, tightening his hand round her throat. He turned and took aim at the bed again. The Pixie got one leg free and aimed a savage kick at his head, but he blocked with his elbow. He looked up. A noise to his right and he could see two of the hospital security running down the corridor, weapons out. He looked at the bed and calculated his chances of killing the woman in the bed in time; not good. He cut his losses. He dropped the Pixie from above his head and turned away.

He walked past the prone bodies of the clantechs in the corridor at a brisk pace, no faster. Kevin met first one guard and turned him and his gun onto the second who fell in a heap. He disarmed the first guard and shot him. From the other end of the corridor, more security. He walked away. He didn't look back and the Pixie, picking herself up with Julia watched him to the lift.

The Pixie turned to Julia, 'Is she ok?' and looked anxiously at the bank of monitors.

'Are you?'

The Pixie shook her head and looked at Sam, 'Never mind me, is she?'

'Yes, he didn't get to her. They tried to upload a wake-up routine into the system, I blocked it. You were quick.'

The Pixie smiled looking down at Sam, 'I was, with your help? What now? Can we get her out?'

'I am trying to talk with her physician, but she has her com off. You might like to check those two.'

She gestured at the two clantechs. The security staff were checking their colleagues but not the clantechs. The Pixie nodded and she went out and bent down over them. One was coming round, helped by a good drug system. The young man didn't respond so the Pixie injected him with something and put him in a recovery position. She left them and came back to Julia and Sam.

'They sent for backup, she'll be ok, he's a bit bashed up. Any luck with the Doc? We could ask Rachel?'

Julia pointed at the door, 'Go get the list I sent you.'

'OK.'

It took a little more than ten minutes before the Pixie was back with two bags of medical supplies and a wheelchair.

Julia waved as she came through the door, past the clantechs in the corridor who were being looked at by some medical staff. A gurney was being wheeled away with the second of the dead security staff.

'I've talked with the clantech Doc and her bosses, they've agreed to let her go,' said Julia.

'That sounds easy.' The Pixie smiled.

'They didn't want the responsibility of someone else killing her. They tried their own termination command, to her implant, it was blocked by someone or something. They've tried a few times, I guess they'll try again. I guess whoever is blocking them will go on doing it, and they'll try some other way to terminate her.'

'A loose end…' and the Pixie looked at Sam.

18

Problems Problems

Xin was sitting in an unusually full meeting room. Almost all the surviving members of China 12 were there. Julia had just faded, allowing the room to speak while she worked with the Pixie to get Sam safe. They all looked grim and most were shocked. Milo was, of course, still in Beijing, meaning Julia was too. But the added advantage of being able to have someone in more than one place at a time was useful to exploit. Cathy was curious.

'But she could still be here in the meeting too?'

'Yes,' answered Milo.

'Do you know what's happening in New York?'

'No, I could but I'm not her. I can't do that and this, for me multi-tasking is two jobs done badly. I can't pay attention to both places at once.'

'So why isn't she here?'

'She knows that certain situations have implications that mean we might want to talk about her, she's giving us that space. Even if she's working in New York, she's still based here, in me. There are limits to what she can achieve, but she's able to give us privacy.'

'Still weird.' Said Cathy.

Rachel smiled and Xin frowned. She turned to Milo.

'The news that Kevin is back but not here, what does it say about Joanna and Mariana? Are they dead? Did he kill them? If they're alive, where are they?' She asked.

The heads round the table all nodded.

'I saw what you saw, I know what you know. If you're wondering if I had something to do with it, I didn't. We should be able to get the DNA results from the forensic company in Brazil, one way or another,' Milo looked over to Erasto Diallo and Rahul Patel, who agreed, 'but if they are alive it's probable that they haven't contacted us because they're afraid of detection.'

'We can protect them, can't we?' Xin asked and looked round the table.

Hoshika shook her head, 'On the evidence so far, not very easily. Particularly not from one of our own. There's a high probability that they can be got to if their whereabouts are known. We have to find out what happened. Who happened.'

Milo sighed, 'That is, of course, what we will aim to do. But picking up the threads of a case from which we have been excluded won't be easy.'

Xi Liang, the group's chemist, leaned in and bowed a little toward Milo, 'Can we know if Julia had anything to do with this?'

Milo thought as all the faces turned to him, it would appear to have been a question for them all.

'Know? No. It's not going to be possible, in the short term, to pick apart what Julia the AI knows or has done and what Julia/Elspeth the human intended or planned or did. We can take it at face value and look at and examine the evidence, but whatever we think, it will be on a "best guess" basis.'

They all then turned to Xin, she agreed slowly, 'We have to be careful, but until we get definite evidence that things are being done to us by Julia, I think we have to exploit the advantages she gives us.'

While some looked troubled most nodded their heads at this. Xin continued, 'However, I also think we should note that we seem to be under attack and that whatever is going on is serious and goes beyond any one crime.'

Erasto agreed and said, 'You should all have received updates in our security systems, changing access codes and we've tightened our anti-infiltration protocols. Julia helped there. Kevin has made no attempt to contact us, so we have to assume he is working against us and helping others.'

A couple of heads were in hands at the scale of what had happened.

Hoshika leaned in again, her specialist area was in probability, 'The whole mess would seem to be related to whatever it was Julia and her sister dreamed up. Should we not go back and speak with the sister?'

Milo frowned, 'We did try to go back and speak with her. But after the attack in Denmark she has managed to drop out of sight.'

'That family seem to be able to make themselves invisible at will.' Cathy observed.

Rahul looked unhappy, 'Not invisible enough, given that two of the three are dead. Though this fail-safe code they've injected into the web is certainly helping them.'

Xin looked round the table again, 'Alright, next moves?'

Liang was insistent, 'We must look for Joanna. I don't know if we can capture Kevin, or even if it would be worthwhile, but we have to find Joanna and help her if at all possible.'

There was general agreement, Milo was thoughtful, 'Of course I think that's right, but Joanna is a formidable op and if she has decided she doesn't want to be found… On the other hand, I don't think that if she is alive she will stay silent forever.'

Wolfgang Schultz, the team's forensic archaeologist, shook his head, 'I think we are forgetting or avoiding the possibility that when Kevin left us, Joanna did too.'

Despite the grim looks round the table, Xin flattened her lips and agreed, 'It is possible. It makes it all the more important to find out who is pulling the strings. This is something that has been happening for some time I think and we happened to trip over it, making us a target.' Koura Aripe insisted.

'Or we were drawn into it…' Rachel suggested and Xin again concurred silently.

'It is obvious that Anna is working for whoever is behind this. While she was working with them, she clearly was not on the Brooklyn Brotherhood's pay roll.' Koura observed.

Milo looked round the group, 'And what about our ordinary work? The day to day of detection?'

'I think we must look at anything that our system bids on as being suspect and part of this, whatever is going on,' said Xin.

'But we take it?' asked Milo

'We take it and consider it a lead.'

'If it's a complex case, do we have the resources to take care of a case and find Joanna?' Erasto asked.

Milo smiled, 'I think we do. If we accept Julia as part of the team until we know she should not be. The Pixie can back me up...'

'Even if she's off saving Sam?' Hoshika asked.

Milo went on, 'She is pretty reliable. Once Sam is safe, and it would be unreasonable to expect her not to take care of that first,' there was general agreement round the table, 'I think she will be available. And once recovered, maybe Sam too.'

Liang shook his head slowly, 'I'm not sure that's a good idea, personal relationships in the field complicate things.'

Milo smiled, 'They do. Can we agree to see how things go?'

Liang said nothing but didn't look any happier. The others seemed to go with Milo.

Xin looked round, 'Is there anything else? No? We have work to do.'

The meeting broke up, as people stood Xin turned to Milo, 'Could you wait a moment?'

Milo sat again and the others left. He turned to Xin.

'I know this can't be easy, but we have to be very sure of what we're doing here. I would like you to keep Cathy in the loop with your... thoughts, on how things are going and how you're feeling.'

'My feelings you mean about...'

'Your guest.'

'Rather, my co-habitant.' And he smiled, she also smiled and then didn't.

'Something worrying is going on, something bad has already happened. We have to be sure of ourselves or else I think we may be lost completely.'

'That sounds very, apocalyptic.'

'I think the situation might just be and we don't know which side Julia is on. We have to investigate her thoroughly. So far as we can see, things are fine, but we can't allow that to blind us to a problem.'

'I don't mind giving Cathy access to my system but sooner or later we are going to have to take a leap of faith.'

'You already have?'

'I have. I did in the weeks after Julia was restarted.'

'That might not have been your decision.'

'I know, but in the end this comes down to perception, is your green the same as my green?'

Xin took a deep breath and leaned back, she thought about something and then smiled at Milo.

'Ok.'

Milo stood, saluted and walked out.

A short while later in his rooms he was looking out of the window at the grounds and Julia appeared. They looked at each other and she cocked her head to one side. He looked back out into the grounds, where a few of the members were walking together.

'Like you said, they're worried.'

'They should be. I'm the only one who can be sure what's going on with me, which side I'm on and where I come from. Even then I can't be sure there isn't some hidden piece of code waiting to be triggered.'

'You reassure me.'

She laughed, 'Would it be better if I told you everything was alright and nothing to worry about?'

'Yes.'

'Everything is alright and…'

'Ok, ok. How are they making out in New York?'

'The Pixie is being like a mother hen, a young, extremely dangerous, in fact lethal, mother hen. But maybe that's not the worst, in the circumstances.'

'I was thinking I'd like to limit your exposure to the world in general, if you're a secret weapon we may as well keep you secret,' suggested Milo.

'And you don't want to have too many people thinking about me in the meantime.'

He looked at her again and smiled, 'Yes, exactly. You said you were designed as a research assistant with one or two tweaks.'

'Yes.'

'Your capabilities go way beyond that, your deductive and reasoning abilities are beyond what is required.'

'Jealous?'

He smiled, 'Pff, you wish. But she really went above and beyond with you, I'd like to know why.'

'I'll put it on the list.'

'Where?'

'Well, after why Kevin's trying to harm Sam, and after who is trying to target China 12.'

'Target China 12?'

'You don't think someone is?'

'I do.'

19

Darkness and Emeralds

The room was dark. There was no technical reason for that, he just liked it dark. It was about ten at night and the sole source of light was the lamp on the table in front of him. Like every house on the island, this one was independently powered by solar cells and battery power. The batteries, discreetly stored on an upper floor, safe from flooding, were capable of delivering about 20 kW and easily able to cope with the normal 12 kW he required daily. The rich smell of African wood filled the room.

Outside, the only light was from the stars, the moon wasn't going to put in an appearance until later. The only sound was the crickets throbbing in the background, their night song a continuing chorus to life.

He was concentrating hard. Jeweller's loupe squeezed tightly in his eye, he went through the stones on his desk one by one. Emeralds. These, smuggled up the coast from Zambia. He had heard about the package and inserted himself into the deal. He had paid for its transit, bribed the necessary officials. He was supposed to hand it on. He wasn't going to do that now. He had sent a message that the transit had failed. An unfortunate accident and the courier had died, these things happen. They'd try again in a few months.

This was one of the earliest batches from a new lode, rivalling, they said, stones from Columbia. So far, he was impressed. He wasn't expert enough to be able to tell if they rivalled Columbian stones, but he knew enough to know they were good, very good. And that in a world where emeralds had become much more scarce, which of course made them fashionable.

He was sorting them into two piles. He had thought "good" and "bad" at first, but now it was "good" and "very good". There were about thirty stones in all, of various sizes. He stopped and took the loupe from his eye as he reached the last one. He stretched and rubbed that eye and smiled down at the dull collection in front of him. Very nice, very tidy. He already knew the buyer and the route. He was adding up the next bribes and transport costs and finally, the profit. Reaching for the bottle of brandy across the desk he poured a good measure and recorked the bottle. It was the good stuff, his second tonight. Tonight was special. He pushed his chair back from the desk. He drank, allowing the aroma to fill the air round him. He closed his eyes.

So consumed was he in the big pay day that he made the mistake he'd never made before. Everything in the room was meant to prevent this mistake. The angle of the desk to the window. The chair not so comfortable, back to the wall but not close enough to lean against it. But the day had been long and anxious, the delivery late and the night was warm and quiet. It was only a moment. He closed his eyes only for a moment. Sleep caught him for a moment, not even a moment. It was enough.

His head bumped against the desk and he could see hands sweep the stones into a piece of cloth. He couldn't hear anything distinct. Then something puzzled him, even as his brain was starved of oxygen, as the blood pooled round his head. His finger, dipped in the blood, traced out a word; "dogs" and then began...

The world faded from him and the mystery embraced him. He had become a case number.

The local police inspector was called to the scene the next morning after the call to prayer. He walked round the body shaking his head. Inspector Mwangi was sad, he was always sad when he found a murder, it was troublesome. He was sad that a person had died, but that was fate. The real sadness arose from the disruption to his life. He liked an ordered life with ordinary crime; arguments between neighbours or debt collection supervision, the odd smuggler. If you were going to have a fuss it should be for some important crime, not this kind of thing. This only brought the smallness of the island to the frowning notice of Nairobi. This kind of thing was neither worth his while nor did it provide the satisfaction of resolution. He knew he was very unlikely to be able to arrest the killer. He knew this man. He knew his business. He had been offered, and refused, his bribes. But all that meant was that he knew the quarter from whence his killer probably came and the end of the case as a practical investigation. He felt like shouting at the dead, demanding to know what he thought he was doing. Amateur.

He turned to the forensic expert over from Malindi. She, like he, was in a bunny suit. He hated theses suits, they made him hot and he felt trapped, he looked ridiculous. He pointed to the dust on the desk, 'Can you guess what this is?'

She looked closely at it and turned her face up to him from the level of the desk. 'No.'

'Not at all? A guess, I won't hold you to it?'

'Then what value would it be?'

He took a deep breath, 'A start.'

'But if I'm wrong, it will be a false start and you won't want to unpick your assumptions.'

'I am already making assumptions, false or not.'

She bowed her head and looked at it again. He closed his eyes and then, 'Look, I have been hearing things, I really just want some confirmation. Could it be dust from an Emerald mine?'

'Really, how would I know without testing it? It's dust. It speaks to me through testing and analysis, not by jumping up and saying "I am from…" If I start throwing opinions around I'll be the same as the boys on the beach. Go ask them if you want a guess!'

He made a loud, ill-defined noise and turned to leave and then stopped.

'Can you at least tell me if he wrote that in his own blood?'

'I can tell you, he, or someone, wrote that in something that has a similar colour to oxidised blood that may or may not be from the victim. I am not clever, I cannot "jump" to conclusions. You'll have my report when you have my report; as always!'

He didn't turn again and he stalked out. Just as he reached the door, she shouted, 'Will you be home for supper?'

He didn't stop, 'Yes.'

She continued also, not stopping for a heartbeat, but she smiled. She stood and, walking over to her equipment, which was lined up on a small table made specially for a crime scene. She pulled out a box with a tail of filaments a bit like a tiny broom, hanging from it. The box connected with her implanted system and a display appeared in front of her. She went over to the desk from where the victim had been removed and brushed the dust with the filaments. In the display the constituents of the dust appeared in front of her along with their probable source; an emerald mine: Zambia. He was so damned clever, "I have heard…"

She brushed the writing and it was; blood. Same type as the victim, DNA match. Of course, this would all have to be confirmed, but it would be. What she wasn't finding much of, was evidence of a murderer, apart from the victim, of course. But she would be able to give him a motive and where to look with that "dogs". What was he trying to write next? Looked like the beginnings of an "o". Or and "a" or a "g', for that matter. Now she was jumping to conclusions!

She straightened, a sombre expression on her face. Jumping to conclusions or not, she didn't like where that pointed and she hoped Mwangi wouldn't get all worked up about this. You did not want to mess with them. People who messed with them, wound up like the guy whose blood she had just analysed; dead.

20

A slow Boat

When the selection system came up with the crime number and the details, Xin had to read it twice. Then she shared the news and called in Milo. He did not come alone. Erasto, Rahul, Liang and Hoshika all came in with him. Xin was surprised.

'So?'

Erasto was first, 'Africa?'

'And?' Xin, surprised as she was, didn't like unannounced deputations.

Hoshika held out both hands, 'Is this not exactly what we were talking about? Milo would be isolated and vulnerable.'

'A sitting duck, one might say.' Rahul put in. Rahul was still scarred by the Brazil incident, blaming himself unfairly for the disappearance of his workmates.

Xin held up her hands, 'This is not how we do things. The system, which we set up, has bid for and won a job. At the moment we don't know what it means. I will speak with Milo and we will confirm it to the system when that discussion is over. If people have something to add to the discussion, I am always glad to hear it. But not 'off the cuff' reactions. Thank you.'

They all looked at one another and none too happy, left. Milo watched the door close silently behind them, he turned to Xin, 'That was harsh.'

'I will apologise later. Frankly, all of those questions are running round my head also. What are your thoughts?'

'The same. But I can't see the angle at the moment. I suppose I could be kidnapped.'

'How close are we to knowing the Pixie's availability?' She paused, then, 'Don't we have another name for her? It is very odd to keep calling her "pixie" or "The Pixie".'

'I've asked, about the name, but she evidently doesn't like her given name. I'll ask again. As to availability…'

Julia appeared, 'I was talking with her earlier, she and Sam are settled but the Pixie is very uneasy, they are being watched by clantechs, it will probably be a few days.'

'That is a lot of exposure.'

Milo nodded, 'Yes, but if it's a way of getting us out into the open it's also a way of discovering who is behind it.'

'Even if they haven't set it up, they can read crime boards like anyone else and see we are out there, I don't think using you as bait is clever.'

'I still think we should take it, I need the exercise.'

'Can you speed up the Sam situation?' Xin asked Julia.

'Obviously I can try, but it's about emotion not just logistics. Sam's situation is delicate'

Xin moved on, 'Alright. Milo, you've made the link to Cathy?'

'I have.'

'That should mean we will know what is happening, without your having to call. Good.'

Milo smiled at the implied concern.

'When should I leave?'

'If we're going to treat it as a normal job, then we should do just that.'

'I shall get ready.'

'Good hunting.'

Julia faded and Milo walked out.

Once on the Hyperjet to Nairobi, Milo turned a quizzical look on Julia. She looked back with her usual unexpressive expression, though Milo had noticed a slight change in her menu of looks lately.

'What?' She asked.

'Did you?'

'Did I what?'

'Stop being evasive, you know exactly what I'm asking and that's truer than it usually is between folk.'

She looked at him steadily, barely interrupted by his acceptance of a complimentary drink and then said, 'I didn't choose the job, of course I didn't. Although I have always wanted to see Africa.'

'You're certain about that? Choosing I mean, because I'm feeling a slight sense that that might not be everything.'

'You're probably just sensing what I'm feeling about the Pixie and Sam.'

'Alright. Have you heard anything that might give us reason to worry about this job?'

'I've noticed that we will be the first crime group to visit the island.'

'Oh? Why? Is there no serious crime in East Africa?'

'There's lots, but not much here, at least they've never posted a crime before.'

'Hmm. Are we walking into a trap?'

'I guess anything is possible, but nothing is coming up so far.'

It took two hours to get from Beijing to Nairobi. The heat as they left the air-conditioned atmosphere of the terminal was like stepping into a blast furnace, even Julia complained.

Global warming had hit Africa hard and the tropics hardest of all. Had it not been for the filtration of sea water, Africa at these latitudes would simply have become desert. As it was, economically, a number of countries had done well. Living in a hot house with abundant water had its advantages and they grabbed every one. Automation had suited African life. The concept of a universal income had been quickly adopted and the populations had enjoyed a great cultural flowering. Life was good, at least from what the outsider could see, if you stayed out of the sun.

They had the choice of the overnight train through the national park to the coast or a short hop in a light aircraft to Mombasa, then either the boat or a flight to Malindi and then another to Manda and then a boat. Milo really wanted to go by train, really, really, really. Especially as the carriages were restored and air-conditioned 19th century Pullman coaches. Julia wanted to use any extra time on a dhow from Mombasa. On the basis that they had time but not that much time, he won.

The old "Lunatic Express" had been decommissioned in the early part of the century, but nothing sells like yesterday and a version of the trip had been reopened about ten years earlier. The train left from Nairobi at about five and would stop in the park just before sunset near a new watering point which attracted animals from far and wide. Passengers would drink "sundowners" as the sun set - rather quickly near the equator - and then eat supper.

Milo was enjoying the whole experience and could feel Julia's excitement as Africa's, artificially irrigated, splendour came to life. It had everything, water, wildlife, a setting sun and thorn trees.

'So, this is fun.' Milo observed.

'Fun? It's amazing and the smell of the earth, it's like a dream.'

'Far be it from me to bring us down to earth, but have you noticed anyone on the train who might not belong?'

She turned and he could feel her thinking, 'No. You?'

'Not yet.'

'It's much more likely they'd try pick us up at a pinch point like Manda, I would guess.'

'Hmm, alright. What should we have for supper?'

They ate well and didn't even notice the train moving again as they did so.

At 9.30 the next morning, this train was quicker than its older predecessor, they pulled into Mombasa. They climbed out into the hubbub of an old station creaking with age and already roastingly hot.

The plane to Malindi was prosaic by comparison and it was only two hours later that Julia got at least part of her wish and they were on a dhow from Manda to Lamu. She turned to him, a huge smile on her face as the wind tugged at Milo's shirt.

Milo looked serious, 'Now's the first point where I would expect to have trouble, far from home on a slow boat to murder.'

21

Brotherhood of Doubt

The room was crisp and clean. Brightly lit from windows that stretched along one side reflecting in the shine on the long, heavy wooden table that ran its length. The walls were white, the skirting highly polished mahogany, or something that looked like it. There were no pictures in the room, in fact no ornament, barring a bare wooden crucifix at the opposite end from the door. Highbacked chairs surrounded the table, each one filled with a serious looking, white shirted, crisply suited, middle aged white male. Their hair was cut short and styled in a strikingly similar fashion, that would not look out of place in a high end 1950s business magazine. On the left lapel of each suit a small gold crucifix gleamed, no other ornament was visible. In front of each man was a pencil and a white, U.S. Letter sized notepad and to its right a glass of God's good water, underneath, a white coaster. In the centre of the table, a black, leather-bound Bible.

The brethren were meeting in anxious distress. Things had not gone well and several of the brothers had deep reservations about the current path they had taken. The rumblings had bubbled away in the weeks since Sao Paulo and then Daniel's murder. The opening prayer had just been said and a number of the brothers cleared their throats. At the head of the table, The Elder spoke.

'Brothers, we are at a critical juncture. We meet here to decide which path we should be walking upon in future and to what destination we are heading. Yes, Brother Michael?'

'Elder Thomas, I know there are Brothers around this table,' he held out placating hands, 'I don't doubt your hearts or your sincerity, but they are going to advocate for a continuation along this current path. I have not slept, Brothers, since we put our feet on this road. We have done great harm, to others and now to ourselves.'

'Brother, what would you have us do? Ignore the opportunity…'

Brother Michael held up his hand and the Elder intervened, 'Brother Francis, allow him to finish, it is our way.'

'Thank you Elder. What would I have us do? Repent Brothers, we have left the sure path. What more certain way is there to see the truth in this, than that Americorp, the dark soul of Baal, Prince of the underworld, an organisation dedicated only to Mammon and the pursuit of worldly riches and pleasure, wanted and now has this very system, mechanism, I don't know what. And we, who have given our lives and the lives of our families over to God, we have been instrumental in their cause. Brothers, in prayer and in meditation, we must repent.'

The Elder raised his hand as Michael took a deep breath to continue and he smiled, 'Thank you Brother Michael, eloquent and brief.' Another of the Brothers raised his hand just as Francis thought he was about to have his say, 'Brother Mathew?'

'Thank you Elder. I was deeply moved by Brother Michael's words, deeply moved. And I believe he has struck close to the very nub of our dilemma. We have unleashed onto the world and now helped to deliver, an infernal system. As Brother Michael has pointed out, it has already done harm. Harm to the world and harm to ourselves. How should we, in God's name, respond? What form should this repentance Brother Michael speaks of so eloquently, what form should it take?'

'I agree we have a responsibility for this, but should we run away? Can we? Do we wash our hands of what we have done, as Pilate tried to do? Are we so pure of heart that we can afford to face judgement at the sound of the Trumpet and say, "But I said I was sorry"? Repent, yes, but by being brave enough and, yes, man enough to accept responsibility for what we have done. When a dog bites you, you put it down, Brothers. The Spirit of Jezebel is loose and the Enemy is using it to fight against the righteous judgement that is surely his due.'

'We could retreat in prayer, and many Godly men have done that over the years, but, Brothers, I say we should repent, in action. Rid the world of these people, who would misuse the great gifts which we were given and if necessary rid the world of this very system itself. Thank you, Elder,' and he lapsed into silence, but the table was filled with nods and murmurs of agreement.

Brother Michael looked most unhappy. The Elder cleared his throat once more, he seemed to use it rather in the way a judge uses a gavel.

'So, Brothers, we have heard for and against. Both speak of repentance, both pious men, both strong in the fear of God. With whom does God ask us to walk? As ever you have two stones, one white, one black. As you leave place your hand in the urn and leave one stone, the white for Brother Mathew, the black for Brother Michael. In the name of the Father and of the Son and of the Holy Ghost, thank you Brothers.'

They stood and as one they faced the Elder and bowed. Then, one by one they filed out, first those on the side of the window and then those on the side of the door. Eleven votes, eleven stones and then the room was empty. The Elder stood and walked down to the urn. Lifting it he spilled its contents into the small, clear bowl beside it. The stones flashed as the sunlight caught them as they fell. Ten white stones, one black. The Elder smiled satisfied.

Later that day the Elder was alone in his study. A red bound book nestled in his hand as he walked to and fro silently reciting a prayer. He read, yet seemed to know the prayer by heart. The room was quietly furnished. Everything held the solidity of age, the certainty of the past. A solid knock on the solid door, The Elder stopped.

'Enter.'

The door swung open and Brother Mathew was there, 'Am I disturbing you?'

'Never, Brother, come in.'

Brother Mathew gave the corridor a quick glance, a habit of many years, before closing the door quietly.

'Would you like a drink, Brother?'

A schoolboy grin creased his face, 'That would be very considerate, Elder.'

As the Elder poured two nice measures, 'That was a finely delivered speech this afternoon, Brother.'

'Oh now, Elder, it was a finely written speech for sure.'

As the Elder turned, he grinned and his arm stretched out with the drink.

'Alright I'll agree to that.' They touched glasses and drank, savouring the moment. The Elder looked serious.

'I thought Brother Michael had made an impact, it needed all your skill, Brother.'

'Brother Michael's problem isn't that he doesn't fear God enough, it is that his fear paralyses him, he can never be bold in the fight for the Lord. He doesn't see we've been called to fight and in any fight there is damage and injury, winners and losers. He is all, "Sermon on the mount" and not enough, "Christ in the Temple".'

The Elder looked down at his drink and smiled, they touched glasses again. Silence as they enjoyed the moment.

'You have news, I understand Elder?'

'I do. I have heard about people, people we thought dead and also about a missing part, a part that might change everything.'

'Is that so?'

'It is. But it might need the sort of work to bring distress to the heart of Brother Michael and some other, um… Franciscan, souls. Best we keep this to a few disciples. I'm going to send you along to one of the Brothers who work in the pit. We need to be sure he remembers his place in the world and the cost of forgetfulness. I would like to speak with him here.'

'I understand, Elder.'

They smiled and drank.

22

The Beast in his Den

It used to be the Willard Hotel. The place Ulysses S Grant held court when he was President. Part of the building still was a hotel, though it would almost require a government loan to be able to afford to stay there. A slice of 19th Century Paris in the heart of Washington. Two floors of the building were now the sole domain of the Americorp. The name was so ubiquitous that some people thought "America" was named after Americorp. They provided everything in the society, from air transportation to taxis, from baby-food to anti-aging treatments and the services around the hardware too. People in every stratum of society used their wares if they wanted to, even if they didn't. People thanked them and cursed them in equal measure. They were a transnational organisation holding monopolies in base commodities across the full range of the necessities and pleasures of life.

The Willard was only one of their main offices, but the one where you were to find the power-brokers in the corporation. The very centre of power in Americorp was the man sitting in a straight-backed chair reminiscent of the ones used by the Brooklyn Brethren. Duncan Heath had held the positions of Chair and CEO for decades. For so long in fact few remembered that he had once crawled out of Brooklyn himself, a Brother. About five years earlier and much against his instincts, he had relinquished the role of CEO in favour of one Andrew Donovan. Donavan had been his protégé, a second, or perhaps third, son of sorts. Heath had believed he saw himself in the good-looking, confident young man. He thought he saw a man capable of charming at the dinner table in the early evening and shafting his guests in the late evening. He was worried now that this might not be true.

It was thus a fractious Duncan Heath who swished his brandy around in his glass and peered at the nervous members of his board.

Jones, the Chief Operations Officer (COO), was just finishing a competent but empty presentation about "the situation".

Heath waited as Jones sat and then waited some more. After some minutes he looked up and into the faces of each of the executives in the room. Apart from him, only Jones and Donovan were seated and it was in Donovan's face that he ended his tour.

'That was forty minutes I can't ever get back again, it said nothing but, "we dropped the ball",' he turned to Jones, 'could've just walked in and said that. If you had, I probably would have been just as annoyed but less angry. I have heard nothing yet about what are you going to do?'

'Well, Sir, that is why we're having this meeting, to hear all sides and make the decision.' Donovan offered.

Heath did another tour of the faces in front of him, seemingly failing to find any source of comfort there.

'Is there one of you, just one, who has the first idea of what we've lost here?'

Jones shifted, 'I think we do know, Mr Heath, but we are caught between the conviction that the opportunity is gone and the hope that it still might be retrieved.'

'Retrieved eh? My understanding, from your presentation, is that it cannot be retrieved.'

Donovan cleared his throat, 'That may not be completely accurate. In its current form the system is dead.'

'Current form?'

'An automated algorithm. We put in the parameters, time and so on, the target destination and the system guides the people to the correct choices. We now believe that there is another part to the original system, an AI.'

'Why d'you think that?'

'Jones here observed the number of corrections the system needed in order to keep it from reaching absurd results and he concluded that it needed to keep reaching for new inputs and from wider sources in order to keep going forward.'

'So, why not just build one? We've thousands of the damn things.'

'We think it was designed to work within an organic system, a human mind.'

'Why? That sounds… why would it work better than an AI on its own, the brain would slow it up…'

'There was an example from a play, or maybe it was a poem, I don't know. Observing human behaviour logically can skew your results. Without going into the detail of the example, it was possible to infer from human behaviour the opposite of what the traffic system was telling them. AIs have difficulty holding two competing ideas at once, when choosing one idea over another is a matter of an illogical, emotional response to an outcome foreseen but neither clear nor definite.'

Around the room most were trying to work this out, Heath leaned in, 'You mean to say we're selfish and not always rational when viewed from the outside?'

'Yes Sir, that's it. As I hope I conveyed in the presentation earlier, the rational argument for coming to the US was clear and I think unanswerable, but Dr Armenta's insecurity led her to make an, outwardly, irrational choice.' Jones leant back in his seat, feeling perhaps, he had won something. Heath looked unconvinced and took another pause and another mouthful of brandy.

'Are you suggesting we build this thing? Or saying we can't?' Turning to Donovan and then round the room. Donovan shifted, 'I think we could, but it might take years. We believe however, we have found what and where the original was, and we think it still exists.'

'Oh?'

'I'd like to adjourn the board at this time Mr Heath.'

Heath waved his agreement and, when no one moved, raised his head frowning without looking at anyone in particular. The meeting broke up. Jones stood and Donovan gestured to him. Waiting until the room had emptied, Jones walked to the door of the adjoined room. As he opened it Donovan turned to Heath, 'You are going to meet the person who nearly stopped the deployment of the fail-safe which is stopping our system working at all.'

'Alright then.'

Jones said something to the person in the next room through the doorway and held back the door. Anna May came into the room, a patch over one eye and a stick, black with a silver handle, in her left hand. She had a pronounced limp. Heath stood as Anna made her way across the room. The injuries had obviously been extensive, but apart from the limp she moved easily enough.

'Mr Heath, Anna May. Anna, this is our chairman, Mr Duncan Heath.'

She gave Donovan a resigned and pitying look which Heath couldn't fail to notice before they shook hands.

'You've been working hard for us, and at some cost I understand.' He gestured to her stick and patch.

'I failed, Mr. Heath, these are just reminders of that.'

He appraised the unapologetic but frank response and sat, he pointed at the chair Jones had been in.

'Drink?'

She accepted, 'Jones knows what.' And Jones was over at the table filling glasses.

'You have more to tell us about this AI, I gather?'

She gave Donovan a look, 'It was the AI that was the cause of the failure to stop the deployment of the fail-safe.'

Heath considered this and then with a frown, 'So where is it stored? From where is it working? I thought China 12 deployed the fail-safe. Am I wrong Jones?'

Anna grinned, 'Starting at the end first, China 12 did deploy the fail-safe, but they did so because of the AI. Currently the AI is stored in Milo Talbot's head and we think it has embedded itself in his brain.'

'How do we know this?'

'Julia Church's cousin, who I eliminated in Marseilles, had notes on his brain implant. The device I used to bring him down also downloaded his storage system, not all of it but enough. We also found notes in Church's apartment. They were useful, but it was only because I saw the AI actually working that we realised what it might do.'

'Might?'

'Can't be certain unless we have it.'

'So let's get it.'

Donovan shook his head, 'Not so straightforward, we think it's still in Talbot's head.'

'Buy him. There isn't a person alive who can't be bought. We just need to find the price.'

'I'm not sure Milo is inclined toward money.' Anna said.

Heath laughed, 'I never mentioned money, he has a price, trust me. And if we can't meet it, we only want his head, isn't that right?'

He turned away from Anna, 'Listen Donovan, we have the resources and the personnel, if this thing is in his head, then we have to have his head, understand?'

'Yes sir.'

'As you seem to know what you're about, I think, if you can still work with Jones, you and he should take stay in control of the operation, Miss May. If you can't work with him, then you alone. Donovan will ensure you have everything you need.'

23

Lamu

The trip from Manda to Lamu, even by dhow, is not very long but the change of pace is instructive. Lamu had had an interesting history from it's heyday in the 18th century as a centre for poetry and the arts, to its nadir in the early part of the 21st Century, after the failure of the Chinese "String of Pearls" plan, following the rise in sea levels.

A lot of the archipelago had gone and on the island itself parts of the old town and much of the north east of the island had been saved only by the construction of levees which held back the seas. Most of the current inhabitants were seasonal workers catering to the still functioning tourist trade and those who for one reason or another wanted to keep formal authority at arm's length. They lived under a different kind of authority, in some respects more free, in others more brutal.

The wind driving Milo and Julia toward the jetty near the old town was warm and scented. Julia kept prodding Milo to do something or other. To stand, so that she could feel the breeze, or to take a deep breath the better to get the scent of where they were. He indulged her as a parent does a child, though the thought he was experiencing these things for and with another person was… strange.

As they approached land they could see various people crowding on the shore. Some straining to see relatives, porters from the hotels awaiting guests, some of the town's traders waiting for goods to be delivered. At the back of the crowd was a tall man in a smart, crisp green uniform, standing erect and aloof. Milo turned to Julia, 'I don't know if he has an implant but no sudden appearances.'

'I'll remember. He looks pretty sharp for a country policeman.'

'I think this place is just the old centre, the rest of it is spread round lots and lots of little islands.'

'Doesn't look much.'

'Used to be more. You're a researcher do some research.'

'Ok.'

The boat swung into the land, making its last tack. The sail dropped and lines were slung out and caught as it drifted the last metres in. With a surprising lurch they came to a halt and some passengers squealed. From the look on the master's face, he liked that bit, it could almost have been deliberate.

Milo hung back, letting the crowd get done those things he would otherwise have to clamber over or wade through. He watched the man they were due to meet, or the one he thought they were due to meet and was reassured by his calm sense of self possession. Finally a space cleared and Milo made his way to the gangway and land, his baggage on his shoulder, he thought he looked very seafaring. The uniformed man stepped forward, a broad smile and an outstretched hand.

'Milo?'

Milo dropped his bag.

'Inspector Mwangi?'

They shook and the inspector pointed the way to the town.

'Have you eaten? That journey from Mombasa can be very dusty. Leave your bag here, I'll get someone to take it to the hotel.' He gestured to one of the men on the shore with his chin and then turned away. Milo looked round and there was already someone heading his way.

'That would be lovely, thank you.'

They walked on quietly, the inspector evidently wondering how to say something.

'Milo, I don't want to be impolite but, do China 12 often pick up jobs like this one?'

Milo frowned, 'I don't understand, "like this one"?'

The inspector's eyebrows rose, 'We don't put our crimes up on the boards, I understood that agencies like yours get their work from the crime boards.'

'We do, we did.'

They arrived at the building that had a large sign beside it saying

"General Store" and under that in small writing, "police bureau". The inspector pointed inside. They made their way through the bustle of what appeared to be the main store in the town, which made Milo feel he was in an old movie about an even older time. The crowd opened before them and closed behind. A narrow passage and a staircase to a nice wide room with a wide-open triple door to a balcony. A fan, that must have been decades old, spun in lazy circles producing little effect. The inspector showed Milo to a chair and then went to collect a prepared tray with cold drinks and some light cakes. He put them down on the table in front of them and sat. Both men were already covered in sweat.

'As you can see, Milo, we are a small operation. An inspector normally has many men to run around for him and I do have some, but not here. Well, I have one here and he is seeing to a problem at the donkey sanctuary.'

'The donkey sanctuary?'

Julia appeared beside him, '*World famous, at one point they had three thousand donkeys. See, researching.*'

'Oh yes,' said the inspector, 'it's quite well known. At one point it had three thousand donkeys.' And Milo smiled.

'Please take your drink, and these cakes are local, not at all heavy.'

Milo did as asked. The light lime drink perfectly slaked the thirst which had been growing. He then bit into the cake. Light, as described and flavoured with coconut. Milo was just thinking "how nice" when, '*Oh wow, these are delicious!*' Julia, with her eyes closed, savoured the taste, Milo jumped. The inspector turned.

'Everything alright?'

Milo coughed, 'Fine, just after the journey a little fatigue, throat dry. The cakes are very nice.'

'*Oh be a little more enthusiastic.*' Julia said. Milo wished he could kick her and as soon as he wished, she turned with a broad grin.

'Yes, they are a favourite of mine.' He reached out for another. Milo waited. Without looking at Milo the inspector said, 'You see, I don't want to think that Nairobi doesn't trust us to solve the case. We do not have a poor clean up rate,' he turned to Milo, 'although we don't have many murders, so it could be an experience issue.'

'Inspector, as far as I know this crime was lifted in the usual way by our system. There was nothing particular in the way we have been employed.'

The inspector was looking out of the window again, unhappy, 'Right, right. Good.'

Milo finished his drink and was about to reach for another cake when the inspector turned and with a sad smile, 'I suppose you want to see the crime scene?'

Milo's hand shot back, seemingly unnoticed by the inspector and he nodded quickly. Julia looked at the cake longingly and Milo looked a little embarrassed.

'Oh, yes of course.'

They stood and Julia looked at the inspector, '*He doesn't look like he's thrilled to see us.*'

Milo thought, '*No, not very. He seems very worried about us being here at all.*'

Julia cocked her head, '*Something to hide?*'

The inspector held out his hand, 'This way.'

They headed back through the shop and took a right down a little alley, reaching a small square at the end of it. Diagonally across that and out through another small street and past several more houses. The walls on either side were fresh, of white stucco. At regular intervals they passed a door, finely carved in dark wood.

'*Are you looking at these doors?*' Julia asked, '*They're famous. They do look pretty magnificent. And the cats, did you see the cats? Some of them have different coloured eyes, they look like Egyptian temple cats…*' She grinned, '*Research.*'

Milo turned to look and the door was indeed magnificently carved. A dog poked his head round the door and barked loudly. The inspector frowned at it as the chorus was taken up by his friends round about. Milo shook his head.

'*I'm sorry.*'

'*Sorry?*' asked Julia.

'*For opening my big mouth.*'

The inspector stopped and tore off old "crime scene" strips. He pushed the door and stepped back.

They stepped into a garden. Two large trees, the one on the right very old, very tall - Milo wasn't sure what kind. The branches were strong with clusters of bulbous fruits, he supposed they were fruits. The other tree was a coconut palm, not as large but also very tall. Milo stopped to look up at it. Julia was also looking up, '*Did you know that 150 people aren't killed every year by coconuts?*'

Milo frowned, '*What?*'

'*Yeah, it's pretty amazing. Some people thought that that many people were killed every year by falling coconuts.*'

'*But they're not.*'

'*Nope.*'

Milo closed his eyes and took a breath. He walked on to the house, passing a well with a rusted grill, the overgrown garden crowding in on top of it. More tapes at the front door which the inspector tore away before pushing the door open. He again stood back. Milo stopped walking and he looked at the inspector, 'Inspector, you've already looked at the scene?'

'Yes.'

'Your thoughts?'

The inspector became a bit stiff, 'You should look. I understand that usually the local police are for enforcement only in these cases.'

'You've never had an outside agency deal with a case here before?'

'No, never.'

Julia looked at Milo, '*Duh! He has said as much.*' She said.

Milo took a breath, 'Ok, we like to talk with the local police anyway, they know the area and they always have an opinion, right or wrong, and that's useful. We put the crime, any crime, in a broader context of human behaviour and narrow down the probable causes and perpetrators from there.'

The inspector considered this, 'Right. Whereas someone like me works from the known workings of the local community and the known behaviour of the people in my district and go up from there. Not so different.'

'Not so different, but, our system should catch your knowledge and eliminate prejudice built up from knowing your own people too well.'

The inspector relaxed a bit, 'Take a look and then we will talk.'

Milo walked in, scanning the room which was very bare and empty of furniture. The walls were covered in large ceramic tiles varied in colour, making brilliant patterns. The floor bleached and dry, as though it had been thoroughly scrubbed over and over. The inspector watched Milo and offered, 'Flooding. Living quarters are above.'

Milo looked up at the raftered ceiling and they headed for the stairway, which was a rough wooden affair nailed to the wall. A counterweighted trapdoor rose up above them as the inspector pressed down on a lever to the side. They stepped up into the room and the inspector let down the trap.

Milo looked round the room, while furnished, it was pretty sparse. One wall was covered in a light cotton cloth, patterned in an African style which Milo presumed, and Julia confirmed, was local. There was a long table made of some sort of dark wood, old and well-worn on one side, that seemed to serve as a dining table. A desk, again dark wood, large, heavily carved decorations on the sides. On the top, an old large white blotter and a single lamp, several pens and a Jeweller's loupe. One side of the blotter was covered in some sort of dust. At one point the dust had stuck in a puddle of what appeared to be dried blood. There were no communication devices and no com loop in the building.

At the back of the room was a rough kitchen with an induction plate, common in this sort of small kitchen and a sink. Two or three plates and a couple of glasses were there, unwashed. If there were cooking utensils, they must have been in what appeared to be storage with a cloth curtain pulled across it.

Milo turned to the inspector.

'Where did he sleep?'

The inspector pointed up to the floor above and Milo followed the gesture.

'A bit of a bare existence, did he rent the place?'

'No, he owned it. He wasn't a full-time resident, I think this was a holiday home, from his family. He had a practice in Nairobi, architecture.'

As they were moving about the room, Julia was looking at the forensic report which had come in as they entered the building. She turned to Milo, 'He was a mixed-race Kenyan, great-great-grand parents were colonists from Scotland, had a farm up by lake Naivasha, he had a relationship with someone in Nairobi but it ended a year ago. 47 years old and his practice was struggling, several loans, payments being met but his accounts are not awash with cash. Several staff layoffs in recent months. Found on the desk, throat cut, one carotid artery and his windpipe, this is the probable cause of death. The dust is from an emerald mine in Zambia, no emeralds found, is that what the inspector is worried about? Some writing, "dogs" on the blotter, written in the victim's blood, possibly by the victim. Some hair samples found in several parts of the room, track to the cleaner and her family. No other DNA apart from the victim's found. Murder weapon not found. Victim had an implant which he seems to have used for all coms, am getting the most recent and decrypting them now, that will be a while.'

Milo smiled and to the inspector, 'Good forensic report.'

'*That was a summary*.' Said Julia, Milo ignored her; as much as he could.

'Good, I haven't read it yet.'

'He was killed here?'

'That was where he was found, so probably, there was no sign he was moved.'

Milo rubbed his chin, 'And no emeralds?'

'No.'

'That is what seems to be the motive.'

'I would say, probably.'

'Probably?'

The inspector looked unhappy again, rather, dissatisfied and frustrated.

'Look, Milo,' he stopped and looked directly at Milo and frowned, 'I have been calling you Milo, the file said, is that right?'

'Yes, perfect.'

'Good. Milo, I should tell you that I believe I know who did this, or who is responsible at least.'

'Oh?'

'I also should tell you that I don't think there is any chance they will stand trial and this investigation is highly dangerous.'

'Who?'

The inspector walked to the table quickly and tapped his finger on the blurred word on the blotter.

'I think the victim told us.'

'"dogs" like the ones outside?'

'Yes and no, the "Dogs of Lamu", they are a gang. Their boss is here in Lamu, he lives about three houses away, if you shout you can call him over. They run most of the criminal operations along this coast of Africa, from Somalia to Zanzibar.'

'We should talk with them.'

'No we should not. They are very dangerous, very bad men. For very little money there is nothing they would not do.'

Milo turned and looked round the room and then at Julia, '*Is that why we're here? Has someone manipulated our system to get us isolated. Have the Dogs of Lamu been paid to kill us?*'

24

TLC

The Pixie was just sitting looking at Sam, as she had been for the past 17 minutes. Sam finally turned to look at her.

'Are you going to do that all day?'

'Probably.'

'Shouldn't you be checking something or other, or preparing my medicaments?'

'Medicaments? Do you mean medication?'

'No, medicaments, it means, "medication", just older.'

'So, like you.'

Sam just looked at her in silence.

'What? You are.'

Sam stayed silent and her face slowly became sad and then her head dropped and she pushed out her bottom lip and the Pixie cracked.

'No. Stop, I'm sorry, you're not older and I couldn't love you any more, no matter what… Stop.'

Sam grinned, 'Huh, "older" indeed. I could be deader, thanks to you and your friends.'

'No, please, I'm sorry, I know you could, but you're not.'

Sam laughed and held out her hand and the Pixie grabbed it, 'I'm sorry, that was mean. It wasn't your fault, or your friends, it's the kind of thing that could have happened on any assignment.'

'But it happened because you trusted them and their judgement.'

'Yeah, but they were reasonable. And they helped out the other evening.'

'I guess.'

They were sitting in an apartment in New York, in northern Manhattan just below the Cloisters. Manhattan had not fared badly from the flooding, unlike the neighbouring boroughs of Queens and the Bronx. Manhattan had become very exclusive, Brooklyn very religious and the others very poor. The apartment was comfortable 1930s design in old wood, well looked after. Like most buildings it had been updated in its heating and lighting but discreetly, so that it still looked much as it had just after it had been built. Sam was sitting up on a couch surrounded by pillows. The Pixie was sitting cross-legged on a table not far from her. The apartment was a place used by China 12 and others when staying in the city for longer than a week and it was well-known to anyone who cared to find out about such things, but surveillance was straightforward and access easy. From Sam's point of view, it was also close to medical help should it be needed.

The Pixie was there to take care of, and protect Sam, but they knew that this would be a sort of long term "interview" for China 12.

'Thought any more about it?'

'About whether the two women were dead?'

'Yeah.'

'I have. I've run through what I can remember, it's a pity base purged the clips of the evening, but my strong impression was they'd had it. He shot her square in the back and her suit was not in the best shape. But who knows, maybe they're out there.'

'They still haven't managed to get the DNA records from the forensic company.'

'You never knew them, right?'

'It was before I knew anything about them.'

'She seemed a good type.'

'Huh, maybe I'm glad she's dead…'

Sam held out her hand and the Pixie took it, 'What I can remember is how angry I was, you just don't turn on your partners.'

The Pixie leaned over and kissed Sam on the forehead. Sam winced. 'Sorry.'

Sam smiled and again, 'Worth it.' The Pixie laughed. Sam turned serious, 'How long are you going to have to be here?'

'How long are you going to be unwell?'

'You know what I mean.'

'If you could travel we could get you to Beijing and then I'd know you were safe.'

Sam smiled again, 'Do you think they'll let me go?'

'I don't think. We're not going to give them any choice. It's like your "termination system", execution system more like. Julia can switch things off. If you're well enough we can get you out, I'm pretty sure. But, you know what our former bosses are like; they will be upset if we try to go too fast and they'll be very upset if anyone else tries to get hold of you.'

Sam nodded, 'Yeah, too much coding access from my implants now that Julia's disabled the internal kill switch. They have too many secrets to hide.'

The Pixie touched her hair, 'Good job we have Julia around.'

Sam smiled, 'She is a pretty nifty friend.'

'Yeah, dangerous.'

'I'm surprised she isn't causing more of a stir. My lot would love to have something like that.'

'Julia hasn't been around that long, so not many know about her, I guess. Wow! A world full of Julias - that would be a bit wild.'

Silence. Sam thinking about something and the Pixie worried about what to do if... Finally, Sam looked up.

'Who is he anyway?'

'Who?'

'The guy who tried to kill me?'

'Kevin? I never met him. Like I said, he was an op in China 12. You know more about what happened that night than we do and certainly more than me. It looks like he's gone rogue, or he did. Look, I'm not really supposed to talk to you about him, the doc said it wouldn't help you recover.'

'They always say that, but the trouble is I just go on thinking about it. Do you have any pictures of him?'

'Yeah.' And the Pixie connected to Sam's system and shared a few images of Kevin's face.

'Good looking bastard. I do remember some bits, I saw him in a street, I must have been on a "watch only" brief. I don't remember too much after that street bit, he was outside, rain, I thought he spotted me. Next thing I do remember well was the fire and him shooting his partner, or I think they were together, that's the strong memory I have of it. They were together and there was someone else.'

'That would have been the client maybe?'

'Maybe, I think it was another op though, it's all a bit mixed up. Was the client a woman?'

'Yeah.'

Sam's face scrunched up and she tried to piece it together and then she shrugged.

'No good. So, Kevin, is he any good?'

The Pixie grinned, 'Not good enough.'

'Don't, you can never tell. Is he going to stop? Do they know?'

'If he is helping someone trying to find out if Joanna and Mariana, the op and the client, are alive, then they might try again, see if you know something. If he was trying to kill you because he thought you were the only one who knew he was alive, then that's blown and he won't come back. China 12 thought maybe, that he wasn't alone.'

'So who else?'

'I don't know. It's all above my pay scale and even the brainiacs seem a bit confused. It hurts my head. I just wish they'd point me at something and say "kill that".'

'You know it's never that simple and you're easily bright enough to deal, or you wouldn't be a pixie, and you wouldn't be with me.' Sam said.

The Pixie smiled and they touched heads lightly, 'That's just having really good taste in women.'

'That too.' Sam was quiet again and then a little sad, 'Do you think we have a chance?'

The Pixie smiled a smile of utter confidence, 'Are you kidding? China 12 are the best, Julia's a ghost and you have me.'

'Silly me, who could stop a ghost? Are these people dangerous? Really? You were up against them with Anna, what do you think?' Sam asked.

The Pixie gave it serious consideration, 'I think they have money behind them, money is always dangerous. I think they want something, we thought we'd stopped it, but maybe not. I wish I knew what, 'cause then I could blow it up. If they think whatever it is, is still worth something, they'll keep coming. But, that doesn't mean we have to be involved.'

'I think even if we're not working on this, we'll be seen as something that has to be cleaned up anyway. I've seen things. They don't know I can't remember. You've seen things and banged up one of their guys. People like this don't like that and they don't like loose ends.'

'And China 12 are better cover than being friendless.'

'Better cover than being dead anyway.'

Across the street from the apartment, another building, another apartment. This one was about ten years old. The room was utilitarian. A wide-open expanse, clear but frostable® windows, a bare kitchen with signs of being currently in use. Along one wall were several monitors keyed in on two people, Sam and The Pixie. Two combat ready operatives were there watching, one was standing chewing a bar, the other lying in a large armchair. The walls were playing out some animated game.

The automated system opened the door and another two came in carrying packs. The new ones were both male. The older one looked round the walls and back at the op lying on the couch.

'Change that out, you're supposed to be professionals.'

The op on the couch stood and looked round the walls and they switched to a neutral grey.

Then he and his companion lifted packs of their own and headed out the door. Nothing else was said. The new ops took up position. Just before the door closed the walls changed again to another more graphic animated scene. The door closed. The older op sighed and the walls changed to a rural scene, he then asked, 'How long did you say?'

'They told me, "in the next few days", that's all.' And he began to walk along the bank of monitors in the glass of the windows showing the view through the walls and windows of the apartment across the street.

'So, could be us, could be them.'

The first one nodded slowly.

25

The Brother's Rep

Jones was sitting in his work-chair in his home apartment. His chair was designed to dynamically sustain long hours sitting while maintaining circulation and exercising the muscles. While working on sensitive material he used only his implanted systems, connected to the net link in this single room. He trusted no one and was terrified his secret might slip out.

The proverbial knock on the door came as he finished his latest note on Anna May's little project. Donovan had put him in as liaison between Anna and their several partners. She had freelanced for them as they had tried to stop first Julia Church and then China 12 deploy the system which was preventing their social control program from working. The effort had been a near miss, but it had been very close. This time it had to work.

He called up the "welcome" camera, as it was called and looked at the dark-suited gentleman standing waiting at his door. He knew where he was from of course, but this wasn't the usual way things were done. No, this was very unusual. Jones didn't recognise him. He hesitated, simpler just to get rid of him, but you couldn't tell what might happen next. He waved the door open and the two connecting doors opened with it.

Standing, Jones walked through to the reception area and, arm out, greeted his visitor.

'Jones. And you are?'

'From Brooklyn.'

Jones eyes flickered away and then back at the man's face, 'Yes, I understood that, but we haven't met. You are Brother…?'

The man stopped shaking Jones hand but held it still, 'You don't recognise me then?'

'Should I?'

'Should? I suppose not, but we have met before, several times, Brother Mathew.'

No instant recognition in Jones' eyes and Mathew smiled a tight smile.

'Doesn't matter, Dominus Vobiscum Brother,'

'Et cum spiritu tuo. Are we back in those days Brother?'

'Some of us never left.'

'Would you like something to eat, drink?'

'A glass of water, thank you.'

'Of course. I haven't yet eaten, I hope you don't mind.'

'Not at all.'

Jones turned and walked smartly to the kitchen and Mathew followed. Once there Jones busied himself, first getting a glass of water then pulling out food from the fridge and throwing together a salad and dressing, all from fresh ingredients. He waved to a stool by the island as he worked and Mathew sat and watched.

He took a long draught from the glass and then, still watching Jones, 'I have never mastered the art of cooking, my wife does it so well. You seem to be very at home here, no wife?'

Jones looked up and smiled, 'No, no wife, never lucky in love.'

'Pity you couldn't try gambling.'

'Never inclined to, though I'll bear it in mind if I should lose my faith.'

'You haven't then?'

'Eh?'

'You haven't lost your faith, Brother?'

Jones stopped, the sharp knife in his hand poised in mid-air.

'No, Brother.'

Mathew took another draught from his glass finishing the water and he placed the glass carefully in front of him. He seemed to be contemplating it. Jones waited. Mathew looked up.

'There are those who fear you have become detached.'

'Oh?'

'Yes, they consider the life you lead, your involvement with technology, your increasing material wealth, expressed in the,' he waved his hand around the kitchen, 'contemporary distractions of men's toys. Not a single sign in this place that it is the home of a Godly man, Brother, I looked.'

'I entertain people back here from work, it would raise suspicions.'

'We have others in the corporation who have not lost their pride in their faith, Brother.'

'Not in as influential a position. You know who was a member and how sensitive he is to reminders of the Brotherhood.'

'Sadly, yes. Of perhaps greater concern is the lack of information to have come from you in the last few months.'

'There has been little of benefit to the Brotherhood to tell.'

'Not that Miss May has taken thirty pieces of silver from Americorp?'

'I believed Daniels knew that.'

Mathew agreed, 'A fatal error.'

'He was my friend too.'

'What about the news that the China 12 operative still has that AI in his head?'

Jones looked at Mathew for several long seconds, 'I only heard about that myself a few days ago. How did you find out?'

'Not from you obviously. You've known for several days?'

'I was checking it out, checking it was true.'

'You are the liaison of a new group who are to find this… Milo person, for the Americorp.'

'How could you have known that?' His eyes rose and checked out the internal security systems and then dropped back to Mathew's face. Mathew was smiling.

'No Brother, we don't have to spy on you. You are not our only source in the Americorp, I would have thought you knew that.'

Jones shrugged.

Mathew's smile dropped, 'The Elder is worried, Brother, he believes you may need a retreat, just to remind you of your priorities.' Mathew's voice became more insistent.

'I can't possibly take time away. If I am to continue to be of use to the Brotherhood, and I do want to be of use, then I can't just leave, not like that.'

'It isn't really a suggestion Brother Jones, the Elder feels it imperative.'

Jones' eyebrows shot up and he glared at his "Brother", 'No. I said no. I know you don't, or won't, understand this, but the real world outside of Brooklyn doesn't work like that.' Said Jones, his voice rising.

'What is the real world to people like us? We don't work on corporate time, we work on God's time, his schedule, his priorities. If it's part of his plan then the interruption won't be a problem, if it is a problem, then your position isn't part of the plan.'

'Brother, in all humility, I think God reveals as much of his plan to me as to anyone else. This situation is screaming at me that I should stay where I am and fulfil the work I've started. Until I see a compelling indication from God that things should be otherwise, I'm going to stay and do that.' Said Jones calming down.

'Brother, the Elder has told me what has to happen. He has told to me God's plan, or as much of it as I need to know with respect to this problem. You are part of it but it has become clear to the Elder, and it is now clear to me, you have lost your way.' Mathew said.

While he said this his hand slid into the right-hand pocket of his suit, his fingers bulged through the fabric as they curled round the weapon. Jones watched the movement, he understood what it meant. He had to make a decision, though it wasn't if he should leave or not, it was more to decide if he should stop what he knew was about to unfold. He had been told this moment would come. When you are told the future, was that prophecy or a plan? If he said something, was that a sin or was saying nothing the sin?

A sin of omission. He considered what he would do once it had happened. He ran through the chemicals in his store in the basement. He was watching Mathew and knew the man was oblivious. He thought of telling him and then not telling him. It was possible that Mathew would not lift the weapon out from his pocket, it was likely that wouldn't save him. Jones became disinterested, but for old time's sake.

'Brother, stop.'

'Brother, you need to see a compelling reason, I have been told to show you one. This is something I regret. Rest assured I will use it if called on to do so.' Mathew insisted quietly.

'I wouldn't do that.' And he gestured to the pocket with his head. Mathew allowed a brief smile drift across his face and that shut Jones up.

The response time was satisfyingly short. Mathew raised the gun, the house scanning system picked it up and knew, from the heightened pulse and body temperature as well as the enlarged pupils, that the intent was to use it. No countermanding command had issued. The gun was not even fully pointed at Jones when the system fired and hit Mathew once, verified the kill and went back to surveillance mode. Mathew looked at Jones surprised, and then fell off the stool. Jones mixed the dressing for his salad again, poured it onto what was left and tucked in.

Lifting the bowl in one hand and the fork in the other he walked round to the body. Looking down, he prodded at it with his foot, just to be sure, and then leant back against the island. He had thought of doing this at the door, but he knew it would be complicated. Dominos knock down other dominos and the race begins. Now his name would be on a list, probably at the very top. He squinted, looking down at Mathew trying to remember where they had met. Was it significant? He ran through various events while still in Brooklyn, a young man on the rise, filled with the fire of conviction, Mathew could have been him twenty years earlier. Nothing came to mind and he stretched his neck and shook his shoulders.

That would be a problem for the future. He was staring at tonight's problem and it didn't make him feel happy. He had run through his stock of chemicals, but that was very messy. He knew, as few did, that Heath had once been a Brother. He had left when he'd had a falling out with the then Elder, and to many people's surprise they had just left it at that, why?

Was Heath still in contact with the leadership? In that case he was screwed. Unless this little demand had been a way of shoving him completely into Heath's camp. If Heath helped him out, he would owe him everything.

He knew that his apartment's cameras had captured in holographic detail everything that had happened and that he hadn't been responsible for the system taking out Mathew. It was illegal after all, to pull a gun on someone and everyone knew about security systems. Everyone except people brought up without technology. So he wouldn't be guilty of any crime, but, that wouldn't mean anything if someone wanted him put away. Mathew hadn't been briefed about the security system. That couldn't have been anything except deliberate. He looked down again at the body and pity welled up inside him, and disgust. This was how he had lost his "faith", the sheer cynicism of the leadership.

So his next path was to throw himself at the feet of Heath, was it? Ok, then what? Try to stay alive long enough to figure out where to get off the roundabout.

26

Dinner and the Lamu Lockout

Milo was standing in the middle of a wide covered terrace. There were long trailing bougainvillea flowers all around the edge of the arches supporting the upper floor with mangrove beams from swamps long since drowned. Along from him and straddling the arch nearest the open door was a table set for supper. A tall, languid woman in startlingly beautiful African colours carried a drink to him and he took it with a smile and slight bow.

'I should have said so earlier Dr Abebe, your forensic report was very thorough. We found it very impressive.'

'We?'

Milo was caught, he had been thinking about Julia, but he stammered out a, 'Yes, my colleagues in China 12 have seen it.'

'Dr. Lopez-Real by any chance?'

'Yes, her too, well in particular as she is our forensic, um, expert…'

'Oh good. When I was told China 12 were to be involved in this, I had hoped they would send her. I'm sorry Milo, Rachel Lopez-Real and I were at university together when I took my doctorate.'

'Were you close?'

'We socialised together, you know, young women about town, endless parties and fast cars, the usual.'

Milo was a little surprised, trying to align his serious friend Rachel Lopez-Real and this description. As a result, he was a little at a loss for words. The inspector came out with a tray of food and he placed it in the middle of the table, saved. Dr Abebe grinned.

'That's what we dreamed about anyway, mostly it was meeting in breaks from the lab or the library and complaining about supervisors over a drink in the evening.' She said.

Milo laughed. The Inspector looked up and was presented with two grinning faces.

'Is my wife charming yet another guest?'

Milo grinned, 'We were talking about her hell-raising days in Rome.'

'Ah, Rome... It's too hot in the summer and too wet in the winter, but it has some nice ruins.'

'Yes, I was one myself for a while.'

'Really Milo, when?' Dr Abebe asked.

He waved his hand vaguely in the air, 'Decades ago. Lost in the mists of time. That food looks pretty amazing.'

The Inspector beamed, 'Do you like East African food, Milo?'

'I haven't had too much of it to be honest, but if this is typical, I like what it looks like.'

'Yes, it is very typical, we eat like this all the time.' Mwangi said with a broad smile. His wife snorted.

'We'd be bankrupt if we did. This fish, Milo, is from farms up in the Rift valley, the Tilapia, and your drink is some of our best palm wine.'

Milo looked at the milky honey coloured drink in his hand and took a sip. His expression changed and he smiled.

'Wow! That was unexpected. Is this a traditional drink?'

'We've been making alcohol from palm for centuries, but it was a little while after specialist Japanese Saki began to be popular around the world that one of our ministers decided that anything they could do, we could do better. I think he was right.'

'I hope they built statues to him.' Milo said and took another drink.

'He ended his career in jail on corruption charges, but he was alright in the end.' The Inspector laughed. They sauntered over to the table and the doctor arranged them in seats.

Julia appeared in the last, unused seat, but only to Milo.

'*This looks inviting, I can't wait for us to taste it. The wine is, mmmm, too.*' She smiled and Milo looked at the colourful dish in front of him.

The food was as good as it looked, finely spiced, laced with coconut, perfectly cooked. The palm wine was delicious and they had various flavours to try with each course. The evening was long, the conversation good, the atmosphere warm. They sent him away with the aroma and taste of perfect Kenyan coffee. As he walked through the small town's back streets to the hotel, he realised he was feeling a little tipsy. He shook his head and then stopped.

'Hey.'

Julia appeared. He gave her a serious look and she smiled affectionately.

'Did you… muck about with the alcohol suppressant system?'

Julia moved her head up and down, slowly, but very seriously, her smile gone.

'Research.'

'Research?'

She nodded again, 'Research. I needed to know how much cognitive impairment occurs when alcohol is consumed and the nature of that impairment.'

'You wanted to know what it was like to be drunk.'

Julia smiled and held out her hand again, 'Yep.'

'That's very adole, adolescences… adolescent… of you.'

Julia very seriously, 'Yep.'

Milo turned and headed away from the hotel, stopped and turned back in the right direction. Julia walked with him. He stopped about twenty metres later and glared at her.

'You don't look drunk.' And she didn't, she looked perfect, just a tiny bit slower if you knew her, a little more ready to smile maybe. Milo knew her, but he was drunk. They set off again.

Back in the inspector's house the high-flying couple were cleaning up. She was washing and he was drying things and putting them away. She handed him a glass with an ornate coloured stem and stopped.

'Was Milo drunk?'

He continued drying while he considered the question, then.

'Yes, I think so. The Milo of earlier in the day and the one at the end of the evening was different, slower.'

She nodded, 'I thought so, but I thought it was…'

'Travel and tiredness.'

'You don't think it was something else?'

'Such as?'

'I don't know.'

'I think he was just a little drunk.'

'That is very odd.'

He agreed.

'Do they not have systems to stop that, like ours?'

'Yes, they do, I think they do. They must have.'

Dr Abebe was washing again but thinking, remembering.

'Aaah, of course they do, I remember Rachel wanted to test her system against my system, but it didn't work.'

Now Mwangi stopped and gave his wife a stern look, 'I thought it was all study and libraries.'

She smiled and reached out with a wet hand to his face, leaned toward him, kissed him and looked at him with wide eyes.

'It was, we experimented in our boring one room studios, took notes and everything.'

He frowned at her and kissed her back and then wiped his wet cheek dry.

Milo's hotel was in the oldest surviving part of the old town. It had sea on two sides, with a third protected by a high levee which ran on back along the eastern side of the island. Their room was large and the bed very comfortable, despite looking like something out of the latest holo-film of Treasure Island. The large double window doors opened, like the ones in the inspector's office, onto a wide veranda. The sound of the crickets was drowned out by the lapping of the high tide below, which was relaxing nevertheless. Before going to sleep, Julia had restarted the alcohol suppressant bots and the world had returned to normal. Milo was tired but grateful for that at least. It was 11pm in Lamu and 4am in Beijing.

Three and a half hours later, give or take, and Milo woke up. He smelled the unfamiliar room, felt the unfamiliar sheets. What was the sound? Traffic? Of course, central Paris, always the rumble of tyres on the streets.

'Milo?'

He turned over. Julia. He smiled to himself, his head still felt funny, like it had earlier in the evening.

'Hey.'

'Are you… alright?'

He smiled again, reached out… weird. 'I'm fine… is there something wrong with my hand?' he looked at his hand.

'Milo? What do you mean?'

He reached out to touch her but kept landing on nothing. He sat up and looked round the room. He frowned, something was different. He thought to ask Julia and looked across the bed. She was gone.

27

Tap Tap Tapping

It was early, but she had been awake for about two hours and was worried. Something was happening and she now couldn't find Julia.

Liu had been talking with Julia regularly, once or twice a week, over the past few weeks. They had agreed that she could keep an eye on the two pixies in the US. This gave her a real connection to what might have been her life, had China 12 and her father not intervened. They had even been introduced. Also, because someone had already tried to harm Sam, it was pretty exciting, much more than schoolwork.

The other thing, this she had set for herself, was to track down the man who had attacked Sam in the hospital. It was proving difficult but she had some leads. It hadn't stopped there, she now had a list and a routine. She was keeping a watch on the Beijing compound. Not because she'd been asked, but she felt a sense of belonging that filled the space left by her withdrawal from the internal security program.

Her last little project, and this was one Julia had given her, was to try to find out if Mariana and Joanna were alive. She had searched every possible avenue and come up blank. If they were alive, she was impressed with how well they hid, but then maybe they cheated by being off grid; but completely off grid.

Something was definitely up with the people who were watching the pixies in New York, she had presumed they were pixies as well, she knew in the US they were called Clantechs too, but their recent activity made her reconsider. There had been a sudden increase in chatter around their position, encrypted of course, but she didn't need to know what they said. She had warned the Pixie and Sam yesterday. That was strange to her, their names. She wasn't sure why The Pixie called herself that but she thought it was kind of cool and Sam was American, so that was different and so it was cool too. Having warned them they were being watched, meant it wasn't urgent. But, Julia had impressed on her the need that she be told if something changed, something was happening. And something was happening now and Julia had disappeared.

She considered raising China 12 directly but she wasn't sure of her position. Had Julia told them about her? Or had she just told the pixies in the US? She didn't want to get anyone in trouble. Julia had been in Kenya, which was very well connected. She'd been excited about experiencing Africa which was kind of weird, she was an AI after all. It was interesting too though, the experiencing bit that is, the Africa bit was just interesting and not weird. But when Liu got up this morning, Julia wasn't there and now she was worried.

She had a sudden sense of how her father might have felt when she left to join the Chinese version of the pixies. Caring about someone in trouble who you can't help, sucked. But couldn't she still help the pixies? If it was seven o clock in China now, what time was it in New York? 7pm, they would be awake and, if what she'd learned when training was right, the others wouldn't raid before 3am. The brain is at its slowest between 4 and 6am, which is why most raids happen then. She'd read that, in the old days it was when most driving accidents happened.

Telling them now would give them nearly eight hours to get ready or get out. She decided that had to be her top priority and she called the Pixie.

'Hi. Liu? How are you? Is everything ok, you look worried.'

That annoyed Liu, she'd been trying for calm and relaxed. 'Um, yeah, it's just, I'm seeing a lot of noise from your friends across the road and they just had new arrivals but no one left.'

'Ok, what does Julia think?'

'I can't seem to find Julia, she was on a few hours ago but now… I can't find her.'

The Pixie had a think about that one and Liu could hear Sam asking something. The Pixie turned back to Liu.

'Sam can hear us too, alright?' the Pixie asked.

'Sure.'

'Julia doesn't normally go off at all, so something is up, it might have nothing to do with us, or it might,' The Pixie said.

'Yeah, I thought that,' and Liu smiled.

'What do you think?'

'I think they've made a decision and I wouldn't say it's to leave,' Liu said.

'So you think they're going to retire us?' the Pixie asked.

'It's what we would do, I mean, in the training program.'

A voice, without Liu being able to see her, 'Hi, Liu, it's Sam, we'd be thinking on the same lines, but with China 12 involved… and they must know they're being watched.'

'The Julia thing could be them, and they might suspect or even presume they were being watched, that's what we've been trained to do. But they don't know it, or if they do, they're not doing anything about it.'

'They may not be the only surveillance team.' Sam said.

'Julia couldn't find anyone else.'

'She'd be the first to say that that isn't conclusive,' answered Sam . The Pixie got tired of waiting, 'We have to make a decision, guys.'

Liu and Sam together, 'Move.' And the Pixie smiled.

'Ok. Where?'

'How is Sam?'

'Not as bad as she's pretending to me, not as good as she's pretending to herself.'

'Hey!'

'Yeah, but how far does that mean?' asked Liu.

The Pixie looked across at Sam and seemed to try to consider. Sam said something that again Liu couldn't hear. The Pixie thought some more and then she turned back to Liu.

'We don't really have many options. We've prepared two routes and two destinations, but the longer one will take a lot of prep and Sam is … Ow! In great shape. I just don't know if it's great enough. On the other hand, without Julia to run shotgun the shorter option is risky if they track us quickly.'

'Julia set up a program that should let them think you're still in the apartment for about two hours after you've left, it's pretty cool, I think it is anyway. But if you don't leave early enough that won't matter.'

'Ok. That's it then. Will you contact Beijing? And keep trying for Julia, tell her, "it's sunny side up!"'

'"It's sunny side up"?'

'That's it.'

'Ok.'

They broke communications. Liu sat back and was relieved but had a new thing to worry about, would they make it? She took a deep breath and started the program Julia had set up for contact with China 12. It took a few seconds.

'Hello?'

'Hi.'

Cathy O Shea was sitting at a table, breakfast in front of her. Liu's rumbling tummy reminded her she'd been up for hours and hadn't eaten and Cathy's meal looked delicious.

'You are? Oh, hold on, you're Feng Liu, Milo knows you. How can I help; actually, how are we talking?'

'Hi, yes, sorry, I am Feng Liu, Milo got me back from... some people, with the help of Zang Xin, I am very grateful.'

'Good and now the other questions?'

'I have been helping Julia.'

'Oh?' and Cathy frowned.

'Helping her to watch over Sam and the Pixie.'

'I see. Has something happened?'

'Something, yes. Sam's former colleagues are, we think, about to attack her and Julia is missing.'

'Julia's missing? You know she's in Africa?'

'In Kenya, yes, we keep in touch, but not now, she's gone missing.'

'Ok, I'll ask my friends here to look into it. Now, what's this about the Pixie?'

'They've decided to move.'

Cathy looked alarmed, 'Is Sam up to that? They shouldn't be concerned unless it's real important. It might look important but not be so urgent, you know? I'll talk with Milo when he's awake, it won't be for another few hours, maybe two I guess.'

'I know. But the Pixie and Sam are in danger, they have to move, so they're moving, we talked it through.'

'You did?'

'Yes.'

Cathy was halfway between smiling and being worried. 'I should speak with Xin about this, are you going to be available? Won't you have school?'

Liu's turn to smile, 'I'll manage to get a day off. I'll let you talk. Julia said to speak with Rahul? Is that right?'

'Rahul, yes. I'll contact you in a short while, or perhaps Xin will. Thank you.'

'Find Julia for me, she can help the Pixie and Sam, I'm worried they might…'

Cathy smiled again, 'Don't be, we'll take care of it.'

Cathy broke the link with Liu, who sat back. The teenager realised she was hot and sticky and that call had done nothing to reassure her.

28

Looking for something to Kill

There was a stack of counters on the windowsill in front of him. A little further along to his left was a bowl filled with more counters. He was watching the street below intently. The street was a narrow alley running behind the houses. There were three dumpster collecting points, each containing two dumpsters side by side ready for the monthly collection of organic and non-organic recyclables. Waste collection, like sewage treatment had moved on. Kevin was counting. He had a timer up in his ocular system and he was watching the end of the street. The timer was counting down the last few seconds from whatever point it had started at.

'Come on, come on.' The timer stopped and he heard a beep. 'Shit! Again!'

The timer reset to two minutes and began to run down. A young woman with a red top passed the end of the alley lit by street lights, 'One.' As he watched he took three counters from the stack in front of him and tossed them into the bowl. Another red dressed young woman passed, 'Two.' And then another, 'Three.' Unconsciously, his hand gripped and squeezed the edge of the sill. 'Come on.' His eye flicked to the timer, "forty seconds". He moved closer to the window.

A loud noise behind him as Anna came into the room. The regular 'tic' of her stick hitting the ground added a rhythm to her step. She stopped and glared at him waiting. He held out his arm to her with one finger pointed straight up, his muscles tensed.

'Yes! Four!' The timer zeroed again. He took three counters from the bowl and added them to the stack and stepped back.

'Are you ready to go to work now, Kevin?'

'Sure, what's up?'

'To begin with, the targets of our job here are getting ready to move.'

He flashed a look at the monitors and then out of the window and frowned, 'I've seen nothing.'

'No.' She let that one hang there. He looked out of the window again, then back at her.

'Was there something to see?'

'Not out there. But on screen four, if you'd been awake, you'd have seen three clantechs go into the surveillance base.'

'I did see that and flagged it, but they've been doing that for days and days.'

'Oh? Seen them come out then?'

He thought and looked at his clock and then a quick scan of the monitors.

'Oh.'

'Oh is right. They're getting ready to take down our potential little treasure trove as well as our possible leverage over China 12 and you're sodding about doing what? Pretending you're in some casino?'

'It keeps me alert.'

'No Kevin, it stops you being alert.'

'Ok guv'nor, it's a fair cop, won't happen again.'

'I know, and if you ever tell me to wait with that gesture again, outside of combat…'

'Right.'

'Right?'

'Sorry.' She held him in a long stare.

'We bought you Kevin, I expect to get my money's worth,' and she looked him up and down, then, 'It's likely the clantechs won't move for at least seven to eight hours. I don't know if they're likely to catch our targets by surprise. Given they have Julia watching, I doubt it.'

'But then we have hours, and we're already prepped.'

'The targets won't wait until the clantechs hit them. I expect them to have been warned already, possibly some time ago. That means we also might have missed them already.'

'Shit.'

'So why are you just standing?'

He jerked into action. There were two heaps by the door. One, a pack, obviously full; the other weapons and the ammunition to go with them. Kevin had the pack on and was snapping the clips that held the straps when Anna turned, making quickly for the door. Thanks to her suit, her slight limp and stick didn't hamper her at all.

'But we haven't because one of us was paying attention, they're moving right now.'

'How can you see them? I don't see anything?'

'I put up a drone over the back door, they have a car coming.' And she was through the door, gone.

Kevin cursed and lifted the weapons, clipping on the ammunition as he ran out the door.

'They'll bloody spot that straight away and why don't I have access…' He was muttering as he headed for the stairs.

Anna was taking them two at a time, they were three floors up. Kevin had caught up as they burst through the back door of the building and the small yard to the open gate. Anna stopped and looked round the edge of the wall. She was silent for a minute, then two. Having been rushed outside, Kevin began to get antsy.

'So, are we moving or what?'

Anna looked back at him, 'You have the drone image available to you now, tell me what you're seeing?'

Kevin called it up and watched, the drone was following a cab which had reached the end of the alley and was waiting to join the traffic.

'The cab, I presume that's them, you've slaved it to their images. But it's getting away.'

'Take a look at the heat signatures of the cab.'

Kevin squinted as he did that.

'Now wind back to the point where they are coming out of the building, about ninety seconds.'

'What the hell? It's fake. But how could they do that?'

'Julia is how. She must have prepped it before today.'

'They saw the drone, I thought they would. When did you put it up?'

'Saw the drone. The drone is irrelevant. I think you'll find every camera centered on this alley and those ones on the street at the end are picking up this feed in sequence. She might even have one with them rushing out of the front door. We have nothing on the front door, do we?'

'They'd never leave that way.'

They looked at each other and at the same time they turned and ran back to the house. This time Kevin was leading and he threw himself at the door, flinging it back and standing out of the way as Anna rushed through. She took the steps outside in one go, stumbling slightly as she slammed her stick into the pavement for support. She scanned the street. It was empty, or practically so. She looked up and spotted the street cameras. It took her a moment but then she turned to Kevin.

'Just checking.'

He watched her as she was running backward through the recordings on her implant. Her eyes flickered in a pattern familiar to him. He scanned the building opposite and his eyes settled on the screened windows of the apartment where he knew an assault team was prepping for the incursion to eliminate Sam and the Pixie. He could practically smell the atmosphere in the room, he'd done it so often himself. He could feel his stomach muscles tighten; he needed a holiday.

'Got them. I can't fault their procedures, it took me four passes before I recognised what I was looking at. According to the timestamp, they left about twelve minutes ago.'

'So, have we missed them or did the cab have a destination on the top?'

She sighed heavily, 'Neither, nor. We have a tracking relay on the street cameras. I've tagged the cab and it can show me the route, stops and current location. The only problem will be if Julia interferes again.'

She looked at him and then at what he'd been looking at, 'Anything?'

'No, just remembering.' Then he frowned and looked back at Anna.

'If the pixies have left, why don't that lot react?'

Anna frowned now as well, 'I'm guessing they're being fed the same sort of bullshit we were fed.'

'So if she could do it for them, why don't they pick up the missing heat signature?'

Anna flicked her head at the street cameras, 'They don't have thermal cameras, invasion of privacy laws, our drone was strictly illegal.'

While she was talking a cab drew up alongside, she spun round on her stick as the door slid open. Anna climbed in and Kevin followed. Once inside, Anna reached up to the control unit and stuck a small white "pill" on the side and then sat back. The cab rolled forward. She relaxed.

'I'm feeding the connection details to the control, we should be behind them in a few minutes.'

'Ah the wonders of modern tech, I could have used one of those a few months ago and maybe one that disrupts the same feed.'

'It will do that too and it saves all the usual messing about. They should be including this stuff in the next implanted upgrade. The problem they used to have was heat, not that much out here but too much for our little heads. Roll on the day when they can just replace the lot, eh?'

'You mean the organic brain?'

'Yeah, the meat.'

'Won't happen.'

'Why?'

'We animals are pretty efficient and the implants increase that efficiency but we're also selfish, so I don't see anyone queuing up to get their brain taken out.'

'Why'd you think it will be voluntary?'

He snorted at that, 'And I don't think we're even close to being able to do it at all, we'd see proper humanoid robots first and I don't see too many of those. Do you?'

'Maybe you're right. Maybe.'

She had been watching the progress of the two cabs while talking and she leaned forward looking through the front window, 'There.'

Kevin leaned forward, 'Any projected destination?'

She slowly shook her head, 'Too many. But it looks like it might be somewhere in Queens if they go right it'll be the Bronx.'

'So not a known safe house, but it makes more sense, to go to the poor districts.'

'No, not a safe house.' Anna said, still working on the connection.

'It shouldn't be too heavily defended, unless they have more people there.'

'I think that's unlikely, they've been abandoned by the US clan-techs, I think this pair are flapping in the wind.'

'Apart from China 12 you mean.'

'They aren't here are they?' Asked Anna.

'Except for your friend Julia that is.'

'I'm ready for her.'

'You think.'

Anna said nothing but looked ahead at the cab, several cars in front of them. Kevin followed her gaze. The cab they wanted was highlighted in green by their interior systems, appearing as a normal cab with a slight green glow. Anna sat back, it might be a long trip. Her hand caressed the top of her stick absentmindedly.

'It's the Bronx, the edge of it, beyond the flood waters.' Anna observed.

Kevin ran through his pack in his mind and then drifted to his current state of operation. It had been quite a while since he'd had a real workout and that one at the hospital had caught him by surprise. That little Pixie had had a fury he'd rarely met since the war. Normally you were faced with people who made calculations based solely on the profit and loss of any given situation and he had usually meant a loss to whoever the China 12 was after. That was then. For the Pixie in that hospital ward the "loss" column was a lot steeper and a lot simpler. When Anna's little trick didn't work, there was nothing for him there, especially once they'd seen his face. If it hadn't been for pride he'd have cut out sooner. Anna nudged him.

'This is it, they have to be close to home.'

'Why do you say that?'

'Because this little scanner is also tracking the com link between the cab and base and it just gave base a seven-minute note.'

'Meaning?'

'Meaning that in seven minutes or so, the cab would be available for hire.'

'They don't know they're being followed.'

'They don't know they're being followed.' She confirmed. 'I'm going to back us up a bit. When they stop, we stop.'

'You're not going to try catch them in the open?'

'If we were going in for a kill, that would be exactly what I would do, but we don't want to kill them if we can help it, do we?'

'Ok.'

'Once we tag the building, you go for the back entrance.'

'If there is one.'

She turned and gave him a surprised look, 'These people aren't stupid, it won't be "if" there's a back entrance, it's more like how many. Just like you on any op.'

Kevin took a deep breath. The last thing he wanted to get was another supercilious lecture from this… person. She was beginning to get under his skin but the last thing he wanted was for her to know that. He was out of shape and his head was out of the game and he knew it, he had to pull himself together before someone else knew it too. "*Just think of the money*" he repeated to himself… The cab slowed and pulled over to the sidewalk. They waited.

About a hundred metres ahead, the Pixie climbed out of her cab, just stood at the kerbside taking a long, slow look up and down the street. She walked across the pavement to the bottom of the steps up to an old house and checked either side, then on up the steps to the front door. She disappeared from sight for a moment, then reappeared. Moving quickly now, she met Sam who was climbing carefully out of the cab and together they turned toward the house.

Anna and Kevin moved too. Once out of the cab they split, Kevin heading to the rear of the buildings along the street. He saw Anna walk steadily in the direction of the house. He cut down the back alley. Counting the houses and then shaking his head as the target house started to glow green; they take the challenge out of it.

He stopped at the back gate, tall, wooden, worn. His system scanned the gate. The inside of it was reinforced with high tensile carbon rods. Developed in the last decade, they had a structure similar to wood but many times stronger and it was one of the many steel substitutes available. So there was no going through that easily. Over? Anna's additions to his system meant he could pick out the alarm's scanning beams. Anna's voice broke in on his thoughts.

'We won't hit together. You go first and then I'll hit them from here, they are just at the bottom of the steps and their cab's pulled away. I want to hit them at the top of the steps. You have about 90 seconds.'

'Do you know if the house has invasion suppression systems?'

'I can't see any.'

'No.'

He didn't add, "You're not supposed to see them".

He took out a small pistol and fired a bolt into the wall then screwed in the end of a cable attached to his suit. He gave the rear a last look, stepped back to the far side of the alley, checked up and down and ran for the wall. The jolt hit as he crested the wall but lasted less than a second as the system ran to earth through the cable and fused. He could hear it reset and begin to charge again, as his feet hit the ground. Running to the back door, he ploughed through it. Automated firing systems hit him from left and right. His suit flared as the points struck by the projectiles resisted. It did knock him back, but it didn't stop him and he was on the stairs and about halfway when he heard the noise of the fight ahead.

His instinct was to go crashing through the door but he could hear Joanna's voice in the back of his mind saying, "information is power", and he stopped. Edging the door open, he took in the room first one way then the next. Anna was lying on her back, her stick at his feet near the door, with the Pixie in Kevin's path between them. Sam was away to his left, leaning against the wall and she was pointing something in his direction, though what, was obscured by the Pixie. Having been thrown into the house, Sam had obviously surmised the next most likely threat was from the rear door. Could she see that the door had moved?

Anna spun on her back and to her feet, clearly her damaged leg didn't interfere with her ability too much. Drugs, along with the suit he presumed. The two women circled each other, Anna favouring her right side a little. Sam, now clearly visible, weapon in hand, kept her attention focused firmly on the door. Kevin waited. He knew his chance would come in just a few moments.

Anna made the slightest of gestures to her right, but the Pixie wasn't to be baited. Instead after a moment she suddenly dived to that same side, feet first along the floor and took Anna's legs from under her. No sooner was Anna down than the Pixie was up and over her. Sam flicked a look at the fight and Kevin was through the door and on top of her.

He knocked the gun out of her hand. She brought her other hand round on the instant and drove a knife into his ribs, the suit deflected the blow. Catching her wrist, he depressed the thumb and the knife fell to the floor while his other hand completed the movement by bringing a blade to Sam's throat.

'Stop!' He rotated round, curling her wrist into her arm in the process and now the others could see he had Sam. 'We'd like to speak with her, but you'll probably do just as well.'

The Pixie turned and let out a guttural animal sound, half anger, half fear. Her hand was on Anna's throat, pressing it into the floor and in spite of the command the pressure on Anna increased rather than diminished.

'I'm not going to shit about.' Kevin insisted. The Pixie smiled, let Anna go and stood up, 'Good girl.'

The Pixie's smile stayed fixed on Kevin, Anna didn't move.

29

Dissociative Disorder not otherwise Specified

'But it's not possible. Has he gone "off"?' Xin was perplexed to say the least.

Cathy and Rachel had been explaining to her what they thought was going on but were also trying to get to grips with it themselves. It wasn't going well.

They had called in Rahul and Hoshika, who had yet to arrive, but were going through the possible scenarios with Xin. The first was that something had gone wrong with Milo's com software. Then they had tried to check out the hardware, but they quickly ran up against the problem that it wasn't just Julia who had gone missing, Milo was too. Cathy suggested contacting the local police but Xin thought that made them look like amateurs. They had called up the last logged contact with Julia and Milo, which had been the previous evening and then the automated tracking system. It was when they looked at that that they became seriously worried.

Rahul came in and looked across the worried faces.

'Is there something wrong? Something I've done?'

'No Rahul, nothing you've done,' Cathy assured him, 'but something is wrong.'

'Oh?'

'Milo is missing.'

'Not possible, well unless… but even then…'

Hoshika walked in and looked around, she turned her head to one side.

'What isn't, or might be, possible?'

Rahul was running through the possibilities in his head, 'Milo is missing.'

'How? What about our auto tracking?'

Rachel shook her head, 'Nothing.'

'That shouldn't be possible… Should it, Rahul?'

'No. After Sao Paulo we made sure that it would be always on unless the op…'

Xin frowned, 'So why would he switch it off and why is there no tag on the system saying he'd done it?'

Rahul pursed his lips and thought. Turning slowly, he looked to Hoshika for ideas but she was practically a mirror image. She turned to face the other three.

'When did you discover this, if there was no tag? How did we find out?'

Cathy quickly explained about her strange breakfast with Liu, her conversation with Lopez-Real and then the bringing of the problem to Xin.

Xin pointed at them and said, 'And I called you two.'

'Right. You've tried a system check and to com directly? Are there any local problems that might have caused this, revolution, nuclear war?' Hoshika asked.

The three shook their heads as one.

'We should contact the locals.' Rahul put in.

Xin sighed, 'Doing that hardly instills confidence that we know what we're doing, does it?'

'That may be moot if the problem is that he's dead.'

Hoshika shook her head, 'Still wouldn't explain why his tracker is off. He must have done it. Maybe someone has arrived that he's worried might be able to use the system.'

'Then where has Julia gone?'

'Julia is missing too?'

Cathy coloured, 'Ah, yes, that was the trigger for the concern, Liu had been talking with Julia and now she couldn't raise her.'

'That's serious. Julia doesn't work that way, she wouldn't just go "off", not even sure she can.'

'Yes, that's the other thing, the Pixie and Sam might be attacked by the US authorities.'

Xin stood, 'What?'

'Sorry, I got a bit caught up in trying to talk with Milo about it. Liu thought, you see, Julia had been working with her to keep an eye on the Pixie and Sam, so when she picked up a lot of chatter from the US side she thought it a prelude to a raid.'

'Has anyone told the Pixie?' Rahul looked alarmed as he asked.

'Yes, she had already warned them but wanted Julia to help.'

Xin faced Rahul, 'Could you check out the situation over there, contact Ms Feng? Cathy, you and Hoshika try to work out what the hell is going on in Lamu and, if necessary, contact the local inspector. It is nine seventeen now, meet again at ten and we can decide what to do.'

Rahul was already walking through the door and the others turned to leave. Xin sat down.

'Dr Lopez-Real, could we have a few words?'

Rachel stopped then turned and walked back to sit opposite Xin. Xin rearranged some things on the desk in front of her before coming to the point. She looked up.

'Doctor, you probably understand more about the way Milo's implants work than anyone here.'

'Oh, I think Erasto and Rahul would disagree with that.' Xin held up her hand and smiled.

'In fact, I know they would not. Could this be a serious problem with Milo and the way his implants are working? Have we pushed him out into the world too fast?'

'Technically, no I don't think so. His system was stable and working very well for… pretty well all of the time he was under my post-op supervision. I looked at the most recent readouts right up to last night and it was rock steady. I think Julia has helped with that.'

'Right. I suppose that's good news but it means that the most likely cause is from an outside agency. It's not as if we lack candidates though.'

'It looks that way, but I'm sure he'll come through, he's been doing it for a while after all.'

Xin smiled, 'True. Thank you for that.'

Rachel waited and then realised that that was the end of the conversation. She had known and worked with Xin for about eight years and still couldn't see the end of a conversation coming. She smiled and with a sharp jerk of the head stood up and left.

Cathy and Hoshika were looking at data they had pulled down from Milo's and Julia's feed. They had been going through it in silence for some time when Cathy leaned back in her chair.

'I can see nothing that would account for the blackout. I've been through it twice. Something this big should surely be... big.'

Hoshika shook her head, 'On the contrary, it most probably is something really small.'

Cathy just turned to look at her, saying nothing, thinking thoughts ranging from the pathetic to the violent. Then she sat up and frowned.

'We have to get in touch with the locals out there.'

'Why? Xin didn't seem at all keen.'

'If we can't contact him, he must be in the same position. But he hasn't tried to contact us at all. Unless there is a local problem, surely that's the first thing he would do.'

Hoshika considered that, 'That would be logical. Who do we get in touch with?'

Cathy called it up on her system, 'There's an inspector Mwangi who seems to run the regional police force.'

'Then let's...'

Rachel walked in 'Something I just realised.'

They turned and Hoshika said, 'Cathy realised something too.'

Rachel stopped and 'Ok...?'

'Milo should have talked with us by now, why hasn't he?'

'He might not be awake yet?'

Cathy and Hoshika looked at each other. Cathy smiled, 'What time is it in Lamu?'

'Four forty-four.'

'Oh' said Hoshika, she didn't look at all happy. Cathy frowned and Lopez-Real held up four fingers. Cathy closed and then opened her eyes in recognition of the sign of bad luck, death.

'Ok, what was your realisation?' Cathy asked.

'I think I know the local inspector's wife, we were in college together in Rome.'

'Who is she?'

'Dr. Miriam Abebe, she's a forensic pathologist, very bright.'

'What's she doing in the sticks, if she's so bright?' Cathy asked.

Rachel gave her an arch look, 'I don't think she'd think of it as the "sticks". But she's there because that's where her high school sweetheart works, he's the regional police boss.'

'Inspector Mwangi?'

Rachel shrugged and then they all stopped and stared. No one said anything for a moment, and then a few more moments, then Julia stopped blinking and looked back at them.

'Why were you blinking?' Hoshika asked.

'Was I? Artefact of my confusion, I'd say.' Julia answered.

'And you're confused?' Cathy asked.

'I am, I'm not sure what's happening.'

'But you're here, where have you been?' Rachel blurted out.

'I don't know. Everything went dark.'

'Would that have been, half past seven in Beijing?' Rachel asked.

Julia looked at her blankly then flickered, then, 'Sorry, yes, 02.27 local time.'

Hoshika looked at her feed, 'You're in com with us now, the connection seems stable, but Milo still isn't.'

Julia looked uncertain and then, 'He's out of com with me too.'

Cathy and Rachel looked at each other, 'How can that be possible? Is he alright, is he alive?' Rachel asked.

Julia seemed to be gaining some stability, 'Yes he's ok, still alive. This is possible because of what I am. I'm not independent. He can just switch me off or shut me out.'

The three women wondered what to say. This seemed to be causing Julia some anxiety or pain, could an AI experience emotional pain?

They were back in Xin's meeting room. Four people and an AI, all looking unhappy. Xin stood and walked round her desk.

'It seems to me that the person who has all of the answers is Milo, why can't we talk with him, Hoshika?'

'I don't know. He's managed to shut down tracking and com, neither of which should be possible without it raising a flag at our end. We do know where he is and we know he is moving because we can now track Julia.'

'Tell us again exactly what happened before everything went black, Julia.'

'He woke and looked round, I got the strongest feeling of confusion and then Paris, he seemed to think he was in Paris, then he said my name and I thought he wanted something done. But then he didn't say anything to me and everything went black. It's taken me this long to reestablish the link to com. I have very little access to most of his systems.'

Xin paced up and down and then searched the faces of the others, looking for a spark of some insight. Cathy sat up.

'Did anything happen earlier in the evening? Did he have a fall or... anything really, it might not have seemed serious, he might have brushed it off, anything?'

Julia looked guilty, 'I shut down the alcohol suppressant in his system during dinner. I was curious about what being drunk felt like.'

Xin's eyes squinted, 'Curious about being drunk?'

Julia looked stricken, like a teenager caught raiding the drinks cupboard. Xin turned to Rachel.

'Would that be enough to affect his system?'

'How drunk did he get?'

'Tipsy, I think you'd call it.'

'So?' Pressed Xin.

Rachel shrugged, 'Not normally, the system actually should be unaffected. But this isn't a normal situation. What do you think, Cathy?'

Cathy tried to run through what she knew and what she didn't.

'Hoshika, does everything look normal from what you can read through Julia's system?' She asked.

'We're getting the base readings. Thanks to the fact that Julia has entered his organic system we can also see some of the physiological readings too. The implanted system is nominal, Milo's body appears stressed, but then we've seen Julia is upset, so I don't know what's him and what's her.'

'Rachel?'

Rachel looked at the readouts, 'Milo's physical condition is good and his normal readings are usually on the very low side, so these are quite high, for him.'

Cathy thought for about a minute, when she looked up every face was creased with anxiety.

'I'm sure you've heard of dissociative identity disorder.'

Xin and Hoshika looked blankly at her.

'Really? Multiple personality disorder?'

They both nodded.

'When Julia stopped the system that suppressed the alcohol in his body, the alcohol suppressed his pre-frontal cortex and also his temporal cortex. This might mean that his decision-making and his memory were abnormally affected for a time. Julia's presence may be being seen by his mind as a disorder, what people with this disorder call an "alter" and so, because his mind wants to, and it seems it can, he suppressed her.'

30

The Menacing Streets

The sound of the sea woke him. The high tide had reached its peak and the waves shook the hotel as they crashed into the relatively new sea wall. It wouldn't be long before there was another new sea wall, probably the last.

His head hurt. He looked around the room and felt an extreme sense of dislocation, his eyes finally settling on the first thing he recognised, his shoes. He stayed there on his elbows and stared at them. They were more worn than he remembered, not much, but he thought they were fairly new. These were definitely worn and coated with what looked like, dust, or sand?

Looking down over his sweat covered chest, he puzzled at the light sheet draped across his lower body. It was heavily patterned in bright colours, bunched around his waist, it looked damp. A noise caught his attention and his eyes searched for the source. Two circular fans turned slowly and pointlessly overhead. For all their slight effort the air was still, the room was hot, close.

He tried and failed to place where he was and why. He had a powerful feeling that he was in Paris and that there should be someone else with him. He listened intently for the sounds of someone moving about. If there was someone, their presence was masked by the sea. The sea! So not Paris.

The loud and strange sound of the morning call to prayer drifted across the crashing waves, adding to his confusion. The lilt was both reassuringly familiar and very alien and disturbing.

He began running through everything he could remember from the night before. A confused series of images tumbled through his mind and he couldn't hold down any one for very long or place them. He wondered if there was a shower in this place.

He swung his feet over the edge of the bed and dragged his sheet covering with him and it bunched in his lap, falling to the ground as he stood. He stared at it again, pooled round his feet as it was, and tried to place it, tried to feel himself dragging it over his body the night before as he climbed in the bed. He failed.

He took a deep breath, pushing down the rising sense of panic. Scanning the walls, he spotted a likely doorway and walked unsteadily toward it. The door was dark wood, heavily carved, with a rough iron handle. It gave off a wonderful smell and he leaned in, taking his fill of it. Smell, so often evocative of a particular time or place, brought nothing.

He pushed the door and was relieved to see a shower room in front of him. He reached automatically for the light and surprised himself by finding it, but then thought it might be in a very similar place in lots of bathrooms. Then he remembered something, his bathroom had no light switch, most bathrooms had no light switch. He held out the cord in his hand and ran his thumb over the green glass tied to its end.

Green, emerald green, that meant something... A shower, that really meant something.

He had dragged on his clothes, having washed, shaved and pushed his hair about with a comb. The call to prayer had finished and he could hear people beginning their day. He tried to take in the image in the mirror. It looked more or less as he thought it should, maybe a bit better, that was a relief. The clothes were new, not his usual style, but everything fitted him well. They were light, natural fibres, pale colours, so probably bought for... wherever this was. Nothing came to him. He tried to take a run at it, starting trial sentences but ran into empty space each time.

He practised an easy, friendly smile, 'Hi, how are you? By any chance do you know where this is? No, not a damn clue.'

Someone was missing. Who? Male? No. Female? Maybe. Friend? Closer. Lover? Who knows. Relation? Felt like a relation, he knew he used to have a sister, but he had a strong sense she was gone, so...?

He stood up and walked over to the window. The veranda was wide and went right over the sea, or would have at high tide. The water was beginning to retreat. Along the horizon he could see the still darker western sky, the final stars fading. He guessed he was on either a peninsula or an island. Looking north he could see along the coast, small fishing boats and numerous pleasure craft, so a tourist spot. They all looked old from this distance, so a tourist spot past its heyday. To the south he could see the mainland, or what he took for the mainland, catching the increased light from the not yet risen sun. Wherever this was it was nice, was he here on holiday? He tried to rush at it again. He was in…?

He turned to look east. The blue sky and the rim of gold that spoke of the day to come and suddenly it hit him. He was really hungry.

He was downstairs, in what looked like the dining room, but there was no one about. He could hear people moving in the back of the hotel and he walked closer to the sounds.

'Hi. Anyone there? Hello?'

The noise continued as before, no-one answered. His eye caught movement out of the window and he stepped across to see if there was someone there. He looked out of the window and immediately dived back and to the side. Someone was there alright, someone he knew. Someone he liked, he didn't remember her dressed like that. Not strictly dressed for the climate, she was in a dark suit he'd seen her in that last time they'd met. Where was that? Denmark came to mind, but why Denmark? He wasn't sure why but everything in him warned him to keep out of sight until he could figure out what Anna was up to. He was now pretty sure he wasn't there on holiday. And she wasn't friendly. Whatever it was he should really contact base. What time was it there? His system was offline, weird.

He moved away from the window and scanned the room to see if there was anything to eat. There was a roll of bread on one table, probably left from the previous evening, he grabbed it and the water jug on the sideboard. He had to find out where he was. Working, he was now certain but where?

He walked back to the doorway leading to the reception and looked round the door. He wasn't worried that Anna would harm him, he felt in good enough shape, but he needed to know what was happening before he broke cover. Had he followed her here? Was she alone?

The reception area was clear and he walked across to the empty check-in desk. He began to look through the papers and brochures, they still had those, on the side. There were ones with elephants and lions. He stared at them, so he was in Africa. But where, it's a big place? He kept turning over leaflets. Ok, here it said he was on Lamu.

'Can I help you Milo?'

His head shot round at the request, the receptionist smiled broadly and looked questioningly at the jug in his hand and the half-eaten roll. The receptionist knew him, but Milo couldn't place when they'd met. He searched the man's face, was he honest?

'Are you looking for breakfast? Think the kitchen can do better than water and a stale roll. If you'd like to go through to the dining room, I'll get a menu. I hope your early morning is due to the beautiful dawn here and not a sign you slept badly, Milo.'

He seemed ok. Milo, caught between trying to explain the roll and jug, and gratitude that there was another person, looked down at the roll and then back up at the smiling face.

'Great. Thank you. Um, I slept very well, in fact so well that, um, how long have I been here?'

'In the hotel? You checked in yesterday morning.'

'Alone?'

The receptionist frowned, 'Yes, alone. Are you expecting anyone else?'

'Has Ms May checked in yet?'

'No, there is only one other room occupied, an nice couple, regulars, down from Naivasha, Mr Nightingale and Ms Monley, they used to own a place down in Shellagh but then the sea level...' He looked down at the monitor set in the desk, 'No new arrival is booked in.'

Milo shook his head, 'Thanks, I'll just...' and he pointed at the dining room.

Walking back into the room he'd just left, he picked a table near a window but outside of its direct line and sat facing the door, his back to the wall. If Anna saw him she could probably take him out through the wall, but this was his best chance until he'd worked out what was going on. The receptionist had called him Milo and he thought that was right, it fitted, and he could remember base and where he'd been. So not total amnesia. What else could he remember? The thought of his two dead friends swept over him, what was it that had happened in Brazil? The question ran round his head as the receptionist came over with a menu and held it out.

'Thanks.' He gave it a quick glance over, 'Fruit salad and yogurt, orange juice and coffee. You couldn't make me a quick omelette by any chance?'

'Of course. Plain, mushroom, with fruit, how would you like it?'

'Plain is fine, thanks.'

'And the coffee?'

'Strong, black and more of it.'

The man smiled, 'As much as you like.' And he turned away.

Milo thought he caught movement and his head snapped round but it was the frond of a palm tree waving in the sea breeze. He reflected on his order, the sugar jolt might wake him up. But fruit on an omelette? He pushed the thought away. What was he doing on Lamu? Where the hell was Lamu? He tried his system again but it was still offline. Was this something Anna had done? Was she leaving because she'd done to him whatever it was she'd come to do? He was about to stand when the receptionist was back with a tray of food.

'Ah, thanks. Tell me, when is the first way to get off… Lamu?'

'I hope you're not leaving us so soon, Milo. The first boat to Malindi is not until eleven, though I suppose you could hire a boat across, but the boat owners won't be down for another hour at least, no call for it in the off season, unless you already made an arrangement.'

'Right, no,' and he smiled, 'not leaving yet.'

'Good. There is another boat to Manda at two. The omelette will be right along.'

Milo watched him go and turned it over in his mind. He idly took a spoonful of the salad and yogurt. The full flavour hit him, stopped him in his tracks, he wasn't sure he'd ever tasted anything so good, wow. He shovelled two more heaped spoons of it into his mouth and just savoured the fullness and range of fruits in it. He kept going as his thoughts drifted again to his predicament.

He had to get in touch with base. What was the local law enforcement like? Malindi? That rang a bell, and Naivasha… the lake, he was in Kenya. He repeated that to himself again and again hoping to jog something free but it still meant nothing.

If Anna was here following him, he was in trouble, that might be his problem after all. If he was following her, he had to find out what had happened to him and why he was here before the consequences became too high. He had to presume that Anna would have at least equal standing with local law enforcement as he did, until he could speak with base and find out what was up. He'd steer clear of them for now. Breakfast first, then find Anna.

The omelette arrived.

31

Pieces in a Puzzle

'Suppressed her?'

Cathy nodded slowly, still thinking. Hoshika looked Julia up and down then turned back to Cathy.

'She doesn't look too suppressed.'

'I am though.' Julia said. 'Milo's cut contact with me and everyone else. I've opened this com but I've been trying to open my link with him for hours.'

Hoshika frowned, 'I thought you were part of him, organically.'

'I am.'

'But it's possible to shut out parts of your mind, close away things you don't like or are afraid of.' Cathy said.

'Is he afraid of you?'

'I don't know. Why would he be?'

'Good question.' Hoshika was on the sceptical side here.

'First, I'd like to know which parts of Milo's brain you are in?' Cathy asked.

Julia would have taken a deep breath if she could. 'Ok. I was uploaded as an extra measure in the event that something might happen to Elspeth. She adapted me from her AI assistant, giving me more autonomy and a survival subroutine.'

Hoshika's eyebrows couldn't rise any farther, 'A survival subroutine?'

'Yes, I might have been faced with someone attacking me to prevent the deployment of the fail-safe.'

'Right, so what then happened? Were you designed to grow into his system?' Cathy put them back on track.

'Yes and no. I have the ability to connect to the organic brain dynamically. I wasn't designed to do so explicitly, but if the host and I get on, it is part of the progressive routine. In this case I did so quickly, because I had to. When I was triggered, I found Milo's system was too confined to allow me to unpack my memory or a number of my functions, including as it happened, my main purpose.'

'To deploy the fail-safe.'

'Exactly. I had to make a decision, so I entered the hippocampus.'

'To get access to memory?'

'Yes, and to force the brain to grow neurons.'

Hoshika turned from Julia to Cathy, 'Is that possible?'

'I can't do it. I know they have done it in vitro and in some animals but it's not quick.'

'I needed speed. I began to develop molecules, in the way you have molecular factories for making the chemicals used in alcohol resistance, that way I could use the code Elspeth had already stored in DNA. That was one of the ways she had delivered the system. I also needed rapid access to that memory.'

'So where else?'

'Where, was dictated by need. I avoided motor systems but not sensory systems.' She stopped and if a holographic projection of an AI could look guilty, she looked guilty.

'What?' Cathy, Rachel and Hoshika exchanged a worried glance.

'After; after Denmark when Milo had agreed to work with me, I wanted to feel things, learn in the way you learn, through your senses. My first experiences had whetted my appetite.'

Hoshika looked shocked, 'Oh my God, you wanted to be a real boy!'

'What? No… Oh you mean like Pinocchio, yes, I guess that is… no that's silly, not like Pinocchio.' She shook her head as though resetting.

'I am connected with, but I don't control, parts of the frontal lobe and the parts of the parietal that concern sight and sense,'

'The sensory strip.' Rachel put in.

'Yes. I haven't gone near motor functions, but I am in the occipital and temporal lobes, I only take a feed from these. There is some feedback to Milo but that's mostly leakage, not an active open com route. Obviously, I'm mostly in his cerebral web that you implanted

163

in your last surgery. I use the new processor there for most of what you would call "cognitive" activity.'

'The extra processor; they said it was to protect from future attacks like Anna's,' Cathy said.

'When I was in the Pixie's processing unit after Denmark, I hacked the supplier's system and enhanced the spec.'

'Anything else?'

'Is that not everything, everywhere?' Hoshika blurted out.

'Yes and no.' Cathy answered. To Julia she asked, 'You haven't taken over these systems?'

'No, my programming prioritises the host before anything. I will look for a way to survive, but if nothing presents itself, my programme terminates. When it comes down to it, I'm still mostly a research assistant.'

'But growing.'

'Yes.'

'And you've done some housekeeping?'

Julia looked wary and that guilty look again, 'A bit, he's not as young as he looks. I've added some newer elements, one or two small things, very small, to taste for example, as Elspeth and Milo like different things. He seemed to like it. I thought he did anyway.'

And bizarrely she looked glum. Cathy, Rachel and Hoshika stared.

'Do you know what state Milo is in now?' She slowly shook her head.

'How can that be, you seem to be all over him?' Hoshika asked again.

'Mostly, as I said, I am in my processing unit. The programme allows him to shut me off, my primary purpose is to assist. The thing is, if he has locked me up here in the implanted system, he might also have shut down his own access to the memories we had together.'

'What might that mean?' Cathy asked

'If he has, he might not have a memory of anything since Anna's attack or even earlier.'

Cathy ran through the notes she'd taken on her own system and

Hoshika tried to make sense of what she'd heard. Julia just looked still and glum.

Finally, Hoshika stirred, 'It's nearly ten, we have to take this to Xin.'

Rahul was talking with Liu, trying to work out if her presence in the network was a good thing facilitated by Julia, or a bad thing aided and abetted by Julia. He was looking over coding for a set of programmes the pair had developed for the Pixie. They seemed to be just what Liu said they were and nothing else. After the death of the ops in Brazil he was very wary, especially when people were offering to help for free.

'Would you explain what they are doing, these programmes? This one is what, a masking program?'

'In a way. We didn't think it would be...'

'We?'

'Julia and me.'

'Right, but no-one else knew you were doing this?'

He knew what a talent Liu was but having read the report of her recruitment into the Chinese "Pixie" program, he knew she could be headstrong.

'The Pixie did, but I don't think Julia told anyone else.'

'Not even Milo?'

'I don't know.'

'Alright, the programme.'

'Where was... right, we thought the US pixies would pick up on any surveillance we did of them beyond taking the street cam feed and monitoring from the Pixie's apartment and voice traffic, so we went the other way.'

'There is another way?'

'We knew the Pixie and Sam would be watched so we created a programme to provide the illusion that they were still there.'

'What about thermal cameras, wouldn't they pick it up?'

'We blurred the reception from any heat signature at the beginning so they would rely on other means and then we fooled the other means.'

She seemed pretty pleased about that one.

'Right, good. What's the other programme for? I didn't see how it could be used.'

'It's incase they are attacked by Kevin again. This invades his system, Julia got quite a lot of information about him from the China 12 database but when they met at the hospital she was able to see the updates he had gotten from whoever he's working with now… This will allow us to hijack his implant and paralyse him, for a few minutes anyway.'

'Can it be used against the US pixies?'

'Maybe, it's designed for Kevin or comparable systems. But it would be worth a go, it might take more time. The trick would be to stop them killing you, before you stopped them from moving. The stiller you are, the better it works. We sort of thought it would be good if they were hiding.'

'I can see that,' he was scrolling through the code again, 'that is pretty clever. Does Sam have this too?'

'No, we can't use her implant yet.'

'How long is "a few minutes"?'

'We know his system will find a way round it, so maybe three or four, maybe two though.'

'Ok. Have you been keeping tabs on what's happening in the US with the Pixie and Sam?'

'Yes, I was, but not since Doctor O Shea told me to wait until someone spoke with me.'

'Oh. Perhaps we should get in touch with them now.'

'Right.'

Rahul waited. Nothing happened. The panic he had gone through trying and failing to contact the ops in Brazil began to rise again.

'Hi? Anything? Are they not responding?'

'You want me to do it? I thought you were saying you would do it.'

'No. You have been doing this, you should go ahead, I'm waiting for you.' Rahul snapped.

'Alright. It was a misunderstanding. I'll do it now.'

'Sorry. I'm… worried.'

'No worries…' and she smothered a slight snigger.

Rahul waited but the silence grew. He could see Liu's projection and she was still, then she frowned and looked at him. She shook her head.

'What?'

'Nothing is what. They aren't answering.'

'Why?'

She glared at him in the way only a teenager can, half anger, half scorn.

'Sorry, I'll give it a go. Sam's not connected, that's right isn't it?'

'I said we can't use her implant yet. Because she had a head injury and you guys arranged for a new implant to be put in, it's still too early.'

'Alright, of course.'

Rahul tried the connection sequences they'd put in after Brazil. He could connect but was getting no response. He saw they couldn't access the emergency flag system which had been in place for a long time, but the newer systems were open still. Someone had suppressed the older protocols. "Kevin" he thought.

He had their location and he could read the Pixie's life signs, which were… elevated. That, he thought, was not good. Something was going on. On the other hand, she was alive.

'Ok. I can't do it either. We'd better kick this upstairs. I should be able to send Milo, but I don't think I can at the moment.'

Liu looked concerned. 'Has something happened to Milo?'

'He's in Africa at the moment.'

'I know, but I can't raise him, or Julia. Is he still cut off?'

'Yes, we are aware of the problem, we're sorting it out, don't worry.' He was looking at his systems com net now, worried, he looked at Liu again, 'Look, it's almost ten so I have to take this to Xin, could you keep trying to raise him? Xin might be in touch with you, ok?'

'Yes, fine.' Liu was chewing the corner of her mouth when Rahul broke off.

Looking at her com systems she tried and failed to raise Julia again and then Milo. She began to mutter to herself.

'Just don't die, just don't die, just don't die…'

32

Show me Yours

Kevin strained to see Anna.

'Is she alive?'

'For the moment.'

'What have you done?'

'Let Sam go.'

'What have you done?'

'You don't have long. She can't breathe. Her own implant is blocking her body's involuntary functions, she will die. Let Sam go.'

'No. Why don't I just kill this… Sam?'

'You know I will kill Anna if you do. You won't get to me in time, then you'll have no payday. And even if you run, I will make it my life's work to kill you, slowly.'

Kevin was still watching Anna, with the knife tight to Sam's throat. Sam started applying slow pressure to Kevin's hand, meaning she might have bought herself a second. Would that be enough? The Pixie tensed, she watched and tried to edge a foot closer to Kevin, but his eyes snapped back as soon as she moved. She watched him try to evaluate the situation. She knew she wouldn't have much more time because she felt Anna's system finding ways round the block. If he didn't buy it soon, she was going to have to make a decision and Sam's life would depend on the outcome.

Kevin's hand relaxed the hold on Sam's neck and she pushed the knife away. He held out his hands and stood to try to see if Anna was alive. The Pixie put herself between Kevin and Sam, who leapt away and was racing to the back door. Kevin took a few steps towards Anna, reaching for his gun, getting ready to fire on both of the pixies if she should prove dead.

Anna's body arched and she gulped in a huge breath and obviously tried to speak but only croaked loudly. The Pixie was through the back door after Sam, who was already halfway down the stairs, she pulled the door behind her. Kevin whirled toward the door, gun levelled.

'Stop them, you fool.'

Anna was recovering and rising. Kevin fired at the door, splintering the wood. On the other side, Sam was at the bottom and the Pixie was diving down the steps, having bolted the reinforced door. They were across the backyard by the time they heard the windows above smash under fire from Anna's gun. Moments later she was through the window and dropping down on a wire. Sam was at the back gate, dragging it open as Kevin followed Anna. They touched the ground firing as the Pixie reached the gate and flew through the narrowing gap, and Sam dragged it closed. The Pixie fell as Anna's bullets hit home.

'Bitch!' Sam screamed and she ran, stumbled, for the Pixie and grabbed her arm.

The Pixie flipped over and blinked, Sam dragged her to her feet and they wheeled away from the gate. A cab turned into the alley and rolled towards them. Behind them they heard a bang and someone made a noise as though punched. Sam smiled, the Pixie looked back but the alley was empty. They had gained, perhaps, fifty metres and the cab had turned sideways with the door sliding open.

Another bang, louder, and the gate to the house blew across the alley, hitting the far wall, throwing up dust and smoke. Kevin stepped out, gun levelled, and he fired. The needle gun rounds hit the cab and smashed the windows, the chassis began to disintegrate and the Pixie went down again. Sam turned and fired back at Kevin, the wall to the right of his head began falling apart and he ducked for cover. The Pixie was on her feet again and they both rounded the cab and made for the end of the alley.

Kevin stood. Looking back as she fled, the Pixie could see he was in two minds. She guessed Anna had run into Liu's defences around the rear wall and come off second best. There was always the chance she had doubled back and would be waiting for them at the end of the alley. Kevin was either wondering if he should join Anna at the other side of the house or get medical help. They were about to find out.

The Pixie flew out beyond the end of the alley first and into the broad, normally quiet, suburban street. Sam more cautious and labouring, waited for gunfire, none came. A second cab drew up to the kerbside instead and the door slid open; the Pixie waited covering the street. Sam, most of her reserves of energy gone, dived into the vehicle and lay on the floor looking like she wished there was some means of getting more air into her lungs. The Pixie slung herself into the seat and the cab began to move as the door closed.

Doing a U-turn it began to gather speed as it headed for the front of the house they'd just left. The Pixie's eyes were fixed to the front door that swung open and closed, but stayed empty as they passed. She slumped back in the seat and looked down at Sam, whose colour was developing a more normal shade and who was looking up at her. Both were still gulping in huge mouthfuls of air. The Pixie frowned and reached out to Sam who turned her head a little to face her. Sam grinned. The Pixie leaned back and smiled. Their eyes locked and Sam began to laugh. It was infectious and they took a few moments to calm down. The Pixie still smiling, 'Back in the game then?'

'I guess, I'll probably pay for it this evening. Not sure why, but the new system came fully on as we were on the stairs.'

The Pixie grinned, 'I can think of a reason.'

'What happened to Anna? She looked like she was ready to come through that wall when I slammed the gate.'

'Can't be sure, but at a guess that was part of Liu's preparations, they were set to shut off if they detected either of us but come on if it was anyone else. The back wall was live, she must have run straight into it.'

'Clever girl. Glad she's on our side.'

'Course she is, we're the good guys. How are you feeling, can you do a test?'

Sam stopped for a moment and looked into the middle distance as she checked her system and her body. She refocused on the Pixie and smiled.

'I'm pretty sure I shouldn't do that too many more times in the next few days, but everything is looking good so far.'

The Pixie smiled and pushed Sam with her foot.

'You staying down there 'cause you don't want to kiss me, or what?'

Sam rolled onto her side and pushed herself up off the floor and across onto the seat. She wasn't quite there when the Pixie slid her arm under Sam's and enveloped her in a kiss. This took many more seconds than you might expect, given the circumstances… Sam poked the Pixie with her finger and they broke apart, the Pixie frowned.

'Just want to get onto the seat so as the support doesn't actually stab me. Also, bruising…'

'Oh, sorry, are you ok?'

Sam climbed up beside the Pixie and smiled.

'I'm fine.'

The Pixie leant back and shrugged, 'Huh, serve you right for looking so delicious.'

Sam punched her on the arm and then held up both hands as the Pixie turned on her.

'Still a patient!' Sam said.

The Pixie leant back and smiled, and then slid her hand into Sam's. After a few seconds, 'Where is the cab going?'

'Where did you order it for?'

'I thought you ordered it.'

33

Thirsty

Milo had been following Anna for about an hour. Keeping out of sight and about forty metres away, he watched her back as she rounded another corner. Pleased he hadn't lost his ability to remain at a fixed distance from a target, he was still a little frustrated. He only ever saw her back and, slightly obliquely, her face covered always by a small curtain of hair. He was pretty sure she didn't know he was following but she was doing a good job being discreet in any case.

She was heading through the town, only stopping occasionally at a shop or a market stall and talking with no one in particular. He guessed she was waiting to be contacted, expecting to be taken away, in which case he'd be certain his current state of isolation would be explained. Or on the other hand, she might eventually be picked up for a meeting with someone local. If the latter, the intrigue might increase but it might be the reason he was there in Lamu. That was the question really preying on his mind, why had the computer picked up this job?

Every now and then he passed someone he thought might be her contact, they plainly were in touch with someone and watching, but each time she walked past them. He wondered if perhaps someone else had marked out Anna's presence and was following her. As soon as he could contact Beijing he'd run image searches on the people who he'd suspected were connected and perhaps that way figure out what was going on.

He was getting tired and very thirsty. If she didn't stop soon, he'd have to work out a new approach or give up the chase. Right now a partner would be very handy. As he walked he tried to design the perfect partner. He'd usually worked alone with China 12, but had had partners in the past. Working relationships could be tricky if you got off on the wrong foot. Perhaps he didn't need a real partner, a virtual one might do just as well, better in some ways.

He saw a small drinks-seller up ahead, he'd have to stop and hope Anna didn't stray too far, or if his luck was in… It was, she stopped outside a cafe a bit farther along the narrow street, eyed the menu and then went in. He headed straight for the drinks stand. The old seller turned and smiled.

'Jambo.' *Why didn't that translate?*

'Good Morning, do you have a light drink, even water?'

He was aware of his need for something a bit more isotonic than water but it would do in a pinch, and this was a pinch.

'How about a nice cool lemonade?'

'That sounds perfect, thank you. Do you need cash?'

The man laughed as though it was the funniest thing he'd heard in years.

'No, no cash thank you, too dangerous. No way to get rid of it here, only the fancy people and the casinos use cash in Kenya.'

The transaction was swift and Milo gulped down the drink happily. He asked for another and looked round for a place to sit. The vendor cheerfully offered a new drink and a small coconut sweet cake. Milo spotted behind him, by the door of a walled garden, was a small wooden seat. Grateful for the rest and the shade, he sat. Watched by the smiling drinks seller, he poured the fresh drink down his recovering throat. Looking down the street toward the restaurant Anna had entered, he saw no sign of her leaving yet, and he leant back against the wall. Its cool surface, not yet warmed by the sun, was heaven and he closed his eyes.

It was cold and dark. Milo blinked, reached up to pinch his eyes between forefinger and thumb and blinked again. It was dark but he could make out shapes, a table, a high window. He wasn't sure what had happened. Had he fallen asleep? Slipped off the seat? It was nighttime, he could hear the crickets singing, but he was indoors. He moved and took in he was not on the ground but on a low cot of some kind and that he hadn't got there by himself. He swung his legs over the side of the cot and put his feet on the ground. He leaned forward and was about to get to his feet when a voice came out of the darkness.

'Steady, it can leave you a bit dizzy.'

Milo sat back and searched the space for the owner of the voice. 'What can?'

'The juice. Delicious isn't it?'

'Who are you? Where am I?'

'Do you want to ask all of your questions in one go? If you do, I'll go and get a note pad, my memory is not that good. If we work together though, I am sure we won't need a pad.'

Milo waited and turned to face the corner the voice spoke from. He could hear him breathing. The idea that Milo was imagining things occurred to him.

'Alright, who are you?'

'That's better. You see, working together, I tell my people all the time, you get much further this way. I am Doctor Peter Kimani, not a medical doctor, but a Doctor of Philosophy. Given how things have turned out in my life, that is quite funny.'

Silence as Milo waited for more information but that was it.

'I can see how hilarious it might be, but you'd have to explain it and that would spoil the joke.'

'Oh Milo, not lost your sense of humour, that is good, because you will need it.'

'Where am I?'

'Still on Lamu, not very far from where you bought that nice drink.'

'Why did that man give it to me?'

'"That man", is my father, he has been selling drinks from a stand in Lamu since he was seven years old. The lemonade was delicious, no?'

'It was, but why the extras? He'll run out of customers if it's in every drink he sells.'

'You are right, that was a "special" reserved for important clients. He gave it to you because you are important, Milo. Certain people want to speak with you.'

'Who?'

'Can't you guess? On second thought, don't try after all, because the list got longer, just today in fact. About two hours ago you went from important, to very important. Aren't you pleased you are going up in the world and you have only known me a short time?'

Milo frowned, 'Did you bring us here?'

'We did.'

'Anna organised it.'

The good doctor paused and then, 'Who is Anna?'

'The woman who's paying you to hold me in this lovely room.'

Doctor Kimani paused again and went on slowly, 'No, you are wrong. The first people to ask us to bring you here were old friends of yours and China 12. They had a nice little company going along the coast, and across the Mediterranean.'

'The Somalis? Is Anna working with them?'

'Milo, there is no Anna. There are no women called Anna involved here.'

'But I saw her, I was following her before you knocked me out.'

'Following? You were not following anyone.'

Milo's frown deepened and he glared into the shadows. Kimani stepped out into the moonlight. He was short, slight, bespectacled and very young.

'You say you're a doctor?'

He bowed to Milo and grinned.

'But I am. I was the youngest to graduate from my class in high school and took my doctorate at nineteen years, well… just twenty.'

'Then…'

'… What am I doing here?' he finished Milo's thought. 'I had a scholarship from Imperial College London. Each summer vacation I came back here, at first the whole eight weeks, then just under half that; I had friends, I wanted to see London. It then became just a few days.

After my undergraduate degree I thought I would go and see the world, shake off the terrible dust of my homeland, my home island. I found myself standing in a queue for something or other in some place I didn't know and I asked myself, why am I here?'

'Philosophy will do that.'

Kimani smiled patiently at the old joke.

'Yes, Milo, but I just meant geographically, why was I not at home? Why did I think I could enjoy life more thousands of miles away from my family? I was seventeen and I was lost.'

'Betterment? I'm sure they were proud of you.'

'Yes, I suppose. No, they were. But I went home. I finished my postgraduate degree, in record time as well, and then came back home to stay.'

'Then what?'

'I taught in the local school. While I was teaching I looked, really looked, at what I was doing. I looked at what the people I was teaching were actually doing.'

'Making their way, I guess.'

'Becoming low level criminals. There are no jobs in my country anymore Milo. Oh yes, we can get by on government handouts, but the people have nothing to do.'

'That is the sad truth for millions across the world, doctor Kimani, but what I'm doing has nothing…'

Kimani held up his hand.

'There are two worlds Milo, do you see that? Your world, the small world. Filled with important people barely touched by the real world at all. Then there is the big world, most of the people on this planet are in the big world. They exist all around your world but are not seen by it at all. Sixty or seventy years ago, people your world called criminals, began making my world. It has its own money, its own com system, its own transport system and its own laws. It's true things can get a bit rough.' He paused and considered, leaning his head to one side, before going on.

'Sometimes we interact, our two worlds. That is not a very pleasant experience for either of us, often people die. When it happens, my world has to see that we get something out of it, at least. It is that kind of world.'

'There has always been an underworld. Victorian London and nineteenth century New York were famous for it.' Milo objected.

'Except that now it is your world that is the "underworld". We are the normal world. You think of countries as lines on a map. My countries are lines of relationships, they stretch thousands of miles across borders we do not recognise. We don't have your pretend elections, but if I get it wrong, how long do you think I will keep my position? When I lose power millions will notice, but you wouldn't ever have heard of me.'

'So the Somalis want their pound of flesh?'

'The north-eastern cartel want justice. But they might have a new way of getting it. A profitable way and a very satisfactory business proposition as well.'

'Oh?'

'Someone wants your head Milo, or what's in it. You have a valuable head, it seems, and we are in a position to sell.'

His broad grin almost lit the room.

34

The Interview

The door opened and he walked into a large reception area where the young housekeeper was waiting. She made no gesture but turned and walked away, Jones followed. The reception area was wide and tall, wood tiled and probably the oldest place he'd been in, outside of a public building. This was his first visit. They walked down a long corridor to the side of the main stairway, past several sets of doors and double doors to his right and left. Finally, she stopped and he was shown through a heavy wooden door and found Heath sitting in a room that was surprisingly small.

The wall to his left was lined with books, as was the fashion among the rich, some were leather bound and clearly old. The wall to his right was covered in pictures and paintings and an old fireplace with a stone mantle taken from some ancient ruin. The grate was empty. Beyond the windows, which filled the end wall of the room, he could see parkland stretch away into the distance, trees on the right and a hint of water.

The room was not painted in modern nano-particulate paint which would have allowed the style and nature of the room to be changed on command. Jones had the impression he was in a living museum exhibit. Given he had been brought up in the Brooklyn Brotherhood who'd turned their backs on anything from the twenty-first, or even the second half of the twentieth century, it was surprisingly shocking to him to feel he was somewhere that was… old.

He turned and found Heath watching him and he straightened involuntarily, like visiting the school principle for the first time, he wasn't used to being nervous.

'So they came a calling?'

'Yes sir.'

Heath pushed out his lower lip and raised his head toward the drinks on the side table. Jones went over and poured a whiskey, 'I'll take one of those too.' Jones poured and brought the glass over to his boss. They touched rims and drank.

'They came to me once, about thirty years ago. They seem to think, "once a Brother…" I gave them the bum's rush and they took it with good grace I guess, they didn't pull a gun on me anyway. Seems times have gotten more desperate.'

Jones nodded. He couldn't precipitate whatever was coming, couldn't let on he knew. Partly of course because he didn't know; he didn't know why or what they would use the opportunity they had created, for. He was however, beginning to see a larger part of the map. Americorp and the Brotherhood were closer than he ever had suspected or ever would have. He knew the Brotherhood didn't own Americorp. But could it further the aims of the Brotherhood? Twisted, but a means to, what many brothers would see as, a moral end. Or was it that the Brotherhood supplied an arm's length committed cohort available to do the corporation's work? On the other hand, this could be an alliance of opportunity. They had squabbled over the system created by Julia Church and her sister, now they would fight together to take control of it.

He realised Heath was watching him and took another drink. The old man smiled, as if confirming something he had been thinking.

'It is alarming, even when you are unhurt, to be faced with gunplay. I'm sorry they did that to you. Let's see if we can make it worth your while, eh?'

Jones smiled genially at his boss. Heath sat and pointed at the other armchair. Jones had the sensation he was in a remastered holo of a really old movie and half expected the surroundings to be drained of colour. He sat.

'These are dangerous times, Jones. The world is going through momentous changes and we are struggling to stay on top. When I say "we" I don't just mean Americorp, I don't even mean just America. I mean people like you and me, right minded people, people who should be on top. I intend for us to stay on top. Are you with me?'

Jones struggled to stop himself from saying, "What…?"

'Yes, sir.' And then almost an afterthought, 'All the way.'

Heath's eyes hovered nervously around Jones' face.

'Good. This little project has grown in importance. We thought it might just be a means of giving us a market edge. I think Donovan still thinks that.'

He said that in a way that suggested his low opinion of the company's CEO. He took another mouthful of whiskey and savoured it.

'It's more, much more. If the research we've seen is right, it could be the key to the next fifty years, hell, the next thousand years, why not?'

Jones was wondering who "we" were exactly, while Heath seemed to be almost talking to himself, his eyes on the empty fireplace his thoughts, who knew where. They came out of their own speculations at about the same time and their eyes met. They both drank, Heath finishing his and gesturing that Jones should get a refill. Once over at the sideboard, Heath called, 'Bring back the bottle.'

Jones handed over the generous drink with the bottle and sat again.

'So you can see,' Heath went on, 'the stakes are high.'

'Yes indeed, sir, but, if you don't mind my asking, who are "we"? I mean who is on our side and who are we against?'

'Do you not understand the war that has been raging across the world for the last hundred years, son? I know you've been working for this corporation for some years now and you've done well?'

'Yes sir.'

'You'd like to preserve the fruits of your success and rightly so.'

'Yes sir, I would.'

'There are those on this earth who believe that despite their not earning it, they should partake in your success and they want to use our systems against us. They had it good for a while, nearly succeeded, but we don't need 'em anymore. This planet only needs about a ninth of the people it currently holds, the rest are superfluous.'

'Sir?'

'Oh, I'm not saying we should go around killing them, but there's no reason for us to get too excited saving 'em either.'

Jones took a drink, finishing what he had and took a larger refill.

Heath held out his own empty glass.

'We'll need some of the healthy ones for planetary exploration, the Mars thing is doing alright and Mars is full of the resources we need. It's also closer to the asteroid belt and our operations there. We have plans to crash a few large asteroids into the place maybe even make an artificial shield against solar winds. Do you understand?'

Jones's sheltered upbringing had left him hungry for information, so he had been consuming these prospective plans for years. This drew him in, in a way little else could.

'Yes sir. It's very exciting.'

'Exciting? Profitable, that's what it is and that's exciting. But we won't need more than a few hundred thousand, put them places where it would be silly to risk expensive machinery until plans were well advanced and of course we'd need breeding stock for the future. That's why we have our genetic selection programs. But most of 'em are just hungry mouths, a drag on progress.'

'I see, sir. What do you propose to do?'

Heath gave Jones a quick look, checking how the pitch was going down.

'Not too much. We don't want to precipitate a war or anything like that, costs too much damn money. General life spans are shortening again and fertility is falling, though of course that particular problem is wider than just the surplus.'

'The surplus, sir?'

'Keep up Jones, who've I been talking about? The surplus population, the ones we don't need.'

'Of course, sir.'

Heath leaned his head on one side and looked at Jones, his eyes drifted up and down. Jones shifted, worried that he might have dropped into the "surplus".

'Jones, I know with your background in the Brotherhood, you might have some qualms about this. But after last night the Brotherhood might take a more aggressive view of your continuation here with us, an aggressively less supportive view.'

'I do understand that, sir.'

'If you have doubts, you have to let them go and get on board.

Being part of this group is no different than being part of the Brotherhood in earthly terms, it's just that the "us" is a whole lot more comfortable.'

'I am on board, sir.'

'Good. There won't be any getting off now, you might have one or two unpleasant duties but a lot more pleasant ones I assure you. And you can drop the "sir" Jones, one of us, is one of us.'

'Yes si… Mr Hea…'

'Duncan.'

'Duncan.'

Heath smiled, lifted the bottle and poured two good measures. They touched rims again.

'Who's like us Jones? Damn few and they're all dead.'

Then he coughed, 'Or they will be…'

35

Hot Pursuit

Even once Kevin had pulled Anna up off the dirt of the yard, it would be fair to say neither one was particularly happy. The electric jolt had done Anna's injury profile no good at all and Kevin had to help her through the back door and up the stairs. As they climbed, she was recovering.

'We have to be clear of here before the police arrive.'

'Can't Americorp put the fix in?'

She gave him a sideways glance, 'Yes, but it isn't going to do either of us any good if our employer has to dig us out of the shit a week into the job, will it?'

He stopped and looked at her, 'Then I'd say we were going the wrong way, no?'

She sighed impatiently and her jaw set. They turned and headed down. By now Anna had recovered enough to make it on her own. As they got to the rear gate a cab was rolling up and she was already checking the local camera loop. She frowned.

'They're heading back toward the safe house, which doesn't strike me as very clever.'

Now Kevin frowned.

'In what?'

'A city cab.'

'They couldn't have fallen for that old one?'

Anna had to think about what he meant and looked again at the images on her system.

'Just looking up ahead of them. Wow, are they not being discreet. I don't think we're going to have any trouble with the local sheriff. That does explain their lack of interest.'

'Ambush?'

'Usually ambushes are hidden, jump out at you unexpectedly sort of affairs, no?'

'Usually.'

'This isn't one of those. Look.'

Kevin patched into her feed and his eyebrows shot up. 'Overconfident, much?'

'They're certainly presuming they have already caught their rabbit.'

'Can we catch up?'

Anna checked the map and their relative speeds.

'We can push this a bit, but I'd say they are travelling at the limit of what these things are capable. The American clantechs want to get their man as quick as they can.'

'Shortcuts?'

'They're taking them all, I think. Unless those two can think of something, they are walking into a world of trouble.'

'Any point in following?'

'We can verify the dead. They might leave the younger one's memory core intact and we could get that, it would have new access codes, might even be able to get us into Milo's head.'

Liu was looking at her monitoring system with growing agitation. She had been watching as the Pixie's life signs had spiked and then spiked again. Sam's had been a bit less erratic but then had gone off the scale and she took the executive decision to bring her system online. She was pretty sure Dr Lopez-Real would have something to say about that but so far the reads were stable. She had been able to track their geo position, but then that was being suppressed.

At that point Liu had taken a step back and mapped what was likely to have happened. Deciding they must have taken some kind of transport, she triangulated what cab they had likely climbed into and was now following that through the street cameras. Further confirmation was the fact she was being blocked from tagging it. Pixie training was useful.

Like Anna, she had looked ahead once she realised the direction they were taking and had seen what lay ahead. Like Kevin she was surprised they had fallen for the ruse. Now the question was what to do, was there anything she could do?

She guessed the two Pixies would be blind, if her system was being blocked then it was because theirs was being suppressed. She also guessed that they would have put two and two together by now. What were they likely to try and how could she help? If she couldn't help them directly, could she interfere with the planned attack? She could slow them down maybe, buy them time.

She could see the clantechs were manipulating the traffic system to get the cab to them as quickly as possible, so she started there. Liu began by blocking the best routes with traffic, which pushed them away from the main drag and outside of the best roads. After a few minutes they got stuck in a jam. The flooded sections of the Bronx and Queens, and the consequent reduced river crossings had helped by creating dead ends. But the nighttime traffic was light and that didn't help at all.

She checked back to make sure the US group hadn't decided to move toward the cab which was now only four kilometres from where they were waiting. Not yet worried, they were obviously confident they were in control of the evening, though they had twigged that something was up.

Liu now tried to break the suppression field round the cab, easiest when it was static. They were using an old protocol to do it, lazy, she thought, but it might just be…

'Hi, guys, are you there?'

'Yes, Liu, can you see what's going on?' The Pixie practically shouted at her.

Liu quickly laid out what the raiding party were doing right then and what she had done.

'Where are Anna and Kevin?'

'I haven't checked.'

'They must be watching this too and I'm pretty sure they will want to get to us first.'

'I'll look, it will take a minute or two.'

'Don't. Can you break open the cab we're in? Knowing who's going to kill us isn't as interesting as knowing how to get away.'

'Right. I have a little worm going at it right now.'

They waited.

Anna had picked up the disruption in the traffic flows not long after Liu had started to clog up the main routes. She began to work out where it was they might be stopped and to plot a route getting as close to that point as she could.

'We might get them yet.'

'Oh?' She fed Kevin the images of what she was doing and he sat up. He watched for a minute and then turned.

'The question will be, how do we get them out? If the traffic is gummed up... how are you doing that by the way?'

'I'm not, it's someone working with them, I imagine we know who, otherwise there would be an escape route.'

'So?'

'So there's no point in getting killed over it, we won't try to get them out.'

'Kill them and download their system files?'

'We'll take their heads if we have time, keeps the implants fresher and the analysis is that much better.'

'That's pretty grim.'

'Oh please, you didn't take trophies in the war?'

'No, and I didn't let soldiers under me do it either. Your enemy might be just that, but they're allowed a certain respect.'

She smiled and reached over touching his chin with her forefinger, 'Look at you being all honourable.' She focused on the task in her head, 'But taking the money to stab your friends in the back all the same.'

Kevin quietly seethed but said nothing, she shot him a quick glance and noted the silence and the slight change in colour.

'Come on Kevin, war might demand a certain nobility, but no matter how much, it's papering over the shit it really is. This is business. If we can get them out, we will. Not because it's noble, but because it suits us. You take prisoners in war when you have the bandwidth, not because it's noble but because you want, if it comes to it, to be held and not shot out of hand in your turn. In this game, there are no turns.'

He looked at her and it was obvious he was making an effort, but there was recognition of what she was saying too.

'You're right, I guess. I never thought I'd long for the simplicity of war, but right now, I'd take it.' He offered.

'Yeah well, right now we have an intercept point and we'll have to be quick. The clantechs haven't decided to move yet, but it won't be long before they do.'

The cab slowed to a stop and the door slid back.

'Right guys.' Liu had come back to them.

'Yes?'

'I found Anna and Kevin and they've started to move.'

'How far away are they?'

'Anna doesn't look in great shape, but that might be the camera, these aren't very high res.'

'How long?'

'Hard to say, at a guess fiftee... uh oh.'

'What?'

'The clantechs have started to move, they're farther away but I think they'll move quicker.'

Sam and the Pixie looked at one another, 'How long?'

'Just wait... I think they'll all get to you within a minute of each other, clantechs first.'

'How many?'

'Um, five or six, wait, six. They're not going to mess about.'

'Can you get us out of this thing?'

'No, I have a feeling they're hoping to take you inside the cab, so it's locked tight.' Liu said.

'Ok.'

'What are you going to do?'

'This.'

The Pixie aimed her weapon at the windows and door. Liu could see the Pixie and Sam pressed into the far side of the cab, Sam being caught at the periphery of the Pixie's ocular implant. Liu had to suppress the audio pick up of the com quickly as the interior of the cab exploded with the noise of several weapons being discharged at once.

Liu called up the street cam and watched as the side of the cab disintegrated and the door collapsed in a misshapen heap. The cab alarms went off and people in traffic around them, dived for cover. The walls of the houses splintered and became pockmarked and the very few pedestrians fled. Sam and the Pixie stepped into the street.

'Are you guys ok?'

'A few cuts, but yeah, fine.'

The women surveyed the street, looking for a point they could defend and a way out. They were in one of the poor areas of New York. The Bronx, like most of the districts, had had its ups and downs, this was one of the downs. This part was in the down side of one of those downs. The houses were crowded in a way that would have been familiar to a nineteenth century anti-slum campaigner and the street furniture was neglected and in a wretched state. To Liu it looked like an edgy holocast set, in the rundown west, but she filtered that out. Liu only had eyes for the women she was helping.

'Sorry, but that was awesome.'

The Pixie looked up at the street cam and smiled, then continued her search.

'That will bring every cop in the district down on us. We need a way out, girl, and fast.'

Liu saw Sam nudge the Pixie and point up the street. The Pixie's eyes narrowed as she looked and they made for a corner shop.

'Liu, can you find us a piece of transport, probably a delivery van or something like that, or a bike. And a route out of here?'

'Right away.'

They had reached the corner shop and Liu watched as Sam headed in while the Pixie turned her eyes on the street looking for the trouble she knew was on its way to her. The shop disgorged its few customers and, a moment later, the shopkeeper. Shops tend to be for the top of the market which this was not, or for the people who couldn't afford direct delivery or for the few who just liked to shop. This was a low-end corner store and heavily shuttered.

'Guys, you have company coming from the cross street thirty metres north. Six, heavily armed, I think one of them is calling for backup.'

'Thanks Liu.' The Pixie went into the shop.

'Uh guys, Kevin and Anna are about another block away. Anna has picked up the pace... Guys?'

36

Where are we Going?

Rahul had outlined the situation in the US as it was when he left Liu. He thought it containable. Julia wanted to check things out but she was working only from Milo's implant and couldn't stretch her resources. She was reassured by Rahul that Liu would tell them if anything happened.

Turning to Milo and his situation, Rachel, who had gone through his records, didn't think Milo was physically in poor shape but she and Cathy were worried about his mental state.

'The brain is annoyingly difficult. It operates at a few points off a critical state pretty well all of the time, this is what allows us to make decisions in the way we do. Humans aren't alone in this. For us though, the consequences of having doubts about the reality our minds construct can create an avalanche of decisions to provide us with a new, stable reality.'

Xin and Hoshika looked at each other, frowned and turned to Cathy. Cathy took a deep breath.

'What I'm trying to say is that at any point our grip on reality depends on our being able to believe in that reality. If we start to question it in a profound way, we remake it, sometimes from the ground up.'

Xin touched her fingertips together and leaned forward.

'Are you saying he's gone nuts?'

Cathy closed her eyes and coloured, 'Would you describe what you do as "sums"?'

'No.'

'Right. No, he's not nuts, but he's trying to integrate two real and very distinct people in a single mind and there might be the odd bump in the road.'

'This is a bump?'

'I think so.'

Julia held up her hand as though she was in class, Xin lifted her chin.

'I should say, I'm trying to work out what and who I am at the same time, this may not help. Help him, that is.'

Xin smiled and then turned to Cathy and Rachel, 'Is Julia, um, hitting a "bump" also?'

Cathy looked first at Julia and then at Rachel.

Cathy answered, 'I doubt it, Julia has a programmed personality, it's pretty settled. That isn't to say she couldn't develop problems as her world view develops but it's being played against a very firm baseline.'

Xin smiled 'Good. One problem at a time is easier. The next thing should be to locate Milo and find out if he is alright. Can we do that, Hoshika?'

Julia looked at Hoshika, Rachel and Cathy, 'I think I should be able to locate him,' she said. He, we, are still on Lamu. I don't want to push it though, if it makes things worse, so Cathy and Rachel will have to work out my approach to him.'

Cathy smiled, 'Yes, we can do that, it should be straightforward and we can give you warning signs to watch out for.' Turning to Xin, 'I think this is a temporary thing, an adjustment, but we shouldn't do things to turn it into something worse.'

'Yes, alright, thankfully he isn't in a particularly dangerous situation and I gather we know the local pathologist?' Rachel smiled broadly. Xin noted that and turned again.

'Hoshika, what do we think is…'

Liu appeared in the room looking a little panicked. Xin stood, as did Rahul. Liu bowed to Xin and then more quickly to the company.

'I'm sorry to interrupt Zhang Xin, but Sam and the Pixie are about to be killed.'

Cathy and Rachel now also stood. Julia disappeared.

'What's happened?' Rahul asked

Liu gave them a quick recounting of what had happened as far as she knew and outlined the position the two ops were now in.

'The clantech group are opening fire right now, we have to do something.'

'What?' Xin asked and looked at Rahul. Julia reappeared.

'Right, I think there might be things we can do to keep them alive, but the really difficult problem will be to get them out of the city. The raiding group have called for backup and the New York policing authority have begun to head in their direction. It looks like they had been cleared out of the district in preparation for the attack earlier.'

Xin thought for a moment and then 'Erasto, could you join Rahul and Julia?'

He appeared in "holo" looking concerned, 'Problem?'

'Maybe. Ms Feng here has been monitoring our colleagues in the US. It seems the situation has begun to get out of hand. We might need an extraction from New York in a hurry.'

'I'm really more of an engineer than a military expert, you know.'

'I do know that, but you are one of the few on hand who has any practical experience.'

Liu cut in, 'They don't have lots of time.'

Rahul turned and started to walk, 'Ok, Erasto, meet me in Ops room two, you know what node that is Julia?'

'Yes.'

'Liu, that was where we were speaking before, it's wired directly to the satnet system so we should have the clearest view of what's happening.'

Rahul hurried through the door and the images of the other three snapped off. Hoshika, Cathy, Xin and Rachel were left looking at the empty space. Xin reacted first and turning to Rachel, 'Will Sam hold up?'

'She is at the edge, Liu sent me a message she had brought her system online, it was inadvisable but better than the alternative at that moment.'

'But will she pull through?'

'If this doesn't last too long, possibly. Her system can help, but it can also create the conditions for a sudden collapse.'

'Can we help?'

'The people you've sent to help are the best placed to do that, I can't do anything for her medically from here.'

'Then let's address the things we can do. We need Milo fixed. If Julia is busy with the women in New York, we nevertheless have to have a plan for when she is free. Hoshika, you'll have to do an Erasto here and work across fields, when Julia is back we need options for finding Milo, not just for speaking with him. Rachel, you know his implanted system best, see if there isn't a way of breaking in without breaking him. It might be the moment to contact your friend if you haven't already.'

They nodded, no one moved. Xin looked at them quizzically, Hoshika spoke, 'Are you not worried about Liu?'

Xin thought about it, 'That is an issue. I have put it to the back of my mind. Perhaps that's a mistake.'

'I understand she is clever and Julia has vouched for her, but...'

'But, we can't be certain about Julia.'

'It might also be that Liu, even if she is well-intentioned, is being used.'

'By?'

Hoshika shrugged and held out her hands.

Xin pursed her lips, 'When we get some space, might you and Rahul look into it? By the end of this we should have a better understanding of where exactly Julia stands and what we can do about her.'

'That might be too late.'

'True, things are getting difficult and we may have no time at all. But we must save Milo and Julia, that is a priority.'

Hoshika looked at the other two women and their worried faces but she moved and they were all out the door at a fast clip.

37

Fort Apache, the Bronx

Sam was not feeling at the top of her game. The injuries from Anna's assault were mending but not mended and both her own doctor and Dr Lopez-Real had told her to take it easy. She was pretty sure this wasn't what they had meant.

The clantech (retired) was exhausted but watched while the Pixie blocked the main entrance and the one large window not shuttered. She was drinking from an energy pack she'd taken from one of the shelves, feeling it replenish her energy reserves. She turned round, taking in the whole store. At first look it wasn't unusual for a District Local. You could find DL stores right the way across the country; it was a franchise operation and for many the only path to basic goods.

The shop was in darkness, they had killed the lights on the way in and now they were on partially enhanced nightlight. They had to be careful as the street, like many a poorer area, was permanently lit. In rich areas lighting only came on for pedestrian traffic and the rich had a nice night sky to look at. The poor had either this or, from one AM till six, total blackout. For them to see in both the dark and the light took a careful balance of the enhanced system. It would still give them an advantage over people coming from outside.

She turned away from the main shop and her eyes settled on a plastiwood partition about halfway down. While it was usual to divide the shop into storage and retail, this place seemed to give too much of the space to storage. Her eyes drifted back across the shelves the Pixie wasn't tearing down. Products were very densely stacked, nothing out of place but no clear reason to do things this way, it made things harder to get at in a shop that was for quick in and out purchases.

Getting up, she walked slowly to the partition and took out her needle gun. The sliding door suggested another attempt at saving space. She edged to one side and pushed it open a sliver and waited.

Nothing. She scanned the opening quickly and then stopped.

She pushed back the door and looked round the room behind it. She was looking at a caged room, about the same size as the shop. Along each wall were racks and racks of weapons. Stacked on the floor in front of the racks were boxes of ammunition and heavier types of ordinance right up to a small, light, particle beam. At the back were stacks of large black cases. Flicking her eyes along the walls she thought these might be for hand guns and the like. To the untutored eye it looked like a small army could be armed from here. To Sam it screamed "gang world".

'Pix,'

The Pixie didn't even slow down as she heaved another case in front of the window, ''Sup?'

'Pix, you're going to want to take a look at this.'

The Pixie stopped and turned as something in the low, quiet voice suggested trouble. She stepped back to look at her handiwork and seemed happy, then walked back to Sam's side. She stopped and stared.

'What the actual…?'

'This may not be the best news.'

As though she hadn't heard, the Pixie grinned.

'Why? I was worried about the state of our supplies if we have a full unit of your friends coming, but this evens it up a bit. Is that a particle beam? Holy shit!'

'No, this is bad news. This stuff belongs to someone and they aren't going to want people seeing it. Especially not my people.'

'If it was so important why'd they run away?'

'Yeah, they shouldn't have, so someone will die for that little mistake. They probably went to get help. There must be another way in.'

'I got to say, I'm not going to let these sweeties go to waste. We need them and they'll probably want to kill us anyway.'

She took out her sidearm and fired at the locks on the door of the cage, which fell apart, and she kicked the door open. Walking in, she headed straight for the particle beam and crouched down beside it.

'Pix, I wouldn't.'

'Why? One shot of this and your folks will think twice about it before rushing in.'

'I think they'll just stand back and take down the block.'

'Nu uh, didn't you see what was upstairs?'

'No.'

'There's a clinic. Local Doc shop.'

'Shit. That's why they have this place here, it's a "Patch and kill" for the gang. They are really going to be pissed when they find out we're here.'

The Pixie opened her mouth to say something, but whatever it was was interrupted by a crash as a small black cylinder came through the window. The projectile hit the cases the Pixie had piled up at the front of the shop and there was a 'pop'. The women looked at each other, 'Gas!'

Together they pulled out small black and silver implements that went into their mouths and over their noses. The Pixie stalked to the window and ducked down as two more canisters came through. The gas filled up the front part of the shop, obscuring the view. Sam joined her, carrying a large old-fashioned fan. She plugged it in and flicked the switch, and the air cleared a little. The Pixie looked at it appreciatively. Gun fire came in, dissolving the glass front and they ducked down behind the massed heavy cartons and cases.

The Pixie used her com, '*Your friends are serious.*'

'*Always.*'

The Pixie rose, looked, and dived back down, counted three, popped back up and fired. Back down, moved and then up and repeated the exercise. She crouched down next to Sam.

'*They're going to come in through the front, all six are out there. That is of course if Liu was right about the numbers.*'

'*That's a bit weird, must be in a hurry.*'

'*Or they don't think you're up to much.*'

'*We need to make some space.*'

They heard a shout from outside and then a small explosion at the front of the shop. Sustained gunfire began to dismantle the improvised barricade of cases and Splinters of material went everywhere. Sam and the Pixie fell back.

38

Getting ready to Leave

Milo had eaten. He was staring at the shine from the empty plate as the moon began to assert herself outside. The dim sunlight from the high window had faded as the day wore on and he knew no more about Kimani's plans for him.

Kimani would not be drawn on what he had been offered for Milo's head. He wouldn't even say if he had been made the offer directly, only that 'there were interested parties'. Kimani seemed to think Milo knew why they'd be interested in his head, and what was inside it and Milo worried away at that problem. He reasoned that if it was in his head, he should know about it.

He had paced the room, idly tried the door, even tried to get to the window. He knew the effort to escape, whilst an obligation to his pride, would be futile. All the while he teased at the puzzle of his head. Why? What could suddenly be so valuable that people were willing to forego revenge to realise the price of it? What was he not remembering? He was beginning to feel that perhaps there was a gap in his memory which was larger than just how he had arrived in Africa. How long was the gap and what was causing it?

Now, plate on lap, he was sitting. He touched his head, feeling for scarring or bruising. He cast his mind back to the morning and his image in the mirror, he remembered that. Nothing in that to show he'd had a trauma to cause this. He stood and went through as much as he could recall of the last twenty-four hours.

This morning was clear. The middle of the night, he remembered waking and had the strong sense he was not alone, but who was with him? Anna? Kimani was adamant she'd had nothing to do with his kidnapping. He'd been pretty straightforward about his organisation, proud even, what did he call them? "The Dogs of Lamu" because of the way they hunt, he'd said. They'd hunted him that way, shepherding his path, until the moment came. Odd, because he wasn't aware of it, of them, only of following Anna.

Then he remembered thinking it was Paris he'd woken up in. He had a pretty clear memory of waking in Paris, there had been a woman there too... She was just out of reach like childhood birthday parties. He thought he had a grasp on her face and then it drifted away like mist.

He had to pin down facts. What was certain in his mind? He worked for China 12, he was an operative for their agency and they were based in Beijing. He could reel off the names of the others who worked there and the two who had died. He went to Paris to try to deal with the pain of grieving and then... He knew it was something in those days that were the source of the blank.

He could feel his sense of anxiety rise and he began to sweat. Alright, did he know anyone here? Not that he could think of... This was beginning to get frustrating.

Someone at the door popped the electronic locks and the door swung back. Kimani was there with a tray, two glasses and a bottle of what looked like good malt whiskey. Behind him in the corridor were two very large men. They looked bored, leaning against the wall, waiting for an argument.

'I don't have any ice, but I understand you drink it neat, is that right?'

Milo frowned and then slowly moved his head in the affirmative. Kimani kicked the door shut behind him. He walked over to the cot and set down the tray.

'You will drink with me?'

'It's a bit early.'

Kimani frowned and looked up at the window, 'How do you know?'

'It feels too early.'

'Sundowners, traditional in these parts, if you're the right sort of person. You're the right sort of person, aren't you Milo?'

'Aren't we both?'

'Some don't think me part of that club.' While he talked, he poured, two good measures. If he'd run a bar he'd not be in business long. He offered Milo the tray and Milo took a glass.

Kimani put down the tray and then raised his glass.

'You seem a nice enough fellow Milo. If we were on the same

team, I think we'd get along, be friends even.'

He held his glass out to Milo, who held his eyes as he reached out to touch his glass. Milo was aware he was not being offered the drink for friendship's sake or because he was a nice chap and Kimani so chummy. The tray had been offered to him with great ostentation, lots of "look we're drinking the same drink" which obviously meant both were spiked and Kimani either possessed the antidote or there was another element Milo couldn't see. But, the whiskey was good, so at least, if they poisoned him, they were doing it with a little class. Milo savoured the drink and held the glass up to the now bright light of the moon. Kimani smiled.

'It is Tullamore Dew, Irish. You are Irish, I hear, no?'

'A long time ago.'

'We are from the soil that nurtures us Milo. Mark Twain had a lot to say about the drinks Irish men should drink, he seemed to think you should stick to your whiskey.'

'But you're not from Ireland.'

'Ah well, to be African is to be nurtured by many mothers and yes, I am mixing my metaphors.'

'What does it do?' Milo asked looking at the drink. Kimani smiled.

'It creates a convivial atmosphere.'

Milo felt the faint buzz from the drink as Kimani watched, still smiling.

'We would like to move you from here tonight and we don't want a lot of fuss. Knocking you out and carrying you is too difficult and it might damage whatever is in that head of yours. You don't want to tell me what it is by the way?' and he waited. Milo shrugged and smiled faintly, he took another drink.

'The drink contains a compound that stops your alcohol suppressant from, well, suppressing the alcohol. You will be easier to handle.'

'Drunks are difficult to handle.'

'You won't be drunk, just a little mellow.'

'Who are you handing me over to?'

'I don't truthfully know. Some middle ranking expendable

nobody from a large corporation which I'd rather didn't exist.'

'The corporation must have something to gain by paying for me.'

'Yes, they must.'

'It must be a reasonable sum too, or else your friends wouldn't want to play.'

'It is, and before you say it, that obviously means whatever it is is valuable. But, unless we can find out what it is and if we can use it, there is no point in saying no, is there?'

'I guess not.'

'I wouldn't be too particular about it Milo, it means you get to live a little longer.'

'I can drink to that one!' and he did, knocking back the end of the glass. Kimani became a little colder and, taking Milo's glass, he walked out of the room. Milo watched him leave and tried to analyse his condition, the alcohol certainly worked.

The room turned and he suddenly felt a little queasy. He moved slowly over to the cot and sat down. He thought that this would have made him a "cheap date" years ago. Closing his eyes, he lay back on the bed and took a deep breath. This was a distinctly unpleasant feeling, not mellow at all. He was pretty sure this was not what he remembered about being drunk, or even a little tipsy, maybe it was whatever they'd put in the drink to suppress his body's system. He opened his eyes, feeling a sudden need to throw up, and tried to rise. At about half way up his head started to pound and he was finding it difficult to breathe. Then everything went black.

'Milo, Milo, you must wake up now. It's time for us to go. We have some friends you have to meet.'

Milo's eyes blinked open and he stared at the face in front of him. The room was dark and Kimani was perhaps an inch from his face. He took a deep breath. His head was fuzzy, but at least the room had stopped turning. Kimani moved back and stepped away. His two helpers from the corridor reached in front of him and lifted Milo from the bed and onto his feet. Turning him round, one of them lifted a glass of water to his mouth and the other fastened his wrists together with crude twine. Milo was recovering but still feeling the after-effects of the whiskey. The room was clear but distant, he didn't feel much like making a fuss.

'Come on, it's not far but it will take a few minutes to get there.'

Milo assembled a response to this and it came out in a word, 'Where?'

'A boat. We are taking you on a nice boat trip. Quiet and discreet, tourists pay a lot of money for this experience, and we give it you for free. You are a lucky man Milo, very lucky.'

Milo stared at him but had to concentrate on keeping upright. He failed and had to be helped by one of Kimani's men. He shook his head and tried to remember just how much he'd had to drink. He could remember one glass but he felt like there had been more.

'Come on, we have to catch the tide. How often do you under-worlders hear that, I wonder? I am reconnecting you with the earth Milo, I hope you appreciate it.'

Milo didn't feel that appreciative as they staggered out the door together, Milo being half carried, half walking on his own.

The fresh air hit him full on. The night wasn't that cold but stepping outside brought home just how close the air in the dark room had been. Milo shook his head. He had been trying to work something out before he'd closed his eyes, what was it? It was something to do with his past, the people in his past. Xin? No. Rachel Lopez-Real, he liked that name, it made him think of far off days, was it her, she was a doctor? No. Julia… Who was Julia? A girl, yes, but he thought the name might have been a clue. They were stopped at the corner of the street. Kimani said something and the big man behind him grunted and pushed Milo forward. He caught his foot on a football, the leavings of a child's game, and stumbled. Milo staggered forward for a few feet, the man beside him reaching out to steady him, missed, and then he fell. Kimani glared at the heavy and touched Milo with his foot. Milo didn't move.

'Milo, get up.'

Still nothing. Kimani bent down and tried to turn Milo onto his back. With help Milo was lying face up, a cut on his forehead. Kimani bent over him and then reached out for his neck.

'Damnation.'

39

Who knows what the Cavalry looks like

The firing had been sustained and the Pixie's case and carton barrier had fallen apart. Even the shuttering had taken a battering and it was made from carbon reinforced steel, but it had held. Given that the Pixie and Sam were crouching down on either side of the shop entrance behind the shuttering, that was just as well. The gas had cleared though, which allowed the women remove the breathing masks. Sam's head ached and she was having difficulty with her right side, Anna's having shot her before, being an uncomfortable counterpoint to her current situation.

Outside, the unit attacking them had divided in two to create a crossfire, making any attempt to get back to the weapons and ammunition at the back of the shop extremely difficult. Sam looked up at the shuttering on the other side of the heap that used to be the glass front. She lay back against the wall, trying to see the top of the shuttering. It didn't look great, she thought, in fact, it wouldn't last long. The shuttering itself could withstand the attack without too much of a problem, but they were methodically hitting the masonry around it and pretty soon that would collapse. The structure might follow. So much for them caring about the doctor's surgery upstairs.

The Pixie waved at her. She pointed above at the shuttering and Sam gave her a thumbs up in agreement, her companion suggesting they were thinking along the same lines. Signalling that they should shove the remainder of the casing into the gap that had appeared behind the front door, she also pointed to the wall behind her. Sam was puzzled and then realised what she was getting at. The wall along from the Pixie was less pockmarked than the one behind Sam, with cover for a few moments from the cases the Pixie might get to the back unscathed. With more weaponry they might stand some chance. Sam nodded her agreement.

Using their feet, they shoved the cases together and to a greater depth than they had been earlier. The movement brought an increased frenzy of fire from outside. The Pixie set off on her belly, dragging herself forward with her elbows. Sam flattened herself against the wall and into the corner and watched anxiously the progress of her lover.

The shelves above the Pixie crumbled, showering her with the food cans and bottles from above. She kept going and was clear in about two body lengths. She pushed herself up to her knees and felt for her head, where one of the cans had drawn blood.

Looking less than pleased, she got up and headed for the cage and kicked the gate back. Above her, Sam spotted street light coming through holes in the wall and she knew they wouldn't have long. The Pixie reappeared, dragging an old, heavy gauge machine gun from the back, already loaded most definitely not locked. The fire on the wall above her head increased as those outside could see they were about to make a breakthrough. Sam, seeing the fire outside drawn to the iminent breach in the wall, scrambled back to the rear of the shop. The shuttering on that side collapsed. The Pixie immediately opened fire.

'Sam, get back here, take those grenades!' The Pixie shouted over the firing.

Dragging herself through the detritus of the wrecked shop, Sam reached the box the Pixie had kicked and began to pull out several grenades. She realised they were in a sort of "eye" of the firing, a point between the crossing lines from outside, and she stood.

The Pixie's firing had destroyed the window and wall on the right-hand side of the shop. The shuttering came down with a crash but it suppressed the firing outside that had collapsed the wall on the left. The building's structure was now precarious, with the upper floors cantilevered over the walls on the sides of the shop. Beams were exposed on either side.

Sam angled herself at a point where she could see an area in front of where she thought the left-hand unit must be, then she armed and threw four explosives in quick succession. She had no idea whether they were even in the approximate direction of their attackers but it would mean they knew that those inside weren't helpless and rushing the doorway might be fatal for some of them. She was also aware such an attack on them was likely to be successful.

The firing outside stopped. The Pixie grunted.

'Suck that.' She didn't say it loud but with a fair amount of conviction and Sam smiled. The air around them was filled with dust and paper drifted down from walls and shelves. The silence almost hurt.

'What do you think?' Sam asked. The Pixie wore a grim look Sam knew and wasn't encouraged by.

'I think they'll take a step back and might collapse the building like you thought, bastards. The question is how?'

'Rockets maybe?'

'A bit sledgehammer, don't you think? Do you Americans only think in big, "destroy everything" kinds of ways?'

'It's effective.'

'Yeah, but…'

'Did you see the other way out?'

'Is there one?'

'Must be. Gangs wouldn't have just one way, especially with the arms dump. Thinking about it, the police must know about this and been bought off.'

'So the police might be heading this way too? To save us or kill us?' Pixie asked, Sam's look spoke volumes.

'Everyone round here must know about this place.'

'So why didn't your pals wait for the cops?'

'If the gangs have bought them off, they'll as likely kill that unit as help them. Not too much trust between branches of the state.'

'You too, huh?'

'We don't really exist, remember? The cops don't think we'll accept responsibility if they act on our behalf.'

'Would you?'

'No.'

'So who do we think is going to come piling in, from wherever it is that they have of getting in and out of here? Cops or gangs?'

'Which would you prefer?'

The Pixies' eyes scanned the street in front of them. Sam could see it wasn't possible to get at them where they were, at the back of the shop, from an elevated or too steeply angled a position. If the unit attacking them wanted to shoot them, they'd have to move to directly in front of them. That is unless they made a deal with the locals, police or gangs, to take them from behind. They needed to know what was happening. Sam nudged the Pixie.

'While you're wondering, get hold of Liu and ask her what's going on.'

'Yeah, 'cause I hadn't thought of that. In answer to your question; the cops. I know what they're likely to do. About the other thing, the com is always open, they must be doing something.'

'Shit, this is not the moment for your pals not to be on the ball.'

'Faith, dearest one.'

Movement outside and the Pixie opened up again, a brief burst. She looked down at the magazine.

'Nearly out, can you see the box with more?'

Sam looked round her and spotted the opened box. With a quick look back at the shop front, she darted over to the box. She scanned the back of the shop and could see a door, but it was heavily bolted and had cases in front. Bending down to take a fresh mag, she saw the edge of a slab of concrete. At first blush it looked like the rest of the floor. But the attack on the front had disturbed the boxes on top and a crack had appeared.

'Anything happening, Pix?'

The Pixie frowned, 'Not yet, but I don't think...' she opened up again, 'I'm out.' And she leant forward to detach the spent mag. Sam grabbed the new one and moved the three steps back to the Pixie and they swapped, both watching forward all the time.

'Hold on.' And Sam stepped away.

'What?'

Sam was over at the crack in the floor and running her fingers along the edges of the boxes. The boxes were fixed in place, but it took only a few moments to find what she was looking for. A sharp 'click' and, even as the Pixie opened up with another burst, the trap swung open, the boxes moved with the door. Sticking her head down the hole, Sam looked and listened and then came up again.

She reached for the box of grenades and began to pull them out.

'We have a way out, for a few minutes anyway, unless it's booby trapped. I wouldn't think it will be long before it's full of someone though, and it's probably booby trapped.'

'Why isn't it already?'

'Booby trapped?'

'Full of people.'

'I'd say negotiation.'

'Hold on, they're getting ready for something.'

Then suddenly Julia was there, first in the Pixie's implant and then in Sam's.

'Everyone still alive?'

'Yep.' The Pixie snapped out and flicked a quick look at Sam, who was looking surprised.

'Ok, we are trying to find out, oh, you have the trap door, good. We've been hearing about it. There is a lot of chat going on about the tunnel it leads to, some people are very annoyed that you're here.'

'No shit.' And the Pixie opened fire again. This time it was returned. Heavy fire came in from both sides. The bullets were traveling along the wall closer and closer to Sam's and the Pixie's position. They were still at oblique angles, avoiding the Pixie's big gun.

'They're coming in.'

The firing became pretty intense and the walls were pared back to the bare brickwork, the air thick with dust and the exhaust from the Pixie's big gun. The Pixie was hunched down behind the gun, firing first to one side, then to the other. Sam was crouching and setting grenades along the edge of the trap door.

And then suddenly the progress from the guns in front stopped. The firing went on but not into the shop. Sam looked at Julia, who shook her head.

'We're still trying to contact the gang whose place this is.'

'Who's firing then?'

'And who are they firing at?'

Julia froze for an instant and then, 'The cameras outside are showing the clantechs under attack from two sides, they appear to be gathering to withdraw, not far, but to a more coherent position.'

'Who then?' The Pixie asked, crouching down and leaning out, trying to see what exactly was happening.

'The gang have most to gain, they won't want a clantech unit getting in here, not with all this stuff.' Sam answered.

'They've been pushed back to one side and are consolidating their position, one of them is hurt. Monitoring suggests they're calling for back up.' Julia offered a running commentary.

Sam and the Pixie turned and stared at one another, Sam looked back at the street, 'It's Anna.'

Julia froze again and, coming back, turned, 'Plausible, and there's evidence someone, not police based, has contacted the gang. The police are getting a lot of traffic from what we are presuming is a national agency.'

'They're probably pissed that the cops haven't arrived yet.'

'Can we leave?' the Pixie asked.

Sam looked at the tunnel for a moment, 'I don't fancy going in there until I know we're not going to be followed in or ambushed. You know how long it is?'

Julia pointed, 'It's about seventy metres from the bottom of the steps here to the exit, the exit appears to be inside a house.'

Sam and the Pixie exchanged another look and the Pixie shook her head.

'We've got to talk to the guys who own this.'

Julia agreed. There was sound from below and a drop in intensity from the gunfire outside. Sam's head snapped round to stare at the open trap and she lifted one of the grenades she had lined up on the lip. The Pixie looked out at the front of the shop and waited for the assault she presumed was about to begin. Julia froze and unfroze again.

'They're coming from the right. You were correct, it's Kevin and Anna, they have some cops with them who look like they're going to screen the assault unit.'

The Pixie gave Sam a quick look, 'Try to hit us at the same time?'

'I'd say that's the plan.'

The Pixie ducked down, 'I love you Sam.'
'Love you too, Pix.'

40

In a tiny Cafe in a changed Town

The late dinner rush was fading and the staff could do the little things, like make sure they had enough cutlery before they had to set up for waiting clients. Or check the departing kids hadn't unscrewed the salt. The evening was humid and she was tired, but she was also relaxed and enjoying life and those were things she'd not expected to be true just a short while ago.

Mariana was totting up her tips and making her way over to where Joanna stood at the cash desk. Joanna was the main reason they had landed the jobs. Her size and attitude had impressed the owner enough that she was ready to take a chance on the two tired women who'd just wandered in, had a short meal and asked for a job.

About a week after she started, Joanna had stopped an argument between two angry male clients without having to resort to any more violence than a few whispered words in their ears and a hand on the arm. The owner kept asking what it was she'd said, or promised or threatened them with. Joanna though, just looked bewildered at the idea she had said anything beyond asking them to keep down their voices.

Mariana smiled at the memory. She knew it was nothing that was said to either man. She had seen Joanna's fingers slide round the upper arms of both men and she knew that would be enough. Mariana liked to call them Joanna's 'magic fingers'.

They had not gone all that far since landing in the main container port at San Jose. The port, like the reconstruction in Sao Paulo, was a result of the arrival of new sea frontage in places that had been dry land in earlier years. In order to lessen the pressure on the new levees, they had dug deep water channels and new docks. There were advantages and for a while there were new jobs. However, as the work progressed, more of it could be done by robots. The people, like the jobs, had drifted away.

Mariana and Joanna were working in one of the sectors of the economy in the US that still valued inter-human contact. Even here on the smaller meals like lunch and breakfast, the service was automated. The US had gone, outside of the big cities, one of two ways. Ultra modern, embrace everything tech, or ultra off grid, no tech almost medieval. The area of overlap was medicine and in the end each side of the community both despised and needed the other.

The restaurant was a classic crossover venture. The "Techs" would enjoy the luxury of being served by people and having "old time" meals cooked in a traditional way on traditional implements. The "Meds" wouldn't buy their food in a restaurant any other way. For the Techs, it was a risky occasional treat; for the Meds it was Tuesday dinner.

'You ok little one?' Joanna asked smiling.

'I'm better than ok, big one.' Mariana answered.

Joanna laughed and Mariana put her tips in the pool to be divided among the waiters and the kitchen staff.

'Been a good night.'

'Very busy.' Mariana turned and looked over the emptying space. 'It's a good place this. The right sort of size and the right kind of food for the area. I think Pat's done well with it.'

'She's certainly doing better than average, I think she'd do even better if she had someone who could make great desserts.'

Mariana turned back and stared at Joanna, a question being asked without being asked. Joanna said nothing but kept counting the money and dividing it into discreet piles. She finally looked up and smiled.

'No, I haven't heard anything. But you know she said she wanted to head up here and she was putting her stash aside to open a club.'

'But that was in the big city.'

'What's left of it.'

'Sure, but it still has people who have money to spend, places like this…'

She waved her arm around. Joanna leaned forward and lowered her voice.

'We came here because it was near a way out, it was smallish but not too small and there were no local boys trying to control the world. Her priorities won't be any different. I'm just saying they'd fit in pretty well.'

'Yeah, I get that, but wouldn't it make our situation worse?'

'Maybe, maybe not. She's a pretty dependable type, she's resourceful and tough enough.'

'Why're you bringing it up? You've heard something?'

'No. Not really, it's just about the time I would have thought she'd make a move if she was going to make a move.'

Mariana frowned and, still in a whispered voice, 'She had a pretty sweet deal in Rio, why leave? I mean, even if it was the long term plan?'

Joanna stopped counting and thought, and then, 'We'll go for a walk and I'll tell all.'

Cleaning up and dividing up the tips was a straightforward ritual. In a short space of time Joanna had earned the trust of the owner and the staff. She was a straight edge in a crooked world, was the general opinion. A lot of people looked at Mariana and wondered how they'd ended up together. Joanna was gregarious, easygoing and very physical, Mariana was quiet, bookish and more likely to lecture you than hit you. No one actually asked.

They were walking away from the restaurant. The evening was warm and, as it often was these days, close. The sky was cloudy with some clear patches showing stars over the darkened city. They came to a junction, right turn and they would head up the hill to a tiny cabin which they rented from the restaurant owner, left would bring them down into the dock and the robotised wharfs and storage facilities. Joanna pulled Mariana left and they walked down the empty road.

After a few silent steps Mariana gave up, 'Ok, what?'

Joanna gave her a quiet smile, 'You were right, I lied, I did hear something. I didn't tell you at first because it wasn't complete and it didn't sound too good.'

'That was about six days ago, wasn't it?'

Joanna's turn to frown, 'Yes…'

'I thought something was up, you had two bundles ready for a quick departure, discreet, but they were there.'

'I put those away very carefully.'

'Yeah, but I only have one belt and two pairs of jeans that need a belt. You took my belt.'

'You'd have needed the belt.'

'I did, that was why I went looking for it.'

'You didn't say.'

'You didn't say.'

'True. You're pretty sneaky.'

'What did you hear?'

'Kevin found them.'

'Shit. Are they ok? I mean I presume they are… what happened?'

'Not quite sure on the detail, but they took care of him.'

'She's quite the badass, your sergeant.'

'I wouldn't get the wrong side of her. Anyway, he ended up on a ship to, I'm not sure where, and they decided that they'd had their lucky break and it was time to leave.'

'Just because he'd turned up, a bit extreme, no?'

'She didn't survive the war and then the peace in that place, by pushing her luck.'

'Then you've heard she's coming here?'

'No, I haven't but I think we'd do well to keep an eye out for them. If they're being hunted it's because of us and them not knowing where we are won't help them.'

'Might help us though.'

'Not as much as having friends. She isn't coming here without knowing the landscape, if she is coming here. I trust her, but she might have friends here who are less than trustworthy and who might be able to put two and two together.'

'So her friends might sell us out. But then we should get out, no? Before anyone has a chance to put us in the same frame.'

'You've become much tougher than the day I found you on the floor of that house.'

'You've shown me how insecure we are, unless we are careful. Always have a way out.'

'True, but make friends where you can and keep them if you can.

These guys could plug us into a network, a network that the people we're running from can't see, because they don't look.'

'You mean like the restaurants in the favela?'

'Yeah, like them, like the one we work in now. The sergeant is an expert in navigating through the kinds of people we need, most of whom would sell us for a spare kidney. We can't become invisible to everyone without an invisibility cloak.'

'The sergeant has one?'

'Is one.'

Silence descended as the port came into view. To the right the road became a grass bank, uncared for and untended and below that was a tree-line, there to keep the bank from slipping. They could see the whole of the basin, the machines working away, at this distance silently, ceaselessly. The ships waiting in a short queue for space to become available, the ships preparing to leave, all watched over by automated systems and robot security. In the whole five square miles of industrial landscape five people extracted gainful employment and one of them had received notice of termination of employment a week ago. They sat.

Mariana had hoped to find a space on the colony ships to Mars, but faced with the DNA screening they had decided against it for now. She leaned against Joanna as they watched the silent choreography below and examined each movement for the sign of humanity on the ships. Joanna groped in her pocket and pulled out a bottle, uncorked it and handed it to Mariana. She took it and drank, and smiled handing it back.

'I never drank spirits before.'

Joanna grinned and looked at her, 'You never did lots of things before. Have I corrupted you beyond redemption?'

Mariana shook her head and leaned back against Joanna, 'You saved me.'

41

The Call that kept Calling

Liu was looking at the virtual screen her headband offered her and tried to quell the rising panic. She had been watching Milo's life signs for hours and they had been fluctuating, Dr Lopez-Real thought that he had drunk something or that he had been given something, but, about ten minutes ago, they had become very erratic and then stopped. She had sent an alert to Beijing, but had heard nothing back. She had tried to contact Julia but again, nothing. She knew they were busy and why, she had after all been the one worried about the Pixie and Sam, but now Milo was in trouble and there didn't seem to be any reaction.

She thought about it for a few minutes. It was getting to be time to eat and she would have to take a break, as her father always insisted on eating their evening meal together. Normally she liked that, it was the one part of the day when he was hers and nothing else got between them, but tonight… On the other hand, she knew he was someone who knew a lot; would he help her or would he blow up if she asked him about the problem in front of her? He liked Milo and trusted him. Milo had found her earlier in the year and brought her home. She cringed at the memory of her naive idea of what it was she was getting into and her anger that he had pulled her out. Her father had been grateful to Milo then, but she knew what he thought of her online activities, he might be angry.

She got up and took off the headband, breaking her contact with China 12 and Milo, she would ask her father. If she was lucky and she explained it properly he might not be annoyed at all. She had to risk it either way.

Making her way to their dining room she ran into Liang Li, her father's assistant, constant shadow and, as Liu could see, adoring, unrequited lover. Liu liked her and thought it was a shame her father couldn't see what just about everyone else could. Liang bowed and

Liu copied her.

'Did Baba have a good day? Is he in a good mood?'

Liang smiled, 'Your father is always in a good mood for you. He sees you and his whole face lights up.'

'I wish that was true. All I have to do is tell him what I've been doing online and his face changes.'

'You should understand. He was worried when you disappeared last time, he thinks it's dangerous for you.'

Liu's head bowed a touch, 'Yes, I suppose, but it's the world for most people nowadays, he is far behind the times.'

'He likes to think he's ahead of the times you know, he thinks the world will come to its senses. I think he's right.'

Liu smiled broadly, 'I know you do, and I think… I think it's right that you do. Is he waiting for me?'

'As always.'

They parted and Liu pushed on the door, which opened with a whisper. Feng stood with his back to the door, looking out of the window. Like his office, one wall gave out onto the roof garden which was in a traditional Chinese design. He turned at the movement of air that signalled the arrival of his daughter. He, as promised, with the broadest of smiles, turned and bowed to her. She stopped inside the door and, as it closed, she bowed back.

Online, Liu was a strong, brilliant mind able to assist her more experienced friends. When with her father, she was a fifteen-year-old anxious for the good opinion of her sole parent.

They walked and met at the table where an evening meal had been set out ready for them to eat. They sat and she offered him selections from some of the dishes in front of them. He watched her and smiled in a way that was more profound than the broad smile he had shown her as she came in. Realising she was being watched, Liu looked up.

'How was your day daughter?'

She bowed her head and then frowned, 'It was good, but… I have something to tell you, but you mustn't be mad.'

Now it was his turn to frown, 'Why would I possibly be mad at my dutiful daughter?'

Liu looked as though he had shouted at her, but took a deep breath.

'You remember when… earlier in the year I…'

'Yes.'

It would not be fair to say Feng looked annoyed, more anxious, but for Liu this was a bad sign.

'This is not the same. I was curious. I wondered, was Milo right? About the, um…'

'Pixies.'

'Yes, them. But I didn't go back to them, I found my own sources.'

'And?'

'He was right, I was childish.'

Now Feng looked surprised, 'No, not childish, they work very hard hiding what they are. It is part of what they are and they are important to the state.'

Now Liu looked surprised, 'You found out more?'

He smiled, 'You don't get all your curiosity from your mother.'

She smiled and then thought and the smile faded, 'I was curious about China 12 as well.'

He answered, slowly, gently, 'And, what did you find out?'

'At first not very much, they have a very strong reputation, they are very clever.'

'So I understand.'

'I tried to find out directly from them.'

'By asking?' Silence. 'Liu… by asking?'

Now quite slowly, 'Not officially.' She was looking up at him trying to gauge his response but his face was a blank wall.

'What did they do when they caught you? I presume that is what this is about.'

'No, that is, this isn't about them catching me. They did, but they didn't mind. I was caught by an AI.'

'A what?'

'You know, an AI.'

'Like the ones that control traffic flows or production schedules?'

'In a way, but she is so much more than they are.'

'Is she military?'

'No, not at all.'

'Alright, an AI caught you, I have to say I'm surprised, I thought you were better…'

'I am. So I was surprised too, but she's not ordinary, I wish you could meet her.'

'You keep saying her.'

'She is a she, Julia.'

'She has a name?'

Liu went on enthusiastically, 'She is amazing, just like the cleverest person you ever met.'

'And she's on the China 12 system?'

'Oh no, she's in Milo.'

'In? Did you say, "in Milo"?'

'Yes, she's in his system and in his head.'

'So I might have met her when Milo was here?'

'I don't think so, she hasn't been in there for all that long, he's having problems.'

'I'm not surprised. These kinds of experiments, I'm not sure they're ethical.'

'She's not an experiment, it's hard to explain, but she's not an experiment. China 12 didn't develop her.'

'Who then?'

'I think she did herself, or the person who did is the same as Julia, I'm not clear.'

'Fine then, I don't feel so bad about my confusion.' And he scratched his head in the finest traditions of the Chinese comic theatre. Liu laughed. Feng didn't seem too put out.

'That is the problem though, something has happened to Milo, I'm not sure what. I tried to find Zhang Xin and Dr Lopez Real and Julia, but I know she's helping the Pixie in New York, and Sam. And I looked for Dr O Shea, but I can't find them. And Milo seems to be… dead.'

'Dead?' Feng frowned again and leaned forward. 'Are you sure?'

'No. But his life signs are gone,' She began to tear up, 'and Baba, I don't know what to do or how to save him.'

Reaching over the table, Feng took her hand and squeezed it.

'First we will eat,' he held up his hand to pacify the onrush of objection, 'we need to make the best decisions, I don't need to tell you what happens when your blood sugar drops.'

She nodded and began to eat, quickly, and he smiled.

'Then we will find out the right people to help, they may not need our help, you know, they are very clever people, these China 12.'

He fell to eating and Liu was thinking about who he could speak with and her smile telegraphed the confidence she wasn't feeling. Milo might already be dead and did that mean Julia was too?

42

The Old Friends

It was four thirty AM in Lamu and they had been talking for a while. Hologram to hologram. Old times, the exciting time we… did you really marry him after all? The decline in standards. They knew they couldn't dwell, they both knew there was a great big African elephant in the room, they even knew its name.

'But really Doctor, you are calling about your missing colleague.'

'Really Doctor, I am.'

'Lovely though it is et cetera, et cetera.'

Rachel smiled, 'Lovely though it is.'

'I can tell you we are as puzzled as you probably are. I presume you are and this isn't some clever China 12 technique.'

'We are. We are not that clever.'

'What do you know?'

'Nothing.'

'Really Mwangi is the one who should be telling you this.'

'Can he?'

'No, he is out and, unless something new has happened, I know as much as most.'

'Ok. Last we knew he was going to have supper with you both.'

'He was, he did, and it was a very nice evening. He's a very nice person.'

'Did anything odd happen?'

Dr Abebe thinks and then looks up at Rachel, 'I'm not sure how to put this.'

'He was drunk?'

'You know?'

'We guessed and it has been confirmed.'

'But, how?'

'His alcohol control system was suppressed.'

'Deliberately?'

'Yes.'

'Did this have something to do with his disappearance?'

'We don't believe it was done to cause the disappearance, but we think they are connected.'

'How?'

'Long story. We need to get him back and I'll tell you then.'

'Does it have something to do with an AI?'

Rachel stopped in her tracks and gave her friend a long look.

'What do you know about that?'

'Nothing. We have heard there is a group here who want to acquire some AI and they think Milo is part of it or he has it. They want to sell him, someone has put a price on his head.'

'On his head?'

'Mwangi thought it was just a figure of speech, but about an hour ago he heard it wasn't. They really are prepared to pay for just his head, if that's what they can get.'

Holograms can't go white, as the transmission system colour balances the image all the time, but if they could, Dr Abebe would have seen her friend go white.

'Do you know who?'

Dr Abebe shook her head. 'No. The group here are a well-organised gang. They like to think they are an alternative government, but really they are criminals with a bit of philosophy on the side.'

'Do you know when he disappeared?'

'We got a report that he had breakfast at the hotel, but he was behaving strangely. And then some people reported a man chasing about town hiding in doorways. When Milo was late for his meeting with Mwangi, he put two and two together. Then we got the news about the dogs.'

'The dogs?'

'The dogs of Lamu, they are the gang we think have him.'

'So, if you know them, why can't you take them into custody?'

'We can't just "take people into custody", even if we had the right to do it. They are a very influential group and they are centred on Lamu, but they are not only here, they work up and down the coast.'

'Has he been taken off the island?'

'We don't think so. Mwangi has a couple of boat patrols on the coast and he's managed to get the government to send a few men to watch the landings.'

'I didn't think the island was that big.'

'It isn't, but the inspector doesn't have many resources and the rising sea level has made lots of little islands.'

'Does he have enough to make a search of the place?'

'No, he doesn't. Do you not have a tracking system? You should have one for when your people go into the field.'

'We do, Milo's shut down. We've lost all of the tracking we're used to having.'

'How?'

'Normally, that would only happen if he died.'

'He's dead?'

'We hope not. The system should have told us that if he was, but it didn't, it just stopped, we don't know why.'

'Can it be blocked?'

'Yes, but this didn't seem like that, we pinged his system and got a response but nothing else.'

'Do you know where he was when it happened?'

'We think it was near where your small landing is, to the north west of the town. Given what's happened, we aren't confident in any of our information.'

'Alright, I can't do anything for you right now. When Mwangi comes home, I will get him to speak with you. If I can get a message to him, I shall.'

'Thank you, I'm sorry for getting you up at this hour.'

'No, I was up already waiting for him to come home. Relations with the dogs do not usually become violent, but this has been a bit different. It was lovely to speak with you again, Rachel.'

'Lovely to speak with you too, and thank you again.'

Dr Abebe smiled and the connection was broken. She stood looking at where her friend's image had been and then shook her head.

Outside, the inspector was hurrying down one of the narrow streets. The town was quiet and the street deserted. Behind him, a fresh-faced young man in a uniform. There were no stripes or pips on his crisply pressed shirt. He hurried to keep up with the boss. The boss had a face like thunder.

He had dragged constable Maina out of bed to make this search. He usually made any night round with Maina, the town was quiet with him there, not readily explicable but it was the young man's gift.

Rounding the corner at the end of the street and heading to the right. He passed by walls that were now too close to the water's edge and would, in the next few years, be undermined by it. The surface of the road was broken and suffering from repeated flooding. The old, formerly white, walls were discoloured up to the inspector's hip. Straight ahead in the gloom of the earliest morning light and that of a setting three quarter moon, a lone figure sat on the end of the latest makeshift pier. At this distance he looked like a young boy from a story book, lacking only a fishing rod and a straw hat. The inspector slowed down and then stopped. He looked back at the young man with him.

'Wait here, keep your back to the wall and your eyes open.'

'Yes sir.'

The inspector walked forward and looked about him as he went but the man was alone. Without looking round, the man called out.

'Inspector, how nice to bump into you, and so early in the morning. I didn't think you were a restless sleeper like me, do you have a guilty conscience?'

'Do you, Dr. Kimani?'

He turned a little and inclined his head, 'I think we both know I have a guilty conscience, and plenty to be guilty about. I feel we would disagree about which things they are.'

The inspector came to a stop behind Kimani and noted that all the boats he'd seen much earlier in the evening staked to the shoreline still were there bobbing on the flowing tide.

'Will you not sit down for a moment?' the doctor asked, and the inspector sat, being careful to keep his shoes away from the waves.

'Do you still have him?'

Kimani smiled, 'Direct as ever, Inspector. Perhaps that is why we chose our respective paths.'

'Do you?'

'I might ask who, but that would only draw out the conversation and I was just thinking of leaving. I have been here for a while.'

'Is he alive?'

'Why Inspector, how do you think we treat our guests?'

'I know you don't answer your local police inspectors.'

'Very well. Yes, we do still hold Milo in our care. Yes, he is still alive, I think you must have heard something, I will have to make inquiries about that.'

'I have heard something, but not from people round here. He is still alive, what happened?'

'We don't know. He is alive but not conscious, I won't hide the fact we are concerned.'

'You might not get your payday?'

'You speak in disparaging terms, you forget that this man has done many people great harm.'

'He stopped violent thieves from taking what was not theirs.'

'He prevented the people's defenders repossessing material stolen from them, inspector. The ships, run by robots. Their cargo made by robots and the material mined or grown, by robots. Even the security was performed by robots. The only human involved on the ship was given a good meal and offered a trip home. He refused and we left it at that. We defend the powerless, Inspector.'

'You oppress and violate the people you claim to defend. They do not get a say in your overlordship and you make no attempt to allow them a say in how you run things.'

'You might say the same of every king in history. You might say the same about you and your officers.' He twisted round and waved at the young man leaning against the wall. 'Officer, is that young Hasani Maina? Come here.'

He pushed away from the wall but didn't move forward. The inspector lifted his chin and Maina made his way uncertainly toward them. He had begun to sweat and seemed a little tense.

'Relax, young man. How is your sister?'

'Doing better now, thank you.' Kimani nodded slowly.

'Officer, you respect the inspector?'

'Yes sir.'

'Of course you do. Tell me, did he ask you if you wanted to come out this evening and roam around the town?'

The young man smiled broadly and shook his head, 'No sir, of course not.'

'Of course not.' Kimani smiled turning back to the inspector, 'You would be outraged if this young man thought you should consult with him over any decision. Over the biggest decisions I make, we ask everyone their opinion. Can we hold an election? No, you wouldn't permit it. But we have our ways, older ways.'

'A democrat now? A few moments ago you were a king or perhaps a chief.'

'No, I am no king. A chief? Perhaps, but the tribe,' he held out his hands to the wide world, 'but the tribe is not as you suggest. I do not believe you are here to debate my ethics, are you Inspector? You are here to retrieve the oppressor's dog.'

'I am here to rescue a man kidnapped by people who wish him harm. Who have you sold him to Kimani?'

'There are parties interested in talking with Milo, it is true. I understand it is for some software he knows about or has. Dangerous software.'

'And they will kill him to get it?'

'If the army of Uganda kill someone you have sent to them are you responsible? No? I do not answer for the actions of another, Inspector.'

'Who are they?'

'In truth, I do not know.'

'They might be the very people you say you are against.'

'They have made a business arrangement through our friends to the north.'

'When are you…'

'Inspector.'

The young officer called out. The inspector looked up at him and saw him point out over their heads. A boat was headed their way, the white sail billowing out, catching a breeze that would die

223

when the headland cut it off. Several heads could be seen above the gunwales, one had a white hat, perhaps being held on with a hand. The inspector looked back at the rising Kimani, and suddenly they were surrounded by men.

'All of your questions will be answered Inspector, you will be my guest.'

Against his back the inspector could feel a hard, small point being pressed with a force that implied he shouldn't argue.

43

What we Know and What we Don't

'That was how we left things.'

Xin looked perplexed. She did not enjoy it when things were outside of her control and events of the last few days' had been spinning fast, with no sense of how they might be slowed down, much less controlled. Rachel had just finished telling the group about what she and Dr Abebe had discussed, which seemed to be nothing and everything. They now believed Milo had been bought by someone, and possibly because of Julia. Though that was based solely on the speculation about why they would want his head. They were coming to the conclusion that events in New York and Kenya were linked, but in what way was less certain.

Xin turned and looked at Rahul. He shook his head.

'The situation doesn't look great. They are trapped, we think, there appears to be a fight over who will get them. There's a way out but it's controlled by a gang who are based in the Bronx. Julia thought they might be the power in control of the neighbourhood rather than the police.'

'Can we talk to them? Cathy, is there a way to speak with them that would be more persuasive than we are being at the moment?' Xin asked.

Cathy shrugged, 'I think the most important question is, can we speak with them at all? If we can, who is in charge?'

'If I remember my geography, the Bronx is close to Brooklyn. Are the Brotherhood involved in this?'

Rahul shook his head, 'We don't think so, but, like I said the situation is confused at best. Just to make things more difficult, Anna has resurfaced. And the way the pixies go about things, they don't tend to bring order.'

'We need a plan and we need one now. We have to get them out and we have to get Milo back. We have to do it quickly… We seem to be falling apart.'

Instead of a clear voice, she looked from face to face and found confusion and fear. Then a call came in and she looked at the ident of the person calling. Xin looked round the room, 'We seem to be running out of options. I will have to take this. Please give me the room and half an hour.'

They left the room in silence. Xin waited until everyone had left before answering the call. A tall man in a grey suit appeared in Holo in front of her. The suit was cleanly cut and the fabric of a mix that suggested it had cost a lot. However, it had an old-fashioned look deliberately harking back to the founders of the state. His hair was glossy and slicked back, again in the style of the founders of the state and the party. He bowed to Xin.

'Speaker.'

She bowed. 'Minister Deng.'

'I hope China 12 prospers as ever.'

'Thank you Minister, we do.'

'I understand there have been some recent setbacks.'

'Some unexpected events, Minister, but we are a resilient organisation.'

'Is there anything that would benefit from the assistance of the state, Speaker?'

'I don't understand.'

'It has been drawn to our attention that one of your operatives might be unwell and in need of assistance in another country.'

Xin looked at him warily. She considered the possible sources of his information and the consequences of her accepting his offer. "One"? Clearly he knew about Milo at very least. Something else was behind this, he would not normally be so direct. She had to calm herself, perhaps it was a good thing, well intentioned. Was there something to be done that would help, or would the undoubtedly heavy hand of the Chinese state put Milo in even greater danger?

'It is true that Milo has been taken sick, Minister, we are currently in touch with a local doctor to ascertain what exactly the problem is.'

'Speaker, be assured that we will always be here to support an organisation such as China 12.'

'Thank you, Minister.'

'Do you wish for our assistance?'

He was putting it to her directly, this was very unusual. If she were to turn it down it might imply that such aid was not welcome, which of course it wasn't. But to accept…Was there a middle way? She hated this kind of tiptoeing around issues, she would have liked just to say, "thank you, no thank you", but it was not how things were done.

'Minister, I wonder at the effect of such generous assistance to us. Other governments might draw the conclusion that we were not as independent as we maintain.'

'The safety of your personel would be a paramount concern to the people's government.'

'Of course, Minister, but we cannot alert the government every time one of us gets into a scrape.'

The minister agreed but without his customary smile. Something was behind this offer, he had not left as she expected he would, having been turned down. She saw the signs of his approaching the topic again.

'I appreciate your candour, Speaker and I agree this could not be a regular offer, but it does sound as though this is a life or death situation.'

That shook her, "sound", either they were listening and the China 12 systems had failed to pick up the bugs, or someone from inside had spoken to them, this had not come as she had at first supposed, from outside sources and chatter on open coms. He was confident he could interfere with China 12, with her! This was outside of agreed protocols. He was driving at something else.

'I think I can assure the minister that it is not quite so dramatic.'

'Our understanding is, that it is. There is another aspect to this situation, Speaker.'

'Oh?'

'Intelligence sources indicate to us that Milo is a target, not simply for his own sake but for sophisticated technology that could be of assistance in the defense of China.'

Now Xin was really worried and perplexed. The only technology Milo was carrying was the implants that were part of most military operatives. Yes, he had bespoke systems, but they were largely for personal defense and for coms. What the hell was he talking about? This was outside of his remit for China 12.

'Minister, I don't know what you are referring to?'

'The AI he is carrying. Are you suggesting you do not know about it?'

Xin frowned, 'No Minister, we know all about it, but it isn't a system currently with military applications. It was developed as a research assistant.'

'We both know it is far more than a research assistant.'

'Truly Minister, that is what we know about it. We did not develop the system, in fact we came upon it by accident and we are still working out what it can do.'

'Let me tell you that our information is that it is highly sophisticated and has a highly adaptive system.'

'The point might be a bit theoretical in any case Minister, as it is what seems to have caused Milo's problems.'

'It is? You're sure?'

'No, not sure but, confident in our evaluation.'

'If that were true it would make the retrieval of Milo's systems a national priority.'

'Minister, I respectfully remind you that we are an independent organisation. The minister must know our nature and the nature of my role here. We are outside of the jurisdiction of the Chinese state.'

The Minister paused. He frowned and someone else, out of the image, must have spoken to him. He paused and his eyes dropped, before looking back at Xin.

'Speaker, we are offering our assistance for you, as an independent organisation who find themselves in need. If you decide to accept our offer, let me know. But you should know that the window is closing.'

He bowed and, just as Xin was about to speak, he cut the com. She stared at the empty space for a long time. This was unprecedented and she was shocked. Her mind was racing.

She didn't know to whom she might turn. None of them was a programmer and most programmes were now being written by AIs themselves. She certainly didn't have the expertise she needed to pick apart Julia. She needed more time. She could always ask Julia herself, but if she was more than they had supposed, would she tell them, did she even know? How much should she tell her colleagues about what had just happened?

There was the line, she'd have to share it with them. If the Chinese decided to send a special forces extraction team, she couldn't claim it was out of the blue. This was a delicate situation, to say the least. Perhaps it would be best to ask the minister for help. Could she go to the Party secretary? Would that not let them in and abandon the independence she relied on? It would have to be a joint decision. When? Both of the problems facing them were critical and who could she trust?

That was the other issue, how had the government received such a complete description of their situation and from where did they get the impression that Julia was a weapon? She called three of her colleagues to the meeting room.

Dr Erasto Dialo was the first to appear and Hoshika and Rahul came in together. Xin had said nothing at first and they stood waiting looking at one another. Finally, 'I have had a rather disturbing call from the Chinese Minister for the interior. He offered us assistance in getting Milo back.'

The others looked at one another again as she stopped, seemingly to think, holding up one hand to forestall any questions.

'The Minister seemed to know rather more about what was happening to Milo than I was comfortable with, but not only that, he suggested he knew things about Julia that I had not even suspected.'

Frowning, Erasto asked, 'Such as?'

'That she is a powerful... he did not use the word "weapon", but said she could be used in national defence.'

Hoshika shook her head, 'How? And, how did he say he knew this?'

'He didn't say how she could be used nor how he knew, he

seemed to think I would have known her purpose.'

'What did you say?'

'I didn't know what to say. I declined the offer of assistance, but he left the door open and said that it would close soon.'

Rahul looked alarmed, 'What did that mean?'

'I'm not sure, but I'm not reassured.'

'Are we being threatened?' Erasto asked.

'Again, I'm not sure. He would never be so direct normally, it just isn't...'

'How things are done,' observed Hoshika. 'So what should we do?'

They each looked to the other and Xin had the powerful feeling that they had few choices, none of them good.

'Obviously I will not be taking up this offer of help. If they decide to intervene, I do not know what we can do, except make our protests heard. It will, however, damage the prestige of the government if we shout about it.'

'What can they know that would make this worth their while?'

'I hoped that one of you might be able to speculate on what Julia could be, and why it would make Milo such a target?'

Rahul rubbed his chin, 'We know she is an AI and that Elspeth was very brilliant. The idea that she could operate as an independent research assistant, is bold to say the least. We know she is capable of thinking independently and that she is growing in her abilities.'

Hoshika nodded, 'All of that begins to make her commercially valuable, I can think of dozens of companies that would love to have such capabilities available to them.'

Erasto pitched in, 'Anything as multi-talented as that could be deployed as a military asset, but she wouldn't be necessarily any better than a specialised AI. In which case, why the fuss?'

'They think they know something and they are fairly sure of what they think. Whoever the source is...' Xin worked through the problem.

'Wants the same thing?' Rahul asked.

'Maybe they've picked up chatter surrounding the price put on Milo's head and decided there is a military aspect to it.' Suggested

Hoshika.

Erasto shook his head, 'I think the only way to find out is to ask Julia directly.'

'But can we trust the answer?' Xin asked.

Rahul agreed, 'She hasn't lied to us yet.'

Xin sighed, 'No, but she can be careful with the truth she tells us.'

'That is so, but that might be as much about protecting us as protecting herself.' Hoshika said.

'How so?'

'If she is as powerful and resourceful an AI as the government and others seem to think, we would be, as it seems we are, in the way.' Hoshika answered.

Xin touched her fingertips together thinking, 'And to some, that might make us an inconvenience to be brushed aside.'

'With the clean sweep of a government brush...' Rahul added.

44

Taken from Behind

The firing was constant and destructive, but careful. The lines of holes that ran along the tops of the walls had advanced and dropped in height, driving the Pixie and Sam farther and farther back into the structure and closer together. They were now inside the cage. It seemed that Anna and Kevin knew the layout of the inside of the shop, as their firing hadn't encroached on the cache of weapons at all.

Julia had kept them informed on the positions of their assailants but knowing where they were did not allow the Pixie to fire back at them. She also told them that the cops had formed a ring holding the clantechs in position but that there were also plenty of officers left over if Sam and the Pixie had managed to break out.

From the gang there was no word. Several members were in the tunnel below them and Sam had the impression they had set charges along the floor beneath. The gang had then pulled back a little and seemed to be content to let the fight above play out. They had also heard movement from the building above and Julia told them that the doctor's surgery and the rooms above had been cleared with minor, if any, injuries.

The Pixie fired occasionally, seemingly to keep her hand in, but they were largely spectators as Kevin and Anna made careful progress toward the shop. Sam had set a charge on the rear door, anyone coming in that way would get an unpleasant welcome and she had hunched down behind a set of metal cases piled up against the edge of the cage. About two feet behind her was the opening to the tunnel and she watched for movement constantly. She looked round at the Pixie.

'What d'you think they're going to say?'

'Come out with your hands up, or shit like that.'

'Why that? They'd know we won't.'

'Yeah but, it's what people do, always worth a shot.'

'And then?'

'Your rockets or a big ol' charge down our throats.'

'What, you think they'll rush us?'

'No, an explosive charge.'

'Don't they want us alive?'

'In an ideal world. It's not an ideal world.' The Pixie fired again. Julia's image, which had remained largely frozen, moved. The Pixie turned a little.

'What's up?' she asked.

'They've stopped coming forward. I've been trying to speak with Kevin, but he's ignoring it. Anna's system has shut me out, she seems to have shut all coms down in fact. They are speaking.'

'You can't hear them?'

'I cannot.'

Sam stirred, 'What about the gang?'

'They are called the "Order of Jonas", seemingly a reference to the person for whom this neighbourhood is named. Their command structure is very… confused.'

'Will they let us out, or turn us in?'

'That is a very good question, Sam, but I think they are simply worried about their arms and are debating how to kill you.'

The Pixie grinned, 'Don't sugar coat it Julia, Sam likes it straight from the hip.'

'I'm sorry, if that was undiplomatic, I am working off limited resources at the moment.'

Punctuating her words with gunfire, 'Same…old…story.'

'You know you stand no chance of hitting anyone with your firing?'

'You see those cabs over there?'

'Yes.'

'They were stopped by the first round of fire from the unit outside.'

'Yes.'

'Can you read what I wrote on the doors?'

Julia froze and then unfroze, ', "P, a heart, and S",'

233

Sam stirred and twisted round, 'Aw. You didn't!'

The Pixie grinned, 'No trees around.'

Sam shook her head, 'So embarrassing.'

'Nothing else to do.'

Julia looked at them and then smiled, ', "A term of affection associated with adolescent courting rituals", I forget you are young.'

The Pixie frowned, 'Is there something up with you? You've become a bit strange.'

Julia mirrored her frown, 'Yes, there is something up with me.'

Sam turned to look at the Pixie again, and then at Julia, 'Serious?'

Julia looked as though she was fading out of com, but her image stayed, a bit like a ghost.

'I think it might be serious, yes, but I'm not...'

She was gone.

'Julia?' Sam looked at the Pixie, who shook her head.

'Do you think it's Anna? She's pulled shit like this before,' Sam asked.

The Pixie shrugged, 'No idea, could be. But it looks like we're on our own. Is there any food back there?'

Sam scanned the cage, 'Uh, that might be something, I'd have thought there's more out front.'

'Hang on, what's that?' and she was pointing to a smashed set of boxes in front of her on the right.

'I think that's old-fashioned cereal, you know, like breakfast stuff. I wouldn't call it food.'

'Is there milk or something in the fridge?'

They both turned to look at the fridge which was in the corner, up against what was left of the partition wall just before the cage. It wasn't in great shape and was on the left hand side of the shop. The Pixie looked at it and then at Sam.

'Pix, don't.'

'Worth it.'

The Pixie came out from behind the gun and scanned the opening of the shop onto the street.

'Julia would be useful right about now.'

'This is stupid.'

She crouched down and edged forward to the front of the cage and got ready to make a spring for the fridge. She was just rising when there was a huge burst of gunfire and an explosion. She immediately threw herself to the ground behind the cases that covered Sam. Sam dragged her over and the gunfire grew in intensity. Then Sam frowned. She edged her head up above the level of the cases and then back down.

'It's not at us.'

'What?'

'The firing's not at us. I think the unit might be trying to break out from behind the cops. I bet they know they've got another group coming.'

'Or no one's coming.'

'Yeah, just as likely, I guess.'

'Who's gonna win?'

'Depends on how many cops there are.'

A couple more explosions and then silence. One or two more shots and then nothing. They look at each other.

'If it's my colleagues they'll be heading this way, so I guess…'

The Pixie's com went off and she jumped. Sam then also jumped and pulled up a grenade she had beside her. The Pixie held out her hand, 'Sorry, my com.'

'Who? Beijing?'

'They would just com, I think it's that… Person who's trying to kill us.'

The Pixie answered, 'Yes?'

Kevin appeared and seemed to look around. Sam couldn't see him, or hear.

'I like what you've done with the place, much brighter.' He remarked.

'You going to surrender?'

'Yeah, that's likely.' He answered.

'Listen, either come in with your hands or your guns up, otherwise, go to hell.'

'Anna wants to talk.'

'I want a unicorn for my next birthday.'

'It doesn't have to end badly you know, just listen to her and you can still die with your boots on in ten minutes.'

She looked at him coldly and then at Sam who was trying to work out what the chat was about and which way it would go. Looking at Kevin the Pixie tilted her head at Sam, 'She let her go?'

'It could be negotiated.'

'What happened out there?'

'Her friends tried to get rid of our friends, they didn't.'

'Ok, you both step inside to that first set of shelves. If I see anyone other than you two, this place comes down on all of us.'

'Fair enough. Shelves? Is that what they are?'

'Why doesn't Anna just com?'

Kevin smiled at that, 'She doesn't like your friend, not her, the ghost.'

The Pixie nodded, 'Good.' Kevin disappeared from the com and the Pixie turned to Sam.

'They want to talk. They're coming in.'

'Why not just com?'

'Julia has Anna nervous, that was Kevin. They'll come in as far as the shelves over there.'

'Are they the shelves?'

'Yeah, look, I've said if I see anyone else I'll bring the building down. So, if I shout, you dive for the tunnel and I'll set off one of those grenades.'

'As I have the grenades, I'll do that bit and you dive for the tunnel, I'll be right behind you.'

They made eye contact and then the Pixie grinned, 'You mean you want me to clear the path in the tunnel while you take your time behind me?'

'That's it.'

They turned to the front as a noise alerted them to Anna and Kevin's arrival. They picked their way through the debris, Anna leaning occasionally on her stick. The Pixie stood and Sam joined her, a primed grenade behind her. Anna stopped. She didn't look around.

'Here's the deal. I don't particularly want either of you dead. I don't need either of you alive but you're more useful to me if you are. Kevin suggested to you I think that I could let one of you go.'

The Pixie agreed, 'Yeah.' and Sam gave her a sharp look. Anna shook her head.

'Not happening.'

'Then good luck with whatever you're going to say next, 'cause it's in the same boat.' The Pixie smiled as she said it.

'Hear me out. What the people behind me want is that AI. She's of no use to you and she… Look, she's just a bit of code, certainly not worth dying for. I don't even have to kill Milo to get her. But I do need to have Milo, and you guys are going to be the easiest way to persuade him to come.'

'Yeah, I guess he would do that for us. Why do you think we're less than him?'

She smiled, 'This isn't your fight, it isn't even his. The folk behind me have deep pockets. They've bought Kevin here, he's evidence that they keep their word even when people fuck up.'

'He does that alright, but China 12 can give us the kind of life we'd like, and we'd be respectable.'

Anna laughed, 'Money can buy you "respectable". I think Kevin's counting on it. Why get yourselves stuck in the middle of this? Milo and I know each other, we're friends, you saw that, you don't know him at all. Kevin does and he was happy to stab him in the back, so how good a person can he be?'

'Kevin?'

'Milo.'

As she spoke, the Pixie noticed that Anna had turned so that the hand nearest her sidearm was shielded by her body. Trained as she was, she could see the muscles in her upper arm flex to take hold of the weapon. As she moved, she spoke.

'The truth is Milo is a pretty ordinary old guy, outside of his time and not worth…'

And everything went to hell as gunfire exploded, three loud shots. Sam lunged for the Pixie and then tilted back for the tunnel, but missed. Catching her weaker side against the trap, they twisted away and landed awkwardly between two sets of cases. Sam lifted her hand above her to grab one of the cases, it was covered in blood.

45

What Just Happened?

Rachel was concentrating on readouts from four sources. She looked up as Rahul walked in, her eyes showing her confused state.

'Julia isn't relaying via Beijing. That's right isn't it?'

'Yes, the lag would be too great, I mean, not awful, it's just…'

'No, that's not it, the readouts from her are as though she was, I don't know, she's not talking with New York or something?' She shrugged.

Rahul dragged up the feed onto his system and looked, his expression mirrored Rachel's.

'What's happened?'

'Nothing that I know of.'

'She's told you nothing?'

'Nope.'

'And the Pixie hasn't said anything?'

'Not to me, or to us as far as I can make out.'

Rahul gave her a long look, his concerns about his fellow members of China 12 rising as she watched, and she was doing nothing to lower it.

'Should we try to raise them?' he asked.

'What if they're in the middle of something?'

'Like?'

'Like trying not to be killed.'

'Right, good point. Has anyone else seen this?'

'It's only just begun to do that.'

'What do you think?'

'It looks like Julia's back with Milo, but Milo's feed is not showing up much more activity than before.'

'But more?' He examined the feed from Milo, flicking up through the diagrams and graphs which were updating every half second.

239

He turned back to Rachel, 'It looks different to me.'

'It is, I said, but not very much. It might indicate he's recovering or that his system is beginning to fail. If the monitoring of his more general system woke up we could tell, but not on this.'

'But Julia looks like she's back with him, she'll know.'

'She might, if we could get hold of her.'

'You tried?'

'I tried.'

He went back to go through the sets of numbers again.

'Her numbers look ok, very stable, would that be the case if he was dying?'

'Good question.' She went through the numbers herself and her head nodded slowly up and down. 'It does look hopeful.'

Rahul called on his com, 'Cathy, could you come join us?'

She appeared in Holo and was walking, 'Sure, on the way. What's up?'

'Could you take a look at the read outs from our four colleagues, please?' asked Rachel.

She called them up as she was walking and after a few moments she frowned, Rahul smiled in recognition.

'You got to Julia's?'

She stopped walking, 'No… I… the Pixie's readouts are odd.'

The others quickly looked at those and then each other, Rahul shook his head.

'What is going on over there?'

Cathy said, 'Right, I see what you mean about Julia, is she back with Milo?'

Rachel answered, 'That's just it, we were trying to work out what the change in her relaying meant. She's clearly stopped speaking with New York, hasn't she?'

'I'd say she has,' and she looked up and started to walk again smiling, 'clearly.'

'Should we risk trying to contact New York?' Rahul asked.

Cathy thought, 'If they haven't started screaming about what's happened to Julia, I'd say they have other, possibly bigger issues. So, no.'

'Unless they can't com out. We might still com in though.' Rahul worried.

'I think the idea that Julia should talk with them on her own was a good one. Given the situation and without knowing how it's changed, I'd worry about doing the wrong thing.'

Rachel agreed, 'The ops are funny about contact, it's either too much or not enough. Without knowing how to judge what's going on, I wouldn't open a com. If they can, and they need to, they'll com.'

'Alright. Where were we on the gang, had anyone managed to get them to answer?'

Rachel shook her head, 'No. We keep asking but they just close down the line.'

Cathy walked in and closed the Holo com, 'If there's a firefight going on in their place the gang would be loath to trust an outside com. Easiest way to get spiked, according to the Pixie.'

Rahul shook his head, 'So there's nothing we can do, again.'

'That's about it. Now, Milo might be a different matter. What do you think about sending something to Julia now she's just with him, and seeing if we can wake his general system?' Cathy asked.

Rachel moved her attention back to Julia and Milo and nodded her head. She looked across at Rahul.

'What do you think?'

'Any chance we can kill him?'

'Do you want to?' Cathy asked, surprised.

'No. That's why I'm asking, I especially don't want to kill him.' He shook his head. 'We can send a ping to Julia, no one will notice, I think, it will be smaller than the signal we're already getting from Milo's system. That way, if the cause of the reduced feed is that it's being choked, we should still get her to acknowledge it.' Rahul sent the ping. The other two looked at him, 'What?'

'Anything?' Cathy asked.

'It might take a minute, maybe even two. It depends on what's happened.'

They waited. Cathy looked around then at Rahul.

'You were called into the Xin meet?'

He nodded.

'And?'

'And, someone from the Chinese Government wanted us to hand over Julia.'

Rachel and Cathy both looked surprised, and together, 'What?'

Rahul went on, 'And, if we can't do it, just her on her own, Milo too.'

The women looked at each other, Cathy was first, 'What did Xin say?'

'She told them to take a hike of course.'

'And they went?'

'So far.'

'Meaning?' Rachel now anxious.

'Meaning they seemed to give her an ultimatum. I don't know what they'll do after that. They were offering help.'

'Help?'

'Yeah, for Milo in Kenya.'

Cathy was getting more animated, 'Why did they think he needed help?'

'He does.' Rahul answer simply.

'Yes, but how did they know?'

Rahul shrugged, 'Someone must have told them.'

Rachel looked shocked, 'Do you mean someone here?'

'Where else?'

Cathy coloured, 'Like a spy? Couldn't they have been monitoring our system?'

'No, they can't monitor our system and they didn't. It's being checked, but after a quick look I can tell you they didn't find out that way.'

'Who then?' Cathy was slowly becoming more upset, 'And why?'

'Who? There is one person who might have. Why? That is an altogether different question.'

Rachel bit her lip and and looked at her, 'Liu.'

Rahul agreed and looked at Cathy, who sighed, 'Are you sure?'

'No, and I don't want to go round shouting about it until someone has spoken with her, but she is the only one who might really have had that kind of contact with the Chinese Government. On the other hand, we don't know why or that she even knows what she has done.'

Cathy looked thoughtful, 'She's young, it might have been something she mentioned in passing or even just trying to do the right thing.'

Rahul pulled a face, 'The oddest thing about it was that they had very strange ideas about what Julia was. Xin was surprised by that.'

Rachel was puzzled, 'Like what?'

'Not sure, something like an uber AI, a weapon maybe. Erasto and Hoshika are checking back through what we know.'

'A weapon? I mean we know she's not your normal AI, but I don't get the sense that she's dangerous. She can do all that, being everywhere at once, but that's hardly very particular.'

Rahul smiled, 'It's always the quiet ones.'

Cathy poked him, 'How long's it been? With your ping?'

Rahul frowned, 'Too lo… Oh, there. She's still with us anyway. And she sent a ping, so she's active. Oh, and that's different.'

'Can we talk to her?'

'I'm pretty sure not really.'

'Why?' Rachel asked.

'I'd say that, if she could have, she'd have opened a com rather than pinging back. It sort of says she's either very taken up, or she's constrained in some other way.'

'That just says she can't or won't talk with us, but could we send her a message?'

'Oh, I see what you mean now. I guess we could try. If we kept it simple it would stand the best chance of getting through. Also, no point in sending something that needs an answer.'

'Yes. What do we want her to do?' Cathy asked.

'Tell us what's going on and how Milo is?' Rachel answered, which drew a look from both the others. She sighed, 'I know, but it's what we want from her right now.'

'Is it?' Rahul wondered, 'We really want her to do something, like get back the general monitoring of Milo's system. One ping for yes, two for no.'

'Oh God, we're in one of those young teen adventure books, "one knock for yes…" '

Rahul gave her an annoyed look, 'It's a practical answer to limited com capacity. How am I going to ask this… Simply?'

'How about asking, "get monitor gen online" and then your com system, one ping; and all that.' Rachel suggested.

'Ok, we might have more freedom in the information we send her, it's just she may not be able to answer back.'

Rachel gave him a long look but said nothing.

'I'm just saying.'

'Send it and we'll see what she can do.' Cathy intervened, before it came to blows.

Rahul sent the message and they waited. It wasn't too long this time before the ping came back, a single ping.

'Good,' Rahul looked at Rachel and smiled, 'she seems to think it's possible, I wonder if,'

The data started to stream in and Rachel stiffened, scrolling down the columns of numbers. Rahul looked across at Cathy, trying to get a sense of whether the news was good or bad, but she was similarly engaged in scanning the streams of data and looking worried and saying nothing.

46

In the Dark

Alright, she could hear too.

When? She'd suddenly found herself back with, she didn't know where at first, but it turned out to be Milo, it had taken a few moments to work it out. Having cameras and the bleed from the Pixie's implant meant she had visual data to work with, once back here it had been the darkness that had allowed her to work it out. She had reached for the first node to access but found nothing. She rooted round and decided that she must have been pulled back by Milo because she could feel herself breathe, slowly. She checked Milo's system, it was down. She was still locked out of his physical systems, and then one word hit her, "doh"! She could feel the breathing; it was dark because he was down, not her.

Working out which senses she could access had taken a while, but it came down to certain tactile senses, and then the ping had come in. It took another moment to work that out. She realised that something was blocking the outbound signal. She had to make a work-around for that. The ping allowed her to work back to an access point and she connected via the low orbit com satellite, one of a net around the world that enabled high capacity transmission. It was about ten years old.

She noticed, as the response went back when she connected, that it had a very tiny payload. So she sent a ping of her own, bigger. She hoped that whoever had pinged her in Beijing - she could see that much though not who - would see the increase in size.

Then the message asking for Milo's monitors. Why were they off? They were on now. What kind of shape was he in? She imagined the dead were worse off. Hold on, she had data on this, and she went back to his post-op readouts. That was the official low point he was at death's door then. She could do something about this, and that was when she realised she could hear. If she gave Milo a jolt now, he would alert whoever she was hearing to his consciousness. Ok, let's not do that. She could access pretty much everything in here, so voice recognition?

One person she knew straight away, Jones. What's he doing here? Are we still in Lamu? The others, one was the inspector and the last came up as someone she'd not met - a Dr Kimani. If the inspector is here, we're probably in Lamu. Alright, what did they want? Was Milo in a hospital? No electronic data. Kimani was speaking.

'Mr Jones, before we get down to business, would you like something to drink after your long journey?'

'That would be very welcome, thanks. I have to say I'm surprised to find you here, inspector.'

'As am I, Mr Jones.'

She could hear glass and then drinking, then Kimani again, 'The inspector is a guest, a most honoured guest.'

'I see,' this must be Jones again, 'Should we discuss the nature of our business here Dr. Kimani?'

'Don't worry about the inspector, he will not interfere, either now or later. Is this not correct inspector.'

'Probably.'

Jones seemed satisfied from the noise he made, 'Alright then, let's get down to brass tacks. He is still alive, but not in great condition my guy says. What happened?'

Julia could imagine the shrug and the hands held out, 'We are not sure. He collapsed, that is all we know.'

The inspector cleared his throat, 'Actually that is not all.'

'Oh?' Jones.

'The inspector cannot know anything, Mr Jones, he has not seen Milo for at least thirty-six hours until just before you arrived.'

'But I do.'

'Alrighty, let's hear it?'

'I have had several reports of Milo being out of sorts for at least a day and half. It is probably how he fell into Kimani's clutches in the first place.'

'What's wrong with him?'

'I understand he has technology inside him, and we believe it might have gone wrong.'

Julia thought she had gone deaf again, as silence followed you could cut with a knife. Finally, Jones cleared his throat and spoke at the same time as Kimani, she was now pretty sure he wasn't a doctor of medicine and this wasn't a hospital.

'I'm telling you the inspector knows...'

'Doctor Kimani, you should have alerted us to this problem. Even if the inspector is wrong...'

'I'm not - I heard it from Beijing.'

A short silence, then Jones again, 'Right or wrong, it would have been better for us to know and I could have had an expert with me, rather than a paramedic.'

'The first I knew about there being a problem with Milo was when he collapsed a short while ago. I still do not believe there is a problem with him or his system.'

'Where is the nearest operating theatre?' Jones asked.

The inspector spoke, 'There is one down the coast in Mombasa.'

'Actually, we have one across the way near Malindi. Yes Inspector, we even have access to medicine you know nothing about.'

Julia checked Milo's vitals, he didn't appear to have something wrong with him an operating theatre would fix. She had to wake him. She'd already considered the inadvisability of waking him with a jolt, but did she have any other options? Then she had a strange feeling, a sort of tingling.

She knew the inspector had an implant and she had already encountered Jones'. But they were being blocked by whatever suppression system was being used wherever they were. But someone had an active implant and it was really good. Kimani. The technology was different from the sorts she was used to, but she was a quick study.

His system was open. Why? Because it was totally independent from the normal systems, she guessed. She acquired the com protocols and she suddenly found she could not only com to, wow, lots... everywhere. Could she contact base? Probably, but that could wait, she needed a medical database and that was what Kimani was contacting right now. While she searched, she analysed. Their system shut off every time it was not being used, it had an immediate call up, the main processor was quick too. She saw the data she needed and the AI controlling it. By contrast with the rest of the system and the hardware in particular, this was a bit more, ad hoc. Frankenstein's creation came to mind. The AI was a bit old fashioned too.

What did it know that she could use? Her appetite was voracious. There. She thought she could nudge Milo awake. She checked his vitals, which hadn't made a lot of sense a few minutes ago, but now… Ok, Milo, he looks like he's gone into shock. The idea of giving him a slap did occur but that could wait, she had to time this right. Two stages, one for "the talk" the second to act. She was still admiring Kimani's implant when he shut it off and everything went quiet. That was a shock. But she smiled to herself, too late.

She could wake the system up herself now, but thought that had better wait until she was ready. Waking it up would probably alert anyone who could connect to it. Right Milo, oh, turned out the slap would have been bad, medics take all the fun away. Gently, memories that could stimulate and reassure. She wondered what omelettes smelt like, and then decided that cooking fat would do. What music did he like? Daisy Griffiths eh? She wondered who Daisy was when she was at home, but that was another one for the future. It was beginning to get a response. A minute or two later and his consciousness had risen to the point where, 'Hello?'

'Hi.' Julia knew she shouldn't shock him or go too fast.

'Julia?'

'You know me?'

'Of course I do, I'd say we're joined at the hip, if we weren't joined at the head.'

'You really do remember me.'

'Ok, now you're beginning to make me worry. Why's it dark?'

'You collapsed, you're still unconscious.'

'I'm a pretty good conversationalist for a bloke who's unconscious. Am I talking to myself?'

'No, I woke you up a bit, so we could talk.'

'Why did I collapse? Am I dying?'

248

'No. I don't think so at least, you don't want to die do you?'

'I don't think so. Is there any reason I should?'

'No. Don't think so. Look, you had a bit of a breakdown.'

'What? A breakdown? When? Why? What kind of a breakdown?'

'Yes, all of those.'

'Har di har.'

'I got you drunk.'

'Oh yes, I sort of remember that. Is Anna here?'

'…No… I think she's in New York.'

'You think?'

'Sorry, she is in New York, trying to kill the Pixie and Sam.'

'What?'

'Sorry. Let's not go into that just yet, I'm not supposed to shock you.'

'Way to go.'

'I was speaking with Dr O Shea, she thought my making you drunk triggered a sort of dissociative disorder episode, I'm not really sure that's a thing, strictly speaking.'

'Look at me, making medical history.'

'Yes. Anyway, it was sort of in that area, she thought, you know multiple personalities. She thought you had been spooked by my being there the next morning and had shut me out of your systems.'

'I can do that?'

'It seems you can.'

'Cool.'

'Not cool. But it does answer who's in control. You are, in case you missed that.'

'Nope didn't miss it, not at all.'

'Anyway, you went a bit doolally and then fell into the hands of a Dr. Kimani, reading your mem files, which are a bit patchy I have to say. He is from "the Dogs of Lamu", which manages to sound a bit pretentious and down at heel at the same time.'

'I see what you mean.'

'By the sound of things, they have sold you to Mr Jones, remember him?'

'Should I?'

'New York, he was the guy in the suit trying to get into my systems, very rude.'

'Why has he bought me? I mean he could just hire us.'

'As I understand it, he wants to get to me.'

'How?'

'How indeed? It might be they want to remove your head and somehow extract my programming.'

'This is beginning to sound uncomfortable.'

'And impractical.'

'Oh good, that's a consolation. We should think of trying to get out don't ya think?'

'That is sort of the plan, but I have to wake you up first.'

'Contact the inspector, his partner's a doctor.'

'As she's a pathologist, I'm pretty sure she'll get to you in the end.'

'Great. You're a consolation in hard times, you are.'

'Also, the inspector has been captured too, he's in the same room we are.'

'Can you talk to him?'

'If things are going to move, I think you should be awake first.'

'Great, then wake me up.'

'Not so simple.'

'Why?'

'You won't be able to just get up, I think. And you may not remember this conversation, and that's important because I don't want anyone to know you're awake until we're ready to make a move. I'm guessing we'll get one chance. It'd be a shame to wake you up only to have them shoot you dead.'

'Only one way to find out.'

47

The Gentle Questioning

'What we really want to know is how much you told him about Julia? Did you go into detail about how she works. Indeed how much do you know about that?'

Rahul was speaking with Liu in a secure Holo. It was early in the morning and she was a little spooked. She had been very forthcoming about her conversation with her father and very surprised that the government had been so rude in their enquiries and offers of help. She also said she thought her father would be too. They were now trying to find out what it was the authorities knew, or thought they knew, about Julia and if what they knew came from Liu in the first place. Rahul had reassured her, after the initial enquiry, that she was not to blame for what had happened and that as far as they knew Milo and Julia were in no more danger now than they were before.

'I only know what Julia has told me, which I think is about the same as she's told you.'

'Is there anything else that you might have surmised, given your training for the pixies here in China?'

'I don't understand what you are asking?'

'Have you speculated, on your own, or say with your dad, about what Julia is or what she might be, or could do?'

Liu thought about it and very slowly shook her head from side to side.

'I'm still not sure what you mean by "What she might do"? Do you mean beyond what she does? Because what she does is amazing. She is the full package, you know. I don't think there's anything like her out there.'

'Did you say that to your father?'

'Which?'

'There's nothing like her.'

'Um, no, I don't think so. I was more worried about Milo. I kind of think if he's alive she can take care of herself, but we hadn't heard from him and then she went. I thought the only reason for that could be if he was dying, or maybe dead.'

'I see,'

'Is he dead?'

'No, he's not, and she isn't either.'

'You've spoken?'

'No, but we have commed and we have Milo's monitoring stats back up, so we know his condition.'

'Is he going to be alright?'

Rahul grimaced slightly, 'We don't know, we think so. A little while ago his numbers changed. We are hoping that indicates he is coming out of his coma.'

'Coma?'

'Yes, sorry, he was in a coma, Dr Lopez-Real thought it was shock, but he's showing encouraging signs now.'

'Did I help? Or make things worse?'

'We don't think you made things worse anyway. What we really need to know is where the idea of Julia being, I don't know, a weapon maybe, came from?'

'When I was looking at the chatter about the price on Milo's head it was all about something special in him. I thought that was Julia.'

'I'm sure he'd be very happy that you think the only thing that could be special in him was Julia. Though I think she'd agree.'

'I didn't mean that I…'

'Sorry Liu, I know, I think you're right, it was Julia. What is so special that they'd want to buy him?'

Liu obviously concurred with his questioning. 'And why does the government think she might be a weapon? They must think she's pretty important if they're prepared to be so forward.' She asked.

'The game you played in, that was run by an AI, wasn't it?'

'Yeah, but not like Julia. It could learn and respond to what you were doing but its parameters were much narrower. Julia's parameters change, she's like a real person and she draws from everywhere.'

'So do you think they could copy her?'

'I'm sure they could copy her base code, of course. But from what she told me about herself, she's now in Milo and so she's growing in a way not really thought of by her designer.'

'Like a person but much, much faster.'

'And everywhere, if she wants to be.'

'Not quite, she has limitations. She seems to be confined by how much power her base program can draw from its home station.'

'Yes, I guess it seems she is. That could be partly tied to the way she's embedded in him, his cells. When he went down, she struggled.'

'How much of this did you share with your father?'

She smiled, partly fondly, part amused, 'You didn't meet my father, did you?'

'I have not had that honour.'

'I wouldn't describe him as technophobic exactly, but his relationship with tech is… I'd say arm's length.'

'Are you saying he wouldn't have understood?'

'No, he would grasp it alright, but he'd quickly have moved the subject on to what it was that was the matter and what I would like him to do. He wants to be interested but unless it contributes to a show for the theatre, his attention drifts.'

'You sound like a teacher from my childhood talking to my parents about history lessons.'

She smiled.

'Right then, not your father. You're not in touch with any of your old buddies from the Game, are you?'

'I'd like to be, but they won't talk to me now, I have a bad reputation.' Liu looked down and went quiet. Rahul realised it was not just the opportunity she'd lost when they'd rescued her from the Chinese pixies.

'I'm sorry.' But she'd already recovered and was looking up, looking forward.

'Don't be. If that hadn't happened I'd never have met Julia, and she's much more fun.'

There was something in the way she said it that made Rahul sit up.

'Liu, what did you and Julia get up to? I mean, if it was so much fun.'

'We watched the Pixie and Sam and we worked out ways to be able to help them. And we looked through your security protocols in China 12.'

He thought there was just the glimmer of something.

'When you did that, did you come across any breaches?'

'I wouldn't say "breaches" exactly. There were one or two people trying to work their way through the system and we blocked them, although they wouldn't have worked out they'd been blocked exactly. Your security was very good, we just made it a little better.'

'The people trying to break in, could they have been government?'

'One was commercial, up until a few days ago we were still watching them. They were just going round in circles. We had talked about making a fake world for them to break into, Julia suggested it. She said we could see exactly what they wanted and where they were from. I was writing sets of algorithms that they could "discover" and...'

'The other one?'

She thought about them for a moment, 'They went round a couple of times, then I think they might have worked out they had been at that level before even though it looked different. I had a go at working out where they were from, they seemed pretty methodical, I...'

'Could they have been government, Chinese government?'

More slowly, 'Yes, I guess they could, after I tried to tag them, they stopped. I'm pretty sure they didn't know about me.'

'Could they have broken in and you not known about it?'

'Me? Yes, they could. Julia, no chance.'

'Why not?'

'What do you know about the China 12 security?' She asked with a slightly condescending air.

'I designed it.'

Now Liu was staring at him in shock. Watching her, Rahul decided that she was replaying the conversation in her head. In Holo, there couldn't really be any other evidence of her embarrassment.

She looked at her feet suddenly.

'I'm sorry.'

'Doesn't matter.'

'I've been very rude, I…'

'Liu, it doesn't matter. This does. We have to work out what the government think they know and from that, what they might do.'

She straightened up.

'Right.'

'Now, why could they not have gotten round Julia?'

'You have a layered system. Like I was saying, when you break a layer the system reroutes you back to another layer. It's clever because you get moved about to different looking systems, but in reality you're not getting anywhere. That's why the methodical hacker was beginning to make progress. Julia added to your system, you had lots of layers, she added maybe ten times more and she gets real-time reports from each layer. She can tell if the hacker is the same person…'

'You mean working from the same place?'

'No, based on their keyboard performance she can judge who exactly they are. She knows if they are right-handed, how they are sitting in their seats, whether they are a male or female.'

'How? There's no physical interaction with keyboards anymore?'

'No, but there are virtual versions of old physical tech and we create images for ourselves to work through, all of that betrays biases which she can work from. It shows her age, gender, and cultural history. She showed me using data from my playing the Game, it was fun.'

'Fun for you two… If even a hint of what she was doing got out. I can see why any government would like to get hold of her capabilities. One last thing, did she provide a secure connection for you too?'

Liu smiled, 'First thing.'

He sat back and took a while to run through where he'd reached. He got lost in his own thoughts and took longer than he'd realised. When he looked up, Liu was still waiting anxiously for a pronouncement on her guilt or innocence and he jumped.

'I'm sorry, Liu none of this is your fault. If anyone is to blame, it's me, I never looked. You said she could be anywhere and know anything?'

'Of course. Any database is available to her and as soon as it is, she's an expert in whatever it is about. If an AI she comes across has learned something, she's learned it too. I think she could have Milo playing the guitar and dancing if they wanted.'

'You don't think she could make him?'

'We talked a bit about that, but I think Milo shutting her out says no, she can't.'

Rahul nodded his head slowly, processing the information he'd heard.

Liu was still anxious, 'Was that alright? Do you know what's happened?'

Rahul smiled tightly, 'Know? Not exactly, but I'm guessing they've put together parts of what they could, and the chatter has done the rest. I have to go, talk with the rest. Thank you - you've been of great help.'

Liu brightened, 'That's ok, I hope I didn't do anything bad.'

'No, nothing bad. Liu, stay in touch from now on. I don't know what people are going to do, but I suspect they'll use whatever they can, to get to Julia. We have to look after each other. Right, got to go.'

He smiled at her and broke the com.

48

The Frog and the Scorpion

The sound of the explosion was still being damped by her system. Sam hoped that it was working well enough to still filter sounds important for her survival through the white noise of the explosion aftermath. The Pixie's voice reassured her.

'What the hell?'

Sam raised her head just above the level of the cases round them. The dust was settling and one or two bits of masonry were still falling to the ground. Her system looked for a heat signature and she could make out a body on the ground a few metres from the cage. She thought that was where Anna had been standing and she looked for Kevin. No sign of another body. Had they been hit from behind? She wondered if her former friends had broken out of the police cordon. If that were the case then where were they? They should really be piling in from their position now they'd made a breakthrough, but there was silence.

'Can you see anything?' The Pixie, lying underneath her, asked.

Sam turned quickly to look at her. 'Mostly, just a lot of dust. There is someone on the ground, I think it's Anna.'

'Alive, dead?'

'Not sure, I'm guessing her suit will keep her alive, but something hit her.'

'Any guesses what?'

Sam had been scanning what was left of the shop and the street outside, now much more visible than earlier. She shook her head.

'I'm not seeing anything.'

'Where's Kevin?'

Sam shouted, 'Anyone alive?'

Kevin's voice came back. 'Clearly you are, what about your friend?'

The Pixie answered, 'I'm fine, don't think much of yours.'

'There's gratitude.'

Sam and the Pixie looked at each other and Sam hissed, 'He shot her in the back.'

The Pixie shouted, 'You did that?'

'I'm responsible for the first three shots, I think your friend did the rest. Nearly took my head off.'

'Missed then.' Sam shouted. 'What now?'

'Well, I'm not going to hang round till she wakes up, am I?'

'She's not dead then?'

'I suppose she might be, but I'm not going to find out.'

'Was this your plan all along?'

'Hardly.'

'What the hell then?'

'She kept going on and on about stabbing people in the back.'

There was a brief silence and then Sam spoke.

'You don't think she had a sort of point?'

'What I think is that I made the best decision available to me at the time. Now though, she might have a point.'

'So no one paid you to do it.'

'No, no one paid me. In fact, it cost me quite a bit of money, Jo'd be proud.'

'Who's Jo?'

'Never mind.'

The Pixie lifted up and whispered, 'The one he shot in Brazil.'

'Oh.'

'What?'

'Nothing. So you off now? What are the police doing?'

'Yeah, I'm going. The cops are staring a lot and holding position. I don't think they'll trouble you for a while, but I wouldn't leave this way if I were you.'

'Right. Thanks. Any more advice?'

Kevin, in a much more subdued tone, 'Yeah, don't turn your back on me.'

Silence followed for a minute then two. The Pixie leaned up again.

'Is he gone?'

'Hey Kevin?' Nothing.

'We could really use Julia about now.' Sam observed.

'Oh, I have coms again, hang on.'

A couple of seconds and Rachel appeared. 'You're alive?'

The Pixie answered, 'We are, I think.'

'Good. Are you both uninjured?' The Pixie looked at Sam, and Sam looked puzzled. 'Sorry.' And she opened the com to her.

'Hi, Doc.'

'Hi, I was asking if you were both uninjured?'

'I think I'm ok, but I saw blood earlier.'

'Yeah, I think you cut my hand when you threw me on the ground. I mean I like it rough...'

The doc coughed. The Pixie smiled broadly.

'So no one badly injured?'

'No.' Sam answered.

'Right. We managed to get through to the gang. How are things fixed? I'm gathering that if you're talking to me, you have a little time.'

'We do, don't know how much, I'd say not long. What did the gang have to say?'

'They'll take you out, we agreed a price.'

'Just like that?'

'They were very accommodating, it was a high price.'

'But a money price?'

'Yes, money. From the sound of it, you've demolished their place.'

The Pixie looked around and agreed, 'Ok, we did change things about a bit.'

'What's happened to the unit trying to kill Sam?' asked Rachel.

'They're being entertained by a group of cops at the moment. But Kevin has gone, so I don't...'

'Kevin?'

'Kevin and Anna, didn't Julia tell you? She disappeared, everything ok there?'

'Here, everything is fine. Something is up with Milo and Julia, we don't know what. Don't worry about that for now. Where is Anna?'

'Kevin shot her.'

259

'What? I thought they were together?'

'They were, they're not.'

'Right, Jonas' boys, the gang, said you have the tunnel wired, do they have that right?'

'-Ish.'

'Ok then, you have to undo that.'

'And they won't kill us?' The Pixie asked.

'We think they're on the up and up. They've been paid a lump of money but they'll get a lot more when you're out and free.'

'That's good. When it's clear, what do we do?' Sam this time.

'I've told them you're going to clear it and they're waiting.'

Sam and the Pixie looked at one another and the Pixie shrugged, 'Not like we have many options.' Sam nodded and pushed herself up.

'Keep watching out front and watch Anna, if she's not dead she won't be out long. This will take about a minute.'

She got to work and the Pixie pushed herself up on one elbow. The street was clear, there didn't seem to be any movement yet, it was likely they were scoping the shop to see if anyone was coming out. Anna had begun to breathe in an obvious way, meaning she was breathing more deeply. She was coming round.

'We don't have long, Sam.'

Without looking up, 'The cops?'

'Anna.'

'Shit, ok, one left.'

Anna's arm moved as she prepared to get up or at least clear her face from the rubble round her. Outside, the Pixie could see some movement as well.

'Things beginning to happen on the street.'

'I'm clear.'

'Let's go.'

Sam swung her legs over the edge of the trap, reaching for the far edge she dropped and swung into the void. The Pixie took a quick look back and could see Anna's dust covered face lifting from the ground. Not pretty.

'Jesus.' She thought about shooting her, then thought better of it given the number of trigger happy people around them. There was a sound from below and she dived for the trap, following Sam who had disappeared. She dropped into the darkness.

As she hit the ground she rolled backward and up onto her feet, weapon in hand. Sam was beside her and her night vision adjusted to the dark. In front were about five people, heavily armed, none smiling. One of them had the butt of a cigar in her mouth, which she shifted from one side to the other without touching it with her hands. She jerked her head up.

'You the two from China 12?'

'Yeah.' Sam answered.

'You fucked up our place.'

'Yeah, sorry about that.'

'There were kids upstairs and a Doc.'

'Anyone hurt?'

'No.'

'I'm glad.'

'You don't know how much. Anyone alive up there?'

'Yeah, she's just getting up and I think the cops or the maybe the clantech unit is coming in.'

She jerked her head and the men behind her parted, 'I'll need your weapons.' And she held out her hands.

'Fuck off.' The Pixie said steadily.

'You want to die here?' the woman asked.

Without taking her eyes off the woman, 'Looks as good a place as any. Is this where you planned to go out?' The Pixie answered with a question of her own.

The woman snorted and shook her head, 'They said you were prickly. Let's go then. We won't have much time and the cops are already pissed at us. At us! Shit.' and she spat.

The men divided and two went ahead, the other two waited until the three women had passed and they fell in behind. They didn't run but they moved at a steady clip, Sam and the Pixie alert for whatever might be about to happen to them. The Pixie took a quick look back behind to see if Anna had followed, but there was no sign of her. They covered the seventy odd metres quickly and a well-lit stairway appeared in front. Another man and woman, again heavily armed, waited.

'We've got 'em.'

The two at the bottom of the stairs reacted not at all as the party approached but watched with unkind eyes. The hairs on the back of the Pixie's neck prickled as they passed and began to climb the stairs. She turned to Sam.

'What time of day is it?'

'No idea.'

'It's one AM, past my bedtime.' The woman informed them.

At the top of the stairs they stepped into a long corridor lined with doors at regular intervals. Every door was open and people crowded in each, silently watching as they passed. They looked like families, from the youngest babe in arms to old folk, weathered and broken by a harsh life. Sam and the Pixie tried hard not to stare back.

They were moving in single file and passing through the gauntlet of silent faces without stopping. Ahead, the door swung open onto another street. They spilled out and down a long set of steps; clean, without having been well looked after. Two vehicles were waiting by the kerb with doors open, waiting for them, along with more armed people of varying ages. They were guided into the back of the second car, a large people carrier. Looking down the street as they did, Sam could see more vehicles stationed at regular intervals. She turned to the woman, still standing in the street, who was clearly in charge, 'Are they petrol-engined?'

'Eh?'

'You know, non-electric.'

'Yeah, I guess, they mostly don't work anyhow. What did you call them?'

'Petrol-engined.'

'I know what an engine is.'

'Petrol, they run on it, it's fuel.'

'Like juice?'

'Yeah, is that what you call it?'

'It's what the old guys call it, I call it broken.'

She walked round to the passenger side of the carrier and checked a young woman in the front, looking over Sam and the Pixie as she did. The rear-door of the vehicle was pushed closed by a man outside it and a kid, not more than twelve, jumped into the driver seat and pushed the start switch, the engine hummed into life. The young woman in the front passenger seat twisted round to stare at them over the backrest. The Pixie watched, fascinated, she nudged Sam and pointed at the lad, 'He's driving us, just like the simulations.'

The older woman leaned in and looked at them, 'You never seen that?'

They shook their heads and she grunted. 'Say, where you from?'

'Me?' the Pixie asked and the woman just stared back.

'Europe.'

'You're the first person I ever met from there.' She leaned over the front seat and held out her hand, the Pixie took it. They shook. The woman looked down at the Pixie's hand as she let go.

'You got an honest handshake anyway. Tamsin.'

'Pixie.' And the woman looked at the joined hands and turned to Sam. Again, holding out her hand, she asked, 'You are?'

Sam took the hand, 'Sam.'

This time the woman pulled her forward as she shook almost banging her into the seat. Sam grunted in pain, the Pixie bristled. The woman smiled and let go the hand. She leaned back.

'You'll pass.'

Sam and the Pixie looked at each other and then back at Tamsin.

'They told us your names, gave us some images but they can be faked. They said that one of you had a bit of trouble on account of that woman back there. I had to be sure it was true.'

'If it wasn't?'

She gestured at the passenger in the front seat and the young woman leaned back showing a heavy calibre weapon pointed at them. Tamsin smiled at the girl, who put the gun onto the floor in front of her. Sam and the Pixie sat back and Sam slid her hand into her friend's again.

Tamsin stalked round to the back of the carrier and gestured over one of the men standing beside the truck behind them.

'Don't let anything get between you and us. If the lead pulls in to the right, it's trouble, to the left and we're stopping as normal.'

'You think there's going to be trouble?'

'I think when you pick up folk like these, there's always trouble. But we're not going to get screwed over,' she looked back in the direction of the ruined store, 'they've cost us a small fortune and a lot of time, if we don't get our money those nice girls don't have a nice future.'

He gave her the thumbs up and she lifted her chin to his companions all armed to the teeth. They piled into the truck and a kid fired up the lights. The man looked at Tamsin in case there was anything else, she looked back at him, her eyes steady in spite of the glare from the lights.

'Stay awake.'

He nodded and she turned then climbed into the carrier.

The small convoy headed into the dark.

49

Sailboats and Fishermen

It was the third night they had waited. It wasn't hard work, the nights were warm, a little humid and they chatted. The second night Mariana brought a bottle of wine and a little food, pointing out that they had to eat and one of them had to be a grown up about it. Joanna laughed but she drank and ate it all the same. They watched the robot boats come and go, carrying merchandise most people around there, either couldn't afford or couldn't afford. It was Mariana suggested blowing some of them up, which drew a surprised look from Joanna. The night traffic had become familiar enough that they spotted the change straight away.

Joanna became rigid and she pointed out the small craft coming round the head of land to the north, as it made its way discreetly along the new coastline. It was moving under sail. They watched and Joanna observed that they would have to tack a few more times if they were to pull into the small, largely abandoned jetty just their side of the freight port. Then she pointed to a group who had appeared on the land side.

The group was moving slowly and too carefully to be honest she said. They watched for a few minutes and then Joanna nudged her.

'Let's go little one, we have people to meet.'

Mariana had learned to trust and grabbed the bottle and what was left of the food, stuffing them into her pack. Joanna was ready and waiting by the time she rose to her feet. They went downhill, through the scrub and the small tree line. They kept the boat and the group in sight all the time, which meant a detour or two so one or other weren't covered by trees. At one point Mariana, struggling to get round one tree when an easier course was to cut through the copse, asked, 'How've we become so dishonest Jo?'

'Sorry?'

'We're moving so slowly we must be the worst of the bunch.'

That earned her a punch on the shoulder, which made her smile. They were much lower now and could see the group was made up of five men. By now, keeping the boat in view was becoming hard. Joanna compromised, losing the boat for a bit but keeping the group in sight. Then as the group slowed, she pulled Mariana slightly higher and behind a hedge of bushes. They had gotten close enough now that they could hear the laboured breathing of some of the men and the odd swear word when they tripped or caught their shins on a stone or branch. Mariana crouched and waited. Joanna, bent behind the bush but still looking over it, watched. Mariana could feel the tense concentration. The men split up. One of them headed round to Joanna's and Mariana's right while the others went down in the direction of the jetty. Joanna turned and smiled, a sure sign of trouble.

'I'm just going to see what this guy is up to. Do not move. That's important, ok?'

Mariana nodded. If there were times she was the grown up, in times like these she felt like the child. She reached up and touched Joanna's arm, 'What if it isn't Sergeant Meier?'

'A sailing boat, this time of night, just here, where I expected her to be? It's the sergeant.'

Mariana nodded again and Joanna headed across in the direction the man had taken. Mariana watched and worried. Joanna moved silently. If Mariana hadn't known she was there, she wouldn't have spotted her. It helped that the port was lit up like daylight, throwing everything else into pitch darkness. By contrast with Joanna, the man was easy to follow. He walked easily and openly and noisily, making the obvious and not unreasonable presumption that he was alone. He had something slung over his left shoulder. After a minute or two he stopped and looked around himself before disappearing down and, Mariana presumed, sitting. She still hadn't worked out what he was doing.

Turning back to the rest of the group, she saw that they had nearly reached the dock. She thought that they must have been visible from the boat, so whatever else this was, it wasn't an ambush. They reached the jetty while the boat was on its final tack and the main sail had been hauled down. Mariana could see two figures on the deck, one hauling in the sail, the other at the tiller, neither seemed anxious. The men at the jetty split up again, two waited at the end of the jetty and the other two made their way slowly down toward the end. Now that she was a bit closer and looking at it, Mariana noticed how makeshift the whole affair was, she had thought it falling apart from age and lack of attention, in fact it had never been much more than it was.

The person on the deck flung a line out towards the jetty and one of the men caught it, tying off on a large, rough cut, tree trunk. The boat slipped into dock being dragged to a halt with a lurch as the rope bit. The man who had tied off stuffed his hands in his pockets and a moment later a small flame sprang up in front of his face and died.

The two on the boat moved around a bit more, securing both ends to the jetty. Neither went below. They stopped, and the one on the foredeck went back to the tiller, while the person who had brought the boat in walked past and jumped down onto the jetty.

Mariana couldn't see the faces clearly, but from the wild hair and the short stature she knew this was indeed Sergeant Meier, late of Rio. The man with the cigarette and she were talking and evidently disagreeing. Meier was shaking her head and she turned away. The man roared.

'Don't turn your back on me.'

The men at the end of the jetty took a step forward and the man with the smoker moved nearer as well. Meier turned back, and Mariana thought she smiled, and held out her hands in placation but she moved no nearer the man. Mariana stole a quick glance back at the person she now assumed was Marcus. He was just sitting there. She couldn't see if he was armed but the men on the jetty with the smoker all now had weapons on show, at least the ones at the beginning of the jetty had guns.

Meier said something to the smoker and he must have given some kind of instruction because the man beside him moved off a few feet. Mariana had seen Meier in action only once and that had come upon her unexpectedly. She didn't think Meier would be unprepared for anything this evening and she thought maybe the men were making a mistake. When Mariana turned back she could see that Meier was again shaking her head and this time it was her that shouted.

'No fucking way, a deal is a deal.'

Then something odd happened. The smoker turned toward the hill. Mariana at first thought she had been spotted and dived down. She peeked out very circumspectly and saw the smoker waving the hand with the cigarette up and down. Whatever it was about, Meier saw it too and ran for the boat. Mariana heard the dull crack and for the second time in her recent life, she heard a silenced weapon being discharged. She looked for Meier and saw her fall. Did she fall? No. The smoker turned back, looking up the jetty.

Mariana could see one prone body with the other man bending over him. He stood and with a second crack he fell. The third goon, it seemed, was also armed and he began to fire up the hill, he got off a single shot before going down. Marcus was now standing and like the smoker, looking up the hill. Meier must have shouted at him because Marcus disappeared below and she climbed off the boat again. The smoker was staring up the hill, or at least that was what Mariana imagined as his face was in total darkness. She saw the cigarette fall and thought he was giving up but he whirled round and faced Meier, who just stood with her hands on her hips. His right arm was rising and he had a gun as well, but a forth dull crack and he tipped sideways into the water.

Meier slowly turned and looked up the hill. Mariana tried to slow her heart down again from the hammering it was still doing. She had realised what might be happening after the third man went down and now looked anxiously over to her right.

Joanna rose into the evening, something in her right hand, and began to make her way back in Mariana's direction. Mariana closed her eyes and breathed a silent prayer from her childhood. She reached into the bag and pulled out the bottle of wine and took a big mouthful. She was putting it away when Joanna appeared at the edge of the hedge.

'Well done soldier. First and most important thing in a skirmish, follow orders. That way you don't get killed by your own side. Shall we go?'

'I knew it was you, you know.'

'Oh yeah?' they began to make their way down to the boat. 'Who else?'

'True, I could have been the other guy and just a lousy shot.'

'Yeah, I guess.'

'I hope Marcus has some food, that kind of thing always makes me hungry.'

A sound to their left and Mariana leapt into the air. Joanna laughed quietly.

'It's a raccoon, there are a couple of them out for a snack about thirty metres to the left there.'

'I forget you can see in the dark, it must be really useful.'

'Yeah, not sure it was worth the seven years in the army, but the kit is pretty good.'

They reached the end of the jetty and Mariana kept Joanna between her and the two bodies at the point where it began. As they walked toward the boat, they could see Marcus easing the body of the dead man into the water as Meier walked toward them a big smile on her face.

'Thought that might have been you sir, fine shooting if I may say so.'

'You may. Bit sloppy not to be better prepared, don't you think sergeant?'

'Marcus was waiting for me to get clear, he has a 50mm beside the tiller, pretty good with it too.'

'Noisy.'

She shrugged, 'All's well and all that stuff. Want to eat?'

'Reading my mind again, Sergeant.'

50

Party Crashers

They say prevarication is caused by wanting perfection and fearing failure. Julia had been hesitating about waking Milo for about twenty minutes, maybe a bit more. Jones, spooked by the condition he'd found Milo in, had opted to wait for "his guy" to come down from Mombasa before Milo was moved. The trip would take the man a little over two hours and he was on his way.

Julia was worried if she woke Milo and it was discovered it would trigger an early move to Malindi. On the other hand, waiting made Milo's waking spontaneously more likely as she had nudged him into a higher state of awareness already. Added to that, Kimani's dislike of waiting had led him to get hold of a local doctor who was prepared to try to wake Milo as soon as he could. Jones was resisting for the moment.

Kimani had used his implanted connection to the com network a few times which allowed Julia to become more familiar with its workings. She was now more confident that she could use the system without alerting anyone. Milo thought she should try make a connection to the inspector. Julia wanted to send a message back to China 12, as she had already managed a rough system with them and wanted to get a message to the inspector's wife. They both worried that they would only get one chance.

'Look, if we don't try something we may lose the chance of doing anything at all.' Milo, "shouted" would be the wrong word, but that's what he did. 'We can make the inspector aware of what's happening and then you wake me up. We'll be as ready as we can be to go with whatever we can do.'

'If I can get China 12 to get Dr Abebe ready to act, she can organise people to help us on the outside, if we get out.'

'If.'

'Ha ha, very classical scholar of you. Getting out is no good if we then get shot getting away.'

'Alright, I don't care anymore, pick one, do it and we can either die in here or out there and one of us can say "I told you so" as we die.'

Julia thought she had now learned people in unconscious states could shout and sulk and neither was very helpful. She tossed a coin.

'Oh, how did you do that?' Milo asked.

Julia, having caught the penny, looked at him, 'Can't you toss a coin?'

'Yes.' He answered, 'But not in my head.'

'I'm pretty sure if I can, you can.'

'Which is it?'

'I said, both.'

'Heads or tails.'

'The coin…' she looked, 'Heads.'

'So?'

'So you get to wake up, after I talk to the inspector.'

'You picked my one?'

'The thought of your dying words was the clincher.'

'When are you going to…?'

'*Hello?*' the inspector's voice cut into the question, '*Who is this?*'

'*Hi, Inspector, I am Julia,. It's important that no one knows we are talking, so continue just as you are for the moment.*'

'*Alright… Julia. Um, who are you? Where are you for that matter?*'

'*This is a bit complicated, but the AI, Kimani and Jones want from Milo, that's me.*'

'*Very impressive. So Milo is alright, are you just pretending to be unconscious?*'

'*This isn't Milo and no, he isn't awake yet. I've got him into a unconscious but not comatose state so he and I could talk, but we're not sure what will happen next.*'

'*Kimani has his doctor here and Jones is waiting for his man.*'

'*I know about the arrangements in the room, I'm talking about Milo. When I wake him, he may not remember our conversation and he may not know to keep quiet.*'

'*I see. Why will he not remember?*'

271

'*Because this experience is a bit like a dream to him, he might remember everything.*'

'*But that's not a guarantee.*'

'*Right.*'

'*Alright, I'll try to manoeuvre myself over to near where Milo is lying. Once I'm settled, you wake him. I can try to cover it up if he's too obvious.*'

'*We can't see, so you'll have to let us know.*'

'*You can't see? Of course you can't. Can you keep the com open? How are you doing this anyway, I can't make contact with my people, there's something blocking me.*'

'*I'm using Kimani's network, they are very confident that, because it can't be detected, it can't be used by anyone but them.*'

'*But you can see it?*'

'*Kimani showed me the way. This com will be open as long as you want it to be.*'

'*Ok, I'm going to move.*'

The room they were in was in stark contrast to the one that had earlier played host to Milo. An upper-floor room, since the rise in sea levels most living areas were on the higher floors, it had all of the appearance of colonial gentility. The decor of the room reflected Kimani's particular life and his position between two worlds. Little in the room was untouched by tech, nothing in the room appeared to be.

Milo was stretched on a delicately carved couch covered in silk cushions and cooled by an Indian punkah which drifted lazily over him. Kimani and Jones were standing on the verandah, looking out over the lightening sky as though watching would speed the journey from Mombassa. The young officer Maini, kneeling and praying in front of a chair by a small window. By the door, two men lounged and chatted. Through the window the sound of Salat, the call to prayer, drifted thinly and was ignored by all but young Maini.

The inspector was sitting by a small table in a corner along from the door and diagonally across from the couch. On the table were three empty glasses. The inspector composed himself and re-emptied his empty glass, carefully examining it before putting it back on the table. He looked across the room at Milo and waited. After about a minute he stood, as though his curiosity had been caught by Milo and he walked over in that direction. The men by the door were immediately alert and stood, the conversation forgotten. He ignored them and walked slowly across to Milo and touched his forehead.

The movement caught Kimani's attention on the verandah and he turned to watch. The inspector, ignoring everyone else, ran his fingers down Milo's shoulder and lifted his hand, sliding his own into Milo's as he sat down. He settled himself as though watching an elderly sick relative. Kimani watched for a short while and then, with a quick look at the men by the door, he turned back to the vigil over the sea.

The inspector relaxed.

'Alright, I'm sitting beside Milo. I have his hand in mine, so I should be able to mask any movement with that.'

'Great, I'll start to try to bring him awake. The big danger is if he starts to speak when he wakes up.'

'Can't you tell him not to?'

'I can try, but sometimes he doesn't listen.'

The inspector stole a look round the room. The men by the door had relaxed again, his position and actions were all too familiar to them and they believed they knew what they were looking at. Kimani and Jones were still looking out to sea, although they seemed to have changed the direction in which they were looking. Young Maini was just finishing and sitting back on his feet, perhaps thinking about his younger sister, who he had mentioned was unwell.

Looking back at Milo, the inspector wondered what he should be looking for. Would the eyes flicker or would the man suddenly sit up? He tried to prepare to take some kind of masking action. As it turned out, the first indication the inspector had was Milo's hand warming up.

'Hello? Milo, are you awake?'

'He is close, I'm trying to tell him to be still.'

'Good God, I feel like hell.' Milo was awake. The inspector smiled

involuntarily and shifted in his place.

'*Why does he feel so bad?*' the inspector asked.

'*Hangover.*' Julia answered, '*He's been mucked about by several different chemicals. I tried to get his anti-intoxication system working, but Kimani's drugs were engineered with that in mind, so I've adjusted things. It didn't really kick in until he was awake. He'll feel better in a few minutes.*'

'*Good. When you feel alright, we can work out what to do next. I'm going to try get Maini's attention, when he's finished his prayers.*'

The inspector looked up again away from Milo and was about to turn to look at his young officer, but he noticed that Kimani and Jones were now at what he was sure was the wrong end of the verandah. They were straining to see something coming from the direction of Manda Island and that couldn't be the man from Mombasa. Kimani turned sharply and glared in the inspector's direction.

'Have you done this?'

The inspector felt his heart rate rise and his grip on Milo's hand tightened. He ran through what exactly Kimani could have seen and he went with, 'What are you talking about?'

Kimani pointed off the verandah out to sea. The inspector frowned.

'*Something's happening. Do nothing until I tell you.*'

He began to stand and the men at the door took a menacing step toward him, Maini, in turn, stood. Kimani made an impatient gesture at the men and they relaxed. Now standing, the inspector walked slowly out onto the verandah and looked in the direction of Kimani's finger.

Out in that direction the inspector could see several small, fast motor launches heading their way. More menacingly, in the air there were four helicopters. These were large robot-driven troop carriers they alone would be able to take control of a small forti-fied town. Around them buzzed swarms of smaller flying drones, autonomous, seek and kill bots which would take out any ariel or ground resistance. All this firepower meant the town might be well armed, it would still fall. Whoever it was, they anticipated trouble and were ready for it. Whatever they wanted, they were serious about getting it.

'Who is that? They're coming from Manda, are they Somali?'

Kimani frowned and looked again at the fast approaching force, 'No, not Somali. If they were, I'd have had some warning in any case. You are saying you know nothing about this?'

Still looking, the inspector shook his head slowly from side to side.

'Not me. They're not ours.'

Jones, who hadn't stopped watching the advance suddenly whipped round to look at Milo.

'They're Chinese. He did it.'

Now they all looked at Milo's immobile body. Jones turned to Kimani, 'Lift your com block.'

'Why?'

'We need answers, now.'

Kimani gestured with his head and the inspector commed with his base. Julia took advantage of the distraction and the open com on her usual network, to send a full message to Beijing including an update about the apparent Chinese intervention, with a query about whether China 12 was behind it. She sent the result to the inspector straight away.

'*China 12 know nothing about it.*'

'*Right, thank you.*'

The inspector turned to Kimani and Jones, 'The intervention is being done by the Chinese government with the permission of the Kenyan authorities.'

Kimani turned to look at Milo.

'Is he awake? Is that what's happened?'

'I don't know if he's awake but I've been told that he had nothing to do with this and neither has his group.'

Jones stepped forward, 'But they are in Beijing?'

'As I understand it, they are completely independent of the government. It is a point about which they have been very exercised in the past.'

'People frequently get exercised about things when they are trying to cover them up. Didn't Shakespeare say that?' Jones pointed out.

'Not as elegantly.' The inspector observed.

'We have to move, unless you want to meet these people?' Kimani said. 'Anyone?'

'Not me.' Said Jones. The inspector shook his head. Kimani began to walk over to where Milo lay, and then jerked to a halt and reached for his head.

'Dr Kimani, let me introduce myself. I am Julia Church.'

51

The Diplomatic Spat

When you're a guest, it is sometimes difficult to know when you should point out that your host is being rude. China 12 believed they had reached that point, or some of them did. All of those not actively monitoring the situations of their operatives were in the room glaring, either at Xin or at the floor. She seemed distinctly uncomfortable and very defensive. Xin was standing, having been using the display systems to illustrate the advantages and problems associated with their situation and the position as they knew it in Kenya. She was answering questions.

'No, we cannot. They have taken this action in another jurisdiction and it is one we can't control nor really object to.' Xin insisted.

'They are interfering with an ongoing criminal investigation.' Hoshika answered.

'That cannot be denied, I'm afraid.' Xi Liang shook his head sadly.

'They can counter that the investigation is stalled by our operative's collapse and they are there to assist.'

'They have no standing. Not in Kenya, not under international law, not even here in China can the army suddenly be deployed in this way.' Koura Aripe offered loudly and very indignantly.

'If they can do that it offers them licence to invade any country in which we are working. How many jobs will we get if we accept this?'

That brought Xin up short, and she agreed none too happily. She considered for a moment or two.

'Alright, I accept there is a problem and they have overstepped the mark. The question is what should we do about it? What can we do about it?'

'That's two questions.' Hoshika noted and Xin rolled her eyes, 'What? It is, and they both need answers.'

Xin looked round the room at everyone present and then at the

Holo presences.

'Would anyone like to offer a perspective on the, twin, problems in front of us?'

Wolfgang Schult coughed, 'I think we should move.'

Xin looked round the faces again, 'Where?'

'Canada?' Schult again.

'Wouldn't we be seen as a US pawn, or in the grip of the American corporate system.' Xi Liang suggested.

'In Canada?'

'Many people think they are simply the same. In any event, certainly not independent.'

'Africa?' Rahul asked. 'We'd have good net connection and wouldn't be seen as anything but neutral.'

'Yes, but the physical connections to the rest of the world would be considerably less efficient, less swift. Where in Africa would also be a problem, it's a big place.' Cathy said, 'and there are those who see growing African power as a threat just as large as the US or China.'

'Or India.' Erasto said.

'Part of the problem is that we sometimes don't see just how lucky we've been here. Our arrangement and facilities are pretty unique.' Xin pointed out.

'Yes, but like everything, it works until it doesn't.' Rachel observed.

'And do we know that it doesn't?' Xi Liang asked.

Xin sighed, 'That is well asked, but this conversation is about what we do if it becomes clear, as seems likely at the moment, that it has stopped working.'

'Why do we need a base at all?' Hoshika asked, 'We can collaborate easily across the network, yes the compound is a real benefit, but not a vital one. It is, in fact, a luxury.'

This produced murmurs of agreement from round the room.

'It still begs the question, where we should relocate to? If any one of us is in a compromised or compromising situation, all of us are weakened. Protecting us while we are on a job is an issue even here.' Xin said.

Again murmurs of agreement.

'I think we should give ourselves a day at least to think about this. I will ask the Chinese authorities what is going on and try to ascertain their intentions. Tomorrow we will know more and be in a better position to make a decision.'

'Kicking the can down the road.' Cathy O Shea said.

Xin held out her hands, 'Yes, but on a deadline and putting ourselves in the best position to make a good decision.'

Cathy and Xin held each other's eyes for a second, before Xin looked away and said, 'Anyone else have anything to offer?'

There was silence.

'Right, we can meet at the same time tomorrow and make a decision about this.'

The Holos disappeared and those in the room dispersed, as she was going through the door, 'Dr O Shea, a word if you have time.' Xin asked.

'Sure.' She stepped out of the way of the few still to leave and waited. When the room was empty, Xin crossed over to her desk and sat, pushing her chair away from it. Cathy said nothing and took a seat. Xin, as ever, thought about what she was going to say.

'I hope Dr O Shea, your words were not intended to convey the thought that I was being less than loyal to the organisation.'

Cathy paused before she replied, making sure she got it equally right.

'They weren't. If there was any edge in what I said it was related to our situation.'

Xin and Cathy exchanged another long look before Xin looked away and took a moment.

'My position here is difficult, Xi Liang and I are vulnerable in a way others here are not. When others say "Canada" or "Africa", there have been times in the last thirty years when such ideas would have been feasible for us. I thought, until this very morning, we were living through such a time. I do not know what has changed. I care about this organisation, about these people, as people do about their blood.'

'I understand Xin, I have always believed that was true.'

'Do you still?'

'Of course. Like lots of people faced with uncertainty, I want a decision. It's childish I know, but it was what was behind my comment, not a criticism of you. I think we both do know what has changed though.' She looked at Xin and turned her head to one side.

'Julia.' Xin answered and Cathy nodded.

'Julia.'

'What is she that people have become so excited about her?'

Cathy shook her head, 'What have they heard, would be a better question. It could be just as she said, controlling the planet is a pretty big prize.'

'But there seems more to it, it's a frenzy. Military intervention is a pretty extreme step.'

Cathy stood, lifted her shoulders and held out her hands in the universal sign for, "I have no idea but these people are crazy, what do you expect from…" Xin sighed. Cathy turned to leave.

'No. Please wait Dr O Shea, I am going to call now.'

Cathy came back and sat down again.

Xin gathered her thoughts about the situation for many minutes. She had to make the call and she dreaded it. She was angry and couldn't show it. She would have to ask questions to which she knew the answers she would get, and she did not believe those answers. She got a final encouraging smile from Cathy.

She called the Ministry for the Interior and was put straight through to the minister; so they were waiting for her.

'Zhang Xin.'

'Minister.'

'Perhaps you are calling about the state of my health?'

'Always a concern, minister.'

He smiled and bowed his head, 'I am very well thank you.'

'Very pleased to hear it.'

'Is there anything else? As you can imagine, I am very busy at the moment.'

'Almost nothing minister, just wondering if you knew, perhaps, about the current state of health of our operative, Milo Talbot?'

He looked as though the question was one on a subject about which he had known something long ago. He gave it due consideration.

'I am surprised you ask me. He is, after all, your man, no?'

Xin said nothing, but waited. The minister smiled and said nothing. The moment stretched for a minute, then two, and then the com was cut. Xin stood, Cathy stood.

Xin turned to Cathy, 'Something has happened. I'm bringing forward our decision, our meeting, to this evening.'

52

Hot Crossed Coms

Heath was awakened by the com, fumbling for the glass of water beside his bed and getting the system to answer the call as he did so. Jones shimmered into view and the lights came up at the same time. Heath blinked as his body was suffused with a drug to get him up to full speed.

'News?'

'Yes and no, sir.'

'That means nothing. Do you have him or not?'

'I am moving with him at the moment but the Chinese government seems to have intervened.'

'China 12. Should have seen that.'

'They say not.'

'"They say".'

'The local police chief, who we also have with us, is inclined to believe them. It appears to be an operation for them to get the AI for themselves.'

Heath sat up fully now and finished the water. He pushed himself off the bed and slipped his feet into a worn pair of slippers. Jones wasn't quite sure where to look, as his boss was naked.

'So, they want her for themselves, I smell faction fighting. What time is it there?'

'9.23 am.'

'9.23? Couldn't be, I mean Beijing, not there! It must be 14.23. I'll get someone on it. Have they taken you in?'

'No sir, we've left the island. It seems these people are a lot more sophisticated than we knew, we're traveling up the coast in a powered dhow. It's a small compartment below deck. They had a water-tight tunnel that allowed us to get out.'

'Small? I hope you're not too claustrophobic.'

'No sir, we won't be in it long in any case. I should warn you though that something is happening between Dr Kimani and Milo.'

'So Milo's awake?'

'Yes sir, he was awakened by the AI just after the Chinese appeared, we left a little thereafter.'

'No matter, whatever China 12 offer, double it, no, triple it. You understand what this AI means, don't you? Not just for the Corporation, but for us, for you and me, the board?'

'I remember sir. The sticking point could be the AI itself, I'm not sure how much she cares about money.'

'Whatever it takes Jones, I told you before, everyone has a price. I understand you can be a persuasive fellow, it's what's in your resume after all.'

'Yes sir. I'll do my best.'

'And Jones?'

'Sir?'

'It's Duncan.'

'Yes… Duncan.'

Jones went dark and Heath stared at the empty spot the Holo had seemed to occupy and chewed his lip. That was not good news. If the Chinese were after her themselves, it might mean that the news was out about what she really was and what she could do. Leaks… he hoped that boat didn't have as many as Americorp seemed to. Jones had to succeed, there were no two ways about it.

Insurance? He had to give Elder Thomas a heads up. He didn't like them but they were useful when everything else went down. He was sure Thomas had control of the wilder elements now.

He put the call through and waited.

'Duncan? This is late.'

'I know, Thomas, and I'm sorry for it. I have some news but it's not good.'

'Oh?'

'Jones may have some difficulty acquiring the AI. It's not certain at the moment but I've just spoken with him and his voice sounded as though he was less than confident.'

'That is bad.'

'Do you have anyone who can do the necessary violence if it's needed?'

Thomas's eyebrows shot up and he shook his head, 'No Duncan, we'd talked about that before we had Jones's system dispose of my last major hawk. I'd have to trawl further down the ranks and that can be uncertain. What's happened to that woman? Donovan's girl?'

'Anna?' She's capable but she's gotten herself injured again. I think she put herself into the field too soon, made a characteristic misjudgement.'

'Women.'

'Don't be too harsh Thomas, it's because of her finding Church's notes that we worked out what this thing could do in the first place.'

'True, but you can't rely on them, Duncan.'

'We won't get into this now. You can't help and I have bigger problems.'

'Sorry Duncan.'

'Sleep sound Thomas.'

He cut the connection, tried to drink from the empty glass beside the bed and then glared at it accusingly. He calculated, it was 14.40-ish in China, so he had a bit of time, but not much. He composed a terse message to an underling on the China desk, reviewed it and then sent. He climbed back into the bed and the lights faded out. His system was flooded with a drug that undid the work of the earlier one and he drifted off.

Jones was sitting squished up in a corner of the space watching Kimani. Two long benches lined each curved side and a set of steps led to a flat sealed door at the top. Kimani was sitting beside Milo at the far end and they were apparently conversing, though quietly enough that it couldn't be heard. Jones had to work out a strategy. He had to work out what it might be that an AI wanted most. Was he perhaps all wrong, was the issue Milo? He didn't think it changed much, as he didn't think Milo was any more interested in money than the AI would be. From his file, a good mushroom and cheese omelette might be more of a bribe.

He didn't think he'd get more than one shot but who should he talk to, Milo or the AI? Which one was Kimani talking to? And, could he talk with just one of them? What were the Chinese doing? Heath could find out, but he's old and frankly a bit slow, he might believe anything the Chinese would tell him. If they were after the AI themselves, how did they find out? So far as he knew, Anna had lifted the only copy of the notes from Ms. Church's apartment in London before Milo had arrived and it had taken them some time to decrypt them, did they have a mole? That would be a complication. One thing at a time, what does an AI want?

Kimani, Milo and Julia were certainly in a conversation and it was one that surprised each of them in turn. Milo still believed the Somali groups to the north, who had their operations disrupted by China 12, to be pirates. He was being presented again with a reasoned argument for why they believed they had a right to the contents of the ships they raided. Kimani showed them evidence of the careful choices the Somalis had made about which ships to intercept. International law was based on the mutual respect of countries for one another and their rights and traditions. Kimani showed how the peoples, he and others represented, were being cast aside as irrelevant to the economy that had emerged since the mid 2030s. These people were large majorities of their countries' populations. To the tech savvy and rich, to their own governments, they were invisible and what you don't see often doesn't exist. Kimani and his allies were intent first of all on being seen.

It was already clear that they had command of very considerable resources and that they were managing, in some cases just about, to piggyback on the economy of the rich. But there was also an independent, older economy growing alongside the more obvious one. He warned darkly of a day of reckoning in the not too distant future.

The conversation turned to Julia. Kimani had begun to be curious about why she was attractive to these large corporations. With the Chinese intervention, his curiosity had exploded into a full-blown need to know. In part, both Julia and Milo were just as baffled about what exactly it was that had produced this increasing desperation to control Julia. Julia herself had been running through her code and through everything she could get hold of relating to her creation, in an attempt to solve the mystery. So far, nothing obvious had jumped out as a compelling reason to commit so many resources to obtaining her. Kimani was distrustful.

'You must be able to tell.'

'But why? Not everyone can see what their skills and abilities are.' Milo asked.

'She is not everybody, she has been constructed and not emerged. She must know herself in ways we do not.'

'That is a point of view certainly, but I am also emerging. Since my joining Milo, and becoming part of his physical structure, I gain experience and knowledge in the same way you do. I am beginning to learn, above all, to know myself.'

'And?'

'And I can't see why they are making a fuss.'

'Are you looking at it from their perspective? What can you do, do you do, that they would want?'

'I am more efficient than the AIs they currently use and I'm more personal. But that's just a case of evolution, they will come up with something as efficient.'

'Then it can't be that. You said you deployed a "fail-safe" to prevent them controlling populations covertly.'

To Kimani, she appeared to think and look at Milo and then at the room.

To Milo she said, '*You know I am the fail-safe don't you?*'

He tried to look calm, and was, as though he was waiting for her reply to Kimani's question.

'*Not as such, I thought we deployed it when we brought two of the heads together. I thought it was in the heads.*'

'*We did, it was. It triggered a subroutine in my code that adjusts and essentially neutralises the web feed, but it's a dynamic operation. Part of my involuntary functions.*'

'*Is it that then? The thing they all want?*'

'*It could be, but it's a bit extreme and Elspeth thought they'd work a way round it eventually.*'

'You'd better answer Kimani, I'm not very good at this.'

'We did deploy it, but that can't be worth the effort they are putting in to get hold of me. They would surely start with finding a way round it?'

If Kimani suspected they were having a conversation without him, he wasn't showing it. The thought did pass between Julia and Milo that he might be thinking that anyway.

Kimani grinned, 'Of course, if we were to work it out and it proved very interesting, you are under our control at the moment.'

And that was when Kimani discovered how little he understood Julia. Suddenly, he found himself in darkness and looking only at her image. He could perceive everything she could do to his implanted system and to the network of which he was so proud and then, just as suddenly, he was back in the sealed compartment. He swayed and looked at Milo. Milo looked back at him, his features calm and utterly untouched by what had happened. Kimani blinked and rubbed his head and slowly he reached for the wall, shaking his head to clear it.

'Why didn't you do that earlier when I caught Milo first?' he asked.

'He was blocking me from doing anything.' She smiled.

'That was pretty impressive and very useful, why not that, as a reason to want you?'

'No more useful than a gun when it comes down to it. Desirable maybe, but worth sending an army after me?'

'Yes, extreme is the word.'

The ship slowed down and the engine noise became quieter, indicating they were coming to a destination soon. Kimani looked up and met Jones's eyes and Kimani realised his conversation with Milo had been watched throughout the voyage, though of course, Jones would have heard only one half of it. Kimani smiled.

'Not too seasick, Mr. Jones?'

'Not even a little Dr Kimani. A very smooth ride thank you.'

'Sorry for the intimate surroundings.'

'I'm not as badly off as some.' And he pointed to the inspector, who was stooped and truly squished in beside his young officer despite being in the centre of the compartment. Kimani's smile broadened.

'The height of inconvenience, no?'

Jones laughed. They lurched forward and the passengers, except for Kimani, had to grab for some support, as the ship came to a stop. Above them, a loud hiss sounded as the seals opened. The light poured in from the midday sun as the hatch slid back and a face appeared.

53

The Breaking of the China 12-1

Liu had been receiving reassurances from Rahul that her actions had been reasonable and the response of the government not her fault. Several times he'd had to say to her to dry her tears and she was at last calming down.

'Still, I'm sorry.'

Rahul wondered sometimes if they'd chosen correctly (he had chosen) when they had set the translation algorithm to "European English". Although each person could alter their own personal preferences, the general setting had been for English and he preferred European to international or North American. At one point he'd tried to allow for nuances of accent and grammatical bias within different languages, but it made comprehension less easy, so he had abandoned the effort. Moments like this though, where Liu's evident distress and her heartfelt apologies were being smoothed out in the translation, led Rahul to think it lacked a necessary emotional component. He thought it would be interesting to speak with Julia about it.

'You have nothing to apologise for, Liu. Neither you nor your father could have imagined the action of the government in this. It has taken us by surprise.'

'Thank you. Could you say sorry to Zhang Xin for me as well? I'll do everything I can to make up to you for it.'

'Don't worry Liu, and pay our respects to your father. Now think about something else.'

He smiled and the com ended. He sat back in his seat and wondered if someone so young could ever understand the cynical minds of older, political folk. Part of him hoped she never would and part hoped she would, really quickly.

Xin was calling them all back to the meeting room. Even though the compound was discreet it was more usual for meetings to take place in Holo, as that allowed people to carry on with what they were doing more easily. If, however, the point in discussion was sensitive, or would take above a certain length of time, the meeting rooms were used. In this instance it was the delicate nature of the discussion that would bring all of them into the shielded room.

By the time Rahul got there the rest of the group were seated and Xin was laying out for them the choices they had. He took his seat beside Cathy and behind Rachel. Across the room were Wolfgang and Erasto, always sitting together in things like this, and beside them Hoshika. Koura Aripe and Xi Liang farther along made up the total group in Beijing at that moment.

The atmosphere was tense. Xin had shared the record of her exchange with the minister earlier that day and people were alarmed about the apparent attitude of the government. There was particular concern for the Chinese nationals among them who were more vulnerable. The others had somewhere else to go and were free to leave whenever they wished, life could be more complex for the Chinese.

'Let me pose then the question that Wolfgang put in front of us, should we leave? If we do, where do we go?'

'I don't think we have much alternative. If our independence is compromised, we are no longer a trustworthy investigative group.' Xi Liang said, shaking his head.

A general murmur of agreement went up. Xin nodded her head.

'This view was where we were coming to this morning I believe. The more vexatious question is where do we go and when?'

'There aren't that many places we can go and still be the group we have become.' Cathy observed.

'Canada. I know I said it this morning, but the Canadian government is trusted and I think we can avoid the taint of US corruption.' Wolfgang put forward.

'No one is suggesting Europe?' Rachel asked.

'Europe has everything we would need but add most of the problems associated with the US, as well as their internal problems.' Aripe said and many heads agreed.

'Australia?' Cathy suggested, 'or New Zealand?'

'Identified with Europe and... let's face it, they're far away from everywhere.' Erasto said.

'That was one of the attractions, I thought.' Cathy said, to general smiles.

'We are running out of options.' Xin noted, 'I think we have to make a decision. The longer the government have to consider what to do, the more likely they are to decide we shouldn't leave at all.'

The first indication that something was happening was the alarms going off. That triggered a visual readout in each of their implants showing them that the compound had suffered multiple breaches. Several of the group stood at once, all turned to face Xin.

'I… What is going on? Can any of you make it out?'

Then, without warning, two Holos appeared in their visual systems, Liu and Julia. Liu noticed and held out her hand.

'You are under attack from military units of the Chinese Government, you have to get out now.'

Xin blinked in apparent shock and then frowned, 'I don't understand, they would never…'

'They have and are doing it, you have no time. There are escape routes in the compound, aren't there?' Julia said.

'Yes, but, if this is a military operation, what chance do we have? Should we not wait? They will free most of us after questioning.' Said Xin.

'From what I can read of the coms, they are not intent on talking. They seem to have come to the decision that getting control of Milo is all important and China 12 is expendable.'

'But why invade the compound?' Xi Liang asked.

'To get leverage over Milo and me.'

'It's true, I intercepted their com after Rahul left, you have to leave.' Liu said.

Julia turned to her, 'So do you and your father. I've got a car for you both coming to the theatre, get him and get out.' Liu looked stunned but then broke off her com.

Julia turned then to the room, 'The rest of you get out now. Get to the south west sector, the tunnel from the refectory to there is perfect, I'll have transport waiting for you, but you must hurry.'

'Can you tell us what's happening?'

'There are two units from the north… they are making contact with the perimeter wall now.' Julia said.

'We must leave right away!' Rahul said and the group began to move to the door which Xi Liang had opened. Xin was not moving. Julia posed the question silently.

'I will wait, I may be able to buy time for the others. Wait for me in the refectory.'

'I don't think they are going to be impressed with people who think they are in charge, they will just scoop you up.' Julia told her.

Xi Liang and Rachel stopped at the door, turned and waited.

'Go on, the refectory, wait there.' said Xin. She seemed as calm as ever even managing the ghost of a smile.

Xi Liang wasn't buying it, 'You must come too.' Xin shook her head and sat down.

'Go. This is where I should be. I have to try.'

They looked at each other and Xi Liang pulled Rachel out through the door.

The first six had hurried away and had already disappeared from sight, by the time Rachel and Xi Liang left the room. He was slow. They tried to follow directly but the wall ahead began to crack and the percussive bangs showed that someone was trying to break through. Rachel pulled Xi Liang down the first turn bringing them further away from the refectory. Several more short diversions and they had begun to jog. The building had become a confusing place of noise, the air filled with dust.

The main group of six were walking quickly along the corridor towards the refectory. Rahul having run ahead, reached the doorway and shoved the twin doors back into their place in the walls. He hurried through and opened the entrance to the tunnel then began pushing the tables and chairs aside. He looked up as Cathy came into the room and then beyond her into the corridor.

'Is Xin coming?'

'I haven't seen her, Rachel and Liang were with her. I think she was waiting for… whoever is in charge.'

Rahul shook his head, 'That won't do any good.'

Cathy held out her hands, 'We can't worry about that yet, I'm sure Julia will look after her.'

'What about Rachel and Liang?'

'I don't know if they stayed or followed us.'

The others were coming along. In spite of the still distant banging they didn't seem to feel the pressure Rahul felt or Julia indicated they should. Rahul looked anxiously up the corridor. Through the windows in the distance, troops could be seen running to cover doorways, taking up positions at corners and generally making a perimeter.

Cathy turned as Xi Liang and Rachel appeared at the end of the corridor alone and she stepped toward them. As one, the group, still not yet in the refectory, stopped and turned to see what Cathy was looking at. Rachel began to wave them on frantically, but suddenly there was a loud percussive bang. All heads ducked at the noise.

A section in the corridor wall, running along between the main group and the last two blew in. Rubble and dust flew everywhere and everyone covered their heads, several covering their ears. By the time Rahul looked up there were two dark, mottled uniformed, figures in the corridor, with weapons pointing at the people lying on the floor. Xi Liang and Rachel were getting to their feet and beginning to raise their hands in the air. The white dust in the air causing them to cough. The masked soldiers said nothing but opened fire.

54

The Breaking of the China 12-2

As the others had left, Xin sat in the meeting room, waiting. She had heard the blasts as the intervention force attacked the building and made a series of other incursions into the compound. Julia appeared.

'Will you get them out?' Xin asked.

'I think so, Liang isn't moving very quickly, but I'm sealing the passages behind him and Rachel.'

'They should wait in the refectory, can you keep them safe there?.'

'Once they're in there I can block the pursuit but keep the exit open.'

Xin smiled at Julia.

'You are useful.'

'Hold on…'

Rahul felt the shock run through his system, somewhere between ice cold water being poured down his back and hot flames being fired at his face, his stomach fell through the floor. He held out his hands and started to shout. Those in front of him not yet in the refectory scrambled to try to get through the door as the troops turned in their direction.

China 12 had given the group members more than a chance to work in ideal circumstances. For some, it had given them the chance to be who they wanted to be, to live as they wanted to live. Compassion for what was going to be lost was not part of the soldiers' instructions. Erasto would have been next to go down but Wolfgang, his longtime companion, his friend, a man he had given up much of his life for, dived in the way of the stream directed at his back and he went down instead. It did no good. Erasto turned, confused, and crouched to try to lift and drag Wolfgang to his feet, as though his friend had tripped and fallen while walking. He seemed not to understand what had happened. That his friend was dead.

The fashionable Koura Aripe, clothes now covered in dust and flecks of blood from the assassination of her companions, saw Erasto turn back and then what he was trying to do. She also grabbed Wolfgang's arm and turned toward Rahul for help. Even as Rahul took a step toward them, he saw them go down in a hail of bullets. Aripe's eyes open and stuck holding his as their life drained away. Rahul froze.

Almost in slow motion, he saw the soldiers lift their attention to him and watched the weapons rise as they prepared to kill him too, the hole in the wall behind them filling with more troops. The briefest of flashes crossed his mind that he didn't care about dying, so great was the pain and shock of having watched his friends being killed moments before.

Then suddenly it was the soldiers grabbing their heads and falling and his confusion increased. Hoshika dragged at his arm and Cathy threw herself at him. Unbidden by any one of them, the doors of the refectory snapped shut, a barrier between them and the troops.

It was like a trance being broken. Cathy hit his chest and pushed him backward. Hoshika's dragging on his arm turned him away from the door and toward the tunnel entrance. Rahul went with them and then was suddenly overwhelmed with the impulse, the desperate need, to run.

They crashed through the doorway into the tunnel and flung themselves along the smooth curving passage. The doors closed with a loud bang. They had travelled perhaps a hundred or a hundred and fifty metres when they began to slow and then to walk, chests heaving, breathing ragged. Hoshika stopped and held out her hands. Their eyes were filled with tears.

'Wait. Xin, I didn't see Xin, we have to go back.' She said.

The others stopped and Rahul looked at Cathy.

'Did you see her?'

'I don't think she came with Rachel and Xi Liang.'

'Why?'

'Try to stop this I guess, I don't know.' Answered Cathy.

Then they were all looking at Julia. In all of the chaos she looked so strangely calm, the holo projection having no emotional content. Her words, however, were filled with urgency.

'You have to go, now.'

'But Xin.' Said Rahul.

'Nothing you can do.'

'The others?' Hoshika asked.

'Gone.'

'Who? Rahul asked.

'Erasto, Wolfgang, Rachel, Liang, Aripe, all gone.'

'You're sure?' Cathy pressed.

'Sure, yes, I'm sorry, I was trying to seal off the corridors behind Liang and Rachel, but the general system is down, I'm fighting blind.'

'The soldiers falling, was that you?'

'Yes.'

'Why? Why are they doing this?' Cathy asked, now shock was lessening and anger swept in to take its place.

'This is my fault.' Rahul said suddenly.

Cathy turned and Hoshika looked shocked. 'Why?' Cathy asked.

'My security system, how did they get through it?'

Julia looked at him, "Rahul, this is not your fault. There was nothing you could have done and your system didn't fail.'

'But then who, and why? Asked Cathy again.

'I don't know. They're trying to get hold of Milo, I guess they think if they leave him no place to run it will be easier.'

'But he would have come back here.'

'No, he wouldn't. They knew that. They want to deprive him of allies. Now, you have to leave. I've stopped the people who intercepted you and some of the others, but there are more.'

'And Xin?' Rahul asked again.

She shook her head and they set off again.

Julia had just disappeared. Xin waited. Julia was a puzzle to her. Sometimes she could be everywhere at once it seemed, other times she could do only a limited number of things. Xin had tried to correlate the demands on Julia's system with what she was doing, but she couldn't make an accurate evaluation without having access to her data from within Milo. She wondered what was going on. Why was Julia taking so long? Then she was back in front of Xin and they stared at each other.

'What?' Xin asked.

'They're dead.'

Xin stood, 'Who?'

'Not all of them, most of them. They just shot them. Didn't ask. Rachel and Liang were surrendering, and they shot them.'

Then Julia was looking at Xin, almost looking through her.

'Why did you stay?'

'What are you asking?'

'Why did you stay behind?'

'I… wanted to buy them time, to escape. Why else?'

'Why else?'

'Are you saying that I knew?' asked Xin.

'Knew what?'

'They would be killed?'

'Not exactly. What did you know?'

'Nothing. Don't you question me, I'm First Speaker.'

'What did you know?'

'I knew nothing about any of this.'

'But you did, you spoke with the minister.'

'Dr O Shea was there too, she saw. The minister left.'

'You asked her to stay. The minister left, after an apparent silence.'

'Yes, it was… odd.'

'Very. But not if you were communicating without speaking.'

'She would have been able to detect that. The com was open. She's not a fool.'

'It struck her as odd when you asked her to stay, that hadn't happened before, and then to witness such a strange departure and now this. Everyone was gathered together, ready, except for you. It was something new, something she couldn't recognise…'

Xin backed away until she hit the wall.

'I was doing the right thing.'

The door crashed open and a special forces officer came in. In his right hand he was holding an old-fashioned pistol. Two more men came behind him, flanking the doors. He stopped and he swept the room, his eyes finally settled on Xin.

'The minister sends his regards, Zhang Xin.'

Xin stood away from the wall and bowed slightly.

'Thank you Colonel.'

'Is that everyone?'

'Is what everyone?'

'We intercepted groups of six and two, moving toward the dining room.'

'I think that would be all of my colleagues.'

The officer looked at her as though expecting more, she shook her head and held out her hands.

'Let me be explicit. I had reports from my men that there was no resistance. But I have just received a report saying that those men are all unconscious, maybe dead. This is your plan, is that everyone?'

Julia, unseen by the Colonel, glared at Xin and shook her head. Xin looked back and smiled, then she shrugged her shoulders. She turned to look at the colonel. Her attitude changed, her voice became harder.

'Colonel, you were given entry codes that should have allowed you to bypass the alarms here. If you had used them, all of my colleagues would have been gathered up in the same net. You were told to take them prisoner, not to kill them. If you're supposed to be following my plan, you failed. You've bungled this, just as the fool that launched the attack in Kenya bungled that.'

'The minister has given me complete authority here. He said the operation should be "clean".' As he spoke, the colonel raised the hand containing the pistol. Xin's hand was already at her neck, clutching a small black stone on a chain, she had worn it as long as Julia had known her. Julia realised in a rush she had seen one like it before. Looking at the Colonel, Xin's eyebrows rose and as he squeezed the trigger, Xin squeezed the stone. Xin watched as he and the men by the door collapsed.

'Your plan.' Julia stated.

'My plan.'

'The minister?'

'Seems to think he can build an empire on my dung heap. He discovered two minutes ago he can't. Factions.'

'Since when have…?'

'Have I been working for the Chinese government? Since always. We weren't dishonest in our dealings with the group or the world, but our aims were always to have, what do they say? "Skin in the game". Then your developer blundered into our arms. It was an opportunity, heaven sent. But…' and she held out her hands at the bodies by the door.

'Milo too?'

'Useful idiot. We found him put out to pasture by the western so-called powers. We took him, reconditioned him and put him out there.'

'Joanna and Kevin?'

'Same as Milo, a bit less stable.'

'Anna?'

'Very capable, a little accident prone.'

'But she works for you?'

Xin didn't answer but a small smile crossed her lips, Julia just stared back. Xin started to walk toward the door and stepped over the bodies of the soldiers as she got to them. She looked down and stopped, turned and looked at Julia.

'Your tricks won't work on me, we adapt.'

'Why the move against us?'

'We thought the Americans would get hold of you, double cross us, couldn't have that. Don't misunderstand, no one was supposed to die tonight, I'm sorry they did.'

'You seem crushed.'

'Collateral damage.'

'Why the frenzy?'

Xin gave a little laugh, 'How little you know yourself. Don't you see what you're doing for Milo? You've entirely changed his system. His entire physical system. He's an old man, benefitting from modern science, yes, but you've made him young again.'

'I don't understand.'

299

'So clever, so stupid. You've made him a young man again.'

'You think I'm the fountain of youth?'

'No, but with your help, or something like you, our leadership will last a lot longer. Decades, perhaps more. With that time and the accumulated experience we have, we can do things others have only dreamed of. But you're more even then that, we think you're using processes we haven't mastered yet, quantum processes.'

Julia considered, 'You're mad.'

Xin laughed, 'You're a unicorn, if we can't develop another like you we'll just track you down. We almost had you here.'

'So, you blew it.' Julia's turn to smile. Xin turned away and as she was leaving.

'We've learned what's possible, it will do for now.' And she left.

55

Temptation

Milo felt the series of blows Julia suffered, as first she saw her friends attacked, then killed. The realisation that Xin was involved in the destruction, responsible for it. To then see that she didn't care that her colleagues had died was devastating. They were collateral damage. As soon as she felt these things, he knew what they were about and he suffered the same shock as Julia. Kimani registered the change in them and, presuming it was related to the events of the previous evening, he called for a glass of water.

They had disembarked from the boat earlier and had evaded the Chinese search conducted from helicopter above and around the archipelago. It seemed that the Chinese had been warned off doing a ground search and Milo thought that just as well when he caught sight of the sheer numbers of people who had emerged, mostly armed. It seemed that the power Kimani had at his disposal was news to the inspector too, and he and the young officer whispered anxiously together.

But now, having had lunch and waiting as various factions debated the position and their possible fate, Milo was thrown into confusion and almost despair at the news from Beijing. They had already decided that going back was not going to be a great idea. If the Chinese were prepared to deploy armed forces in a friendly country in pursuit of Milo and Julia, Beijing was not safe. They had debated where they might go, but Milo pointed out that it would, in part at least, depend on their getting out of where they were.

Milo drank the water offered to him. Kimani watched and waited, wishing to know if he had recovered. As he drank, he and Julia considered their options, '*Should I say what's happened?*' Milo asked.

'*They are going to find out soon anyway, I'd think.*'

'*The question is would we rather tell them or let them bring the news to us?'*

'I think we should tell them.'

'Ok, when?'

'In a few minutes. I don't want to have a divided attention and I have one or two things still to do.'

'Right, let me know.' Milo finished the drink, and as he did he thought about how Julia and he were interrelating, sometimes full-on, sometimes, increasingly, compartmentalised. He smiled and handed back the glass. As he did, he stopped, looked at it and frowned.

'Thank you for that. This is very unusual, is it old?'

Kimani smiled as he took it, 'Not at all. We make them locally.'

'Truly?'

Kimani still smiling, 'Are you feeling better? You went quite white.'

'Yes. I wouldn't say right as rain, but certainly better.'

'Good, we can't have our honoured guests falling ill.'

Milo smiled tightly, Kimani left him. Milo noticed that Jones was talking with someone on com. He couldn't see them talk but people developed a kind of faraway look. It took great self-control to be able to have conversations without others noticing and Milo had managed to learn only recently with Julia's help. The Pixie could hold a conversation both verbally and nonverbally with two different people but she had grown up with the tech so Milo thought she didn't count.

Jones was eyeing him up and Milo felt a conversation was imminent, he wondered if it was about events in Beijing. Julia came back as he thought of it and Milo realised she was keeping an "ear" open to what he was thinking. Jones turned in his direction and slowly made his way over to them. Milo was about to ask Julia if now was the time but she was gone again.

'I noticed you being brought water, is everything ok?'

'Sweet of you to care, everything's fine.' Milo answered.

'Good. I was wondering if you'd be able to take a minute with me.'

'When?'

302

'Anytime that suits. Now if you're free?'

Milo looked about comically, 'It's so difficult, meetings and such…'

'Ok, now then.'

Milo shrugged.

'Have you thought about where you will go now?'

Milo's eyebrows shot up. 'I'm being offered a choice? A short while ago you were going to remove my head.'

'Yes, well, circumstances have changed and the removal of your head was always plan B.'

'And discovering it was out of the question if you wanted Julia…?'

'Played its part.'

'That and Kimani changing his attitude towards us.'

'That and… So have you? I presume China is out.'

'A wise man once said, "presumption and assumption are at the bottom of every screw up" Why would we not want to return to our home?'

'A little dangerous, don't you think?'

Milo briefly wondered what Jones had heard but decided that was paranoia.

'They were merely anxious about my well-being, I understand.'

'Yes. There's anxious and anxious. Anxious with a small army is a little too anxious, I'd say?'

'Perhaps. But you're not seriously offering a less dangerous alternative?'

'A few short months ago I was telling your man, Kevin, that China was not to be trusted. I offered him everything a young man could wish for. I can make you the same offer.'

'That turned out well for him, didn't it?'

'People are free to make the choices they feel right for themselves.'

Julia appeared again in Milo's implant and he felt a wave of distress.

'I think we have to tell them, or they will be telling us.'

'*Something else?*'

'*Something, but I'm handling it.*'

'*Ok.*'

To Jones he said, 'As it happens, we have some news that we should share with you.'

Jones looked concerned and a little shifty. Milo caught Kimani's attention and the inspector's and waved them over. Jones looked put out.

'It's the kind of thing you should all know, at once.'

Milo observed the change in people's attitude and noted the shift in the balance within the group. He wondered how the news would change things. Julia answered the thought, '*They will find out soon.*'

'I've just mentioned to Mr Jones here, we have some news I have had some news. Bad news, as it happens. The Chinese authorities have hit our compound in Beijing, most of my colleagues are dead, some are trying to get away. We don't know how that will turn out, obviously.'

Shock registered on all of the faces, followed almost immediately by suspicion.

'Why?' the inspector asked.

Milo shrugged, 'We're not sure. As best we can understand it, they are trying to isolate Julia and me. I think they believe we will be easier to control and capture if we have no one to assist us.'

'Was the attack here coordinated?' Jones wanted to know.

'No. The government seems to be divided into factions, and one faction wanted to get a jump on another.'

'Do you know who's behind it?'

'We're not sure.'

'*Yeah, I think that was the right thing to say.*' Julia said to him.

'How do we know this is true?' Jones asked.

Milo shrugged, 'Why would I make it up? But I'm sure your sources will let you know shortly in any case.'

Kimani looked at Milo directly, 'They were wrong to imagine that you'd be isolated by this,' he said, 'I think you now have your pick of allies.'

'I'm not sure how much they know about people like you.' Said Milo.

'I'm quite sure they know us little and think of us less.'

Jones agreed, 'You have been an eye opener to a number of us,

Dr Kimani.'

Kimani smiled and turned back to Milo placing a hand on each arm, "Milo I'm very sorry for your loss. I wish there were things I could do and of course anything I can, just ask.' and he bowed slightly.

'*Wow! Has your status ever changed!*' Milo could feel Julia's mixed surprise and outrage as she said it.

He nodded to Kimani but said nothing. The inspector reached out and put his large hand on Milo's arm and just squeezed and Milo's eyes teared up but he swallowed hard. Milo pressed down on every feeling he had rising up inside of him. If they were going to get out of this alive, they would have to have all their wits about them, grief would have to wait. Then something odd happened.

'*Am I speaking to Julia?*' It was Jones. He had managed to separate out the two com signals so that the question was indeed directed to Julia. She opened the com to Milo but blocked any chance he'd have had to give away his "observer status" to Jones.

'*Yes, you are, but how did you manage that?*'

'*You're not the only one with tricks. Can Milo hear us?*'

'*Do you want him to?*'

'*He's your partner, I get that, but if it were possible to speak with you separately…*'

'*Go on.*'

'*You have some choices ahead of you. I don't want to pressure you but we can offer you a lot. I'm not talking about Milo here, it's you Julia we're interested in.*'

'*I don't want to burst your bubble, but I'm pretty happy with my current arrangements.*'

'*Do you know what you are? The things she designed into you?*'

'*People are beginning to insist on telling me.*'

'*She didn't design you to be chained to some old guy…*'

'*Hey, that's a bit…*'

'*He's fine, a great test subject. For what it's worth, I like Milo, but you… We have a program. We've been trying to clone people for years.*'

'*You're not alone.*'

'*Not simply people, our clones have been designed to work from the get-go with implanted tech.'*

'Cyborgs?'

'No, they'd still be people, but we want them to have the chance to be in control of the tech they have inside them. The trouble is we can't get the systems to mesh properly. A lot of them are dying because their bodies reject them. And the ones who don't, we only have one or two who've reached maturity, they suffer from depression and extreme body dysmorphia.'

'I'm not too surprised.'

'Yeah, but see, this is the brilliant bit. You were designed to overcome all that. You can really, not only assist in perfecting the growing clone, but help the emergent personality to adapt to their true selves.'

'Where have you got all this?'

'Anna, she found Elspeth's notes. That's what Daniels was getting from her in Brooklyn.'

'So she was a prisoner?'

'She had been, there was a misunderstanding.'

'Does she work for Americorp?'

'Of course. Never mind her though. You're the prize, you can do everything we need and there are hints at more. You should come work for us.'

'Then why not just develop a version of me yourselves.'

'We're trying, of course, but we... it looks like we're missing something. Our guys can't figure out what. But this is a huge opportunity for you. You'd have your own bespoke body and one that wouldn't age the way Milo has, you'd have the very best available tech, you could design it yourself.'

'But what happens if you get what you want from me and then find I'm a bit inconvenient?'

'That'd never happen. We're too ambitious. The people on the board they want things, things you can't imagine, things...'

'Jonesey, let me stop you there. This won't fly. I won't fly. I'm not a toy or a piece of tech to fit in with your ambitions. I don't want to be a part of making some ubermensch.'

'You want to live in this poor limited way? When you could be so much?'

'*I am so much. I just don't want to be yours so much.*'

Jones blinked while he processed that one. He opened his mouth to say something and then turned on his heel and stalked away. Julia opened the com between her and Milo and there was a significant silence.

'"*Some old guy*"?'

'*I didn't say that.*'

'*No, I heard and just for the record, you said just about what I would have said myself, I think…*'

'*Good, 'cause I can call him back.*'

'*No, I'm happy.*'

'*That deal did sound pretty sweet.*'

Silence.

'*Glad we're on the same page.*' Julia said.

56

Picking up the Pieces

The transport she had arranged for them was a little unexpected; a large robo-trans chicken transport. They didn't recognise it at first as "transport". A sharp "get in" from Julia had them in the back and the truck moving in a few seconds however. It stank. The livestock was absent, which was a blessing, though they soon longed for some sort of seating or even something to stop them sliding about the place.

They were heading north from Beijing. Julia had calculated that this was the least likely, best chance compromise they had of getting clear of the pursuit. That they were outside the city limits and still alive suggested she'd gotten it right.

The trip was a regular for this truck. North of Liaoning and then due south to the Korean border. Hundreds of trucks crossed the border each hour, and Julia would make sure this one was as nondescript as possible. The trip to the border would take ten hours. Once in Korea they could get to Seoul quickly by train, which had been updated since the unification of the country.

In the back of the truck were three broken people, unable to grieve, terrified of what was going to happen next, and not really understanding what had already happened. They were in shock, tired and now bruised. Rahul was still torturing himself about his failure to foresee and stop the attack.

The truck, though by no means a rough ride, was nevertheless bumpy and not a little terrifying in its own right. They sat in a row, backs pressed against the side of the pen, feet braced against the floor. The heat of the vehicle was beginning to penetrate and they began to feel thirsty and hungry. Julia had left them it seemed and they knew neither where they were nor how close they were to where they were going. They had internal chronometers, but time seemed amorphous, stretching out in an endless series of moments and passing with a rapidity they couldn't follow. They wanted to stop. To get out and breathe, to shout and scream at the heavens. They were terrified that they would be stopped and tried to keep as silent as the dead they had left behind. As each minute passed, they felt a minute safer and a minute closer to losing everything. Tears came where no words would.

Julia appeared and tried to explain what the plan was. Explained that she wouldn't be able to keep in touch all the time because of the history of the region as a zone of conflict. She tried to reassure Rahul again but wasn't sure how much to tell them while they were still on the run. They were confused and wanted to quiz her about what had happened and what was going to happen, but none of them could articulate a single question.

The convoy containing Sam and the Pixie had reached Columbus, Ohio and was heading round on the ring road. They had avoided entering any of the big cities on the way and were making good time. The plan had been to deliver them to San Francisco and for the New York gang to get the second part of their payment there. The events in Beijing had spooked Julia, and she now worried that the gang could decide to try change the terms or even cut their losses, if they knew what had happened. She woke the Pixie.

'*Hey, how are you guys doing?*'

'*Mmm, what?*' The Pixie was taking a few minutes to come to, having shut down her systems in an effort to recharge after the previous day.

'*I have something to tell you.*'

'*Ok, you want to tell Sam as well?*'

'*Probably best.*'

The Pixie nudged Sam. By contrast with her companion, Sam was wide awake and ready to go.

'*Yeah? Oh, it's you.*'

Long training meant there was no sign from the outside this conversation was happening.

'*Yeah, me. I have bad news.*' Said Julia.

'*Ok*' The Pixie said.

'*The Chinese Government have attacked the China 12 compound.*'
Now both were alert.

'*What? Is everyone ok? You guys are still in Africa?*'

'*No everyone's not ok. Cathy, Rahul and Hoshika are alive. The others are dead.*'

'Oh my God.' Sam hissed, the mask slipped.

'What?' The driver turned back for a moment and asked.

'Oh, sorry, nothing, I woke up, dreaming. Sorry.'

'Ok. You guys ok back there? We'll be stopping again in about forty minutes to charge. Our solar conversion units don't work so good. Need anything to eat, drink?'

'Nah, all good, we can stretch our legs, when we stop?'

'Sure.' And he went back to driving.

'*Sorry about that. What the hell happened?*'

'*Partly they're trying to get hold of Milo and extract me, and partly there are internal struggles in the factions in the government.*'

'*I thought Xin could control the government and had agreements.*'

'*Yeah, about that. It turns out that Xin was the government. They had set up China 12 so they had a group in play.*'

'*Jesus. So she's alive?*' Said Sam.

'*Yes. It turns out it was her plan, or mostly her plan.*'

'*Hey, I liked Xin. I used to like Xin. How could she do that?*' the Pixie asked.

'*The killing wasn't her idea, I think. The attack was, she was going to try to hold the group to get Milo to return to Beijing.*'

'*Was Milo not going to return to Beijing?*'

'*Not since we were attacked in Kenya, by the Chinese.*'

'*You were attacked in Kenya? I can't let you guys out of my sight, seriously.*' The Pixie said.

'*Where are the others now? Does Xin have them?*' asked Sam.

'*No. They're on the way to Korea in the back of a truck.*'

'*Will they make it?*'

'*I hope so.*'

'*Hold on. If China 12 is done for, who is going to pay these guys for us?*'

'*Right, now we come to the reason why I called.*'

'*We're listening.*' The Pixie said.

'*I think I can get these guys their money anyway, it just won't be from China 12. However, I am going to try to put together another way out, if I can. I won't really be able to do anything effective before you get to Denver.*'

'*We're going to Denver?*' Sam asked.

'*You are. But from then on you have to be ready.*'

'*We will be.*'

Julia was back with Milo.

'*So?*' he asked.

'*So they know. I have to get hold of the cavalry and we have to get out of here. No one's tried to kill you yet?*'

'*No. I think Kimani's taken a shine to us, or he's about to kill us. He doesn't like Jones.*'

'*I suppose that's good. But having one killer like me above another, doesn't fill me with joy.*'

'*I get that, but having one killer stop another killer from, you know, killing me, gives me a little hope. How are the people in the chicken truck doing?*'

'*They will be at the border in three hours. No pursuit so far, that is, nothing beyond the government turning the country upside down looking for them.*'

'*Will they find them?*'

'*It depends. If someone puts the extra chickens together with the trucks then they could, but that requires the system to do a lot of things it isn't very good at, in a short space of time. On the other hand there are some random inspections that could find them.*'

'*So fingers crossed.*'

'*And anything else we've got.*'

'*I was wondering if we should think about the poor guy that got his throat slit over some stones?*' Asked Milo.

Julia thought about it and then, '*Let me do some quick…*'

'*Some quick?*'

'*You know me, research. There, I thought so. He's on Kimani's system. There's quite a bit in fact.*'

'And?'

'Let's see… He was in touch with someone in Zambia about some stones. He didn't initiate it. He piggy-backed on someone's deal. Oh, he was brought in. Ok, lots of back and forth… right, here. Just here he says the shipment's been lost.'

'Who's he sending that to?'

'They're being careful. Apart from this, they're not on the system. Whoever it is has a relative who needs money. Oh, that would… hmm.'

A short silence and Milo waited but then said, 'How're you doing this? Is it not encrypted?'

'Yes…' she answered slowly, 'I decrypt it.'

'Pretty quick no?'

'Using some stuff I found, based on something called "adiabatic computation", not sure I can explain quickly. It's just what I can do, like walking…'

He thought for a moment, shrugged and said, 'Right. So let's look at "dogs" or "dogs?" which do we think it is?'

'I'm pretty sure it's "dogs?", there's no sign that Kimani's lot are in on it.'

'I thought it was on his server?'

'Yes, but he's not involved in all of it, it's used just the way the ordinary net is used, just not by people like us.'

'Right. I was thinking, the victim had dogs?'

'Yeah.'

'When we were out with Kimani, you could hear them all over the town.'

'So you mean he was wondering why his were barking? A bit late to wonder that I'd say.'

'That's just it, maybe they didn't bark.'

'You mean, maybe they knew the killer?'

'The inspector would have a better knowledge of that part, and I think we're out of time.'

Kimani, who had been speaking with the inspector, made his way across to Milo and Julia.

'Well, well, well, what are you two plotting? I presume you are plotting.'

Milo smiled and Julia duly appeared to him.

'Why would you presume that?' She asked.

'Hmm, you are being held prisoner by desperados, your friends have been killed by sociopaths and another sociopath wants to cart you away. If I were you, I'd be plotting.'

'Fair enough, but we have other people in harm's way and we don't feel in immediate danger. But now you've brought it up, what are you going to do with us? Should we start plotting?'

'I have had a chance to evaluate your circumstances in a new light. Fact; many groups who have harmed, and want to harm, the people, also want you. This cannot be good for us. Fact; they have shown their hand dramatically, this is, obviously, revelatory.'

'I think we're all seeing the world in a new light.'

'I believe that's true. I think it's especially true for you and for my friend the inspector. We currently have no use for your technology. I would imagine, useful though you are, we will not have any future use for you. I'm speaking to Julia now. Milo, on the other hand, we might be able to use from time to time.'

'How generous.' Milo said with a touch of irony. Kimani acknowledged it and smiled.

'It implies the Somali group, who had been happy to see you in the hands of the Americorp man here, would be happy to see you set free. Some other arrangement can be made with you.'

'Alright, that is possible and also gratifying.' Milo conceded. Kimani nodded again this time without smiling.

'Do you know what you would like to do? Where would you like to go?'

Milo looked at Julia and she held out her hands, Kimani watched them thoughtfully.

'So you really weren't plotting. I would earnestly advise you to start. We can get you away from here, but Mr Jones has his own ideas. It will help when the time comes if you know what you want.'

He left them. They thought for a little about what he'd said.

'The US is very much the fire from the frying pan, wouldn't you say?' Milo asked.

'Ireland is a bit out of the mainstream, with all due respect.'

'It's part of the Scan-Fed, Scotland, Iceland, Norway, Sweden,

Finland, Estonia and Latvia. They're a big group.' Milo pointed out.

'But they are not easy to get to and you are easily isolated if you go there. Just like you were here.'

'Canada?'

'Possible.'

'The whole group was easily isolated in Beijing. It's not like we can point to a place where the powers that be can't reach out to take us.'

'No, but there are places I can organise help and places where I can't.' Julia said

'And you believe you can in America?'

'I believe it's the epicentre of what's coming.'

He looked at her for a long time, taking in the events of the last few months and then the last few hours.

'What's coming?'

'The decision on how this planet will be governed and in whose interests. To be honest it's been coming for about eighty years.' She said this in a completely passionless factual way.

'Eighty years? What? How do you see that?'

'Since the top point one of one percent started to see their fellow citizens as parasites, and then began to develop ways to eliminate them. It's not here yet, but it's not far away.'

'Shit.'

'Shit indeed.' And she then disappeared.

The crowd had driven Liu and her father apart and was now sweeping them a growing distance away from each other. She was panicking. She could still see him and they made eye contact. He indicated that they should head for the barrier and meet there. She wished she could wear her band, or that she'd had implants put in so they could speak.

They had made good their departure from the theatre, a little after she had broken off coms with Julia and the group. Liang had a car waiting and her father had insisted she come with them. It was around that point Liu realised Liang and her father had finally formed something beyond a working relationship.

The car brought them, through nondescript streets to the smaller of the two rail hubs in the city. It serviced the docks and the football stadium. The plan had been to get to the docks and board a ship. Julia had arranged the ship with some provisioning to be open by the time they got there. It would leave about an hour later. The trouble arrived when the crowds from a football match left and enveloped them up.

Face recognition must have picked them up at some point on the journey, as that explained why they saw half a dozen police transports arrive and spill their passengers onto the sidewalk. It was evident from the way they deployed they were looking for someone in particular. Without her band, Liu wasn't able to take any of the countermeasures she could so easily have used to hide them. Putting on her band now would mark her out straight away.

Her father, who had managed to keep with Liang, was indicating to her the barrier between the crowd and the entrance to the docks. The police did not yet realise where they might be headed and were covering the entrance to the station from which they had just left. Liu, though a powerful fighter and a brilliant mind, was still a slight fifteen-year-old and the crowds were carrying her nearer to where they were going, and they were going back to the railway.

She forced herself to calm down and looked at the movement of the crowd. Realising it was flowing and that she was caught in its current just like a river, she picked an angle across it of about forty-five degrees and struck out in that direction. It was a fight, but she managed to find the edge of the heaving mass and leant back against the fence. She searched again for her father and Liang.

The police had shifted. A thin line had held at the front of the station but now there were a number of smaller squads moving through the crowd. It irritated her to see the people halt and move round these squads and that they weren't having the same struggle as she to get through. A cold hand grabbed her chest as she watched one squad home in on something and then, following what they were seeing, she saw her father.

He was trying to get to the barrier that would let him into the docks, but a squad had seen him and his objective and blocked his path. It took a few seconds before he realised this and he and Liang stopped. They had a disagreement. Liu watched as her father seemingly tried to get Liang to stay with him. She was shaking her head and pulling away. She finally managed it and then deliberately got the attention of the police and they began to follow her. Liu teared up as she watched. She saw her father scan the crowd, see her and then he moved in the opposite direction, like Liang drawing the police away from her. She considered her options.

Her training had taught her to see what the police were doing and she knew to what extent she could influence that. She knew the police would now catch her father. Her heart beat faster as she also realised that the police probably thought Liang was her. Now any cover they might dream up would be destroyed if the police caught Liu as well. She was suddenly grateful that she was a slight fifteen-year-old, and she sank out of sight.

57

The Promise

Running from the authorities is terrifying. The fear of discovery or betrayal is constant and the realisation that your life hangs by a thread leaves scars that can last months and years. Some people never recover. It is also often deeply physically uncomfortable. It's possible you will be in a plane or a train, but if you are, you won't necessarily be in a seat. The thing people rarely mention is the boredom. Waiting for the hammer to fall is both time consuming and the very thing that stops time passing at all. Yet, for the most part, nothing is happening. You can't talk to your companions because you might miss something and that could be fatal. That of course, is if you are lucky enough to have companions. Alone, the hours and seconds drag as you worry about your loved ones and yourself, and every time you wish there was something to do, guilt hammers at you.

Julia appeared back with Milo. He jumped at the sudden appearance and was less than pleased.

'Why do you have to disappear? Can you not multitask?'

'Hey, I'm trying to get three sets of people out of two countries and work out how we're going to stay safe as well, what are you doing this afternoon?'

'Don't get snippy with me, Miss!'

'Snippy?'

'Yeah, snippy.'

They had a glare off until Julia started to laugh and then Milo started to as well. The people in the room turned to look at the man in the seat in the corner laughing loudly all on his own.

'You know they think you're nuts?'

He calmed down, *'I'm not sure they're wrong. Sorry. You gave me a fright and I was worried.'*

'We'll have to find a better way of working things.'

'Why do you have to disappear?'

'I am in Africa, and I'm piggybacking my signal across two other continents, you'd need a bigger head to feed me the kind of juice I'd need to stay here as well, drinking tea with you.'

'Ok. I'm sorry.'

'I know.'

'How are things?'

'Cathy, Rahul and Hoshika are out of China and will board a flight out of Korea in about an hour.'

'Flight to?'

'Glendale International. It was the first one.'

'Ok, and Liu?'

'She's on a container ship, she left Pearl City about three hours ago. I had to change ships because she missed the first one. So she's headed for Japan. I'm tracking what they are doing with Feng and Liang and I might be able to do something for them in a day or so.'

'Right, what about our Pixies?'

'They are just past Denver and I'm hoping for a rendezvous just short of Salt Lake. I have arranged payment for the gang.'

'Oh? How?'

'The United States Government have made a wonderful and generous contribution to the cause.'

'What's the excuse?'

'A few "extras" on a fact-finding mission by a group of senators.'

'Won't that be noticed?'

'It will not.'

'Right then, you asked what I was doing?'

'You were doing?'

'I was. Kimani has definitely decided that we are going to live.' And he smiled.

'We? I was always going to live.'

'Ok, well, now I am too.'

'Jones know?'

'Not yet. But he's going to bring us down to the airstrip at Malindi. Manda is still crawling with troops and surveillance drones. We can fly to Nairobi and then on to wherever we want. Have we decided?'

'*Have we?*'

'*I think we have few options.*'

'*I'll see if we can't coordinate with the others. I've had to blur some identities.*'

'*Is it going to be problematic?*'

'*No.*'

'*Uh oh, here he comes.*'

'Milo, how are things?' asked a very happy Kimani.

'Fine, thank you. Do we have a departure time?'

'Right about now.'

'Tell me, what happens to the inspector and his young officer?'

'They will go home. The inspector and I have reached a new understanding about how we will be dealing with, um, the powers that be and each other'. And he grinned broadly.

'Are you implying that he will be turning a blind eye to your illegality?'

'The purpose of Law, Milo, is to ensure our rights as citizens and to provide for our safety. Not of a particular group, but of the ordinary woman or man, adult or child. Law, is being subverted. We have agreed to return it to its original purpose. That is all.'

Milo smiled, 'If there is anything we can do doctor.'

'I'll be sure to call.'

He held out his hand and they shook. Milo looked down at the hand and then up at Kimani.

'You're not coming?'

'No need and I have things to do. The inspector and his man are travelling with you and will catch a boat back from there.'

'*Should we be worried?*'

'*Not yet.*'

They moved out in a group, with a surly Jones bringing up the rear. The trip to Malindi was by motorised dhow and went without incident. As Milo watched the coast slip by, he was thinking of the trip to Lamu and Julia's excitement.

Chinese troops were still in evidence but they seemed to have decided that the bird had flown, so their presence was token. Out at sea they could see two Chinese warships sailing from the deep water harbour. Alarmingly, they appeared to be heading down the coast as well. They couldn't be sure that had anything to do with them. But the warships increased speed and were soon a long way off.

At Malindi there were no troops at all. Julia used the local net to scan the area and could find no evidence of troops. A plane was waiting for them. Electrically powered jets were the commonest form of short-haul transport in Africa and this one looked like one of the newer types with about twenty seats. They were considered less dangerous and more reliable than the old internal combustion engines now only seen in countries whose economies were in serious trouble.

Two stewards were waiting at the end of the steps and the pilot was just entering the cabin as they came to the edge of the tarmac. There were two more maintenance men coming round from the charging coupling, having evidently just pushed it back from the side of the plane.

One of the stewards walked over to them and stopped, 'Do you have any luggage today?' he asked Milo.

'No, we're just as you see us.'

He smiled and held out an arm in the direction of the plane. Jones was still about ten metres behind them. The inspector coughed and Milo turned round.

'We're going to be leaving you here. The boat will take us back up the coast.' He reached out his hand to take Milo's. They shook and then the inspector dragged Milo toward him and began slapping him on the back.

'This is a proper Kenyan good bye!' He leaned in. 'These men are not who they look like, something's wrong. Don't get on the plane.' He hissed in Milo's ear.

Milo much more loudly, 'Hey, do you think I can get something to eat before we get on board, you know, something really African?'

'Yes, I think there's something in the terminal, or I can ask the staff kitchen to fix something.'

Jones gave some sort of signal and suddenly everyone was holding a gun. Jones smiled.

'What tipped you off?'

The inspector looked round him and finally settled on Jones, 'Your boys pulling out all those guns is the real thing that's done it. But one of my men in the building pointed me in the right direction.'

'Just a tad too late.'

Across the field, two khaki coloured vehicles were racing toward the plane. The inspector pointed at them.

'For you or me?'

Jones looked at them and his expression soured. He lifted his chin at his men and they put up their weapons.

'Where are the crew?'

Jones pointed at the hanger about fifty metres away.

'I presume they are unharmed.'

'They are.'

The inspector waved at one of the vehicles and it broke off in the direction of the hanger.

'You can go with Milo, if that's alright with you, Milo?' Milo nodded, 'Your men stay,' the inspector went on, 'and might have a few questions to answer, but they will leave in a couple of hours.'

Jones gestured to the plane and one of the stewards ran up the steps and leant into the cockpit. The pilot and co-pilot emerged, looking less than happy. The group shuffled off to one side as the first vehicle arrived and disgorged its passengers. Milo turned to the inspector, 'Very efficient.'

'Thank you it really was down to…'

Young officer Maina suddenly shouted something and dived at the inspector, who fell to the ground. As he fell there was a loud shot, then two, and suddenly everyone was all guns again. Milo ducked.

'*Is there nothing you can do?*'

'*Not really, they're all on separate and quite private nets. If you give me a few minutes I might try something.*'

The inspector rolled over and Maina had a gun of his own in his hand. He fired and a man in the building toppled down the steps. Another shot came from behind him and Maina went down in a heap and didn't move. There followed a volley of firing and one of Jones's men went down. Jones started to wave his arms about.

'Stop, stop, that's enough.' Jones yelled. There was a moment or two when it looked like that might not be enough, but then good sense prevailed and guns were lowered. The inspector stood and brushed himself down.

As the inspector got to his feet he yelled, 'A doctor, now!!'

'You alright?' Milo asked him.

'I am, but I'm afraid this young man isn't.' He crouched down and placed two fingers on the officer's neck and took his hand. They waited. Sadly, the inspector got to his feet and shook his head. He turned furiously on Jones, about to say something, but then took a deep breath. He gestured for one of his men to come over as the second vehicle arrived with the flight crew.

'Take Mr. Jones here and see he is comfortably seated.'

Jones said nothing, but flicked his head at the inspector and walked to the plane. The inspector turned to Milo, who held out his hand.

'I'm sorry.'

'Yes, I will have to tell his family and they have been going through difficult times. They're not the first and probably not the last.'

He stared at they young man's face for a moment and then something struck him.

'Tell me, did you have any ideas about that thing that brought you here? Just on the off chance.'

'We did. Whoever you're looking for was probably the original purchaser of the emeralds. Julia did some research and was able to find evidence of messages between the victim and a couple of people. The last message said the shipment was lost. Whoever it was he was working for, this wasn't their normal line of work and they were a bit naive I'd say. But they were powerfully motivated about the outcome of the deal and they uncovered the deception it seems. The final deal was done, by the way. The emeralds have left Lamu.'

'But then, why the "dogs" message? Kimani is adamant that he had nothing to do with it.'

'Yes, we looked again at the message. It wasn't just "dogs" but "dogs?" with a question mark, we thought.'

'I don't understand.'

'The victim owned some dogs, I believe?'

'He did.'

'Are they ok?'

'Yes.'

'We're guessing they didn't bark, no warning. So either they knew the killer or they had another reason not to bark. Drugged, maybe?'

The inspector turned slowly and looked again at his dead junior officer, who had just saved his life. He sighed, then turned to Milo.

'So you're sure it has nothing to do with all this?' and he pointed all round him.

'Sometimes, Inspector, murder is just murder, but what do I know.'

'Yes, thank you, I will give it due consideration.'

Milo turned and walked toward the plane. As they were doing that, another very different conversation was happening, '*Mr Jones.*'

Jones almost tripped over the final step as he climbed into the plane.

'*Yes?*'

'*That was not… cricket.*'

'*You can't blame a guy for trying. How did you break into my net?*'

'*You're wrong, I can blame a guy for anything I like.*'

'*Ok, I'm sorry. Ok? There was no plan to kill anyone.*'

'*Not ok, but I'm not going to touch you. However let me make you a promise, this will have consequences.*'

58

Many Threads

They had been traveling for nearly three days. The occasional stops for food, rest and crew rotation had shown how extensive the network of "gangs" across the states had become. Sam, in particular, was taking notes. This was, after all, her patch and she was more than a little put out that so much could exist that neither she nor the people she used to work for seemed to know anything about. A couple of times the Pixie had had to stop her from practically interrogating the young drivers.

Their supposed guards had been easy enough companions. The woman who'd been in charge back in the Bronx, Tamsin, seemed to know everyone in the country and was a figure obviously well-known, well-liked and respected. The Pixie liked her and they'd had several long conversations about how the gang network survived and how they kept a profile below the radar of the supposed government.

The morning of day three came as ever, with the sun chasing them, appearing in the camera screens of the people carrier. As had become usual, the silence of the morning was punctured by waking and stretching bodies and the demand from the younger gang members for a rest stop. Tamsin cleared her throat.

'Settle down.' And the noise stopped.

'We've had a bit of news in the night. We're going to meet your people in Evanston, outside Salt Lake, in about an hour. From what I've been told, we'll get paid and then you folks can go on about your business, and I hope that's right. Let me be clear, I like you two, but if your folks try to screw us over I won't hesitate to keep my end of the deal. You've seen me with my people and I won't sacrifice my reputation just because you're nice.'

The Pixie agreed, 'We know… In your shoes we'd be the same.'

'Good, then we understand each other.'

'*Did you get a plan?*' Sam asked.

'*Nope.*'

'*We don't know what's happening?*'

'*Not the first idea.*'

'*Do we know who's "our folks"?*'

'*Nope.*'

'*So long as we're this organised, I don't see how things can go wrong.*'

'*Me neither.*' The Pixie smiled and turned to look at Sam and took her hand and closed her eyes.

It was about forty-five minutes later that Julia woke the Pixie up. She didn't open her eyes, training had taught her not to react when in a combat zone, and this was a combat zone.

'*Hey.*'

'*We wondered when you'd call?*'

'*Now.*'

'*Right.*'

'*You're about ten minutes out from Evanston. They're waiting just the other side on the freeway. There are three of them, you'll see one at first.*'

'*Has Tamsin been paid?*'

'*Not yet, I don't think that's going to be a problem.*'

'*Good, 'cause she will kill us.*'

'*You made friends then.*'

'*We did, but this is business.*'

'*They don't have much internal tech so there's nothing I can do about them but I think our insurance is good.*'

'*These guys are organised.*'

'*We know.*'

'*They use an old-fashioned radio set.*'

'*I've listened, the language is interesting, like listening to a play.*'

'*Yeah.*'

'*The contact is out in the open, no node to speak with you, satellite is a bit weak. Stay calm and trust me.*'

'*As if I'd ever do anything else.*'

'*Five minutes, be ready.*'

They were passing through Evanston, which they could see on either side of the freeway. Local traffic was light, as it was still early in the morning, but as this was Utah it would pick up soon. The gang were getting themselves organised and the Pixie could see that they had picked up a further two vehicles, making four in all. Sam stirred and looked out the window and back at the Pixie, who smiled at her.

Utah, like some of the other states and unlike many of the rest, had embraced the circumstances of the changed world and broadened its democratic profile. On the face of it, the impact of middle twenty-first Century tech was light, in reality it was deep and profound. The cars of the gangs that surrounded them were state-owned and run, and the "gangs" wore a uniform. Sam took note again.

Tamsin leaned forward, 'We're about two minutes away. Do not screw around. I'd be unhappy if I had to kill you. I'll be really annoyed if you die by accident.'

Sam smiled and nodded, 'No screwing around, check.'

Tamsin gave her an unamused amused look. The Pixie sat up, anxious to know who it was that was picking them up. They pulled off the main drag onto a small side road sheltered from the highway. Drawn up on the side of the road was another, rather beaten up people carrier and a slight figure beside it waving them down. The convoy slowed to a stop. One of the Utah vehicles overtook them and parked down the road about fifty metres away. Everyone got out of all the vehicles. The gang members and the militia from Utah looked round warily, but the area was flat and the people carrier had its doors open and was empty.

Sam and the Pixie were in the middle of the group from the Bronx, Tamsin just behind them. They stopped about five metres in front of Mariana, who was standing beside the open door of her van.

'You the China 12 woman?' Tamsin asked.

'I'm with them, yeah.'

Something came across the radio in the gang's truck and the operator popped his head round the door. Tamsin looked back and flicked her head.

'Ok then, looks like we're clear. Nice doing business with you.'

She stood aside and whistled and the two in front parted, allowing

Sam and the Pixie walk ahead. Mariana smiled and neither Sam nor the Pixie moved. Tamsin picked up the tension.

'Something wrong?'

'Who're you?' The Pixie asked.

'My name is Mariana, China 12 rescued me in Sao Paulo. Joanna Baines was the op that did it. You're the Pixie, and you must be Sam, Julia arranged for us to get you.'

'She didn't tell us.'

'Um there's been a lot of trouble. Milo's in Africa.'

'What about the others? Did they get out?'

'Julia said she'd fill you in later.'

Sam and the Pixie looked at one another. The radio operative leaned out of the truck again and said, 'Tamsin, could you come here a minute?'

Tamsin gave him and the pixies a curious look and headed over to the radio. She took the beaten up phones from the man and listened and then gave Mariana a sharp look. She dropped the phones, raised her gun and walked forward. Mariana stayed calm.

'You're from China 12, you said that?'

'Yes, I am.'

'Why'd the money come from a government account?'

Sam's head snapped round and then back to Mariana. Mariana held up her hands in the face of nearly a dozen raised guns.

'Like I said. There's been some trouble. Julia has arranged everything and said she said to trust her.'

She said this to the Pixie and the Pixie held her gaze.

'Ok, that was the last thing she said to me, and Mariana was the name of the woman that caused all the trouble in Brazil. She did tell us there'd been trouble. I think we're good.'

She took a step forward and reached out to Sam. Tamsin stepped forward.

'Now hold on just one minute.'

A noise behind her and she looked back. The radio operator was sitting on the ground with a tall woman standing with an automatic weapon pointing at the group behind the edge of the truck. Tamsin turned and there was another noise to her left. A shorter woman with spectacles and strangely coloured hair, also heavily armed, stood and shook her head.

The group from Utah moved to signal their colleagues down the road and Sergeant Meier stepped forward.

'Nuh uh.' She suggested.

'Let's be sensible now. We are who we say we are, well I am.' Joanna said.

Tamsin bristled, 'What is this?'

'It's the exchange. You have your money, it's real, just, not from where you expected. I'm Joanna Baines, that's my old sergeant over there Ms Meier. There's nothing to worry about. You people get back in your carriers and Sam, you and the Pixie get into ours.'

Sam and the Pixie looked again at each other and the Pixie nodded. They were about to walk but Tamsin shook her head and all the gangs guns pointed at them.

'This is not what was talked about.'

'Tamsin, you're Tamsin, right?' asked Joanna.

'Yes, so?'

'The edge of the road is lined with mines, not far, but about ten metres either side of your truck. Like you, I want things to go smoothly, but I'm ready for things to go another way. A lot has happened at our end, but Julia got you your money, it's good.'

'How do I know that?'

'We've been good as our word so far, we're not going to shit about now. Let the pixies go and you go home and spend that money, the folks it came from don't need it.'

Tamsin looked from Joanna to Mariana to the pixies and then at her people. She considered before lowering her weapon and signaling for the others to do the same. The tension drained from her people and the Utah militia. The pixies walked to Mariana and climbed inside the bus. Tamsin was still unhappy. Joanna stepped away from the truck and backed away down the road. She gestured and the gang waited for a final sign from Tamsin. The gang began to grow tense again and one or two hands twitched.

At last, Tamsin pointed to the transport and they walked to their carrier and climbed in. Tamsin walked to the vehicle and stopped at the door. She turned round to Joanna.

'We'll check this out. If it's wrong, you'll find out just how long my arm is.'

'I don't doubt it for a second.' Joanna said.

It didn't take long for the trucks to be gone back toward Evanston, and Joanna and Meier waited until they were out of sight. They walked to their carrier and Meier climbed into the front seat beside Mariana.

Joanna held out her hand, 'We haven't met, Joanna Baines, Rachel Meier and Mariana Armenta. She's the clever one.'

Sam shook, still not entirely trusting, the Pixie more willing to believe. Joanna pulled the door behind her and Mariana started the engine.

As they drove away the Pixie turned to Meier and asked, 'The mines, a bluff right?'

Meier didn't smile but looked back through the window and one side of the road exploded leaving a large crater where the gang's trucks had been.

'In a way, we only had two.'

The Pixie searched the faces in front of her, these were serious people.

'I have a lot to tell you.' Joanna said.

After ten days in a ship alone, Liu would have been happy to see anyone. The tall, slightly awkward man who waved to her in the darkness in San Francisco was not, however, who she expected. For some reason she had expected to see a woman, and one armed to the teeth. She had plotted her revenge and the rescue mission to save her father every single hour she'd been awake and was ready to head back to China straight away.

As it was, Marcus smiled at the shy, slightly aggressive greeting he got and he did what he'd always found worked wonders and opened a bag of food. They made friends over the meal but bonded over the chocolate brownies.

He was only there to meet her, he reassured her, there were plenty of women with guns where they were headed. She accepted that and she ate, but a part of her kept planning.

59

Epilogue

The trip back to Washington had been very long indeed. Jones knew that he'd been picked for two reasons; first, he was ex-Brotherhood and so Heath had a line on him; and second, Heath thought he was a "can do" kind of guy. He thought of himself in the same vein. He had thought, once the trip was over, he would replace Donovan as CEO. Now? This trip had been bruising. Whatever that AI was, he was now sure it was dangerous and he would say so to Heath - Duncan, he had to remember it was Duncan.

The Willard was a wonderful place when you were on the up and on the in, right now it looked pretty cold to him. The young man at the desk looked up and caught his eye and nodded. Jones stood and gathered himself and walked to the lift. Another chance to brood. He was expecting to find Heath with Donavan and perhaps one or two of the other board members but the younger man was it seemed, alone.

Donovan was standing with his back to the long sideboard and he had a drink in his hand. He lifted the glass, gesturing Jones to sit. He looked about as happy as Jones had expected. He drank and stared at his feet. Finally he looked up. Donovan pointed at the chair behind the large desk.

'Do you know he's been here decades?'

'Yes… sir.'

Donovan wasn't really paying attention to him, he was staring at the back of the chair

'I thought this…' He stopped, now he looked up at Jones, 'You've let me down, Jones. I thought you'd bring her home. This was everything his crowning achievement. I read your report…'

He stopped, just stared again at Jones and then took a drink and shrugged. Jones looked round the room and wondered how long the CEO had been here, alone. He hadn't seen anyone come out, though that wasn't so unusual if he'd been having a meeting with Heath, or someone he'd wanted to be discreet about. But he got the feeling he'd been here all the time. As his eyes flicked round the room, they moved across the desk and there in the middle was an old fashioned pistol. When he was with the Brotherhood he'd seen a lot of guns and this one was a German or Austrian make, a Glock, if memory served. Neat, accurate, reliable. Did the boss intend to use it? On who?

Donovan jerked up and looked at Jones again.

'So she got away, again. Our friend Anna missed her target too, we have no leverage and the Chinese made their move…'

His eyes wandered over Jones' face, seeing and not seeing.

'They messed it up too, so there's that… I guess.'

Knocking back the end of the drink he put down the glass. He stood, and walked over to the desk, pushed the papers around a bit and then settled on one, picking it up between forefinger and thumb. He waved it at Jones.

'This is the copy of the notes Anna gave us after Julia's maker, Ms Church, died. It's a promise - a promise that this corporation must have fulfilled. And you know what it is? It's the future. 'Between us, the four corporations, the bank and the Party in China and our friends in Russia, we can reduce overall world population and set up the prospect of sensible global government, even space exploration. It entirely justifies what we've done here. Without it, the future could be in someone else's hands.It could get very messy. Without it we could all go to hell…'

Jones frowned, which hell was he taking about? Was it this world or the next? If it was Heath talking… Donovan walked round the desk and Jones's eyes kept flickering between the gun and his boss. What he did next was not at all what Jones had expected. He pushed the chair with a finger and it turned slowly around.

Jones's heart rate rocketed, he could feel it pounding in his chest, his throat. He was staring into Heath's face. A very dead face. His eyes shot to the gun and back, but he could see no wounds, no blood. Donovan watched Jones and his eyes drifted to the gun. He shook his head.

'No, he didn't do that, I found it there when I came in, he might have been considering it, or considering using it anyhow. But he was just sitting here, I'm guessing the autopsy will say heart attack.' He sighed.

'It's difficult Jones, when you're the boss you have to make decisions, for the future you understand…'

Jones blinked and agreed, a bead of sweat dropping from his forehead as his head moved, still eyeing the gun.

'Sir, Mr. Donovan, I…'

'Jones, I will of course be stepping up to be chairman. The nature of this project is sensitive enough that I am unwilling to allow too many people in on what we are chasing. So congratulations.'

'What?' Jones began to straighten.

'Congratulations.'

'I don't understand?' Jones was lost.

'You, are the new CEO of Americorp. You are, as they say "failing upward".'

'What?'

Donovan smiled and held out a hand, 'Why don't I explain your new role over supper, we'll get someone to clean up this sad relic of what might have been.'

Jones looked round him and took a step toward Donovan. Their hands met, Donovan's hand was cold, in contrast to Jones's hot and distinctly sticky palm.

About four hours earlier in a small hotel in Lagos in Nigeria an average height man with a toned body lifted himself up off a disheveled bed. Two, very beautiful bodies, one male, the other female, were intertwined, sleeping in the bed. The moving body was Caucasian, whose face was sporting a three day beard and who hadn't washed in four days at least.

Kevin walked to the small table and opened another beer. He took a long slug, wiped his mouth, and then belched and smiled. He looked out of the window into the tree lined gardens below and wondered why he hadn't just done this when he'd found himself in Africa months ago. He had a pretty sweet deal with some pretty sweet perks. It had taken long enough, but at last he had the right balance.

Something tickled his head. Something old. He realised it was the alarm systems from his implants. Since he'd been working here he hadn't had to use them but they were always there, a reminder of past sins. Useful occasionally. He looked down. Old laser sighting which produced red dots on the target had been obsolete for decades. New systems were visible only though sighting systems between the weapon and the implant. The counter to that was that they did show up in the ocular systems of military implants.

When he looked down, he saw his chest covered in tiny green spots. His white vest showed them up nicely. He had the immediate impulse to dive, to reach for his gun, to fight his way out. He suppressed it. He took a long drink and looked straight out the window.

'Bitch.'

The shots smashed the window but otherwise made no sound. Kevin's body was thrown back across the bed, landing between his guests. The younger man woke and saw the blood pouring from the wound. He began to scream.

Three refugees were sitting in a cafe in Glendale airport. Glendale had been built to replace LAX after the sea rise drowned the old place. The refugees were waiting to be picked up by, they were not sure who, and they had been there already for a couple of hours. They were still digesting the news of Xin's betrayal. Julia had told them on the plane and explained to an unconvinced Rahul how his system had been cheated.

Rahul rubbed his temples looking at the bleak faces of his companions, and he asked the question that had been going round in his head since the chicken truck.

'Why did we fail?'

'What?' Cathy asked.

'Why did we fail? Why didn't we see it coming? We know more about probability than any group on the planet. How is it we didn't see Xin as a threat? How were we so blind to the Chinese government?'

'You're really asking me that, aren't you?' Said Hoshika.

'Yes, but I've been asking me that since we left.' Answered Rahul. 'I didn't work out the numbers on it.'

'You'll never answer a question you don't ask.' Put in Cathy, 'And we were never looking in that direction.'

'But it was obvious.'

'Only when you look back.'

'People… our friends died, because we didn't ask.' And he put his head in his hands.

Cathy reached across and took his arm in her hand and Hoshika rubbed his back. A movement by the door caught Cathy's attention. Two women, one tall, one short, had just walked in and Cathy smiled a tired smile, and shook Rahul's arm.

'Come, our lift is here.'

Acknowledgements

Finishing a book needs so many things apart from a quiet room and a means to express yourself. While some of these are resourced from inside the self, encouragement, insightful commentary and… spelling, often have to be offered from outside. I am fortunate to have people who are able to supply me with these qualities and who do so selflessly.

On this book Ann Westcott offered a first (and further) critique(s) and loads of insight. Rachel Meier and Marcus Franks, overlooked my ignoring (for the most part) the Oxford comma but gave me a sharp and patient edit. Sally Fegan-Wyles and Nigel Shapcott offered their customarily excellent early and supportive guidance as did Kim Horsford and Andrew Milliken. Wendy Taylor lent me a writer's perspective and Maria Sheehy a thoughtful, considered, reader's. Mark Coleman was very helpful in giving me a more transatlantic view as well as a quick steer on professional vocabulary. Corrie Shapcott and Chrissy Lawrance-Thorne rounded my view of what I'd written nicely.

Daniel de Sybel was thorough and precise in his reading and my use of language.

Dr. Katharine Shapcott was able to allow me expert assistance which I managed both to embrace and ignore, (sorry).

To all of the above my endless gratitude.

You can see, only the errors are mine.

Raoul Morris.

Printed in Poland
by Amazon Fulfillment
Poland Sp. z o.o., Wrocław

60009321R00200